W9-DDO-280

The New Decameron

The New Decameron

Count Jan Potocki

Further Tales from THE SARAGOSSA MANUSCRIPT

Translated by Elisabeth Abbott

The Orion Press

New York

Library of Congress Catalog Card Number: 66–26538
Designed by Wladislaw Finne
Manufactured in the United States of America

Contents

Translator's note

The first portion of *The New Decameron,* this extraordinary collection of tales written by a Polish nobleman, Count Potocki, and first published in St. Petersburg in 1804, was published in the United States in 1960, under the title *The Saragossa Manuscript.* That collection included the first fourteen Days and the "Tales Taken from Avadoro, a Spanish Story."

This collection includes the remainder of what the rather mysterious Polish nobleman called *The New Decameron.* For the reader who has not read the previous stories, we herewith reprint excerpts from Potocki's foreword to *The Saragossa Manuscript:*

"As an officer in the French Army, I took part in the siege of Saragossa. A few days after the town was captured, having advanced to a somewhat isolated post, I noticed a small but rather well-built villa that I thought, at first, had not been visited by any Frenchman.

I was curious and decided to look it over. I knocked on

the door, but seeing that it was not locked, I pushed it open and stepped inside. I called, I looked all around—nobody was there. To all appearances everything of value had been removed; only a few unimportant objects lay scattered around on tables and in drawers. I noticed, however, on the floor in one corner, a number of copybooks filled with writing, and I glanced over the contents. It was a manuscript written in Spanish. I knew very little of that language, but enough to understand that this manuscript might prove entertaining. There was a lot in it about brigands, ghosts, cabalists; and nothing could be more suited to distract me from the fatigues of the campaign than the perusal of a fantastic novel. As I was confident that this book would never be restored to its lawful owner, I did not hesitate to take possession of it.

"In time we were obliged to leave Saragossa and, as ill luck would have it, I was cut off from the main body of the army along with my detachment, and taken prisoner by the enemy. . . . When we came to the place to which they were leading us, the Spaniards began to strip us of our belongings. I asked to be allowed to keep only one possession which could be of no use to them—the manuscript I had found. . . . They asked their captain's advice. He glanced hastily through it, came up to me and thanked me for having preserved intact a work he valued highly, as it contained the story of one of his ancestors. . . ."

The ancestor referred to—and the narrator of *The New Decameron*—is Alfonso van Worden, a captain in the Walloon Guards. At the beginning of the Fifteenth Day, he is in the company of a group of gypsies in the Alpuharras mountains where he has lingered on his way to join his regiment. With him, throughout these tales, we again meet several characters from the previous stories—the cabalist and his sister Rebecca, Alfonso's two entrancing cousins (and later his wives), Emina and Zibeddé and, most important of all, the gypsy leader Pandesowna, really a high-born Spaniard named Señor Avadoro, who entertains the group by telling his story to which newcomers add theirs.

E. A.

The New Decameron

The fifteenth day

I awoke fairly early and went for a walk before breakfast. While still some distance off, I saw the cabalist in lively conversation with his sister and, in order not to disturb them, I turned in another direction. Soon, however, I noticed that the cabalist was hurrying back towards the camp while his sister, Rebecca, was coming quickly towards me. I went to meet her and we walked along side by side without exchanging a word. The beautiful Israelite was the first to break the silence.

"Señor Alfonso," she said, "I have something to tell you that will interest you in so far as you are concerned about my future. I have decided to give up cabalistic lore forever. Last night I pondered this decision carefully. What do I care for the empty immortality my father wished to bestow on me? As it is, are we not all immortal? Shall we not all be united in the Abode of the Just? I long to enjoy this brief life, to spend it with a real flesh and blood husband and not with stars like the Celestial Twins. I want to be a mother, to see my children's children and then, weary and sated with life, to fall asleep in their arms and pass away in Abraham's bosom. What do you say to this plan?"

"I am wholeheartedly for it," I replied. "But what does your brother think of it?"

"At first," she said, "he was extremely angry, but afterwards he promised me he would follow the same course, provided he did not have to give up Solomon's daughter. He will therefore wait until the sun is in the sign of Virgo before he makes his final decision. Meanwhile he would like to know something about those ghosts who played tricks with him at the Venta Quemada, the ones who call themselves Emina and Zibeddé. He hesitated to ask you, for he realized you know no more than he does. Tonight, however, he will summon the Wandering Jew, the man you saw at the hermit's. He hopes to get some information from him."

While Rebecca was telling me all this, we were summoned to breakfast. It was served in a roomy cave in which the tent had been pitched. The sky had begun to cloud over and soon a heavy storm broke. When I realized that we would be obliged to spend the rest of the day in the cave, I urged the old gypsy chieftain to go on with his story, which he did in the following words:

CONTINUATION OF THE STORY OF PANDESOWNA

Do you remember, Señor Alfonso, the story of the Princess of Monte-Salerno that Giulio Romati told us? I have told you what an impression that story made on me. When we went to bed our room was lighted only by the feeble rays of a lamp. I was afraid to look at the dark corners, especially towards a certain chest where the innkeeper was in the habit of storing his supply of oats. It seemed to me I would suddenly see the Princess's twelve skeletal servants step out of it; and to shut out that sight I wrapped myself in my covers and soon fell fast asleep. The braying of mules woke me the next morning and I was one of the first up. I forgot about Giulio Romati and the Princess and thought only of the delight of continuing our journey which proved to be extremely pleasant. The sun, behind light clouds, did not trouble us too much so the mule-drivers decided to make a full day's journey and to rest only at the Dos Leones' horse-pond where the road from Segovia joins the road from Madrid. This plaza offers a refreshing shadow, and the two lions that pour water into the marble basin add to its charm.

We reached there at noon. Scarcely had we arrived when we saw travelers coming towards us along the Segovia highway. On the mule at the head of the procession sat a young girl who looked to be about my age, though in reality she was several years older. The boy leading her mule must have been sixteen; he looked charming and carried himself with an air although he wore the ordinary garments of a *zagal* or stable-boy. They were followed by a lady of riper years who could have been taken for my aunt, not because she resembled her, but because she bore herself with the same air and her features bespoke the same kindness. She was followed by a number of servants.

As my aunt and I were the first to arrive, we invited the ladies to share our meal which was served under the trees. They accepted, though they looked very worried, particularly the young girl. From time to time she glanced tenderly at the young stable-boy, who, for his part, waited on her with the greatest zeal. The older lady gazed pityingly at them both. I saw that she was troubled and I would gladly have comforted her, but as I did not know how, I concentrated on the meal.

After the midday repast we continued our journey. My good aunt let her mule trot beside the lady's mule, but I kept near the young girl. I noticed the way the stable-boy, under pretext of tightening her girth, managed to touch her hand or her foot and once I even saw him kiss her hand.

Two hours later we came to Ohnedo where we were to spend the night. My aunt ordered chairs brought out in front of the inn, and no sooner had she settled herself there with the other lady than she asked me to fetch some hot chocolate for her. I went into the house and while I was looking for a servant, I came to a room in which I saw the stable-boy and the young girl. They were clasped in each others' arms and were weeping bitterly.

This sight broke my heart. I flung myself on the boy's breast and wept so hard that my body trembled from head to foot. In the meantime the two matrons had come in. My aunt was deeply moved. She led me from the room and asked me the cause of my tears. I had not the faintest idea why we had wept and was not in any position to tell her. Meanwhile the other matron had locked herself in the room with the girl and the boy; we heard them sighing mournfully and they did not appear again until dinnertime.

That meal was neither very gay nor very lengthy. When the table had been cleared, my aunt turned to the elderly lady.

"Señora," she said, "Heaven forbid that I should think ill of my neighbor and especially of you whom I consider a good and very Christian soul. It has been my good fortune to dine with you, which I shall deem an honor at any time. Now, however, my nephew has seen this young girl in the arms of a stable-boy—a very handsome stable-boy; I must admit in this respect he is above criticism. You, Señora, apparently do not find such actions reprehensible. As for me, to be sure I have no right. . . . But as I have had the honor of dining with you and as we still have the journey together to Burgos ahead of us . . ."

Here my aunt became so embarrassed she could not finish her sentence. The other lady promptly intervened.

"Yes, Señora, you have the right to inquire about the motives behind my leniency. There are many reasons why I should not divulge them, but I am impelled not to keep anything from you."

At this the lady took out her handkerchief, wiped her eyes and began as follows:

THE STORY OF MARIA DE TORRES

I am the eldest daughter of Don Emanuel de Noruña, judge advocate at the Court of Segovia. At the age of eighteen I was married to Don Henrique de Torres, a retired colonel. My mother had been dead for many years; my father we lost two months after my marriage. My husband and I took my younger sister, Elvira de Noruña into our home. Though Elvira was not yet fourteen at that time, her beauty even then created a sensation. My father had left us practically penniless. To be sure, my husband possessed a large fortune, but owing to a family agreement we were in duty bound to pay a pension to five Knights of Malta and to support five relatives who were nuns, so that our income barely sufficed for our living. However, a pension with which the Court rewarded my husband for his services, put us in a somewhat better position.

In Segovia in those days there were a number of aristocratic families that were no better off than we. United by a common bond, they had made it fashionable to live as economically as possible. Rarely did we visit one another. The ladies spent their days at the window, the gentlemen strolling about the streets. There was much playing of guitars and a great deal of love-sick sighing—and all that costs nothing. Cloth and wool merchants lived in luxury but as we could not compete with them, we took our revenge by ridiculing and despising them.

The older my sister grew, the more guitars gathered in our street. Some of the players sighed to the strumming of others; sometimes they all sighed and strummed together. The town's beauties almost died of envy, but the object of all this adulation paid no attention to it. My sister seldom appeared; therefore in order not to seem discourteous, I would stand at the window and say what one usually says on such occasions. And there I had to stay till the last suitor had gone. My husband and my sister would wait for me in the dining room, and we would spice our modest evening meal with a thousand jests about the bemused lovers. No one was spared and if they could have heard us, I think none of them would have come back. Our remarks were far from kindly, but they amused us so much that we often kept it up until late into the night.

One evening when we were discussing our favorite topic, Elvira suddenly looked very serious.

"Sister," she said, "haven't you noticed that, evening after evening, when all the guitar players have left and the lights in your room are out, you can hear one or two *seguidillas* in which both singing and accompaniment are more like that of an expert than an amateur?"

My husband said that was true; he had also noticed it. I agreed and we teased my sister about her new admirer. We noticed, however, that she did not take our jests in such good part as usual.

The next evening after I had dismissed the guitar players and had shut the window, I lighted the lamp but did not leave the room. Soon I heard the voice of which my sister had spoken. First there was a prelude with numerous variations and then a charming air full of mystery, followed by a song of bashful love, then silence. On leaving the room I found my sister standing at the door listening to the songs. I pretended not to notice her; but at supper that night I was struck by her dreamy and thoughtful expression.

The mysterious stranger repeated his little serenade and we became so accustomed to it that we did not dine until we had heard him. The singer's persistence and the mystery surrounding him aroused Elvira's curiosity rather than her emotions. Meanwhile a stranger, who was turning all heads and setting all hearts aflutter, arrived in Segovia. He was Count Rovellas, whose banishment from Court made him important in the eyes of people in the provinces.

Rovellas was born in Vera Cruz. His mother, a Mexican, had brought great wealth to that house and as Americans were popular at Court in those days, Rovellas had crossed the ocean with the sole intent of becoming a grandee of Spain. As you can imagine, he had been brought up in a world that had little in common with Court life. But there was a splendor in the luxury with which he surrounded himself and his naïveté amused the King. However, as these attributes sprang in great part from his boundless self-confidence, people soon ceased to smile at them. In those days it was the custom for young noblemen to pay court to the lady of their heart by wearing her colors and, on many occasions as for example in jousting, a sort of tilting at the ring, her insignia. Rovellas, whose ambitions ranged far and high, chose the sign manual of the Infanta Maria Teresa, the daughter of the King. The King thought it a good joke, but the Princess felt insulted. An *alguacil* of the Court arrested the Count and brought him to the tower in Segovia. There he sat for eight days; then he was allowed to come out, but was banished from the city. The reason for this exile was, as you see, not altogether honorable, but as it was characteristic of the Count to make everything serve his vanity, he spoke frequently and willingly of this "disfavor," often hinting that at bottom there was an understanding between himself and the Infanta.

In short, Rovellas was well supplied with every form of self-conceit: he thought he knew everything and was successful in everything he did. His greatest pretensions, however, were to bullfighting, singing and dancing. No one was so discourteous as to deny him the last two talents, but bulls are not so amiable. When accompanied by his *picadores,* the Count frankly considered himself invincible.

I have already said that it was no longer customary for us to hold open house except for a guest paying a first visit, for whom our doors were always open. As my husband was distinguished both because of his family and his military service, Rovellas thought he had to begin by calling on us. I received him in my *estrada;* he stood outside. In our province it was still the custom to maintain a great distance between ourselves and the men who came to call. Rovellas talked volubly and quite frankly. In the middle of the conversation my sister appeared and sat down beside me. The Count stood as if turned to stone. He stammered a few meaningless words, then he asked my sister what her favorite color was. Elvira said she had no preference.

"Señora," replied the Count, "as you display such indifference, it becomes me to show my grief and from now on brown shall be my color."

My sister, who was not accustomed to such compliments, did not know what to say. Rovellas rose and asked permission to take his leave. We learned that, from that evening on, everywhere he went, he could talk only of Elvira's beauty. A few days later we heard that he had ordered forty brown liveries trimmed with gold and black.

Rovellas knew that it was not the custom in the noble houses of Segovia to receive regularly, so he contented himself with spending his evenings beneath our windows along with the other noblemen who paid us the same compliment. As he was not a grandee of Spain, and as most of the young men were *titolados de Castillas,* he considered himself their equal and treated them accordingly. But more and more Rovellas's irresistible charm prevailed. All guitars fell silent before his, and he became not only the leader in the concerts but also the main topic of our conversations.

This prestige, however, did not satisfy the proud Mexican; he longed to kill a bull before our eyes and to dance with my sister. He therefore announced with great fanfare that he had ordered one hundred bulls sent from Guarama and was having a one-hundred-foot square in the amphitheatre covered with flooring so that after the bullfight the guests could spend the night dancing. Few words but what a furor they aroused in Segovia! Rovellas turned all heads and, though he had not yet broken all hearts, he had made an exceedingly good beginning.

Word of the bullfight had scarcely spread abroad when all the young men of Segovia started running wildly around, practicing various techniques of bullfighting, ordering scarlet cloaks and garments trimmed with gold braid. I leave it to you to imagine what the ladies were doing! They tried all the latest styles of dress and coiffures—and that is not the half of it. They even sent for tailors and milliners, and those who did not have the money bought on credit.

Everyone had so much to do that our street began to empty of serenaders. Rovellas, however, appeared punctually at the usual hour. He told us he had sent to Madrid for twenty-five pastry cooks and begged us to judge of their skill. Whereupon servants in brown and gold livery entered bearing refreshments on platters of gilded silver. The same thing was repeated the next day and my husband was justifiably annoyed. He did not consider it proper that the entrance to our house should be the scene for open gatherings. He was kind enough to ask my advice on this matter and, as always, I agreed with him. We therefore decided to retire to the little market-town of Villaca where he owned a house and a country estate. Moreover, this solution had the advantage of permitting us to save money; we could omit several bullfights and balls which meant that we would not have to buy any new dresses. As, however, the house in Villaca was in need of some repairs, we were obliged to postpone our departure for three weeks. On learning of this plan Rovellas could not hide his disappointment and still less the emotions my sister had aroused in him. Elvira, who had apparently forgotten the serenader with the charming voice, accepted Rovellas's attentions, but with the greatest indifference.

I must now tell you that my son who, at that time, was two years old, is none other than the little muleteer you see here with us. This child whom we named Lonreto was the joy of our lives. Elvira loved him almost as much as I did and he was our only comfort when we were bored with the stupid performances before our windows.

Just as we were about to leave for Villaca, Lonreto came down with smallpox; you can imagine our despair. We nursed him day and night and during that time the serenader with the melting voice began his concerts again. Elvira blushed, but was wholly absorbed in nursing Lonreto. At last our dear child recovered; our window was opened to the lovelorn youths and we heard the voice of the mysterious singer again.

From the time we opened our window, Rovellas had appeared regularly. He told us the bullfight had been postponed on our account and begged us to name a day. We answered this courtesy as in duty bound and at last the famous bullfight was set for the following Sunday, which dawned all too soon for poor Rovellas.

I shall omit the details of that spectacle: when you have seen many bullfights one is just like a thousand others. You know, of course, that noblemen do not fight the bull the way ordinary folk do. They attack first on horseback with the *rejon* or javelin. After you have made the first thrust, you must receive one yourself, but the horses are trained for that and the thrust merely grazes the animal's rump. Then the noble bullfighter leaps from his horse and draws his sword. For this to be successful you must have *toros francos;*

in other words, the bull must be gentle and without cunning. But the Count's *picadores* were so stupid that they let loose a *toro marrajo* that was being kept in reserve for another occasion. Connoisseurs saw the mistake at once, but Rovellas was already in the ring and he could not turn back. Apparently not realizing the danger that was about to befall him, he let his horse dance around the bull, planted his javelin in the animal's right shoulder, and in doing so thrust his arm forward so that his whole body was between the bull's horns. All this complied with the rules of the art.

The bull started to run for the exit, but turned suddenly, rushed at Rovellas, caught him on its horns and tossed him so high that his horse was hurled over the parapet but Rovellas fell inside the arena. Now the bull stormed down upon him, drove its horns into Rovellas's jacket, whirled him around in the air and hurled him to the opposite side of the amphitheatre. For a moment the animal lost sight of its victim and searched wildly for him. At last, it saw him, glared around wildly, lashed its tail furiously against its flanks, and pawed the ground in rage. At that moment a young man swung himself over the parapet, seized Rovellas's sword and red cloak and planted himself in front of the bull. The animal made a number of sly feints which had no effect on the stranger. Finally the bull lowered its horns, rushed forward, spitted itself on the stranger's sword and fell dead at his feet. Tossing his sword and his cloak over the bull the stranger turned towards our box, saluted us, leapt over the parapet and was lost in the crowd.

Elvira clasped my hand.

"I'm sure that was our singer," she said.

As the gypsy leader spoke these words, one of his men came for him. The chieftain asked permission to postpone the rest of his story until the following morning and went off to attend to his duties as head of his tribe.

"I am extremely sorry," remarked Rebecca, "that the chief's story has been interrupted. We have left the Count lying in the arena and if no one picks him up before tomorrow I fear it will be too late."

"Don't worry," I replied. "You may be sure that a rich

man is not so easily deserted. You can rely on his servants."

"You are right," said the Jewess, "nor does that situation disturb me so much. But I am curious to learn the name of his rescuer and whether he really was the mysterious stranger."

"I thought you knew that long ago," I said drily.

"Señor Alfonso," she replied, "do not remind me anymore of cabalistic lore. I want to know only what I myself really hear and know I want nothing but to make the man I love happy."

"What! Have you already made your choice?"

"By no means. And so far I have no one in mind. I don't know why, but it seems to me I would not want a man of my own faith. However, as I would never marry a man of your religion, I have only the choice of Mohammedans left. The men of Tunis and Fez are said to be handsome and attractive, but if I could find a man with a tender heart I would ask nothing more."

"But where," I asked, "do you get this dislike for Christians?"

"Don't ask me about that! It is enough for you to know that I can change my faith only for the Mohammedan."

We continued to argue in this fashion for quite a while. Then I took my leave of the young Israelite, spent the rest of the day hunting and did not return to camp until supper time. I found everyone in a very merry mood. The cabalist was talking about the Wandering Jew who would soon arrive from the center of Africa, and Rebecca said:

"Señor Alfonso, you will see the man who has known personally the object of your adoration."

Those words could easily have involved me in an undesirable argument and I therefore quickly changed the subject. We were all eager to hear the sequel to the gypsy's story that same evening, but the latter asked to be allowed to postpone it till the next day. We therefore went to bed and I soon fell sound asleep.

The sixteenth day

The locusts that sing so loudly and tirelessly in Andalusia woke me early in the morning. I had become very sensitive to the beauties of nature and I stepped out of the tent to gaze at the brilliance of the sun's rays as it rose above the horizon. Rebecca is right, I said to myself, to prefer the joys of human existence, of the real life, to the empty dreams of the ideal world into which, willy-nilly, we shall all enter sooner or later. Are there not enough of the most varied emotions, the richest impressions on this earth of ours, to fill our brief existence? Such reflections occupied me for some time. Then I saw the others on their way to breakfast in the cave and I followed them. We ate like people whose appetites are whetted by the crisp mountain air. And after we had eaten our fill, we urged the gypsy leader to continue his story, which he did in these words:

CONTINUATION OF THE STORY OF PANDESOWNA

I have told you that on our journey from Madrid to Burgos, we got as far as our second halt for the night, that there was a young girl in our company and that she was in love with Maria de Torres's son, a youth disguised as a muleteer. The Marquesa de Torres had told us that Count Rovellas lay half dead in the arena, when the young stranger killed the bull, which was just about to finish off its victim. What happened then Maria de Torres will now tell you.

CONTINUATION OF THE STORY OF MARIA DE TORRES

While the terrible bull was writhing in its blood, Count Rovellas's servants rushed into the arena to come to his aid. He gave no sign of life; they laid him on a stretcher and carried him to his dwelling. The spectacle was called off and everyone went home. That same evening we learned that Rovellas was out of danger and on the following day my husband sent to inquire for his health. Our page was a long time returning, but at last he brought us a letter which read as follows:

Colonel Don Henrique de Torres:
Your Excellency will see from the following that Heaven in its mercy has left me a remnant of strength. But a greater agony in my heart makes my recovery doubtful. You are aware, Don Henrique, that Providence has bestowed all worldly possessions on me. I am bequeathing part of them to the young stranger who risked his life to save mine. The remainder could not be in better hands than in those of Elvira de Noruña, your incomparable sister-in-law. Be so kind as to assure her of the deep respect she inspires in a man who soon perhaps will be no more than dust, but whom Heaven still permits to sign himself:

Count de Rovellas
Marquis de Vera Longa y Cruz-Vejarda
Hereditary Commander de Talla-Verde y Rio-Floro,
Lord of Tolasque y Riga-Fuera, Mender, Longo,
etcetera, etcetera . . .

You will be surprised, Donna Maria said, that I have remembered so many titles, but in a joke my husband and I conferred them on my sister so that in the end I came to know them by heart.

As soon as my husband received this letter he informed me of its contents and asked my sister what answer he should make. Elvira replied that she would always follow my husband's advice, but that Rovellas's good qualities had made less impression on her than his boundless egotism which was evident in his every word and deed. My husband understood what she meant. Elvira was still too young to appreciate His Excellency's feelings as they deserved, nevertheless she joined us in wishing him a complete recovery. Far from seeing in this reply a rejection, Rovellas now spoke of his marriage to Elvira as a *fait accompli.* In the meantime, we moved to Villaca.

Our house stands in charming surroundings at the far end of the little market-town, almost in the country. It had been put in good repair; but opposite us stood the house of a simple farmer that was decorated with rare good taste. Flowerpots on the doorstep, a beautiful window, a birdhouse and a certain air about the whole place gave it a specially pleasing and well-ordered appearance. We were told that a *labrador* from Murcia had recently bought this house; in our province landowners who are called *labradores* form a middle class between the lesser nobility and the peasantry.

It was already late when we arrived in Villaca. The first thing we did was to go over the house from cellar to attic, then we had chairs set out in front of the door and drank our chocolate. My husband joked with Elvira about the inadequacy of our house—which is really not small—to shelter a future Countess de Rovellas, all of which she took good-naturedly. A little later we saw a cart, pulled by four strong oxen, being driven by a farm hand across the fields on the way home from work. Behind it walked a young man with a young woman on his arm. The young man was a striking figure and as he came nearer, Elvira and I recognized Rovellas's rescuer. My husband apparently did not notice him, but my sister gave me a look I well understood. The young *labrador* greeted us courteously, but the expression on his face was that of a man who does not wish for any further acquaintance; he then went directly into his house. The young woman looked at us attentively.

"What a handsome couple!" exclaimed Doña Manuela, our housekeeper.

"What do you mean, a handsome couple?" cried Elvira. "Are they married?"

"Of course," Manuela replied. "It is apparently a marriage against the parents' wishes, a sort of elopement. But frankly, no one here is fooled by the deception; it's plain to be seen they're not peasants."

My husband asked Elvira why she was surprised, adding: "You might think he was the mysterious singer."

At that moment, from the house opposite, we heard a prelude played on a guitar and then a voice that confirmed my husband's words.

"That is strange," he said, "but since the young man is married, his serenades must have been intended for one of our neighbors."

"True," sighed Elvira, "and I thought they were meant for me."

This ingenuousness made us smile, but after that we did not mention the singer again. We spent six weeks in Villaca during which time the curtains in the house opposite were always drawn, we saw nothing of our neighbors, and I thought they had left. Soon, however, learning that Count Rovellas had recovered and that the bullfights were to begin again, we returned to Segovia. There we found ourselves caught up in a whirl of gaiety and entertainment. The Count's wooing finally touched Elvira's heart and the marriage was celebrated with great pomp and ceremony. They had been married three weeks when the Count learned that his exile was ended and he would be permitted to appear again at Court. The prospect of presenting my sister at first delighted him, but before leaving Segovia he was eager to learn the name of the man who had saved his life. He therefore offered a reward of one hundred gold pieces, that is eight hundred *pistoles* for information about the man. The next day he received the following letter:

Count de Rovellas:
Your Excellency's efforts are in vain. Do not try to learn the identity of the man who saved your life. It is enough for you to know that you have ruined his.

Rovellas showed my husband this letter, saying haughtily that it could come only from a rival. He had not known, he added, that Elvira had had any love affairs and had he known it, he would not have married her. My husband ordered the Count to be more circumspect in his language and he never called on him again.

There was now no talk of going to Court. Rovellas became sullen and bad-tempered; his vanity turned to jealousy, his jealousy to rage. My husband told me about the anonymous letter and we decided that the *labrador* of Villaca must have been a disguised and disappointed suitor. We made inquiries in the neighborhood, but the stranger had sold his house and left town.

Elvira was pregnant so we were careful to keep our knowledge of her husband's attitude from her. She realized that he had changed, but she did not know why. The Count saw her now only at meals. Conversation lagged and the few words he addressed to her were sharply ironical. When my sister was in her ninth month, Rovellas announced that business called him to Cadiz. Eight days later a notary brought Elvira a letter and insisted that she read it before witnesses. We gathered around her and this was what the letter said:

Señora:
I have discovered your love affair with Don Sancho de Penna Sombra. I have long suspected it. However his sojourn in Villaca is sufficient proof of your infamy, which was so poorly veiled by Don Sancho's sister whom he introduced as his wife. My wealth was doubtless the greater attraction but that wealth you will no longer share with me. We shall not live together any longer. I shall acknowledge your existence, but I shall not acknowledge the child you are about to bear.

Elvira did not hear the end of the letter: after the first lines she fainted. That same evening my husband set out to avenge this injustice to my sister. Rovellas had just sailed for America. My husband followed on another ship; they were both lost in the same storm. Elvira gave birth to the little girl I now have with me. Two days later my sister died. Why did I not die with her! Truly, I do not know. I think the very magnitude of my sorrow gave me strength to surmount it. The little girl was christened Elvira and in her I found her mother again. She had no one in the world but me and I made up my mind to devote my life to her.

But first I tried to prove her right to her father's inheritance. I was told I must appeal to the law courts in Mexico. I therefore wrote to America and was informed that the estate had been divided among twenty distant relatives and that Rovellas had not acknowledged my sister's child. As my entire income was not sufficient to pay for six pages of the legal proceedings, I had to be content with registering Elvira's birth and legal status in Segovia. I sold my town house and with my little Lonreto, who was then three years old, and my little Elvira, who was as many months old, I retired to Villaca. My greatest sorrow was to have constantly before my eyes the house in which the accursed stranger with his mysterious love had lived. In the end I became accustomed to it and my children helped me over all my troubles.

However, I had not been in Villaca a year when I received a letter from America.

Señora de Torres:
The following lines are addressed to you by the unhappy man whose respectful love has brought sorrow to your house. My admiration for the incomparable Elvira was, if possible, even greater than the love I felt for her at first sight. I therefore ventured to bring my sighs and my guitar to your street only when it was empty and there were no witnesses to my boldness.

When Count Rovellas succumbed to those charms that meant life to me, I hid in my heart a passion that now could only be considered an offense. I knew, however, that you were planning to spend some time in Villaca and I bought a house there. Hidden behind my shutters I often gazed on her whom I never dared to address, still less to apprise of my devotion. I had my sister with me and introduced her as my wife to avoid any suspicion that I was a suitor.

Our dear mother's dangerous illness sent us hastening to her side. By the time I returned to Villaca, Elvira was already the Countess de Rovellas. Heartbroken at the loss of a treasure I had never dared to claim, I hid my grief in the wilds of another hemisphere. There I learned of the despicable events whose innocent cause I had been, and of the disgraceful interpretation put upon my honorable love.

I therefore declare that the deceased Count de Rovellas lied when he claimed that my admiration for the divine Elvira proved that I was the father of the child she carried. I declare this to be false and swear by my honor as I hope to be saved, to take none other to wife than the daughter of Elvira. This will be proof that she is not my daughter. In witness of this truth I call upon the Virgin and may the precious blood of Her Son have mercy on me in my last hour.

Don Sancho de Penna-Sombra

P.S. I have had this letter countersigned by the Corregidor of Acapulco and advise you to have it notarized and registered by the law court in Segovia.

No sooner had I finished reading this letter than I began to curse Penna Sombra and his secret love.

"You wretched fellow! You selfish, insane devil, you Lucifer!" I cried, "Why didn't the bull you killed kill you instead? Your cursed adoration caused the deaths of my husband and my sister. You ruined the poor girl's life; you condemned me to live in poverty and now you seek a ten-month-old child as your wife. May God punish you!"

When at last I had unburdened myself of my anger, I went to Segovia and had Don Sancho's letter registered. There in my home town, I found my affairs in bad condition, the proceeds from the sale of my house had been seized to pay the pension we owed the five Knights of Malta and my husband's pension had been canceled. I had nothing left but our little country place in Villaca. It was therefore with all the greater joy that I returned to Villaca where I found my children healthy and happy. I retained the woman who had taken care of them during my absence and she, with a lackey and a stable boy, were my only servants. In this way I managed to live without excessive worries. My own background and the position my husband had held assured me of the esteem of the people who were all of them eager to do what they could for me. In this way six years passed and I wish that all my years could have been as happy.

One day the *alcalde* of the village called on me. He knew about Don Sancho's unusual proposal and he handed me a newspaper from Madrid.

"Señora," he said, "allow me to congratulate you on the brilliant marriage in store for your niece. Read this article":

Don Sancho Penna-Sombra has rendered the King the most distinguished service not only by annexing two provinces in New Mexico, that are extremely rich in mines, but also by the skill with which he put down the uprising at Cuzco. As a result His Majesty has bestowed on Don Sancho the rank of a grandee with the title of Count de Penna-Velez. The Count has just sailed for the Philippines in his capacity as Captain-General.

"Thank God!" I told the *alcalde*. "Elvira will have, if not a husband, at least a protector. May he return safely from the Philippines, become Viceroy of Mexico and have our possessions restored to us!"

What I wished at that time with all my heart came to pass. Count de Penna-Velez was appointed Viceroy and I wrote asking him to interest himself in my niece's case. He replied that I did him a grave injustice if I thought he would ever forget the daughter of the incomparable Elvira: he was far from being guilty of such an offense. On the contrary he had already taken the first steps in the Mexican law courts. The case would be long drawn-out, but he dared not hasten proceedings because, as he was still determined to have no wife but my niece, it would not be proper to urge the courts to make an exception in his favor. I realized that the man still held firmly to his idea.

Some time after that a banker from Cadiz sent me a thousand gold pieces, but he would not tell me the name of the donor. Though I was sure it was the Viceroy, I hesitated, out of a sense of delicacy, to accept this money or even to touch it and I begged the banker to deposit it in the Bank of Asiento.

All these matters I kept as secret as possible, but as the sun brings everything to light, people, even in Villaca, soon learned of the Viceroy's desire to marry my niece and from that day she was known as "the little Vicereine." My little Elvira was then eleven years old and I think such brilliant prospects would have turned the head of any other girl, but Elvira's heart and mind were filled with other thoughts that not even vanity could replace. Of this, however, I became aware too late. From her earliest years she had babbled of love and tenderness and her little cousin Lonreto was always the recipient of these precocious emotions. I often thought of separating them, but I did not know what would become of my son. I scolded my niece—with the sole result that she ceased to confide in me. As you know, in this country, romances or *novelas,* as well as novels, are recited to the accompaniment of the guitar as a sort of melodrama. In Villaca we had two dozen volumes of this beautiful literature. I forbade Elvira to read them, but by the time this thought had occurred to me, she already knew them all by heart—and had known them for a long time.

The strangest thing of all was that my little Lonreto had exactly the same romantic nature. They understood each other perfectly, especially as to the best way to hide from me. Their behavior struck me as suspicious and I would have liked to put Elvira in a convent, but I did not have the money to pay for her board. Probably I did not do all I should have and so it came about that instead of being delighted to be called Vicereine, the little creature began to think of herself as a star-crossed lover, a victim of fate, doomed to misfortune. These fine ideas she imparted to her cousin and they vowed to defend the sacred rights of love against the tyrannies of fate. All this had been going on for years before I had the slightest inkling of it.

One day, however, I found them in the chicken house in the most dramatic attitude: Elvira lay outstretched on a chicken coop, a handkerchief in her hand, weeping bitterly, while Lonreto knelt beside her sobbing at the top of his lungs. I asked what they were doing here. They said they were acting a scene from the novel, Fuenderosas and Lindamora.

This time I was not fooled. I realized that they were in love. However, I gave no sign, but I went to our priest and asked his advice. He thought it over a while and then said he would write to a friend of his, another priest, who could take Lonreto into his house. In the meantime I should offer the Virgin a novena and be sure to lock the door of the room in which Elvira slept.

I thanked the priest, made the novena and locked Elvira's door; but unfortunately I did not lock the window. One night I heard a sound in her room. I opened the door and found her in bed with Lonreto. They jumped out in their nightclothes, flung themselves at my feet and told me they were married.

"Who married you?" I demanded. "What priest would dare to commit such a hideous sin?"

"No, Señora," replied Lonreto earnestly. "There was no priest involved. We were married under the big chestnut trees. The God of Nature received our vows as dawn broke and the birds around us were our witnesses. In exactly the same way, Señora, the lovely Lindamora became the wife of lucky Fuendarosas as it is written in black and white in our history."

"Unhappy children," I cried. "You are not married and you cannot be married: you are blood cousins."

I was so crushed I did not even have the courage to scold them. I sent Lonreto from the room, threw myself across Elvira's bed and burst into torrents of tears.

When the gypsy chieftain had spoken those words he remembered that he had an important matter to attend to and asked our permission to leave. After he had gone, Rebecca said to me:

"Those children worry me a great deal. The love that seemed so alluring when it illumined the faces of Mulat Tanzais and my maid, Suleika, was certainly far more exciting when it enflamed handsome Lonreto and Elvira. They are like Cupid and Psyche."

"A happy comparison," I replied. "It also indicates that you will soon make the same progress in Ovid's works as in studying the folios of Henoch and of Atlas."

"I'm beginning to believe," retorted Rebecca, "that the teachings you speak of may perhaps be more dangerous than those to which I have heretofore devoted myself and that like the cabala, love too has its magic."

"Speaking of the cabala," Ben Mamun intervened, "allow me to inform you that the Wandering Jew has already crossed the Armenian mountains and is swiftly approaching."

As I was already so bored with magic that I invariably turned a deaf ear when that subject came up, I left the company and went hunting. And I did not return until it was time for the evening meal. As the leader was absent, I sat down at table with his two daughters. The cabalist and his sister did not appear. This tête-à-tête with the two young girls somewhat disconcerted me, but it seemed to me that not they, but my two charming cousins were the ones who had honored me with their visit to my tent. But what those cousins were, whether devils or human beings, I could not make up my mind.

The seventeenth day

The next morning when I noticed that all the company had gathered in the caves I made haste to join them. We ate a hurried breakfast and, as soon as it was over, Rebecca was the first to urge the gypsy leader to tell us what had happened to Maria de Torres. Pandesowna did not wait to be coaxed but promptly continued his tale.

CONTINUATION OF THE STORY OF MARIA DE TORRES

My grief, Maria de Torres explained, would perhaps have been less had I ventured to ask anyone for advice, but I did not dare to expose my children's shame; I thought I would die of mortification and I blamed myself only. On the third day I saw a long column of horses and mules in front of my house. My servant announced the *corregidor* of Segovia. After preliminary courtesies that official told me that the Count de Penna-Velez, Grandee of Spain and Viceroy of Mexico, had arrived in Europe a few days before and had charged him to deliver a letter to me, but that his esteem for this great lord had impelled him to deliver it in person. I thanked him for his consideration and accepted a letter which read as follows:

Marquesa de Torres!
Today in two months it will be thirteen years since I had the honor of declaring that I would have no other wife but Elvira de Rovellas. On that day when I wrote to you from America, she was seven and a half months old. Ever since then my admiration for her lovely person has grown with her charm. It was my desire to hasten to Villaca and throw myself at her feet; but orders from His Majesty Don Carlos II advise me not to approach Madrid within a distance of more than fifty hours. I shall therefore count on meeting Your Grace on the road from Segovia to Burgos.

With the highest esteem I am
Your Grace's obedient servant
Don Sancho, Count de Penna-Velez

That was the deferential Viceroy's letter. In spite of my anger I could not suppress a faint smile. The *corregidor* then handed me a portfolio containing the sum I had deposited in the bank at Assiento; and, bidding me farewell, returned to Segovia.

I stood there motionless as a statue holding, in one hand the letter, in the other the portfolio. I had scarcely overcome my bewilderment when the *alcalde* arrived to tell me he had escorted the *corregidor* to the end of his territory and was now at my disposal to supply me with mules, servants, guides, saddles, provisions, in short everything I needed for my journey.

I let the good *alcalde* have his way and, thanks to his endeavors, we were ready to set out the next day. We spent the night at the Villa Verde and now we are here. Tomorrow we shall arrive at Villa-Real where we shall meet the estimable Viceroy. But what shall I say to him? What will he himself say when he sees these two young people in tears? I did not dare to leave my son at home lest I arouse the suspicions of the *alcalde* or the priest; but perhaps even more because I was afraid of doing the poor child harm. That is why I disguised him as a muleteer. God knows what will happen now! I want everything to be open and above-board—and I dread it. And finally, I must see the Viceroy, must learn from him what he has done to recover Elvira's property. Even though she no longer deserves to be his wife I still hope she will arouse his sympathy and that he will make her his ward. But how at my age can I have the courage to admit my negligence? Truly, if I were not a Christian, at such a moment I would prefer death.

Here the good Maria ended her tale and, giving way to her anguish, wept bitter tears; even my aunt took out her handkerchief and held it to her eyes. I too began to weep. Elvira sobbed so hard that we were obliged to undo her laces and carry her to her bed; this incident ended with everyone going to bed. I too went to bed and soon fell asleep.

The sun had not yet risen when I felt a tug at my arm. I awoke with a start and called: "Who is there?"

"Speak softly," a voice whispered. "I am Lonreto. Elvira and I have thought of a way out of this predicament, at least for a few days. Here are Elvira's clothes, you are to put them on. Elvira will take yours. My mother is kind; she will forgive us. As for the mule-drivers and the other people from Villaca, they cannot betray us for they will be replaced by men sent by the Viceroy, and the lady's-maid is on our side. Dress quickly, get into Elvira's bed and she will get into yours." As I had no objections to Lonreto's proposal, I dressed as quickly as I could. I was twelve years old and tall for my age and Elvira's clothes fitted me perfectly.

When I was dressed, I went to Elvira's room and got into her bed. Soon after that I heard a servant telling Elvira's aunt that the Viceroy's majordomo was waiting for her in the kitchen which served as a reception room. The next moment, Elvira was summoned—and in her place I appeared. Her aunt raised her hands to heaven and sank down into a chair that stood behind her; but the majordomo did not see this—he was too busy bowing and assuring me of his master's esteem. Then he handed me a jewel case. I received it graciously and bade him rise; a number of the Viceroy's people then came to congratulate me and shouted three times: *"Viva la nuestra vicereyna!"* "Long live our Vicereine!" Last of all came my aunt, followed by Elvira dressed as a boy. It speaks well for Maria de Torres's intelligence that she realized she had no choice but to let us have our way.

The majordomo asked who this lady was. I told him she came from Madrid and was traveling to Burgos to put her son in the seminary of the Theatine monks. He invited her to make use of the Viceroy's litters. My aunt then requested one for her nephew who, she explained, was very delicate and tired quickly. Whereupon the majordomo ordered another litter brought up and then offered me his gloved hand to help me enter mine. Shortly after that I gave the order and the whole column started forward.

So there I was, the future Vicereine, holding a jewel case containing diamonds, riding in a gilded litter drawn by white mules, and accompanied by two knights who kept their horses prancing at my side. It was a very strange situation for a boy of my years, and for the first time in my life I began to think about marriage, a bond of whose nature I was totally ignorant. Nevertheless, I knew enough to be sure that the Viceroy would never marry me and that I therefore ran no risk in prolonging his misconception and giving my friend, Lonreto, time to think of some way out of this sorry affair. For in helping a friend I felt I was doing a very beautiful deed. In the end I made up my mind to be a young girl. And to get into practice I leaned back in my litter, plumed myself and gave myself airs. I also remembered that I must be careful not to walk with great strides and that it was especially important to avoid any violent movements.

I had gone thus far in my reflections when a huge cloud of dust on the horizon announced the arrival of the Viceroy. The majordomo requested me to descend and offered me his arm. The Viceroy dismounted from his horse, bent his knee, and said:

"Señorita, be so gracious as to accept the declaration of a

love that began with your birth and will end only on my death."

With this he kissed my hand and, not waiting for my reply, led me back to my litter, mounted his horse and set the procession in motion. While he trotted his horse beside my litter, I had time for a good look at him. He was no longer the handsome young man he had seemed to Maria de Torres in the days when he rescued Rovellas or walked behind his cart in the village of Villaca. Though he could still be considered a fine looking man, his coloring, bronzed by a tropical sun, was more black than white and the heavy brows that hung over his eyes gave his face an expression that was far from friendly. When he spoke to men it was in a thundering voice but when speaking to women it was in a light falsetto which one could not hear without laughing; when he turned to his servants you might have thought he was commanding an army, and when he leaned down to speak to me it was as though he were about to accept my advice on a campaign.

The more I looked at the Viceroy the more unpleasant he seemed to me. I thought about his character and I was positive that the moment when he realized I was a boy would be the signal for a punishment, the mere thought of which made me shudder. I had no need to pretend fear; I trembled in every limb and I dared not look anyone in the face.

When we arrived at Valladolid, the majordomo gave me his hand and led me to the suite of rooms that had been reserved for me. Both aunts followed me. Elvira started to follow us too, but the servants pushed her aside as if she were a street urchin; Lonreto stayed with the muleteers.

When I was alone with both aunts I threw myself at their feet, implored them not to betray me, and painted a gruesome picture of the punishments which the slightest indiscretion would bring down upon me. My aunt was in despair at the thought that I might be beaten. Her moans and wails mingled with mine but to no avail. Maria de Torres, who was as terrified as we were, thought only of postponing the discovery as long as possible.

At last we were called to supper. The Viceroy received me at the door of the dining room, escorted me to my place and sat down at my left; he motioned Maria de Torres to the place beside him, my aunt the place opposite. This arrangement was carried out with the greatest formality. Then the majordomo showed the other guests to their places. For a long time we ate in silence. At last the Viceroy turned to Maria de Torres:

"Señora," he said, "I was grieved to learn from your letter that you appeared doubtful of my readiness to fulfill my promise to sue for the hand of the enchanting Elvira."

"Your Highness," replied Maria, "my niece would seem to be, and in fact would be, more worthy of your Grace had I thought you meant this in earnest."

"It is easy to see," said the Viceroy, "that you are a European, for in the New World people know that I never jest."

With this the conversation ended and was not resumed again. When we rose from the table, the Viceroy accompanied me to the door of my chamber. Both aunts went off to hunt for the real Elvira, who had been allowed to eat at the majordomo's table, and I was left behind with Elvira's lady's-maid who had now become mine. She knew I was a boy but she was no less zealous in serving me, for she too was terribly afraid of the Viceroy. We encouraged each other and ended by laughing merrily.

The aunts came back and, as the Viceroy did not wish to see us until the following day, they allowed Lonreto and Elvira to join us secretly. What a jolly time we had, laughing like mad, so delighted to have even one day's postponement, and the two aunts almost shared our exuberant spirits.

Late that evening we heard the twang of a guitar and saw the Viceroy, wrapped in a cloak and partially hidden by a neighboring house. His voice was no longer the voice of a young man, but he sang faultlessly and it was obvious that he knew a great deal about music.

Little Elvira, who was adept at the customs of gallantry, pulled off a glove and flung it down into the alley. The Viceroy picked it up, kissed it, and tucked it in his breast.

But scarcely had I observed this courtly gesture than I felt as though I were being given those hundred lashes I was bound to receive as soon as the Viceroy learned what sort of an Elvira he had in me. This upset me so that I had only one thought—to sleep. Elvira and Lonreto took leave of me and shed a few tears.

"Until tomorrow," I said.

"Perhaps," replied Lonreto.

I then went to bed in the same room with my new aunt, undressing as decently as I could, and she did the same.

The next morning we were awakened by my aunt Delanosa who informed us that Elvira and Lonreto had disappeared during the night and that no one knew what had become of them.

At this point in the gypsy's story, one of his men came to report to him. He rose and asked our permission to postpone the sequel until the next day.

Rebecca remarked rather impatiently that someone always interrupted us at the most exciting moments. Afterwards we talked about unimportant matters. The cabalist told us that the Wandering Jew had already passed the Balkans and would soon reach Spain. As I myself am not quite clear what we did that day, I shall therefore skip to the next day which proved to be much richer in events.

The eighteenth day

When I awoke at dawn I was seized with the desire to visit the fatal gallows of Los Hermanos again, a visit that turned out not to be in vain; for there I found, lying between the two hanged men, an unfortunate fellow who seemed to be unconscious and was quite stiff. I fetched water and sprinkled his face, but when I found that he did not recover consciousness, I lifted him on my back and carried him out of the gallows' enclosure. Gradually he came to himself, stared at me wildly and, springing up suddenly, fled across the fields. For a time I followed him with my eyes, until he was about to disappear into the thickets in which he could easily lose his way. I considered it my duty to hurry after him and stop him. The stranger turned and, seeing that I was following him, he began to run all the faster. A few moments later he staggered and fell, hurting his head. I cleaned his wound and bound his head with a piece of material that I tore from his shirt. The stranger did not say a word to me. But as he made no objection, I took him by the hand and led him to the gypsy camp, though even on the way there I could not get a word out of him.

When we came to the cave, I found them all assembled at breakfast. They had kept a place for me and now they made room for the stranger without asking who he was or where he came from. Such are the customs of Spanish hospitality which no one dares to violate.

The stranger gulped down his chocolate like a man who needs something to strengthen him. The gypsy leader asked whether it was robbers who had given him such ugly wounds.

"By no means," I replied, "I found this gentleman lying unconscious between the gallows of Los Hermanos. The moment he came to his senses he ran with all his might straight across the fields. As I was afraid he might lose his way in the thickets I dashed after him, and, at the very moment I reached him, he fell. The speed with which he ran away is the cause of his wounds."

At those words the stranger laid down his spoon and, turning to me, he said:

"Señor, you are mistaken. That is certainly the result of false principles you were taught in your youth."

You can imagine what impression that speech must have made on me. However, I controlled myself and replied:

"Señor stranger, allow me to assure you that, since my youth I have been inculcated with the highest principles which are all the more useful to me as I have the honor to be a captain in the Walloon Guards."

"I meant," the stranger went on, "the principles you employed when referring to the accelerated speed of a body across a sloping plain. When, for example, you speak of my fall and wish to explain the reasons for it, you must take the following into consideration. As the gallows stand on a height, I was obliged to run over sloping ground. One would, therefore, have to describe the line of my course as the hypotenuse of a right triangle, the base of which runs horizontally with the vertical line leading to the top of the triangle, that is, to the foot of the gallows. On this assumption you can say that my accelerated flight across the sloping ground was indeed one cause of my fall, just as the vertical line served as the hypotenuse. This accelerated flight, but not the doubling of my speed, was the cause of my fall—but this by no means prevents me from believing that you are a captain in the Walloon Guards."

After these words the stranger turned his attention to his chocolate and left me uncertain how I should interpret his reasoning. For truly I did not know whether he was serious or whether he was making fun of me. The gypsy leader noticed my annoyance at the stranger's remarks and changed the subject. As the noble traveler, who was obviously a master of geometry, needed a rest, he said, we should not force him to do any more talking today. "If you will allow me, I'll gladly take his place and go on with my story that was interrupted yesterday." Rebecca replied that she knew nothing she would enjoy more, and the gypsy began his story.

CONTINUATION OF THE STORY OF PANDESOWNA

We were interrupted yesterday just as Aunt Dalanosa came running with the news that Lonreto and Elvira had fled with Elvira dressed in boy's clothes. This news was a blow to Maria de Torres, who lost her niece and her son at one stroke: she was beside herself with grief. As for me, whom Elvira had deserted, there was nothing left but to continue to be Vicereine in her place or to submit to corporal punishment, which I feared more than death.

I was reflecting on those horrible alternatives when the majordomo informed me that we were ready to leave, offered me his arm and escorted me down the stairs. I was so imbued with the necessity of playing the part of the Vicereine that unconsciously I clasped my breast and looked so dignified that, in spite of their grief, my aunts had to laugh.

That day the Viceroy did not ride his horse beside my litter. We met him in Torquemada at the entrance to the public inn: the token of my favor I had granted him the evening before had emboldened him. Showing me my glove which he had hidden in his coat, he held out his hand to help me alight, pressed my hand gently and kissed it. I could not repress a sense of pleasure that a Viceroy should treat me in this manner; but I was still upset at the thought of the beating that would in all probability follow these homages.

The two ladies and I spent some time in a room reserved for women, and then we were called to the noonday meal where we were seated in almost exactly the same order as on the evening before. During the first course, deep silence reigned. As the second course was about to be served, the Viceroy turned to my aunt.

"Señora," he said, "I have learned of the trick your nephew and his little groom have played on you. If we were in Mexico, they would already be in my hands; nevertheless I have given orders to search for them. When they are found your nephew will be given a sound thrashing in the Theatine courtyard and the little stable-boy will be sent to the galleys." At the word galleys in connection with her son, Señora de Torres fainted, and the thought of the beating in the Theatine courtyard brought me out of my chair.

The Viceroy was most zealous and gallant in his efforts to help me; I recovered somewhat but for the rest of the meal I was in a sorry state. Afterwards, instead of escorting me to my room the Viceroy led me and my two aunts out under the trees opposite the inn and bade us be seated.

"My dear ladies," he said, "I am aware that you suspect me of a certain hardness in my behavior today which I have perhaps acquired in performing harsh duties but which is wholly foreign to my heart. Moreover, you must not judge me from a few incidents in my life, whose origin and connection you do not know. You must wish to know my story, and I think it is proper to tell you. I hope at least that when you know me better, you will lose that fear of me I have detected in you today."

After saying this the Viceroy fell silent and waited for our reply. We expressed our eagerness to know him better. He thanked us for our interest and began as follows:

THE STORY OF COUNT DE PENNA-VELEZ

I was born in the beautiful countryside of Granada, on an estate that my father owned on the banks of the romantic Genil. Spanish poets, as you know, place the scene of all their pastoral romances in our province. They have persuaded us that our climate is so conducive to love that there is no Granadan who does not devote his youth, and many of them their whole lives, to that passion. When a young man of Granada enters society, his first care is to choose the lady of his heart; if she accepts his homage he declares himself to be her *embecevido,* that is, the fool or dupe of her desires. The lady who recognizes him as such assumes the tacit obligation to entrust him, and no one else, with her gloves and her fan and to prefer him above all others to bring her a glass of water which the *embecevido* offers her on bended knee. Furthermore he has the right to ride his horse beside her litter, to offer her holy water in church and many other privileges of similar importance. Husbands are not jealous of this sort of relationship nor would they have any reason to be; first, because ladies never receive anyone at home, and outside of the house they are surrounded all day long by *dueñas* and lady's-maids; moreover, to tell the truth, women who have decided to betray their husbands would not choose the *embecevido.* They cast their eyes on some young relative who has entrance to their house; and the most depraved women take their lovers from the lower classes.

That, therefore, was the situation in Granada when I entered society. The fashion did not attract me; not that I was lacking in passion: far from it. More than most men I was susceptible to the amorousness our climate arouses, and the longing to love was the first emotion that rejoiced my youth. However, from the very beginning I was convinced that love was something more than this exchange of foolishness in which our ladies indulged with their *embecevidos.* Though it was a truly harmless exchange, it had the effect of confining a woman's interest to a man to whom she could never belong and of weakening her feeling for the one to whom she belonged by marriage. This division disgusted me. Love and marriage seemed to me to be one and the same thing;

and a marriage, enriched by all the attributes of love, became my deepest and dearest desire, the ideal of my boldest dreams. Moreover, I must admit that the more I fostered those dreams, the more they took possession of my whole soul, so much so that my judgment was affected and I could have been considered a real *embecevido.*

When I went to the house of a friend I took no part in the conversation but amused myself by imagining that this house was mine and that it would be the future home of my wife. In my mind I furnished her salon with the most beautiful fabrics from India, with Chinese mats, with Persian carpets on which I could already see the traces of her footsteps. If she went out to take the air, she stepped out onto a balcony decorated with most beautiful flowers and with an aviary full of the rarest birds. Her bedroom, on the other hand, was a shrine which my imagination dared not desecrate. While I was absorbed in those thoughts the conversation would be going on around me. My share in it therefore consisted in giving senseless answers when I was addressed, and always somewhat ill-naturedly at that, for I did not like to have my thoughts disturbed.

If my manner during those visits seemed strange, it was even more so when I went for a walk. If I had to cross a stream, I walked into the water up to my knees, while, in my imagination, my wife stepped from stone to stone, leaning on my arm and rewarding my solicitude with a heavenly smile. I adored our children; I could not meet any of them without almost devouring them with loving caresses. And, for me, a woman who nursed her child was the masterpiece of creation.

Here the Viceroy turned to me with an expression of mingled tenderness and respect.

"On this point I have not changed my opinion. I am convinced that my adored Elvira will not allow the impure blood of a wet nurse to be mingled in the veins of her children."

Those words upset me more than you can imagine. Clasping my hands, I said: "Your Highness, in the name of Heaven, I implore you never to speak of such matters for I know nothing about them."

"My dear young lady," said the Viceroy, "I am distressed to have wounded your innocence. I shall continue my story and shall take care not to make such a mistake again." And with that, he went on as follows:

Because I frequently appeared to be distracted, people in Granada began to think I had lost my mind and in that there was some truth. But they were more inclined to think I was a fool because my folly was different from the folly of my fellow citizens and I would have been considered clever if I had been the official fool of a lady of Granada. As, however, that reputation was not exactly flattering, I decided to leave my homeland for some time. There was also another reason for this move: I wanted to be happy with my wife. Had I married a girl from Granada, she would have felt entitled to accept the admiration of an *embecevido,* and this would have displeased me. I therefore left Granada and went to Court. Here under other names I found the same nonsense: the *embecevido,* which today has come from Granada to Madrid, was not yet in vogue. The Court ladies called their favorite, but unfortunate, lovers *cortejos* and just plain *galanes*—those they treated even worse and whom they rewarded at the most with a smile once or twice a month. But all the men, without exception, wore their ladies' colors and pranced their horses around their carriages, which stirred up such a dust every day in the Prado that no one could live on the streets near that beautiful promenade. I had neither the background nor the money to cut a figure at Court; only in bullfighting did I make a name for myself. The King talked with me many times and many of the grandees did me the honor to seek my friendship. Among others, I was well acquainted with Count de Rovellas. At the time I killed his bull, he was half unconscious and did not recognize me. Two of his *picadores* knew very well who I was, but obviously they were busy somewhere else or they would certainly not have failed to claim the thousand gold pieces the Count offered for information about his rescuer.

One day at a luncheon given by the Minister of Finances I sat next to Don Henrique de Torres, the Señora's distinguished husband who had come to Madrid on business. It was the first time I had had the honor of talking with him; but his whole manner inspired such confidence that I did not hesitate to bring the conversation around to his favorite topic; I mean, to marriage and gallantry. I asked Don Henrique whether the ladies of Segovia also had their *embecevidos,* their *cortejos,* their *galanes.*

"No," he replied. "Our customs do not permit that sort of thing. When our ladies stroll on the promenade (we call it *locodover*) it is not customary to approach them whether they are on foot or in their carriage. We do receive a man or a woman in our houses for more than a first visit; it is customary, however, for our ladies to spend the evening on their balcony which is somewhat higher than the street. The men stand below and talk to their acquaintances. To begin with, the young men stroll from balcony to balcony but they always end the evening in front of the house of a marriageable girl. However, Don Henrique added, of all the balconies in Segovia, mine enjoys the most frequent ovations; they are in honor of my sister-in-law, Elvira de Noruña, who combines all the distinguished qualities of my wife with a beauty that has no equal in Spain."

The Marquis de Torres's words made a great impression on me. Such a beautiful young woman, with such outstanding qualities, in a land where there were no *embecevidos*—this all seemed ordained by heaven for my happiness. Several people from Segovia with whom I talked agreed that Elvira's beauty was incomparable—and I decided to make sure of this with my own eyes. Even before I left Madrid my passion for Elvira had already reached certain proportions. Unfortunately my shyness had increased in the same ratio so that when I arrived in Segovia I could not bring myself to call on the Marquis de Torres or on any of the other people whose acquaintance I had made in Madrid. I wished that someone would speak as well of me to Elvira as they had spoken of her to me. I envied any man who had a great name or a brilliant reputation for, unless I made an impression on Elvira before I met her, I was afraid it would be impossible in future to arouse her interest in me.

I spent several days in my inn and saw no one. Finally as I was being driven through the street on which Don Henrique lived, I saw a sign on the house opposite and asked if there was a room for rent. I was shown a room under the roof, which I promptly took. I called myself Alonzo and said I had come here on business. My entire business, however, consisted only in peering through the shutters! Towards evening I saw you, Señora, come out on the balcony with the incomparable Elvira. What shall I say? My first thought was that I was looking at a great beauty. On closer scrutiny I realized that though the perfect harmony of her features made her beauty less striking, this was the very point on which she had the advantage over other women. You yourself, Señora de Torres, were beautiful, but I venture to say that you could not stand comparison with your sister.

From my attic room I was pleased to note Elvira's indifference to all the homage paid her. But this observation robbed me of any desire to add my name to the list of her admirers, who bored her. I determined to watch her from my window and to wait for a favorable opportunity to make myself known. I admit that I counted a little on the bullfights.

You will recall, Señora, that in those days I sang quite well. I could not resist the desire to let her hear my voice. When, therefore, all the suitors had gone home, I went down to the street with my guitar and sang a *tirana* as well as I could. This I repeated for many nights until finally I noticed that you did not leave until you had heard me. This knowledge filled my heart with an emotion that was ineffably sweet but still far from hope.

At that time I learned that Rovellas had been sent into exile in Segovia and I was in despair for I was sure he would fall in love with Elvira. I was not mistaken. As though he were still in Madrid, he declared himself openly as your sister's *cortejo* (suitor). He wore her colors or what he thought were her colors, and had a motley livery made out of them. From the height of my attic room I witnessed his shameless impudence a long time and I was glad to see that Elvira judged him more by his personal qualities than by the sensation he created. But he was rich and about to be made a grandee; what similar advantages had I to offer? Practically none. Of this I was convinced; and so unselfish was my love for Elvira that I was ready to wish she would marry Rovellas. I no longer wanted to make her acquaintance and I stopped singing beneath her window.

Rovellas, on the other hand, expressed his passion only through courtly gallantries and made no move to win Elvira's hand. I learned that the Marquis de Torres intended to retire to Villaca. For me it had become a sweet custom to live opposite his house. To assure myself therefore of the same advantage in the country, I hastened to Villaca, let it be known that I was a farmer from Murcia and bought a house opposite yours. I furnished it according to my own taste but, knowing that lovers are always found out at some point, I hit upon the idea of bringing my sister from Granada and introducing her as my wife. This, I thought, would allay any suspicion. After I had made all these arrangements I returned to Segovia where I learned that Rovellas was preparing to stage a magnificent bullfight. "At that time, Señora de Torres, you had a two-year-old child. Do tell me what has become of him?"

Maria de Torres could not help thinking that this two-year-old child was the little groom the Viceroy wanted to send to the galleys. She took out her handkerchief and dried her tears.

"Forgive me," the Viceroy said, "I see I have touched on a sad memory, but to continue my story I must speak of that unfortunate child."

You will remember that, at that time, your child fell ill with smallpox. You suffered a tender mother's anxiety and I knew that Elvira, too, spent days and nights at the sick child's bedside. I cannot resist the longing to tell you that in those days, too, a dying man shared your anxieties and walked beneath your window night after night, singing nostalgic romances. "Do you remember that, Señora de Torres?"

"I remember it very well," said Maria de Torres.

Your child's illness, the Viceroy continued, became the talk of the town, for it postponed the bullfights; and his recovery was hailed with joy by all. The bullfight took place, but it did not have a happy ending. Rovellas was badly mauled and would have been killed had I not stepped in front of the raging animal. I thrust my sword in the bull's neck, looked up at your box, saw Elvira lean over to you and speak of me, and the expression on her face made me very happy. Then I disappeared into the crowd.

The next day Rovellas, who had partially recovered, wrote to your husband, the Marquis de Torres, and asked for Elvira's hand. Rumor had it that he had not been accepted, but he himself said he had been successful. When, however, I learned that you were preparing to leave for Villaca, I took that to mean that he had been rejected. I then went to Villaca where I adopted the habits of a peasant. I even drove my carts myself—or pretended to—for in reality I let my servants do all the work.

Several days later as I was returning home behind my oxen, arm in arm with my sister, I saw you with Elvira and your husband, sitting in front of your house door, drinking chocolate. Your sister recognized me, but I did not give myself away. However, I could not resist a little trick which, I hoped, would stimulate your interest: on entering the house, I played some of the songs I had sung during Lonreto's illness. Before I disclosed my identity, I wanted to be sure that Rovellas had been rejected.

"Oh, Your Grace," cried Maria de Torres. "You were certainly not indifferent to Elvira and it is equally certain that, at first, she refused Rovellas even though later she married him—perhaps because she thought you were married."

"Señora," replied the Viceroy, "let us not grumble about the designs Providence had on my unworthy person. If I had won Elvira's hand neither the Assenipols nor the Appalachian-Chirigoas would have been converted to the Christian faith, and the Cross, holy symbol of our salvation, would not have been planted three degrees north of the Red Sea."

"That may be," said Maria de Torres, "but my sister and my husband would still be alive. But, Your Highness, please go on with your story."

One day after your arrival in Villaca, I learned that my mother was seriously ill. A son's devotion prevailed over love and, with my sister, I hastened to her side. My mother's illness lasted three months; in the end she died in our arms. Perhaps I did not mourn her as long as I should have, but in any case I returned to Segovia where I learned that Elvira had become the Countess de Rovellas. At the same time I was told the Count had offered a reward for information about his rescuer. I sent him an anonymous letter and departed for Madrid where I asked to be given a post in America. This post I received without any trouble and I set sail as soon as possible. My sojourn in Villaca had been a secret known only to my sister and me—at least so I thought. But servants are born spies and miss nothing. A servant I had dismissed when I sailed to the New World entered the Count de Rovellas's service, lost his heart to a chambermaid of the first lady-in-waiting at Court and confided to her the whole story of my stay in Villaca and of my disguise. The lady-in-waiting told the *dueña-mayor* and the latter made it her business to tell the Count. The latter put all those facts together with the anonymous letter and my skill at bullfighting and came to the conclusion that I had been his wife's lover. Imagine my astonishment when, on my arrival in America, I received a letter which read as follows:

Your Excellency, Don Sancho de Penna-Sombre:
I am informed that you have had a love affair with the dishonorable person whom I no longer recognize as the Countess de Rovellas. If you consider it advisable, you may look after the child she will bear. As for me, I am following in your footsteps to America where I hope to meet you for the last time in my life.

That letter plunged me into black despair which reached a climax when I learned of the deaths of Elvira, your husband and Count de Rovellas, whom I had hoped to convince of his hideous mistake. However I did everything in my power to refute the slander and to clarify his daughter's position; I vowed solemnly to marry her as soon as she was of age, or at least not to take any other woman to wife. After I had fulfilled this pledge, I felt that I was justified in seeking death, for my religion forbids me to take my own life.

A native leader, allied with the Spanish people, was making war against his neighbors. I enlisted in his service. But before I could be accepted, I must submit to being tattooed all over my body with the outlines of a snake and a frog; the snake's head is tattooed on my right shoulder, the body winds three times around my body and ends at the big toe on my left foot. The native who performs this operation pricks deeply into the leg bones and other sensitive parts of the body and the candidate must not show any sign of pain. I withstood the test: I won the war-club and the martyrdom and I flung myself into battle. We captured one hundred and thirty scalps and I was chosen on the battlefield to be the Casique. Two years later the people of New Mexico were under the Spanish crown and converted to Christianity. The rest of my story you know more or less. I have been given the highest honors a subject of the Spanish King can hope to attain. However, charming Elvira, I must inform you that you can never be Vicereine. The State Council in Madrid no longer invests married men with such great power in the New World. The moment you consent to marry me, I shall cease to be the Viceroy. I can offer you nothing but the title of a grandee, a true and loving heart and a sizable fortune, the origin of which I must explain to you as you will share it in future.

After I had conquered two provinces in northern Mexico, the King granted me the right to develop one of the richest silver mines. For this purpose I selected as my associate a speculator from Vera Cruz. The first year we collected a dividend of three million piastres; but as the grant was in my name, I received six times one hundred piastres more than my associate.

"Pardon me, Señor," the stranger broke in, "the sum due to the Viceroy was one million eight hundred piastres, the sum due to the associate, however, was one million two hundred thousand."

"That is what I mean," said the gypsy leader.

"In order words to put it frankly," said the stranger, "half of the sum total plus half of the difference. That is as plain as that two and two make four."

"You are right, Señor," replied the gypsy leader, and went on with his story.

"The Viceroy, who was eager to give me an exact account of his fortune, said: 'The second year we dug deeper into the earth and had to build corridors, pits, galleries. Our expenses, which up to then had come to a fourth, were increased by an eighth, but the quantity of the ore dropped to a sixth.' "

At those words the geometer took a little tablet and a pencil out of his pocket; as he thought he was holding a pen, he dipped the pencil in the chocolate. Noticing that the pen did not write, he tried to wipe it on his black coat, but instead wiped it on Rebecca's dress and then began to scribble on his tablet. We all laughed heartily at his absent-mindedness. Then the gypsy leader went on with his story as follows:

"That year our difficulties were even greater. We had to send for miners from Peru and give them a fifteenth of the earnings, but we did not burden them with the expenses which that year had risen two-fifths. On the other hand, the quantity of ore had increased six-fourths in comparison with last year's intake."

It did not take me long to realize that the gypsy leader was trying to upset the geometer's calculations. And in fact he went on to clothe his story in the form of an arithmetical problem.

"From that day on our dividends were constantly two-seventeenths less. However, as I had laid aside gold taken out of the pits and added the interest to my capital, the sum total of my fortune amounted to fifty million piastres which, together with my title, my heart and my hand, I lay at your feet."

At this the stranger rose, immediately began to write on his tablet and started to walk back along the path that led to the camp. But instead of going straight ahead, he turned into the path that led to the mountain stream from which the gypsies drew their water. A few minutes later we heard the splash of a body falling into the water.

Rushing to his aid, I jumped into the water, fought against the current and at last managed to pull the absent-minded fellow ashore. While he was being given first aid to rid him of the water he had swallowed, we made a huge fire. At last, after prolonged efforts on our part, the geometer regained consciousness and gazed at us in bewilderment.

"You can be sure," he said in a weak voice, "that the

Viceroy's fortune amounted to sixty million fifty-two thousand one hundred and sixty-one piastres, provided that his share was always one thousand eight hundred to one thousand two hundred of his associate's share, in other words, three to one."

With that the geometer lapsed into a sort of coma from which we made no effort to rouse him for we thought he needed rest. He slept until six o'clock in the evening and woke to babble all sorts of nonsense. The first question he asked was who had fallen into the water. When told that it had been he and that I had fished him out, he came over to me, looking very gentle and courteous and said:

"I really wouldn't have thought I could swim so well. I'm especially pleased to have saved, for the King, one of his bravest officers; for you, Señor, are a captain in the Walloon Guards, you told me so yourself, and I have an excellent memory."

Everyone burst out laughing but the geometer was not in the least embarrassed and amused us with his absent-mindedness. The cabalist was engrossed in his own thoughts and talked incessantly about the Wandering Jew who was to bring him certain information about two demons named Emina and Zibeddé. Rebecca put her arm through mine and drew me away from the others.

"Dear Alfonso," she said. "Do tell me your opinion of the things you have heard and seen since you came to these mountains and also what you make of the two hanged men who give us so much trouble."

"I don't know how to answer those questions," I replied. "I have no idea what the secret that torments your brother can be. As far as I am concerned, I am convinced that I was drugged with a sleeping potion and placed under the gallows. Moreover you yourself told me of the great power the Gomelez secretly wield in this part of the country."

"That is true," said Rebecca. "I think they are trying to convert you to the faith of the Prophet and in my opinion that is just what you should do."

"What!" I cried. "So you share their views?"

"Not at all," she replied. "I have my own ends in view. I told you, didn't I, that I could not fall in love either with a man of my faith or with a Christian. But let us go back to the others. We shall discuss this another time in more detail."

Rebecca joined her brother, and as I walked on in the opposite direction, I began to meditate on all that had happened and all I had heard. But the deeper I became immersed in my thoughts, the more involved it all seemed to me.

The nineteenth day

The whole company assembled early in the cave; only the gypsy leader failed to appear. The geometer had completely recovered and, convinced that he had hauled me out of the water, he gazed at me with the expression of a man who has done a friend a great service. Rebecca was highly amused at his extraordinary reaction. When we had finished breakfast, she addressed us as follows:

"We have lost much by the chief's absence, for I am dying of curiosity to learn how he reacted to the Viceroy's offer of his hand and his fortune. To be sure the noble stranger in our midst could atone for our loss if he would tell us his adventures which are sure to be interesting. He appears to have devoted himself to sciences not altogether unknown to me so that everything that happens to such a man would naturally command my closest attention."

"I do not think," said the stranger, "that you have worked in the same sciences, for as a rule women do not understand the most elementary rudiments of those subjects. But as you have received me so kindly, I consider it my duty to tell you all about myself. I shall therefore begin with the statement that my name is . . . my name is . . ."

"What!" cried Rebecca. "Are you so absent-minded, Señor, that you have forgotten your own name?"

"Not at all," replied the geometer. "I am not naturally absent-minded, but one day, my father, in a moment of distraction, signed his brother's name instead of his own and thereby lost his wife, his fortune and the pay for services he had rendered his country. To avoid a similar catastrophe I have had my name engraved on this little tablet and ever since then, whenever I am obliged to sign a paper, I copy it faithfully."

"But," Rebecca protested, "we want you to tell us your name, not to sign it."

"Of course, you are right," replied the geometer and, tucking the notebook into his pocket, he began as follows:

THE STORY OF THE GEOMETER

My name is Don Pedro Velasquez. I am descended from the ancient family of the Marquis Velasquez who, since the discovery of gunpowder, have all served in the artillery and were Spain's most experienced officers in that arm of the service. Don Ramiro Velasquez, commander-in-chief of Artillery under Philip IV, was raised by Philip's successor to the high rank of a grandee. Don Ramiro had two sons who were both married. Title and fortune always passes to the first-born. But in this case, the eldest son, far from wasting his time on a life of leisure among Court circles, devoted himself to the honorable activities to which the family owed its distinction, and made every possible effort to aid his younger brother.

And so it went in every generation down to Sancho, the fifth Duke Velasquez, the great uncle of Don Ramiro's eldest son. Like his ancestors before him, Don Sancho had the distinction of being commander-in-chief of Artillery and was, in addition, governor of Galicia in which province he usually resided. He married the daughter of the Duke of Alba and this marriage was as fortunate for him as it was an honor for all our house. However, not all of Don Sancho's hopes were realized. The Duchess, his wife, had only one daughter, Bianca. The Duke intended to marry her to one of the Velasquez from the younger branch so that the title and fortune of the Velasquez would pass to that line and remain in the family. My father, Don Henrique, and his brother, Don Carlos, had just lost their father who was descended from Don Ramiro and had held equal rank with the Duke of Velasquez. At the Duke's command, both young men were sent to his house. My father was then twelve years old, my uncle eleven. But their outlook on life was utterly different. My father was serious, immersed in his studies and extremely sensitive, whereas his brother Carlos was frivolous, inconstant and could not spend a moment over a book. When the Duke discovered these varied tendencies, he decided to make my father his son-in-law and, to prevent Bianca from falling in love with a different choice, he sent Don Carlos to Paris to be brought up under the care of Count Hereira, a relative who was at that time Spanish Minister to Paris.

Day by day my father's good qualities, his kindness of heart and his tireless industry won the Duke's affection. Bianca, too, who knew of the choice that had been made for her, grew more and more fond of him. She even shared her young lover's tastes and followed him slowly along the path of learning. Picture to yourself a young man whose exceptional talents encompassed all of human knowledge at an age when most young men are first approaching the rudiments. Imagine also the same young man in love with a girl of the same age, who was gifted with unusual mental capacities, longed to understand him and rejoiced in the successes she shared with him—then you will have an approximate idea of the happiness my father enjoyed in that brief period of his life. And why should not Bianca have loved him? The old Duke was proud of him, the whole province respected him and he was not yet twenty when his fame extended beyond the borders of Spain. Bianca's love for her fiancé was a purely selfish love. Henrique, however, who lived only for her, loved her with all his heart. For the old Duke he entertained almost the same feeling as for the daughter but he often thought wistfully of his brother and regretted his absence.

"Dearest Bianca," he would say to his fianceé. "Don't you think our happiness would be complete if Carlos were here? There are enough pretty girls here to make him want to settle down. To be sure he is fickle, he writes but seldom, but a sweet and clever wife would tame his heart. Dear Bianca, I adore you and I respect your father, but since nature has given me a brother, why does fate keep us apart so long?"

One day the Duke sent for my father.

"Don Henrique," he said, "I have just received a letter from the King, our most gracious lord. I should like to read it to you. This is what he writes."

My Cousin:

At our last council meeting we decided to call for new plans to strengthen the defense of our realm. We see that opinion in Europe is divided between the Vauban and the Cochoorn methods. Kindly set your most experienced officers to work on this matter. Send us your plans and, if we find one among them that pleases us, we shall entrust the author with its execution. Moreover our royal favor will reward him appropriately. Meanwhile may the grace of God be with you.

Your very affectionate
Cousin and King

"Well, what about it?" said the Duke. "Do you, my dear Henrique, feel that you have the ability to enter this contest? I must warn you that your competitors will be not only the most famous engineers from Spain but also from all Europe."

My father thought this over and then replied firmly:

"Yes, Your Highness, although I am a beginner in this profession, Your Highness can trust me."

"Very well then," said the Duke. "Do your best and when you have finished the work nothing shall stand in the way of your happiness. Bianca shall be yours."

You can imagine how eagerly my father set to work. All

day long and all night long he sat at his table and when his weary mind demanded a rest, he spent the time in Bianca's company, talking with her of their future happiness and of the joy he would experience on embracing Carlos when the latter returned from France. In this way a whole year passed. At last plans for fortifications poured in from every part of Spain and from every country in Europe. They were sealed and deposited in the Duke's chancellery. My father realized that it was time to complete his work and he perfected it to such an extent that I can give you only a faint idea of it. He had begun with drawing up the main principle of attack and defense and then introduced the proof, showing on which points Cochoorn agreed with this principle and on which points he departed from it. My father rated Vauban much higher than Cochoorn; nevertheless he prophesied that Vauban would not change his system and in this statement time was to prove him right. All these arguments are substantiated not only by the scientific theory, but in addition by details relating to the condition of the site and the foreseeable expenditure and supplemented by calculations whose accuracy not even the most experienced scientists could conceive.

When my father had written the last sentence, he discovered sundry inaccuracies he had not noticed before. Trembling in every limb, he took his manuscript to the Duke, who returned it to him the next morning with the following words:

"My dear nephew, yours is undoubtedly the best plan. I shall send it off immediately. Now think only of your marriage which will soon be solemnized."

My father fell at the Duke's feet.

"Your Highness," he said, "permit my brother to return, for my happiness will not be complete if I am not allowed to embrace him after such a long time."

The Duke frowned.

"I foresee," he said, "that Carlos will talk us to death with his praises of the magnificence at the Court of Louis XIV, but as that is your desire, I shall send for him."

My father kissed the Duke's hand and went off to see Bianca. From then on he had no further interest in geometry. Love filled every moment of his life.

Meanwhile the King, who held to his decision, ordered all the plans to be reviewed and carefully checked. My father's work was unanimously accepted. Soon thereafter my father received a letter from the Minister expressing the greatest satisfaction and inquiring, at the King's command, how he would like to be rewarded. Meanwhile in the letter addressed to the Duke, the Minister hinted that if he so desired, the young man would certainly be granted the rank of a colonel in the Artillery.

My father took the letter to the Duke, who read him the one he had received. But my father declared he would never dare to accept that rank which, in his opinion, he had not earned and he begged the Duke to answer the Minister in his name. The Duke refused.

"The Minister wrote to you," he said, "and you should answer him. No doubt the Minister has his own reasons for it. As in his letter to me he spoke of you as a young man, your youth probably roused the King's interest and the Minister wishes to hand His Majesty a letter from the promising young man written in his own hand. And finally we can write such a letter without appearing to be presumptuous." So saying the Duke sat down at his desk and began to write:

Most Gracious Sovereign:
Your Majesty's assurance of his satisfaction is reward enough for any well-born Castilian. However, encouraged by Your Majesty's kindness, I take the liberty of seeking Your Majesty's consent to my marriage to Bianca Velasquez, heir to the fortune and titles of our house.

Such a change in rank will in no wise lessen my zeal in the service of my country and of its ruler. I would be exceedingly happy if my work should earn for me the honor of becoming a colonel in the First Artillery in which arm of the service many of my ancestors have served with distinction.

Your Royal Highness, etc. etc.

My father thanked the Duke for writing this letter, went to his room and copied it word for word. As he was about to sign it, he heard a voice calling from the courtyard: "Don Carlos is here!"

"Who? My brother?" cried my father. "Where is he? Let me embrace him!"

"Finish your letter, Don Henrique," said the messenger who was to take it at once to the minister. My father was so excited over his brother's arrival and so nervous at being pressed by the messenger that instead of signing "Don Henrique" he wrote "Don Carlos Velasquez," sealed the letter and hurried down to welcome his brother.

The brothers embraced affectionately, but Don Carlos immediately drew back, laughing uproariously.

"My dear Henrique, you look like the Scaramouche of the Italian comedy as one drop of water is like another. Your ruff surrounds your lower jaw like a barber's cup. Nevertheless I love you truly. And now let us go to the old man."

The two brothers then went to the old Duke, whom Don Carlos nearly crushed with the embraces he had learned at the French Court.

"Dear uncle," he cried. "Your fat ambassador gave me a letter for you but somehow I managed to lose it at my bath attendant's. But after all it's not so important! Gramont Roquelaire and all the old boys send you their warmest greetings."

"But my dear nephew," the Duke interrupted this flow of words, "I do not know any of these gentlemen."

"That's your hard luck," replied Carlos. "They're very nice people. But where is my future sister-in-law? Since I saw her last, she must have become a ravishing beauty."

At that moment Bianca entered the room. Don Carlos went up to her boldly.

"My divine sister-in-law," he cried. "In Paris it is the custom to kiss beautiful women," and so saying he kissed her on the cheek to the great amazement of Henrique who had so far seen Bianca only in the company of her women and had never dared to kiss even her hand. Don Carlos talked a great deal of nonsense which worried Henrique and horrified the old Duke. At last the latter said sternly:

"Go take off your riding clothes. We are having a ball here tonight. And do not forget that what may be considered courtesy on the other side of the mountains, on this side is called impudence."

"Dear Uncle," replied Carlos. "I shall wear a new fashion that Louis XIV designed especially for his courtiers and you will be convinced that he is every inch a great monarch. I shall invite my beautiful cousin to dance a saraband. Though it is originally a Spanish dance, you will see to what perfection the French have brought it."

With these words Carlos went off humming an air from Lully. Henrique, who was greatly worried by this frivolous attitude, tried to apologize for him to Bianca and the Duke, but in vain; the old Duke already had too many reservations about Carlos, whereas Bianca did not disapprove of anything he did.

When the ball opened Bianca appeared gowned not in Spanish style, but in the latest French fashion. The guests all gazed at her in surprise and, although she explained that her godfather, the Ambassador, had sent her this dress via Don Carlos, that explanation satisfied no one.

Don Carlos kept the company waiting a long time. At last he appeared magnificently clad in the latest fashion from the Court of Louis XIV: a blue coat embroidered all over in silver, a white satin sash just as lavishly embroidered, jabot and cuffs of Brussels lace and wearing on his head a white *perruque,* of imposing size. This magnificent costume appeared even more splendid in contrast to the miserable fashion our last kings from the House of Austria had introduced at the Spanish Court. The Spaniards did not even wear a ruff which would have lent them at least a little distinction, but instead a simple collar of the sort worn by *alguaciles* and lawyers of that day, apparel which, as Don Carlos so aptly remarked, reminded one of Scaramouche. Our flibbertigibbet, whose clothes distinguished him from the young Spanish nobles, was even more conspicuous by the manner in which he entered the ballroom. Instead of making a low bow, a courtesy he might have shown, he began at once to berate the musicians, calling out to them at the far end of the room:

"Ho there, you wretched strummers! If you dare to play anything but a saraband, I'll bend your violins around your ears!"

He then handed them the music he had brought with

him, went over to Bianca and led her out on the floor. My father admitted that Carlos was an incomparable dancer, but Bianca, who was naturally graceful, outdid herself this time. After the saraband was over, all the ladies rose to congratulate Bianca on her charming performance. Though to all appearances they intended their compliments for Bianca alone, they kept stealing glances at Carlos as though they wanted him to understand that he was really the sole object of their admiration. Bianca easily sensed their thought and the ladies' secret homage made the young man all the more attractive in her eyes. Throughout the entire evening Carlos did not leave Bianca's side and when Henrique came up to them, he said:

"Henrique, my dear boy, run along now and solve your algebra problems. You will have time enough to bore Bianca when you are her husband."

Bianca's merry laughter spurred on this impudence and poor Don Henrique, completely bewildered, left them. When supper was announced Carlos offered Bianca his hand and took his place beside her at the head of the table. The Duke raised his eyebrows, but Don Henrique begged him to forgive his brother this time.

During the banquet Don Carlos regaled the guests with tales of receptions at the Court of Louis XIV, in particular a ballet called "Olympian Love" in which the monarch played the role of the Sun—a role he, Carlos, could also play to perfection. Bianca, he declared, would be enchanting as Diana; whereupon he proceeded to assign the roles and before the banquet was over, Louis XIV's ballet was completely organized. When Don Henrique left the ballroom, Bianca did not even notice his absence.

The next morning when my father went to see Bianca he found her practicing a scene from the ballet with Carlos. In this way three weeks passed. The Duke became more and more morose and crabbed, Henrique hid his suffering, while Carlos, on the other hand, talked the most ridiculous nonsense which the ladies of the Court considered oracular. Paris and Louis XIV's ballet turned Bianca's head to such an extent that she was oblivious to everything that was going on around her.

One day at dinner the Duke received a dispatch from Court. It was written in the Minister's hand and contained these words:

Your Highness!
His Majesty, our generous lord has consented to the marriage of your daughter with Don Carlos Velasquez. In addition he bestows on him the title of grandee and appoints him colonel in the First Artillery.

Your obedient servant etc., etc.

"What does this mean?" shouted the Duke in a furious rage. "How can Carlos's name appear in this letter when I intend to give Bianca to Henrique as his wife."

My father begged the Duke to listen to him patiently.

"Your Highness," he said. "I do not know why Carlos's name appears in this letter instead of mine, but I am certain that my brother has had nothing to do with this. In the end no one is to blame and it seems as though this change in names has come about quite clearly through the dispensation of Providence. Your Highness must have noticed that Bianca is not interested in me; but that, on the contrary, she is by no means indifferent to Carlos. Therefore may her hand, her title and her fortune be bestowed on him. I renounce all my rights."

The Duke turned to his daughter.

"Bianca! Bianca . . ." he cried. "Are you really so fickle and faithless?"

Bianca burst into tears and fainted. In the end she admitted that she loved Carlos. In deep despair the Duke said to my father:

"My dear Henrique, if your brother has stolen your fiancée from you, he shall not rob you of the colonelcy in the First Artillery, to which I shall add half of my fortune."

"Forgive me, Your Highness," my father replied. "Your fortune, undivided, belongs to your daughter. As for the honor of being made a colonel, the King has done the right thing in granting that post to my brother. Permit me, Your Highness, to retire to a holy retreat to ease my suffering at the foot of the altar and to offer that pain as a sacrifice to Him who suffered so much for us."

My father left the house and entered a Camaldensian monastery where he was received as a novice. Don Carlos took Bianca to wife, but the marriage was celebrated without pomp. The Duke was not present. Bianca, who had driven her father to despair, grieved over the various misfortunes for which she was to blame and even Carlos, despite his customary frivolity, was disturbed by the general air of mourning.

Soon thereafter the Duke fell ill of gout that spread over his body as far as his chest. When he realized that he had only a little while to live, he sent a messenger to the Camaldensians to say that he wished to see his beloved Henrique once more. Alvarez, the marshal of the royal house, brought the message to the monastery. Following the rule that forbade them to speak, the monks answered not a word, but led him to Henrique's cell. Alvarez found him lying on a bed of straw, clothed in rags and bound by a chain around his body to the wall. My father recognized Alvarez.

"My friend," he said, "how did you like the saraband I danced yesterday? Louis XIV himself was pleased with me, but unfortunately the musicians played atrociously. And what does Bianca say? Bianca! Bianca! Answer me, unhappy one!" At this my father rattled his chains, began to bite his hands and was seized with a horrible fit of madness. Alvarez burst into tears, went away and informed the Duke of the sad sight that had met his eyes.

The next day the Duke's gout had reached his heart and they feared for his life. Just before he died he turned to his daughter. "Bianca! Bianca!" he said, "Henrique will soon follow me. We forgive you . . . Be happy!"

Her father's last words struck Bianca to the heart and filled her with remorse. Soon thereafter she lapsed into a state of deepest melancholy.

Young Duke Carlos did his best to cheer his wife, but as he had no success, he left her to her grief. He brought a famous cocotte named Lajardin from Paris and Bianca withdrew to a convent. The post of colonel of the First Artillery was not suited to Carlos. For a time he tried to fill it, but as he was unable to carry out his duties honorably, he offered the King his resignation and asked for another position at Court. The King appointed him Gentleman of the Bedchamber and the Duke, taking Mademoiselle Lajardin with him, moved to Madrid.

My father remained with the Camaldensians for three years after which time, as the result of the monks' devoted care and angelic patience, he was finally restored to health. He then set out for Madrid to call on the Minister. He was shown into the council room where the dignitary addressed him as follows:

"This matter of yours, Don Henrique, has come to the ears of the King who is very angry at the mistake. Fortunately I still had your letter with the signature 'Don Carlos.' Here it is. Now will you kindly explain why you did not sign your own name?"

My father looked at the letter and recognized his own handwriting.

"Your Excellency," he said, "I remember that I was in the act of signing this letter when I was informed of my brother's arrival. My joy at that news was doubtless the reason for my mistake. Nevertheless I cannot blame my misfortune on this error. Even if the commission had been made out in my name, I would not have been able to fill that high honor. But now at last I have recovered my former mental strength and I would be able to fulfill the duties His Majesty had formerly assigned to me."

"My dear Henrique," replied the Minister, "our fortification plans have collapsed and we at Court do not make a point of mulling over past business. However I can offer you the post of commander of the fortress at Ceuta. At the moment it is the only one I have at my disposal. If you take it, you would have to leave without seeing the King. I admit that this post is not commensurate with your abilities; moreover, at your age, I can understand that it is difficult to settle down on a deserted African rock."

"For that very reason," replied my father, "I urge Your Excellency to grant me this post. By leaving Europe I hope to escape the fate that pursues me. In another part of the world, I shall be a new man and under the influence of friendly stars I shall find peace and happiness again."

As soon as my father received the appointment, he made

ready for his journey, boarded ship in Algeciras and landed safely in Ceuta. Filled with joy he stepped on foreign soil with the feeling of a sailor who has come safely into harbor after a dangerous storm.

The new commander devoted himself first of all to reviewing his duties and vowed eagerly to fulfill them. As regards fortifications, he did not have to work on them, for by its position alone the island offered sufficient protection against an attack by the Berbers. He therefore concentrated all his efforts on improving the lot of the garrison and of the inhabitants and making their lives pleasanter. He himself refused all emoluments—something his predecessors had never done—and because of this attitude of his, the entire population worshipped him. Moreover my father took all the state prisoners, for whose care he was responsible, under his protection, often deviating from the strict rules, permitting them to correspond with relatives or friends, or perhaps even contriving various diversions for them.

When everything was running smoothly in Ceuta, my father again resumed his scientific researches. At that time the two Bernouilli brothers were making the world ring with the echo of their controversies. While outwardly my father ridiculed them, he was genuinely captivated by them. Indeed he frequently entered the quarrel by sending them anonymous letters that gave unexpected help to one side or the other. When the great isometrical problem was placed before the four most famous geometers for examination, my father sent them methods of analysis that could be considered masterpieces of inventiveness. However, as the Bernouilli brothers did not realize that the author might wish to preserve his anonymity, first one of the brothers, then the other, wrote to him. They were mistaken: my father loved science, but not the fame it brings. The misfortunes he had suffered had made him timid and nervous.

Jacques Bernouilli died just as he was about to carry off the final victory: the field was left to his brother. My father saw clearly the mistake in his hypothesis of the double root determining the value of the curve, but he did not wish to continue the quarrel in which the whole scientific world was now involved. Meanwhile Nicholas Bernouilli could not keep silent: he declared war on the Marquis de l'Hôpital whose discoveries he claimed for himself; several years later he attacked even Newton. The subject of the new quarrel was the analysis of differential calculus which Leibnitz had discovered at the same time as Newton and which had made the Englishman a national celebrity.

In this way my father spent the most beautiful years of his life observing from a distance that great struggle in which the most renowned minds of those days battled with the sharpest weapons human genius can invent. And yet with all his preference for the exact sciences, my father did not neglect other fields. The rocks of Ceuta were covered with great quantities of sea-animals that are in their way related to plants and form a bridge between two kingdoms. My father had always preserved a number of those examples under glass and delighted in studying their miraculous organism. In addition, he collected a handsome Latin library or books translated from the Latin, which were useful in his historical researches. He had provided himself with this collection to reinforce himself with proofs against the theory of probability which Bernouilli had developed in his *Ars conjectandi.* While in this way my father lived only a life of thought, from research to reflection and back again to research, he practically never left the house. This work and his constant mental efforts helped him to forget the terrible part of his life when misfortune after misfortune had wrecked his mind. But every now and then the heart demands its rights. This happened generally towards evening when his brain was weary from the day's work. As my father was not in the habit of seeking diversion outside of the house, at such times he would go up to the lookout tower and gaze at the sea as it broke and foamed against the dark sands of the Spanish coast on the far horizon. This sight reminded him of his days of fame and happiness when, beloved by his family, adored by his sweetheart, respected by the most famous men in the land, and filled with youthful enthusiasm he had known all the emotions that mean life itself and had immersed himself in the examination of those truths that do honor to the human mind. Then he thought of his brother who had robbed him of his love, of a vast fortune, of a high army post and had left him lying on a bundle of straw, a prey to madness. Sometimes he would take his violin and play the fatal saraband that had won Bianca's heart for Carlos; and at the sound of that music he would burst into tears—and after that his heart would feel lighter. In this way fifteen years passed.

Late one evening the governor of Ceuta came to see my father and found him, as usual, lost in nostalgic dreams.

"My dear Commander," the governor said thoughtfully. "May it please you to listen to the few words I have to say to you. You are unhappy, you suffer. That is no secret. We all know it, my daughter knows it too. She was five years old when you came to Ceuta and since then not a day has passed that she has not heard the people speak of you with the deepest respect, for you are truly the genius of our little community. She has often said to me: 'Our dear commander suffers so much because there is no one to share his sorrow.' My dear Henrique let me persuade you to come to us. That will divert you more than constantly making estimates on breakwaters."

My father agreed to go and see Inez de Cadanza. Six months later they were married and after ten months of wedded life I was born. When my weak little person first saw the light of day, my father took me in his arms and, raising his eyes to heaven, cried:

"O Mighty One! who hath eternity in which to expand to its ultimate power the final phase of all geometric progressions, great God, here is a tender creature hurled into space. If he is to be as unhappy as his father, then may Thy mercy reduce him to a mathematical nullity."

After he had ended this prayer, my father, filled with joy, embraced me.

"No, my poor child," he said, "you will not be as unfortunate as your father. I have sworn by God's holy name that I shall never allow you to be taught mathematics; instead you will be instructed in the saraband, in Louis XIV's ballets and in all the foolishness I can hear of." After these words my father bathed me in heartfelt tears and handed me over to my nurse.

I ask you now to give close attention to the story of my

extraordinary fate. My father swore that I should never learn mathematics, but instead should learn to dance. Things turned out quite differently, however. Today I have a deep knowledge of science but I could never learn to dance—I won't say a saraband, for that of course is now out of fashion—but any dance however simple. I really cannot understand how anyone can remember the figures of a contradance; none of them has the same origin; none is danced according to permanent principles; none can be described by any formula and I cannot imagine that there are people who know all of those figures by heart!

While Don Pedro Velasquez was telling us his story, the gypsy leader entered the grotto. The tribes' plans, he said, made it necessary to break camp and journey into the interior of the Alpuharras mountain chain.

"Thank God," said the cabalist. "Now I shall see the Wandering Jew all the sooner. As he is not allowed to rest, he will accompany us on our journey and we shall all be the gainers from his conversation. He has seen many things and it is hardly possible to have had more experiences than he has."

At this, the gypsy leader turned to Don Velasquez and said:

"And you, Señor? Will you go with us or do you prefer us to give you an escort to the nearest city?"

Velasquez reflected a moment and then replied:

"I left a number of important papers beside the straw bundle under the gallows where I awoke day before yesterday and where the captain of the Walloon Guards found me. Will you kindly send someone to the Venta Quemada? If I do not get my papers back, there is no sense in going any farther and I must return to Ceuta. Meanwhile I could, if you will allow me, travel with you."

"My people are at your service," replied the gypsy. "I shall send several of them immediately to the Venta. They will catch up with us again at our first night's halt."

The tents were struck and we set out on our way. After we had gone five miles we settled ourselves on a mountain peak for the night.

The twentieth day

We spent the morning waiting for the messengers the gypsy leader had sent to the Venta for Velasquez's papers. Filled with curiosity we all watched the road over which they should return—all that is, except Velasquez. On a nearby ledge he had found a piece of slate, polished by the rain, and was now covering it with numbers and X's and Y's.

After he had wrtten a lot of numbers he turned and asked us why we were so impatient. We explained that we were being forced to wait for his papers which were still missing and that when he had finished his calculations, he too, would be just as impatient as we were. He thereupon stopped work on his equations and asked why we did not go on with our journey.

"But Señor geometer, Don Pedro Velasquez," exclaimed the cabalist. "Even if you yourself have never been impatient, you must have noticed this condition in other people!"

"As a matter of fact," replied Velasquez, "I have often observed impatience in others and I have always thought it must be a very unpleasant sensation, one that keeps on growing but in such a way that you can never discover the law of its progress. In general one can say, however, that it is the opposite of inertia. Therefore I, who resist an emotion that is doubly strong, will not reach the first stage of impatience for an hour, by which time you will already be in the second stage. This reflection can be applied to any emotions that may be considered motivating forces."

"It seems to me, Señor," said Rebecca, "that you are exceptionally well versed in the motive powers of the human heart and that geometry is the surest road to happiness."

"In my opinion," replied Velasquez, "the search for happiness may be compared to the solution of an equation of higher degree. You, Madam, know the ultimate exponential, you are aware that it is the quotient of all roots and that before you have exhausted the divisors, you come to the imaginary root and can spend the whole day in the continuous delight of calculation. It is the same way in life. You also come to the imaginary numbers which you have considered real value of the unknown quantity, but meanwhile you have lived and have even been active. And activity is above all the universal law of nature. In nature nothing is idle. You think this rock does not move because the action of the earth on which it lies is stronger than the pressure of the rock, but if you could put your foot under it you would immediately be convinced that it is active."

"Then," asked Rebecca, "can the emotion called love also be appraised by calculation? It is said that when two people live together their very closeness weakens the feeling in the man, whereas it increases the feeling in the woman. Can you explain that, Señor?"

"Madam," replied Velasquez, "the problem you pose proves that the movement of one of the two loves increases while the other decreases. In this way there must be a moment when the lovers love each other equally. From there on the matter falls into the theory of *maximis et minimis* and the problem can be represented in the form of a curve. I have thought of a very agreeable solution to all such problems. Take for example . . ."

As Velasquez reached this point in his exposition, we saw the messengers returning from the Venta. They brought the papers with them. Velasquez took them and looked carefully through them.

"All my papers are here," he said, "except one I do not particularly need, but which had greatly occupied my mind that night under the gallows. However, it is not so important and I shall certainly not detain you on that account."

We therefore set out on our way and traveled the greater part of the day. When we halted for the night the entire company gathered in the chief's tent. After supper we urged him to continue the story of his adventures, which he did in the following words:

CONTINUATION OF THE STORY OF PANDESOWNA

"You left me with the terrible Viceroy who was making me a speech about his fortune."

"I remember perfectly," said Velasquez, "the fortune amounted to sixty million twenty-five thousand one hundred and sixty-one piastres."

"That is correct," the gypsy admitted, continuing his story:

At the end of his speech the Viceroy knelt and kissed my hand. This deference by no means reassured me. I was still afraid of him. The snake tattooed on his skin, the Indians whose skulls he had bashed in, the thought of the beating from the Theatiner monks that awaited me, all added to my horror and I was almost on the point of fainting. Fortunately Aunt Torres summoned enough courage to say to the Viceroy:

"Your Highness, you are frightening this child to death. Please tell us instead what has become of the late Count de Rovellas's fortune?"

"Señora," said the Viceroy, "Rovellas dissipated his fortune by his extravagances. I assumed all the costs of the lawsuit, but the most I could get from his estate was sixteen plantations in Havana, twenty-two shares in the Philippine Trade Corporation, fifty-six in Assiento and a few little effects worth not more than twenty-seven millions in hard piastres."

He then ordered his secretary to bring him a costly teakwood jewel box. The Viceroy was much given to falling on his knees and when they brought him the jewel box he assumed his favorite posture and said to me:

"Charming daughter of a mother my heart has never ceased to worship, deign to accept the fruit of thirteen years' efforts, for that was the time it took me to wrest your property from your collateral relatives."

I did not know whether I should accept the box, but Señora de Torres seized it hastily and—it must be admitted—somewhat greedily.

"Your Highness," she said, "this young person has never seen a man on his knees before her. Permit her to retire to her rooms."

The Viceroy kissed my hand and then offered me his to escort me to my room. Once there, my aunts and I double-locked the door, whereupon Aunt Torres gave way to the wildest joy, kissed the jewel box a hundred times and thanked Heaven for the brilliant future that awaited her niece Elvira.

Almost immediately there was a knock on the door and the Count's secretary entered, followed by a notary who made a list of the papers in the jewel box and asked for a receipt. Fortunately he was satisfied with Señora de Torres' signature. As I was a minor he considered mine unnecessary. After that both the aunts and I locked ourselves in again.

"Ladies," I said to them, "Señora de Rovellas's future is now assured, but how do we get the false Señorita Rovellas to the Theatiner monks, and where can we find the real one and her Lonreto?"

No sooner had I spoken than the aunts began to groan and moan. In imagination my aunt Dalanosa already saw me in the hands of a man with a whip, and Señora de Torres feared for her niece and her son the thousand dangers to which unprotected children are exposed. Both aunts went off to bed in a very sad mood. I stayed awake a long time, worrying about how to get out of the trap, but in the end I fell asleep without coming to any conclusion—and there was only one day left before we would reach Burgos! The part I had to play there worried me greatly; nevertheless I was obliged to get into my litter again, and again the Viceroy let his horse prance beside it, but this time there was a shade of tenderness in his usually sullen expression—which certainly did not give me a comfortable feeling.

In this way we came to an exceptionally shady watering-place where we found a light lunch that the citizens of Burgos had prepared for us. The Viceroy gave me his hand to help me alight from my litter, but instead of escorting me to the table he led me a little farther away, invited me to sit down in the shade and seated himself beside me.

"Lovely Elvira," he said, "the more it is my good fortune to be near you, the more I am convinced that Heaven has destined you to brighten the evening of a stormy life which I have dedicated to the good of my country and the glory of my King.

"I acquired the archipelago of the Philippines for Spain, I conquered half of New Mexico, I brought the rebellious race of the Incas back to their duty. My life was constantly at the mercy of the mountainous waves of the seas, the searing heat of the equator, the unhealthy vapors of the mines I had had opened. Who is to repay me for the loss of the best years of my life? I could have devoted them to the joys of friendship or even to sweeter emotions. Ah, not even the King of Spain and the Indies, mighty as he may be, has the power to do so. But you, charming Elvira, have that power and when your fate is joined to mine I shall desire nothing more. I shall spend my days delighting in you; each smile from you will make me happy and the slightest sign of affection will enrapture me. The picture of this peaceful future, after all the chaos in my past life, enchants me so much that last night I made up my mind to hasten the moment when you will be mine. I am leaving you, beautiful Elvira, but only to go to Burgos where you will see the results of my impatient devotion."

The Viceroy then knelt, kissed my hand, mounted his horse and galloped away. I need not tell you how terrified I was! I was prepared for the most unpleasant scenes; and the least of those prospects, the beating that would await me at the gate of the Theatine monastery, was always before my eyes.

I looked for my two aunts and found them at their midday meal. I wanted to tell them about the Viceroy's latest proposal but I did not have an opportunity: the tireless majordomo insisted upon making me get into the litter and I had no choice but to follow him.

At the gates of Burgos we were met by a page of my future husband. He informed us that we were expected at the Bishop's palace. Only the cold sweat that stood out on my forehead showed me that I was still alive; so numb was I from sheer fright that I fell into a sort of coma from which I did not recover until I stood in the presence of the Bishop.

The prelate was seated in an armchair facing the Viceroy, while a little behind him stood his clergy, and on the Viceroy's side, the most distinguished citizens of Burgos. At the other end of the vast room was an altar decorated for a ceremony. The Archbishop gave me his blessing and kissed me on the forehead.

Overcome by all the emotions that assailed me I fell at his feet and, with unaccountable presence of mind, I cried:

"Monsignor, take pity on me! I want to be a nun, I want to be a nun!"

After I had made this wild plea which echoed through the vast room, I thought it would be a good idea to faint. Rising to my feet, I let myself fall into the arms of my two aunts. They themselves were so nervous they could scarcely stand upright. Through my half open eyes I saw the Archbishop go over respectfully to the Viceroy and apparently await his decision.

The Viceroy asked the Archbishop to sit down again and give him time to consider the matter. The Archbishop resumed his seat, thus giving me a clear view of my noble lover's countenance which looked haughtier and more sullen than usual, an expression that would have caused the bravest man to tremble with fear. For a time he seemed to be deliberating. Then, with a haughty gesture he put on his hat.

"My function here is at an end," he said. "The Archbishop may remain seated."

All the others in the room rose respectfully.

"Gentlemen," the Viceroy now said, "fourteen years ago today a base slanderer accused me of being the father of this young girl. I saw no better way to stop this vile slander than to take a solemn pledge to marry her as soon as she should be of age. While she was growing up, poor and virtuous, the King, in recognition of my services, raised me from rank to rank, finally rewarding me with the distinguished honor that places me so near the throne. Meanwhile the time had come to fulfill my promise. I asked permission of the King to return home to Spain and marry. The State Councilor of Madrid replied in the name of the King: I could return to Spain, but I could continue to be Viceroy only if I renounced marriage. At the same time he advised me not to approach within twenty miles of Madrid. It was not difficult to understand that I had to choose between marriage or the favor of my lord, the King; but as I had given my word, I could not hesitate. When I saw lovely Elvira I realized that Heaven was banishing me from the paths of glory that I might find happiness in the quiet joys of retirement. Now, however, a jealous Heaven has called back to itself a soul too good for this world. I yield to you, Monsignor. Send her to the convent of the Annunziata and may she begin her novitiate there. I have vowed never to marry any other woman; I shall keep my vow. I shall write to the King and ask his permission to throw myself at his feet."

So saying, the horrible Viceroy bowed to right and to left, put on his hat again, pulled it down over his somber face and strode out to his coach. The Archbishop, the clergy and the magistrates accompanied him. My aunts and I stayed behind with a couple of secretaries who promptly began removing the decorations from the altar. With my two aunts I then rushed into an adjoining room where I hurried to the window to look for some possible means of escape that would save me from being sent to the convent.

The window looked out on an inner court with a fountain beside which stood two ragged young boys who seemed to be in great haste to quench their thirst. I recognized the clothes I had exchanged with Elvira; I recognized Elvira herself. The other boy was Lonreto. I let out a joyful shout. The room we were in had four doors. The first door I opened led to a short flight of stairs and on down to the inner court, and my two young rascals, and I rushed down there pellmell to catch them. Dear Aunt Torres almost died of joy when she embraced her son and her niece!

At that moment we heard the Archbishop coming back to take me to the convent of the Annunziata. I had barely time to run to the door and lock it. My aunt called out that her niece had fainted again and was not in condition to receive anyone. In the greatest haste Elvira and I again exchanged clothes. My aunts bandaged Elvira's head as though in falling she had hurt herself, and so well did they cover part of her face that it was almost impossible to discover the deception.

When all was ready I disappeared with Lonreto and the door was opened. The Archbishop had gone, but he had left his first curate to escort Elvira and Señora de Torres to the convent. My aunt Dalanosa went to the inn De las Rosas where we had arranged to meet. We moved into an apartment and for eight days thought of nothing but enjoying ourselves. Lonreto, no longer disguised as a muleteer, lived with us and was registered as the son of Señora de Torres.

On one of my aunt's numerous visits to the convent, the two ladies decided that Elvira should first profess a great longing to take the veil but that little by little her fervor should wane. In the end they would take her out of the convent and seek a dispensation in Rome to permit her to marry her first cousin.

A few days later we learned that the Viceroy was in Madrid where the King had received him cordially, even granting permission for the Viceroy to leave his property and title to his nephew, the son of that sister who had been with him in Villaca. Shortly thereafter he sailed for Mexico. As for me, the adventure of that extraordinary journey had brought to the fore all my harum-scarum, vagabond traits and I hated the thought of my impending seclusion in the

Theatiner seminary. However, as my great-uncle had so ordained it and, after all the delays I could think up, I was at last forced to submit.

As the gypsy leader was speaking, one of his men came to report to him on the events of the day. Each of us gave our opinion of this extraordinary adventure, but the cabalist promised that we would hear far more interesting things from the Wandering Jew and assured us that we would certainly meet this extraordinary man face to face the next morning.

The twenty-first day

As we were starting out on our travels the next day, the cabalist, who had promised us that the Wandering Jew would arrive that morning, could hardly control his impatience. Finally, on a distant hilltop, we saw a man striding along at an unusually swift pace with never so much as a glance at the precipitous mountain path beneath his feet.

"Do you see him?" shouted the cabalist. "Oh, that lazy good-for-nothing rascal! Eight days it has taken him to come from Africa!"

A few moments later the Jew was scarcely a hundred paces away, and the cabalist began shouting at the top of his lungs.

"Well, what's the news? Do I still have a right to Solomon's daughter?"

"Not the slightest," replied the Jew. "Not only have you forfeited any right to her, but even to the power you possessed over the spirits on the other side of the twenty-second degree. Moreover, I hope you will soon lose the power you gain over me so foully."

The cabalist thought this over a moment, then he said: "All the better, then I shall follow my sister's example. We shall discuss this at length another time. Meanwhile, honored traveler, I command you to walk along beside the mules that belong to this young man and his companion, whom one of these days the history of geometry will be proud to recall. You will tell them the story of your life, but I warn you, make it a true story and keep it clear."

At first the Wandering Jew protested, but the cabalist said several unintelligible words to him and the unfortunate wanderer began to tell his story.

THE STORY OF THE WANDERING JEW

My family is one of those families that served the High Priest Onias and, with the permission of Ptolemy Philometer, built a temple in Lower Egypt. My grandfather's name is Hiskia. When the famous Cleopatra married her brother Ptolemy Dionysus, Hiskia entered their service as court jeweler; in addition he was instructed to purchase costly materials and garments and to organize the Court ceremonies. I can assure you that my grandfather was an important person at the Alexandrian Court. I do not say that to boast. What good would that do me? It will soon be seventeen centuries, if not more, since I lost him, for he died in the forty-first year of the reign of Augustus. I was then very young and can scarcely remember him, but a certain Dellius has often talked to me of the things that happened in those days.

Here Velasquez interrupted to ask whether this was the same Dellius who, as Cleopatra's musician, was frequently mentioned by Flavius and Plutarch.

The Wandering Jew confirmed this and went on with his story.

Ptolemy, who could not have children by his sister, accused her of being sterile and after three years broke up the marriage. Cleopatra retired to a seaport on the Red Sea. My grandfather accompanied her in this exile and it was then that he purchased for his sovereign those two famous pearls, one of which she dissolved and drank at the wedding feast arranged by Antony.

Meanwhile civil war broke out in every part of the Roman Empire. Pompey sought asylum with Ptolemy Dionysus, but the latter had him beheaded. This betrayal, which he had hoped would earn him Caesar's favor, had exactly the opposite effect: Caesar decided to restore the crown to Cleopatra. The inhabitants of Alexandria rose to defend their monarch with a passion seldom found in history. However, when that monarch was accidentally drowned, nothing stood in the way of Cleopatra's sovereignty.

Before Caesar left Egypt he commanded Cleopatra to marry the younger Ptolemy, who was her brother and also her late husband's younger brother, which made him also her brother-in-law. At that time the prince was only eleven years old. Cleopatra was pregnant and the child would be called Caesarion to eliminate any doubt as to his parentage.

My grandfather, who was then twenty-five years old, also decided to marry. For a Jew that was perhaps too late, but he had an uncontrollable aversion to marrying a woman born in Alexandria, not because the Jews of Jerusalem looked upon us as renegades, but because we believed there should be only one temple on earth. Our party felt that an Egyptian temple, founded by Onias and formerly a Samaritan temple, would be cause for apostasy which the Jews considered the unavoidable outcome of a general downfall. Those pious reasons, and the evil reputation that tainted all Court circles, impelled my grandfather to journey to the Holy City and there to seek a wife. At the same time a Jew from Jerusalem, named Hillel, arrived in Alexandria with his whole family. His daughter, Melia, was pleasing to my grandfather and their wedding was celebrated with extraordinary splendor. Cleopatra and her young husband honored them with their presence. Several days later the Queen sent for my grandfather and said to him:

"My friend, I have just learned that Caesar has been appointed dictator for life. Fate has raised this man to a rank among world conquerors that so far no one has attained: neither Bolus nor Sesostris, nor Cyrus, nor even the great Alexander can compare with him. I am honored to call him the father of my little Caesarion. This child will soon be five years old: my one desire is for Caesar to see him and embrace him. I have therefore decided to leave for Rome in two months. You will understand that I wish my arrival in Rome to be attended with all the splendor that befits the Queen of Egypt. Even the least of my slaves shall wear garments shot with gold. All utensils shall be made of precious metals and set with costly stones. For me, you will have garments made of the finest tissue from India; as for my jewelry, I shall wear no precious gems save pearls. Take all my jewels, all the golden objects in my palace; in addition, my treasurer shall pay you one hundred thousand gold talents. That is the price I received for the two provinces I sold to the King of the Arabs; when I return from Rome I shall know how to get them back from him again. Now go, and do not forget that everything must be ready in two months."

Cleopatra was then twenty-five years old. Her fifteen-year-old brother whom she had married four years before, loved her passionately. When told of her imminent departure, he was in great despair, and after he had taken leave of the Queen and had seen her ship sail out of sight, he was plunged into such deep grief that his people feared for his life. Three weeks later Cleopatra landed in the harbor of Ostia. There she was met by magnificent barges on which she was rowed up the Tiber and one may well say that she entered the Eternal City in triumph. Where other queens had entered Rome chained to the chariot of a Roman commander, Caesar, who was distinguished as much for his charming ways as for his brilliant mind, welcomed Cleopatra with exquisite courtesy—though perhaps less tenderly than the Queen had expected. Cleopatra, who was more influenced by ambition than by her affection for men, paid little attention to this reserve and decided to learn all she could about Rome. Gifted with unusually keen intelligence, she was soon aware of the dangers threatening the dictator. She warned him of her suspicions, but there was no room for fear in the hero's heart. When Cleopatra saw that Caesar made light of her warning, she decided to manipulate events to her own advantage. Caesar would fall victim to a conspiracy and the Roman world would then be split into two parties.

The manifest leader of the party of Friends of Freedom was old Cicero, a conceited egotist who thought he could accomplish great things by making grandiloquent speeches to the masses. Though he longed to lead a quiet life in his Tuscan villa, he was at the same time unwilling to relinquish the privileges he enjoyed as head of his party. He and his followers aimed at high goals, but as they lacked worldly wisdom they did not know how to attain them. Caesar's friends and the brave warriors who made up the second party were interested only in getting the most out of life and, in playing on the citizens' passions, they were merely indulging their own.

Cleopatra did not hesitate: making her choice, she used all her feminine wiles to lure Antony. She despised Cicero and the latter never forgave her, as is evident from the letters he wrote at that time to his friend Atticus. The Queen, who had seen through the background of this struggle, was not even curious about the outcome, but returned to Alexandria with all possible speed. There her young husband welcomed her with all the exuberance of his youthful passion. The citizens of Alexandria were equally delighted, and in her obvious pleasure at her reception Cleopatra won all hearts. Those who knew her better, however, saw clearly that her joy was more feigned than real, being motivated by her political interests. In fact, after she was sure that the people of Alexandria were behind her, the Queen hurried off to Memphis where she appeared gowned as Isis. The Egyptians were entranced by her. Using the same means, she won over the Nabatiers, the Ethiopians, the Libyans and other neighboring peoples. Then at last the Queen returned to Alexandria.

Meanwhile Caesar had been murdered and civil war had broken out in every province of the Empire. From then on, the Queen became more and more somber, often lapsing into long meditations. Those about her realized that she had decided to marry Antony and rule over Rome.

One morning my grandfather went to the Queen to take her the pearls that had just arrived from India. She seemed to be extremely pleased, praised my grandfather again and again for his zeal in fulfilling his duty, and added:

"My dear Hiskia, here are some bananas which the merchants from Serediva, the same from whom you received the jewels, brought with them from India. Take them to my young husband and ask him, if he loves me, to eat them at once."

My grandfather executed the order but the young King said:

"As the Queen invites me, in the name of the love I bear her, to eat this fruit immediately, I wish you to remain as witness that there is nothing left."

Scarcely had he eaten three bananas than his face contorted, his eyes bulged out of his head, he uttered a terrible cry and fell to the floor, lifeless. My grandfather realized that he had been made the tool of a ghastly crime. He went home, rent his garments, put on sackcloth and strewed ashes on his head.

Six weeks later the Queen sent for him.

"You know, of course," she said, "that Octavius, Antony and Lepidus have divided the Empire among them. As the East fell to my beloved Antony, I wish to go out to meet and welcome him as the new ruler. For this purpose I command you to build a large ship in the form of a shell. Have it completely covered with pearl, both inside and out. The deck shall be surrounded by a golden railing so that I may be seen when I appear as Venus surrounded by Graces and Loves. Now be gone, and see that you carry out my orders with your usual dispatch."

My grandfather fell at the Queen's feet.

"My liege sovereign," he said. "May it please you to remember that I am a Hebrew and that everything that has to do with the Greek gods is blasphemy, of which I dare not make myself guilty."

"I understand," said the Queen, "you mourn my young husband. Your grief is justified and I share it more than I would have expected. Hiskia, I see that you are not made for a life at Court. I therefore relieve you of your former duties."

My grandfather wasted no time in packing his possessions and retiring to a little house he had on the shores of Lake Mareotis. There he devoted himself to settling his affairs, but always with the idea in mind of moving to Jerusalem. He lived in the greatest seclusion, receiving none of his former acquaintances from the Court with the exception of the musician Dellius, with whom he had a real friendship.

In the meantime Cleopatra had had a ship built according to her wishes and sailed on it to Sicily whose inhabitants thought she was really the goddess Venus. However, as Marc Antony had already discovered for himself that the Sicilians were not far wrong in their estimate of the Queen, he sailed away with her to Egypt where their marriage was celebrated with magnificent pomp and splendor.

When the Wandering Jew came to this part of his story, the cabalist stopped him.

"Enough for today, my friend, for we are to stay here for the night. You, however, will spend the night encircling the mountain, but join us again tomorrow. As for the matter I wanted to talk to you about, I shall postpone it until later."

The Wandering Jew glared angrily at the cabalist and stalked off into a nearby valley.

The twenty-second day

We started out quite early and after we had gone a few miles we met the wanderer. Without waiting for us to repeat our request, he pushed between my horse and Velasquez's mule and began his story as follows:

CONTINUATION OF THE STORY OF THE WANDERING JEW

After Cleopatra had become Antony's wife, she realized that in order to hold him, she would have to play the role of Phryne rather than of Artemis. In plain words, she had a most peculiar talent for switching from the role of a tender and faithful wife to that of a seductive vampire. She knew that Antony yielded passionately to the transports of love and she therefore invented endless, seductive varieties of the art to bind him to her.

Soon the Court began to imitate the royal couple; the city followed the Court's example, the entire country followed the city so that in a short time Egypt became the scene of the greatest lasciviousness and license. This shamelessness even spread to several Jewish settlements.

My grandfather would long since have moved to Jerusalem, but the Parthians had recently captured the city and driven out Herod, the grandson of Antipas whom Marc Antony intended to make King of Judea. As my grandfather was obliged to remain in Egypt he did not know where to find shelter; for Lake Mareotis was covered day and night with gondolas and offered a spectacle of the greatest corruption. At last, losing patience, he had the windows facing the lake boarded up and locked himself, his wife Melsa and his son Mordecai in the house. His door was opened only to his faithful friend, Dellius. In this way several years passed during which Herod was crowned King of Judea and my grandfather again made plans to move to Jerusalem. One day Dellius came to see him.

"Dear friend," he said, "Antony and Cleopatra are sending me to Jerusalem. I have come to ask if you have any errands I can do for you. Also I would ask you for a letter of introduction to your father-in-law, Hillel, whom I should like to visit although I am sure they will insist upon keeping me at Court and will not allow me to live in a private dwelling."

At the sight of this man who was going to Jerusalem, tears of nostalgia poured down my grandfather's cheeks. He gave Dellius a letter to his father-in-law and entrusted him with twenty thousand darics with which to purchase the finest house in the city. Three weeks later Dellius returned and immediately sent word to my grandfather that because of important Court matters, he could not come to see him for five days. When this time had passed, Dellius arrived and reported.

"First," he said, "let me give you the contract for a splendid house I purchased for you from your father-in-law. The judges have stamped the document with their seal—in this respect you have nothing to worry about. Now as to my journey: I must confess that I was extraordinarily pleased. Herod was not in Jerusalem. I met only his mother-in-law, Alexandra, who permitted me to take supper with her children, with Marianne, Herod's wife, and Aristobal, who was to have been the High Priest, but who had to step aside for a man of lower birth. I cannot tell you how charmed I was by the beauty of those two young people, especially Aristobal. He is like a demi-god who has come down to earth. Picture to yourself the head of the most beautiful woman and the shoulders of a marvelously well-built man and you will have an idea of what he is like. As I have talked of nothing but those two young people since my return, Antony has decided to have them brought to his Court.

" 'Of course,' said Cleopatra. 'I advise you to do it. But let the wife of the Jewish King come here and the next morning the Parthians will make themselves at home in the Roman provinces.'

" 'Then,' replied Antony, 'let us at least send for the brother. If it is true that the boy is so extraordinarily charming, we shall make him our cup-bearer. You know I dislike having slaves around me and I would be delighted if my pages belonged at least to the best Roman families, for unfortunately there is a shortage of the sons of barbarian kings.'

" 'I have no objection,' replied Cleopatra. 'Let us send for Aristobal.'

"God of Israel and of Jacob!" cried my grandfather. "Am I to believe my ears? An Asmonaer, a pure-blooded Maccabee, a descendant of Aaron—to be cup-bearer to Antony, the uncircumcised, who commits every sort of obscenity! Oh, Dellius! I have lived too long in this world. I shall rend my garments, clothe myself in sackcloth and strew ashes on my head."

And that is exactly what my grandfather did. Moreover he shut himself in his house, bewailed Zion's misfortune and nourished himself only on his tears. Without a doubt he would have perished, had not the good Dellius knocked at his door several weeks later.

"Aristobal will not be Antony's cup-bearer," he said. "Herod has anointed him High Priest."

Comforted by this news, my grandfather opened his door and he and his family resumed their former way of life. Soon thereafter Antony set out for Armenia accompanied by Cleopatra who made the journey with the intention of enslaving Arabia Felix and Judea. Dellius was among their retinue and on his return told my grandfather all the details. Herod had ordered Alexandra locked up in her palace because she intended to flee with her son to Cleopatra, who was curious to know the fascinating High Priest. A certain Kubion discovered this plan and Herod had Aristobal drowned in his bath. Cleopatra cried out for revenge, but Antony replied that every king was master in his own house. However, to calm her, he presented her with several towns that had belonged to Herod.

"Then," Dellius added, "something new happened. Herod took back the towns Cleopatra had stolen from him and, to settle the matter, he journeyed to Jerusalem. The Queen tried to bring things quickly to a head, but unfortunately Cleopatra is thirty-five years old and Herod is madly in love with his twenty-year-old wife, Mariamne. Instead of making a grateful reply to Cleopatra's advances, Herod summoned a council meeting and proposed a plan to strangle the Queen. He insisted that Antony had been tired of her for some time and would not be in the least annoyed by her death. But the council made it clear to Herod that even if Antony would be secretly pleased, he would not forgo this opportunity for revenge and, as a matter of fact, the council was right.

"On our return home, we found unexpected news awaiting us. Rome accused Cleopatra of having bewitched Antony. No lawsuit had as yet been filed, but that would soon follow. Now, what do you say to all that, my friend? Are you still determined to go to Jerusalem?"

"Yes," replied my grandfather, "but not right now. I could not conceal the fact that I have Maccabean blood. On the other hand, I am convinced that Herod will stop at nothing until he has destroyed the Asmoneans, one after the other."

"As long as you insist upon staying here," said Dellius, "grant me asylum in your house. I am no longer at Court. We will both lock ourselves in and not come out again until the whole country has become a Roman province—and that is certain to happen soon. I have entrusted my fortune, amounting to thirty thousand darics, to your father-in-law who has asked me to turn over to you the rent for the house."

My grandfather manifested the greatest joy on hearing his friend's decision and withdrew more than ever from the world. Now and then Dellius would venture out and come back with news of the town; the rest of the time he spent teaching Greek literature to young Mordecai (who was later to become my father). And often he read from the Bible, for my father was determined to convert Dellius. You know what happened in the end to Cleopatra and Antony. As Dellius had prophesied, Egypt became a Roman province, but by that time the cloistered life in our house had become such a habit that those political upheavals made no change in our way of living. There was, however, no lack of news from Palestine. Herod who, it seems, should have fallen with his protector, Antony, won Augustus's favor. The lost lands were restored to him; he conquered many new countries and came into possession of an army, a treasury and such vast provisions of grain that people began to call him "Herod the Great." Had he not been called "the Great," he would have been called "the Lucky" save that the splendors of such a brilliant destiny had been dulled by family quarrels.

As soon as there was peace in Palestine, my grandfather decided to move there with his dear son Mordecai. Dellius had become genuinely fond of his pupil and strongly opposed letting him out of his care. Then suddenly a Jew arrived from Jerusalem bringing the following letter.

Rabbi Sedekias, son of Hillel, unworthy sinner and lowliest of the Pharisees in the holy Sanhedrin, presents his compliments to Hiskia, the husband of my sister, Melsa.

The plague which the sins of Israel and Jerusalem have brought down upon us has carried off my father and my older brother. They now rest in Abraham's bosom and share his glory. May Heaven destroy the Sadducees and all those who do not believe in the Resurrection! I would be unworthy of the name Pharisee if I dared to soil my hands by appropriating the property of others. I have therefore made a careful search to learn whether my father owed anyone, and when I was told that the house in which we live in Jerusalem had once belonged to you, I sought the judges, but learned nothing from them to confirm this supposition. The house unquestionably belongs to me. May Heaven damn all the ungodly! I am no Sadducee.

I have also discovered that once upon a time an uncircumcised person, Dellius by name, deposited thirty thousand darics with my father. But fortunately, I found a somewhat crumpled paper which, I believe, must be the aforesaid Dellius's receipt. Moreover this man was a follower of Mariamne and her brother Aristobal and therefore an enemy of our great King. Heaven curse him together with all the ungodly and all Sadducees!

Farewell, dear brother! Embrace my beloved sister Melsa for me. Although I was very young when you married, I have always been fond of you. It seems to me that the dowry my sister brought your house somewhat exceeded the portion of the estate that was hers; but we shall talk about that another time. Farewell, dear brother! May Heaven make you a true Pharisee!

My grandfather and Dellius stared at each other in utter astonishment. Finally the latter broke the silence.

"That," he said, "comes from not knowing the world. We rejoice in the hope of peace and meanwhile Fate decrees otherwise. People treat you as though you were a dead tree they could cut down or pull out by the roots as they please, or a worm they can crush—in other words, a useless burden on this earth. In the world one must either fight with hammer and tongs or succumb. I have maintained friendly relations with several Roman prefects who went over to Octavian's side. Had I not neglected them of late no one today would dare to wrong me. But I was driven out of the world and forsook it to live with a virtuous friend. Then some Pharisee from Jerusalem appears, steals my goods and chattels and claims to have a crumpled paper which, he says, is my receipt. For you the loss is not so important, the house in Jerusalem amounted to scarcely a fourth of your fortune, but I have lost everything. In any case, I shall go to Palestine."

Dellius made ready for his journey to Judea. One evening as he was walking home through the suburb of Rakotis, a knife was suddenly plunged into his back. He turned around and recognized the same Jew who had delivered Sedekias's letter. His wound took a long time to heal and by the time he was well he had again lost all desire to go to Palestine. First of all he needed the help of men in power and he pondered ways and means of recalling himself to his former protectors. Augustus adhered to the basic principle of allowing kings to rule their own countries without interference. Dellius therefore had to discover whether Herod was favorably disposed towards Sedekias and to this end he sent a loyal and intelligent man to Jerusalem.

Two months later the messenger returned. He reported that Herod's popularity was increasing daily and that the wily monarch was winning over the Romans as well as the Judeans by putting up a statue to Augustus while at the same time announcing that he had decided to rebuild the Temple of Jerusalem but on far more splendid lines than the old one. The people were so delighted that many flatterers were already saying he was the Messiah, whose coming the prophet had foretold.

This prophecy, said the messenger, pleased the Court immensely and a new sect was already being formed. The members called themselves Herodians and the man at their head was Sedekias.

You will understand that this news gave my grandfather and Dellius much to think about, but before I go on with my story, I must tell you what our prophets have said about the Messiah.

After this, the Wandering Jew fell silent. Then, with a scornful glance at the cabalist, he said:

"Impure son of Mammon, a master mightier than thou calls me to the highest peak of Atlas. Farewell."

"You lie," cried the cabalist. "I have one hundred times more power than the Sheik of Tarudant."

"You lost your power in Quemada," replied the Jew and walked away so quickly that he was soon out of sight.

The cabalist looked embarrassed, thought a moment and said:

"I assure you, this impudent fellow has no idea of half the charms in my power, but he shall soon find out for himself.

However, let us talk of something else. Señor Velasquez, did you follow the whole story closely?"

"Of course," replied the geometer. "I listened attentively to the Wandering Jew's words and I consider that everything he said corresponds perfectly to history. Tertullian mentions the sect of the Herodians."

"Señor!" exclaimed the cabalist. "Are you as conversant with history as with mathematics?"

"Not altogether," replied Velasquez. "But my father who, as I told you, approached all mathematical formulas slowly, thought those formulas could also be used in the science of history to ascertain the rates of probabilities between events that have actually taken place and those that could have come to pass. He carried his theory even farther by believing that one could express human acts and passions with the help of geometric figures. To give you a clearer idea, let me show you an example. My father said: 'Antony comes to Egypt, two different passions struggle within him: ambition that drives him towards leadership and love that draws him away from it. I represent two trends by two lines AB and AC that form an angle with each other. Line AB which stands for Antony's love for Cleopatra is shorter than AC, for Antony had more ambition than love. I assume that the ratio is that of one to three. I therefore take the line AB and extend it three times its length in the direction AC, thereby completing the parallelogram and drawing the diagonal which shows me exactly the new direction that has resulted from the forces struggling for B and C. If we suppose more love than ambition and lengthen the line AB somewhat, the diagonal will come closer to the line AB. Suppose, however, we give priority to ambition as for instance in the case of Augustus, then the diagonal comes close to C because there is nothing to divert it from AC. But as passions increase or diminish, the shape of the parallelogram must likewise undergo a change. Consequently the end of the resulting diagonal curves slightly to which one can apply the modern theory of the differential.

"To be sure, the wise man who gave me life considered all these historical questions mere child's play suitable to enliven the solitude of his days, but as the exactness of solutions depends upon the accuracy of facts my father collected all his historical sources with the greatest care. This collection of historic treasures, as well as geometry, had long been a closed book to me for my father wanted me to become expert at dancing the saraband, the minuet and similar frivolities. Fortunately I found my way to the bookshelves and immersed myself in the pursuit of scientific studies."

"Allow me, Señor Velasquez," the cabalist interjected, "to express my admiration of you again for I see that you are as learned in history as in mathematics; for one science depends more on reflection, the other on memory, two intellectual powers that are completely antithetical."

"I don't agree with you," replied the geometer. "Reflection reinforces memory by helping to organize material it has gathered, so that, as a rule, in a systematically ordered memory every concept precedes the results drawn from it. Nevertheless I do not deny that memory as well as reflection can be applied effectively to a certain number of concepts. I, for example, remember particularly everything I have learned from the exact sciences, the history of man and animals, whereas on the other hand I often forget my relation to the objects around me or, in other words, I do not see the most obvious things and do not hear words that ring in my ears. That is why many people think I am absent-minded."

"Indeed," said the cabalist. "I now understand, Señor, why you fell into the water that time."

"One thing is certain," replied Velasquez. "I myself do not know how I got in the water at that particular time, for it was the last thing I expected. Nevertheless I am very glad the accident occurred for it gave me the opportunity to save the life of this noble youth, the captain in the Walloon Guards. However I would rather not be obliged to perform such services often for I know no worse feeling than that of a man who inadvertently swallows a lot of water on an empty stomach."

With such talk we arrived at the place where our evening meal awaited us. We fell to with gusto, but the conversation lagged. The cabalist appeared to be worried. After supper brother and sister talked together at great length. As I did not wish to interrupt them, I retired to a little cave where a bed had been prepared for me.

The twenty-third day

The weather was marvelous. We rose at sunrise and, after a light breakfast, set out on our journey again. Towards noon we halted and went to the table; that is, we seated ourselves on the ground around a leather tablecloth. The cabalist made several remarks that showed he was not altogether pleased with his supernatural world. After the midday meal he began to talk about it again till finally his sister, who thought such monologues would bore the company, urged Velasquez to continue the story of his adventures which he proceeded to do in the following words.

CONTINUATION OF THE STORY OF THE GEOMETER

I had the honor to tell you how I came into the world and how my father clasped me in his arms, said a geometric prayer over me and vowed never to allow me to study mathematics. Six weeks after my birth, my father saw a little ship sail into the harbor and, after it had dropped anchor, send a boat ashore. Soon thereafter an old man, bent with age and wearing the livery of the dead Velasquez, came ashore. He wore a green jacket with facings of red and gold, flowing sleeves and a broad belt from which hung a sword. Looking through a spyglass my father thought he recognized Alvarez. And indeed Alvarez it was. The old man could hardly walk. My father hastened to the landing stage to meet him, but was so overcome with emotion he could scarcely utter a word. Alvarez informed my father that he came from the Duchess Bianca, who had been living for a long time in the Ursuline convent. He handed my father a letter which read as follows:

Señor Don Henrique:

Torn with remorse, I submitted myself to a penance that, I hoped, would hasten my death. Alvarez, however, pointed out that if I were dead the Duke would be free to contract a new marriage which, in view of descendants, might be more fortunate than his marriage with me. Were I to remain alive, however, I could at least insure that you would inherit our fortune. I realized that Alvarez was right, gave up my unnecessary fasting, laid aside the penitent's garb and confined my penances to solitude and prayer. Meanwhile the Duke, who has indulged in all worldly pleasures, began to fail and I thought he would name you as his heir to the title and wealth of our house. But it would appear that Heaven has decided to leave you in a retirement ill suited to your admirable abilities.

I have been told you have a son. My only reason now for living is my desire to restore to him all the possessions you have lost through my fault. In our family the ancestral estates have, from earliest times, belonged to the younger line. As, however, you have not claimed this right, they would be added to the fortune intended for my support. All this is now yours and Alvarez will pay over to you the profits of fifteen years and at the same time receive your instructions concerning further action. Reasons connected with a number of the Duke Velasquez's idiosyncrasies have prevented me from writing to you sooner.

Farewell, Don Henrique! Not a day passes that I do not raise my penitent voice and implore Heaven to bless you and your fortunate wife. Pray also for me and do not answer this letter.

Bianca Velasquez

I have already mentioned the influence memories had on my father's mind. You can therefore judge the powerful effect of this letter which brought to life all those memories again. For almost a year he could not force himself to work at his favorite employment. Only his wife's efforts, her love for me, but above all the theory of the solution of differential equations with which at that time geometry researchers were passionately occupied, managed to give strength and peace to his mind. His increased income permitted him to expand his library and his laboratory. Soon he began to set up a little telescope with fairly accurate instruments. I need not add that he also did not neglect his interest in charitable works. I assure you there is not in Ceuta a single needy or pitiable person for my father applied his brilliant mind to securing a decent income for every man. I could add many interesting details, but I must not digress and forget my promise to tell you my story.

As far as I recall my besetting sin as a child was curiosity. In Ceuta there are neither horses nor vehicles and therefore no dangers for children. I was allowed to run about the streets as I pleased. One day, drawn by curiosity, I went to the harbor and on my way home I followed errand boys into houses, stores, arsenals and workshops where I watched the men at work. I even stopped passersby on the street. In short, I stuck my nose into everything. My curiosity amused the people who were all delighted to satisfy it—everywhere but in my parents' house.

My father had a special pavilion built in the middle of the courtyard in which he established his library, his laboratory and the telescope. I was forbidden to enter the pavilion; at first I did not pay much attention to it, but soon that prohibition whetted my curiosity and was to become the strongest incentive to drive me along the path to science. The first science to which I devoted myself was conchology, a division of natural science. My father often went to the seashore to a place surrounded by rocks where, in calm weather, the water was as clear as glass. There he studied the habits of marine animals. When he found a pretty sea shell he promptly brought it home. As children are naturally imitators I instinctively became a conchologist and would certainly have worked longer in that direction if crabs, nettles and sea-urchins had not spoiled this activity for me. I gave up nature study and devoted myself to physics.

My father, who needed a hand worker to repair, renovate or rebuild the instruments sent him from England, taught this craft to a gunner who showed a certain native ability. I spent almost the entire day in the mechanic's workshop and acquired much knowledge there, though unfortunately I lacked the fundamentals. Although I was nearly eight years old, I could neither read nor write. My father kept repeating that it would be sufficient if I could sign my name and dance a saraband. In those days there was in Ceuta a priest who had been sent there from a monastery as penance, though he was treated in general with great respect. He came to see us frequently. When the worthy priest saw how neglected my education was, he suggested to my father that I should at least be instructed in religion and that he himself would undertake the task. My father consented and under this pretext the priest taught me reading, writing and arithmetic. I made rapid progress, especially in arithmetic in which I soon outstripped my master.

In this way I reached my twelfth year and, for my age, possessed much knowledge. I took care, however, not to parade it in front of my father for every time I forgot myself, he would glare at me sternly and say:

"Learn the saraband, my son, learn the saraband, and leave other things alone. They can only lead to your misfortune."

My mother would quickly motion to me to keep quiet and then she would turn the conversation to other matters.

One day during dinner when my father was again urging me to devote myself more frequently to my dancing, a man, who looked to be about thirty years old and was dressed in the French fashion, entered the room.

He made almost twenty bows one after the other and as he was about to pirouette he bumped into the servant; the soup tureen fell to the floor and broke into a thousand pieces. A Spaniard would have made many and abject apologies, but the stranger was not in the least embarrassed. Instead he informed us in bad Spanish that he was the Marquis de Folencour, that he had killed a man in a duel, on which account he had been compelled to leave France, and he asked us to give him shelter until his affairs were regulated.

Folencour had scarcely finished speaking when my father jumped up from the table.

"My dear Marquis," he exclaimed. "You are the very man I have been looking for this long while. Consider my house yours. Command what you will but do not refuse to concern yourself with my son's education. If with time he could become a little like you, you would make me the happiest of fathers."

If Folencour could have guessed the thoughts hidden behind my father's words, he would surely have rejected the invitation like a gentleman; but as he took this declaration literally, he appeared very pleased and doubled his impertinences by referring to my mother's beauty and my father's advanced years. The latter, however, was still delighted with the Marquis and constantly held him up to me as an example.

When the noonday meal was over my father asked the Marquis whether he could teach me the saraband. Instead of answering, my teacher roared with laughter and when he had recovered from this outburst, he announced that for twenty centuries no one had danced the saraband; now they danced the minuet and the gavotte. With these words he pulled out of his pocket a little violin of the kind dancing masters are accustomed to carry about and began to play the tunes for these two dances. When he had finished, my father said earnestly:

"My dear Marquis, you are playing an instrument that is unknown to all men of good birth and if I did not know with whom I have the honor of speaking I would think you were a dancing master by profession. But even if you were I would still be unspeakably delighted that you are here and would thank heaven that it has answered my prayer. I beg you to take on my son the first thing tomorrow and to educate him after the pattern of an accomplished nobleman of the French Court."

Folencour admitted that in fact family misfortunes had compelled him to devote himself for a time to teaching dancing; he was however well-born and therefore qualified to be the mentor to a young man of excellent family. It was therefore decided that beginning with the very next morning I should receive instruction in dancing and proper deportment in society. But before I describe those unhappy days, I must relate a conversation my father had the evening before with Don Cadanza, his father-in-law. I had forgotten it until today but now I recall that conversation exactly.

That day curiosity kept me at my new teacher's side so that I did not run out on the street, but stayed at home. As I passed my father's workroom I heard him say angrily and in raised tones to his father-in-law Cadanza:

"My dear father-in-law, I warn you for the last time, if you do not give up your secret jaunts and stop sending messengers to Central Africa, I shall be forced to denounce you to the Minister."

"My son-in-law," replied Cadanza, "if you want to know the secret, you shall have it. My mother is descended from the Gomelez; their blood flows in your son's veins."

"Worthy Cadanza," my father interrupted him, "I command here in the name of the King and have nothing to do with the Gomelez and all their mysteries. You may be sure that I shall inform the Minister of our entire conversation, the first thing tomorrow morning."

"And let me assure you," said Cadanza "that the Minister will forbid you to interfere in future in our affairs."

With that the conversation ended. The mystery of the Gomelez occupied my mind the rest of the day and a part of the night, but the next morning the wretched Folencour gave me my first dancing lesson which had a totally different effect from the one my father desired. As the result of those lessons, it was not long before I was able to devote myself exclusively to my favorite study of mathematics.

When Velasquez had finished speaking, the cabalist announced that he wished to talk to his sister about several important matters. Whereupon we separated and each went his own way.

The twenty-fourth day

Again we wandered around in the Alpuharras Mountains until finally we halted for the night. After we had partaken of a bountiful supper, we urged Velasquez to continue the story of his life, which he did in the following words:

CONTINUATION OF THE STORY OF THE GEOMETER

My father desired to be present at my first dancing lesson and requested my mother to accompany him. Folencour, encouraged by such a flattering reception, forgot completely that he had introduced himself as a Marquis and began with an elaborate speech about the art of choreography for which, he claimed, he had a natural talent. Then he noticed that I held my foot turned inwards and went to great lengths to explain that this habit was not consistent with my position in life. I thereupon turned my toes out and tried to walk that way, but Folencour was still not satisfied and insisted that I should walk on tiptoe. In the end, becoming impatient, he seized my hands and to draw me nearer to him, pulled so violently that I lost my balance and came down with a thud on my face. Instead of apologizing, Folencour flew into a rage and used expressions whose impropriety he could better have judged had he been more conversant with the Spanish language. Accustomed to the general courtesy of the inhabitants of Ceuta I considered that one should not let such an insult go unpunished. I therefore went up to my teacher, grabbed his little violin, broke it into a thousand pieces, and declared that I did not wish to receive any lessons from such an ill-bred person. My father said not a word, but rose, took me by the hand and in silence led me into a little room at the end of the courtyard. There he locked me in, saying that I would not be allowed out until I recovered a desire to dance.

Brought up in complete freedom, I could not at first get accustomed to imprisonment and I wept long and bitterly. Streaming with tears I turned my eyes towards a square window in the little room and began to count the panes. There were twenty-seven in the length and the same number in the breadth. I remembered Father Anselm's arithmetic lessons though his instructions had not gone beyond the multiplication tables. I multiplied the height of the square by the breadth and discovered to my amazement that the correct number of panes resulted. I stopped sobbing, my grief assuaged. I repeated the count by subtracting a row of squares once in the length and once in the breadth. Then I realized that multiplying is only a repetition of addition and that the angles can be counted exactly like the length. I made the same test with the flagstones with which my little room was paved, and this time the result satisfied me completely. After that I thought no more about weeping, my heart beat with joy; even today I cannot talk about it without being moved.

Around midday my mother brought me a piece of black

bread and a pitcher of water. Weeping she implored me to yield to my father's wishes and to begin Folencour's lessons. When she had finished speaking, I kissed her hand tenderly and begged her to send me paper and pencil and not to worry about me. Surprised, my mother departed and attended to providing the things I had requested. Thereupon I applied myself to various calculations with incredible enthusiasm, convinced that every moment I was making the most important discoveries. And in fact all these capacities of the numerals were real discoveries for me, as up to then I had not had the slightest notion of them.

Little by little hunger began to torment me; I broke the bread in half and discovered a roast chicken and a slice of ham that my mother had tucked inside it. This sign of kindness added to my delight and full of joy I returned to my calculations. In the evening they brought me a candle and I worked far into the night.

The next morning I divided one side of the square into two halves and saw that by multiplying a half with a half the result was a quarter; whereupon I divided the same side in three parts and got a ninth; and so I gained my first notion of fractions. I made still further sure of this by multiplying two and a half by two and a half whereby the result, of the square minus one half, was two and a fourth.

In this way I pushed my researches farther and farther and found that when I multiplied a given number by itself and raised the product to the fourth power I reached the quantity I would otherwise have attained by addition.

None of my discoveries were expressed in algebraic forms, for I still had no idea of that system. I therefore puzzled them out in particular from the borrowed signs on the windowpanes which seemed to offer clarity and interest. When on the seventeenth day my mother brought me the midday meal she said:

"Dear child, I have good news for you. It appears that Folencour is a refugee. Your father who despises any one who runs away, has ordered him set aboard a ship and sent back to France. I hope you will soon be released from this prison."

I received this information with such indifference that my

mother was surprised. Soon afterwards my father appeared, confirmed my mother's information, adding that he had written to his two friends, Cossini and Hughens, and had urged them to send him the music and dance figures most popular in London and Paris. Moreover he remembered perfectly the way in which his brother, Carlos, entered a drawing room and that was what he had wanted me to learn most of all.

As he talked my father spied the roll of paper sticking out of my pocket and picked it up. At first he was very astonished to see a lot of figures; in particular, to see signs that were completely strange to him. I explained them to him as well as all my calculations. His amazement increased, but I noticed that he was not altogether pleased. After he had mastered my calculations he said:

"My son, if I should add two rows of squares on this window which has twenty squares in each direction but at the same time wish to preserve the shape of the square, how many squares would that give?"

I replied without hesitating:

"I would have two bars below and at the side, each fifty-two squares and up above in the corner a small square consisting of four little squares that would touch both bars."

Those words made my father intensely happy, though he tried not to show it.

"But if I should add a very narrow line below, where then is the square?"

I thought a while and answered:

"I would have two bars of the same length as the sides of the window, but very narrow; but as for the square on the side, it would be so narrow that I cannot even imagine what it would be like."

Here my father dropped down on a chair, clasped his hands, raised his eyes to heaven and said:

"Great God! He has discovered the whole binomial theorem by himself and if I don't disturb him, he will end by discovering all of the differential calculus."

I was alarmed to see my father so upset and on the point of fainting. I loosened his collar and called for help. Finally he came to himself, clasped me in his arms and said:

"My child, my dear child, give up calculation. Learn the saraband, my dear boy, learn the saraband."

There was no talk now of any more imprisonment. That evening I walked along the walls of Ceuta, repeating again and again as I walked: "He has discovered the binomial theorem, he has discovered the binomial theorem."

Without further ado I may admit that with every day I made fresh progress in mathematics. To be sure my father had sworn he would never let me learn it, but one day I found beside my bed Sir Isaac Newton's *Universal Arithmetic* and it was clear to me my father had left it there on purpose. Sometimes, too, I found the door to his study open, and I never failed to take advantage of that opportunity.

Every now and then, however, my father reverted to his original plan, and tried again to make a man of the world out of me; he would command me to make a full turn on my heels on entering a room. He would hum an aria and pretend not to notice my awkward motions. Shortly afterwards, however, he would burst into tears.

"My child," he said, "God did not make you to be a courtier, your days will be no happier than mine."

Five years later my mother gave birth to a daughter whom they named Bianca in memory of the beautiful though somewhat fickle Duchess of Velasquez. Although that lady had forbidden my father to write to her, it was customary for us to inform her of the birth of a daughter. Soon came the answer that opened old wounds; but my father had already grown rather old and the violence of his emotions had become blunted.

Ten years followed in which no special event came to break the monotony. My life and my father's were made pleasant by the new knowledge that absorbed our thoughts day after day. My father also dropped his former manner of treating me. I had honestly not learned mathematics from him for he was concerned only for me to master the saraband. He had nothing with which to reproach himself and he enjoyed talking with me generally about the exact sciences. As a rule these talks spurred on my zeal and doubled my industry but at the same time they instilled in me a tendency to absent-mindedness, as I have already told you, because they absorbed my whole attention. This situation I frequently paid for often too dearly. So one day I left Ceuta (I shall tell you more about that) and suddenly found myself —I had no idea how—among Arabs.

Meanwhile my sister grew more beautiful and more attractive from day to day and our happiness would have been complete if we could have kept our mother with us. But a year later a cruel illness tore her from our arms. At the time my father took his wife's twenty-year-old sister, Doña Antonia de Poneras, six months a widow, into his house. She was a child of my grandfather's second marriage. After Don Cadanza had married his daughter to my father, he had suddenly felt lonely and decided to marry again. However, after five years of living together he had lost his second wife. A little girl, five years younger than I, was the result of that marriage. My young and pretty aunt moved into my mother's house and took over the entire management. She was specially good to me and came into my bedroom at least twenty times a day to ask me whether I would not like to have a cup of chocolate, a lemonade or something like that.

These visits were often extremely annoying to me for they interrupted my calculations. If Doña Antonia made a point of not interrupting me for half an hour, then her maid would come in her stead, a girl of the same age and just as attractive as her mistress.

Soon I noticed that my sister could not stand either the mistress or the maid. I shared her dislike. But with me the reason was the impatience this woman's persistence aroused in me. Frankly, I did not lose much time on their account for the moment they came in I was in the habit of conjuring up imaginary mathematical formulas and the moment they left I returned to my actual figures.

One day as I was busy doing logarithms, Antonia came into my room, sat down beside me and began to chatter about a thousand unimportant nothings and to accompany her conversation with tender glances. As I recognized that she intended to stay a long time I broke off my calculation in the middle of a proposition and began to meditate on the nature of logarithms and the amount of work the famous Baron Napier had expended on setting up tables. Thereupon Antonia got up and to tease me, held her hands over my eyes.

"Now we shall see, honored geometer, whether you can go on calculating."

My aunt's words sounded like both a challenge to and a disparagement of my science. As of late I had been much engrossed with tables of logarithms and, so to speak, knew them by heart. It occurred to me to divide the number, whose logarithm I was seeking, into three components. I found three, whose logarithms I knew, added them quickly and as I freed myself of Antonia's hands, I wrote down the whole logarithm in which I had not made a single error. Antonia was very angry and said as she left the room:

"What stupid fellows these geometers are!"

To be sure my method was difficult to change to primary numbers, but it was rich in ideas and could be used in several cases. I did not understand why my aunt called me stupid. Shortly after that her maid came in and made a few more complimentary remarks of that sort, but I was so upset over her mistress's words that I cut her short without much ado.

Now I come to a period in my life in which my ideas took a new direction, all striving towards one goal. In the life of every scientist there comes a moment, when, strongly impressed by the truth of some principle or other, he seeks not only its results but also a way to use it and develop it into an orderly and original system. At such moments his courage and his work are doubled, he goes back to the starting point and fills in the inaccuracy in the first concept. He thinks over each deduction separately, considers it from all sides, joins and arranges it subsequently as a whole. Even if he does not succeed in developing a system or in convincing himself of the soundness of the principle he has discovered, in any event he will be wiser than at the beginning of his work and will have acquired much knowledge of whose existence he had so far never dreamed. So for me too the time had come to draw up a system. The situation, however, that first aroused these thoughts in me was as follows:

One evening after dinner as I had finished unraveling a very complicated problem, I saw my aunt Antonia come in.

"My dear nephew," she said to me, "the light in this room prevents me from sleeping and as mathematics is obviously such an alluring science I wish you would teach it to me."

As I could not do anything else I agreed. I took a tablet and explained to her two of Euclid's axioms. I was just about to go on to the third when Antonia suddenly jerked the tablet out of my hand.

"Unbearable pedant," she cried, "hasn't mathematics taught you yet how God's creatures love each other in this world?"

At first those words did not make any sense to me, but on further reflection it occurred to me that she was certainly asking me for a general formula comprising all sorts of multiplication employed by Nature from the cedar tree down to the most modest blade of grass, from whales to tiny animalcules that even with the help of the microscope are barely visible. At the same time I remembered various intelligence tests I had made on animals and whose first principles I had recognized in connection with training, tendencies and multiplying. This gradation now opened the possibility of adopting a theory of *Maxima et Minima* and as a result to bring back the whole system to mathematical principles. In a word: it occurred to me to find an equation that would cover the entire animal kingdom if one accepted in all cases the same factors of various values and gradations of activity. My imagination was inflamed, I felt I was in a position to indicate the mathematical nature and the limit of each of our ideas, in other words to apply mathematical procedures to the entire system of Nature. Overwhelmed by the rush of these heady thoughts, I felt the need for a breath of fresh air, rushed out to the city walls and ran around them three times without knowing what I was doing.

At last I felt a little better. The day dawned, I wanted to note down a number of conclusions. While I reflected on them, I thought I was walking homeward. That, however, was not so. Instead of turning to the right from the city walls, I had gone to the left and landed in a trench. My ideas were still vague; moreover I could not put them down on the tablet because the twilight was so dark I could not see the figures. I wanted to get home as soon as possible and began to walk faster, always thinking that I was going in the right direction. In this conviction I reached a breech in the wall through which, ordinarily, guns were placed and suddenly stood on the other side of the fortifications.

Nevertheless, I still did not notice my mistake; paying no attention to my surrounding, I ran straight on, scribbled in my notebook and in this way went farther and farther from the city. Finally I became tired, sat down and devoted myself wholly to my calculations. After sufficient time I opened my eyes and saw that I was surrounded by Arabs. As I knew a little of their language which is frequently spoken in Ceuta, I told them who I was and begged them to take me to my father, who would not fail to pay them a high ransom. The word ransom money always has a good sound to Arab ears. The crowd, now all smiles, turned to their leader, apparently expecting an answer that promised them a rich yield.

But the sheik, gravely stroking his beard, remained sunk in thought a long time.

"Hear, young Nazarene," he said at last. "We know your father to be a God-fearing man. We have also heard various things about you. They say you are as kind as your father, but the Lord has deprived you of half of your senses. Do not worry about that. God is great and gives or takes sense from men according as He thinks best. The insane are a living proof of godly might and of the vanity of human reason. The insane, who know neither good nor evil, are a living example for us of the former state of human innocence. They stand on the threshold of holiness. We call them *marabouts,* the same name we give to our holy men. That is all included in the basic principles of our belief. We would sin if we were to demand ransom money for you. Therefore, with all the respect and honor due to people like you, we shall accompany you as far as the first Spanish outpost."

I must admit that the sheik's speech threw me into the greatest embarrassment.

If, I said to myself, following in the steps of Locke and Newton, I based the principles of the former on the calculations of the latter, should I not arrive at the outer limits of human understanding? Have I taken such bold steps into the depths of metaphysics that people say behind my back that I am crazy; that they relegate me to the category of creatures who scarcely belong to the human race? If that is so, then the devil with differential calculus and all those problems on which I hoped to found my fame! And seizing the tablet I smashed it into a thousand pieces. Whereupon even more hurt I cried:

"Oh, my father, you were right when you wanted me to learn the saraband and lead a life of frivolity." At that I unconsciously danced a few steps of the saraband as my father was in the habit of doing when he recalled his former misfortune.

When the Arabs saw me smash the tablet on which only a few moments before I had been writing so busily, they cried out respectfully and with pity:

"God is great! All honor to the Lord and His prophets! Hallejujah! *Allah Kerim*!" Then, taking me gently by the hand, they accompanied me to the nearest Spanish outpost.

At this point in his story, we thought Velasquez seemed very downcast and distracted and, noticing that it was hard for him to continue, we urged him to postpone the rest till the following day.

The twenty-fifth day

We journeyed on through beautiful but deserted country. As we went around a hill I became separated from the caravan. I thought I heard groans coming from the depths of a thickly wooded valley that ran the length of our route. The groans grew louder. I dismounted, tied my horse, drew my sword and thrust my way into the thickets. But the deeper I penetrated into the woods, the farther away the groans seemed to be. At last I came to an open glade where I saw that I was surrounded by eight or ten men, all of them armed with muskets aimed at me.

One of the men shouted to me to hand over my sword. In answer I rushed forward intending to run him through. He, however, laid his musket on the ground and offered to surrender on condition that I would make him several promises. I replied that I would neither surrender nor promise anything.

At that moment we heard the shouts of the travelers calling me to return. One man who was apparently the leader of the gang, said to me:

"Señor caballero, your friends are looking for you, we have no time to lose. May it please you to leave the camp within five days and journey towards the West. You will meet persons who have an important secret to entrust to you. The groans you heard were merely a trick to lead you to us. Don't forget to come at the right time." With these words he made a brief bow, whistled to his men and disappeared along with his followers. I joined the caravan but did not think it necessary to mention this strange meeting. A little while later we halted for the night and after supper we urged Velasquez to tell us the rest of his adventures which he did in the following words.

CONTINUATION OF THE STORY OF THE GEOMETER

I have already told you that, after observing the general situation in the world, I felt that I had discovered methods of calculation heretofore unknown. I have said that the effect of my aunt Antonia's extraordinary question was to focus my thoughts and arrange them in a system. And finally I described how, convinced that people took me for a mad man, my mood of spiritual exaltation became one of deepest despair. I must confess that this despair lasted a long time and was very painful. I no longer dared to look my fellowmen in the face: it seemed to me they had banded together to ostracize and humiliate me. I gazed in disgust at the books that had given me so many pleasant hours; they now seemed to me only an accumulation of superfluous words. Moreover, I could not bear to touch my little slate; I stopped calculating. My brain went slack and lost its ability to function. I was too weak even to think. . .

My father noticed my desperate condition and asked the reason for it. I held out for some time, but in the end I repeated the Arab sheik's words and described my tormenting despair on first hearing myself called insane. My father bowed his head and tears streamed from his eyes. After a long pause he looked at me pityingly.

"My son," he said, "you are only called insane. I was really insane for three long years. My absent-mindedness and my love for Bianca are not the only causes of our troubles; our misfortune comes from another source. Inventive and moody in her methods, Nature enjoys violating her soundest principles. She makes personal interest the hub of all human actions, though now and then she does produce exceptions in whom there is no discernible selfishness because the full force of their thoughts and calculations are directed outward. Some are in love with knowledge, others with the welfare of humanity. They commend discoveries by foreigners as warmly as though they were their own, or they recommend beneficial constitutions for the government as though they alone were to derive advantage from them. The habit of self-sacrifice influences their destiny; they are incapable of seeing in men the instruments of their own fortune and when Fate knocks at their door, it never occurs to them to open it. There are very few people who can truly forget their own interests. You will find selfishness everywhere; in the advice men give you, in the services they do you, in the connections they seek, in the friendships they form. Absorbed in their own profit no matter how far distant it may be, they are indifferent to everything that does not concern them personally. If, on their way through life, they meet a man who has a poor opinion of his own worth, they cannot understand him and falsely attribute to him a thousand hidden reasons for this; he is possessed of a devil, he is insane. And they drive him out of their circle and banish him to a lonely African rock.

"My son, we both belong to that accursed race, but we also have our pleasures in life and I must take care that you learn to know them. I did my best to bring you up as an ignoramus and a gay blade, but Heaven, far from supporting my efforts, has instead endowed you with a sensitive soul and an enlightened mind. I shall therefore tell you about the joys of our life; they are neither blatant nor dazzling, but pure and sweet. How happy I was when I learned that Sir Isaac Newton had once praised one of my anonymous works and had expressed a desire to meet the author. I did not make myself known, but I was encouraged to go on to further efforts, enriching my mind with a multitude of ideas hitherto unknown to me. So imbued was I with those ideas that I could not refrain from rushing out and proclaiming them to the rocks of Ceuta, confiding them to all Nature, laying them as a sacrificial offering before my Maker. The memory of my sufferings mingled sighs and tears with those lofty emotions, but even in that memory I found a certain joy because it reminded me of all the suffering around me that I could alleviate. I thought of myself as aiding the purposes of Providence, the works of the Creator, the progress of the human spirit. My mind, my ego, my destiny did not seem to have individual shape, but were part of one great whole.

"Thus the age of passion went by and I found my way back to myself again. Your mother's tender devotion showed me a hundred times a day that I was the sole object of her love. My mind, which had closed, responded gratefully to the sweetness of our life together. Little incidents in your childhood and your sister's replenished the flame of my deepest emotions. Today your mother lives only in my heart and my enfeebled mind can add nothing more to the treasure of human knowledge. But I see with joy that every day this treasure becomes greater and I follow in thought the progress of that growth. Pursuits that keep me in touch with the general mental trend prevent me from thinking of my weakness, the sad companion of my age, and so far I have never felt bored in my life. You see, my son, that we too have our joys and if, as I had hoped, you had become a gay young spark you would also have had your worries. When Alvarez was here, he told me things about my brother that roused my pity rather than my jealousy.

" 'The Duke,' he said, 'knows Court life well. He easily unravels all sorts of intrigues, but every time he seeks the highest office, he realizes that he lacks the wings to fly. He was ambassador and represented his King and master with tact and honor but when the first difficult situation arose they had to recall him. You know too that he was one of the cabinet ministers and performed his duties no worse than others, but in spite of all the efforts of his subordinates to relieve him of as much work as possible, he could not cope with it and had to resign. Today, though he is no longer an important personality, he is still able to devise trivial opportunities for approaching the monarch, thus showing the world that he is still in the King's favor. In spite of all he is overcome with boredom. Though he has many ways to avoid it, he invariably succumbs to the iron grip of this monster. To be sure he avoids it by being interested only in himself, but this conspicuous narcissism has made him so sensitive to every untoward incident that life has become a burden to him. Meanwhile many illnesses have shown him that this sole interest of his can easily elude him, and this thought poisons all his pleasures.'

"That is all Alvarez told me about him and from it I realized that, in being forgotten, I am perhaps more fortunate than my brother, surrounded by the riches I have escaped.

"If the inhabitants of Ceuta think you are mad, my son, that is because they are dull-witted. Not until you go out into the turmoil of this world will you know to the full the injustice of men. You must arm yourself against it. Perhaps the best means would be to return insult for insult, in other words, to fight the unjust with their own weapons; but the art of fighting discreditably is not for men of our calibre. When therefore you see that you are being oppressed, go away, retire within yourself, nourish your mind with its own riches, and you can still be happy."

My father's words made a strong impression on me. I took fresh courage and started to work on my system again. At that time I had daily begun to be more absent-minded. I seldom heard what was said to me, except for the last words which were then deeply ingrained in my memory. I replied logically, but as a rule only an hour or two after the question had been asked. Often I set out without knowing where I was going so that it would have been well if, like a blind man, I had had a guide to accompany me. But this absent-mindedness lasted only while I was organizing my system. After that it diminished as I paid less attention to my work and today I can say flatly that I am completely cured.

"So that's it, or almost so," said the cabalist. "Allow me, Señor Velasquez, to be the first to congratulate you."

"My sincere thanks," replied Velasquez, and he continued:

Scarcely had I finished my system when an unexpected event brought about a change in my fate that now made it difficult for me, not only to set up a system but even to devote myself to calculations for ten or twenty consecutive hours. In short, Heaven had decreed that I should become Duke Velasquez, a Spanish grandee and the owner of an enormous fortune.

Four weeks had passed when Diego Alvarez, the son of old Alvarez, came to Ceuta with a letter from Duchess Bianca to my father. The letter ran as follows:

Señor Don Henrique:
This letter brings you the news that in all probability God will soon call Duke Velasquez to Him. The laws of our Spanish nobility do not permit you to be the heir of your younger brother; therefore both fortune and title fall to your son. Now that the fortieth year of my penance is drawing to a close I am extremely happy to be in a position to restore the possessions that you were deprived of through my frivolity. But as we both will soon stand before the gates of eternal glory, the things of this world can no longer concern us. Forgive the poor sinner Bianca and send us the son Heaven has bestowed on you. The Duke, by whose sickbed I have sat now for two months, desires to see him.

Bianca Velasquez

I must admit that this letter filled all the inhabitants of Ceuta with joy, so greatly were my father and I beloved. I myself, however, was far from sharing the general happiness. For me Ceuta was the world I left only in dreams. If sometimes I let my eyes wander over the broad regions beyond the ramparts settled by Moors, to me they were only scenes in another landscape. As I could not walk in those distant parts, they seemed to me made only to be looked at. Besides I thought it would be impossible for me to go anywhere else. In all Ceuta there was no wall on which I had not scribbled an equation, no hidden corner where I had not indulged in thought. To be sure, Aunt Antonia and her maid sometimes bothered me, but what were those little annoyances compared to the absent-mindedness to which I was condemned? If I could not reflect and reason, if I could not continue my calculations, there was no happiness for me. Such were my thoughts as I was about to leave Ceuta. My father accompanied me to the river bank and, laying his hands on my head, blessed me.

"My son," he said, "you will see Bianca; she is no longer the alluring beauty who was to have been your father's pride and joy. You will see her features wrinkled with age and worn from many penances; why did she repent her mistake so long when your father had forgiven her? As for me, I was never angry with her. Even if I never served the King in any honorable post, on the other hand in these forty years among the rocks of Ceuta I have fortunately been able to help a number of honorable people. They owe Bianca their full gratitude; they have often heard of her virtues and they all bless her."

My father's voice was choked with tears; he could say no more. All the inhabitants of Ceuta assembled for my departure: in every eye one could read their sadness at the separation, but also their joy at the brilliant turn my destiny had taken.

We set sail and landed the next morning in Algeciras. From there I journeyed to Cordoba and then to Andujar where I expected to spend the night. The local innkeeper told me extraordinary tales of spirits and ghosts to which I paid no heed. I spent the night there and set out early the next morning. I had two servants with me; one of them rode ahead, the other behind me. Depressed at the thought that I would have no time to work in Madrid, I took out my little tablet and applied myself to the usual calculations, especially those that were still missing in my system.

I was riding a mule whose even pace favored my work. I do not know how much time passed in this way; then suddenly my mule stopped short. I was at the foot of a gallows on which hung two corpses whose grimacing faces filled me with horror. I looked all around and, not seeing either of my servants, I began to shout for them at the top of my voice, but in vain. I decided to ride on along the straight road ahead of me. It was already late at night when at last I came to a large, well-built inn which, however, was deserted. I put the mule into the stable and I myself went into the central room where I found the remains of an evening meal, namely a partridge pie, bread and a bottle of Alicante wine. As I had not eaten since leaving Andujar, I thought my hunger entitled me to the pie, especially as it lay there without an owner. Moreover, I was very thirsty and I proceeded to quench my thirst—perhaps too generously. The wine went to my head, which, however, I realized too late.

There was a very decent bed in the room, so I undressed, lay down and fell asleep. Suddenly, I don't know why, I was wide awake and I heard the clock strike midnight. I thought there must be a monastery nearby and decided to have a look at it the next morning.

Shortly after that I heard sounds from the courtyard and I thought my servants had returned. But how great was my astonishment when I saw my aunt Antonia enter, followed by her maid, Marika. The latter carried a candlestick with two candles, my aunt held a roll of papers in her hand.

"My dear nephew," she said to me, "your father has sent us here to deliver these papers to you."

I took the papers and read the title: "The Exposition of Squaring the Circle." I knew my father had never dabbled in this superfluous question. In amazement I unfolded the paper, but to my indignation, I noticed at once that the supposed squaring was the well-known theory of Dimostratos, authenticated by proofs in which I recognized my father's hand but not his head. In fact I discovered that the accompanying proofs were only miserable paralogisms.

Meanwhile my aunt, who did not see a chair anywhere in the room, sat down beside me on the bed. I was so distressed that my father could lapse into such a mistake that I did not hear a word she said. Unconsciously I moved towards the wall as Marika lay down at my feet with her head on my knees.

Then I read the proof through again and—I don't know whether it was the Alicante wine that had gone to my head or whether my eyes were bewitched—in a word, I cannot understand how it happened that the proof did not seem to be so faulty and after the third reading I was completely convinced by it.

I turned the page around and found a row of wonderful formulas that stood for squaring or straightening all sorts of curves and finally saw the question of isochromes solved through the principles of elementary geometry. Astounded, delighted, drunk with excitement I shouted with every fresh glance at the paper:

"Yes, it's true! My father has made a most important discovery!"

"Then," said my aunt, "you should thank me for the trouble I took to cross the sea and bring you these papers."

I embraced her.

"And what about me," Marika cried. "Didn't I cross the sea too?"

I therefore embraced Marika too.

My traveling companions held me so close in their arms that I could not break away from them; however, I did not have the slightest desire to do so for strange emotions I had never known before now took possession of me. A new sense awoke in me and I sought in vain for some theory to explain it. I should have liked to understand these new impressions, but could not form any notion of them. Finally my feelings increased to a degree which in geometrical progression runs into infinity. I fell asleep and awoke filled with horror under the gallows, where I saw the two grimacing hanged men.

"That is my life story. All that is lacking is to complete the theory of my system, in other words, to apply mathematics to the general scheme of the universe. I hope, however, that someday I can share it with you, especially with this charming lady who, for a person of her sex has, it seems to me, an unusual bent for exact science."

Rebecca thanked Velasquez and asked him what became of the papers his aunt had brought him.

"I don't know what happened to them," replied the geometer. "I did not find them among the papers the gypsy brought back to me, and this I greatly regret, for I have no doubt that if I were to examine the alleged proof again I would immediately discover the errors. That night my blood churned in my veins; the Alicante wine, the two women and a sleepiness I could not control were certainly the cause of my failure. But what still surprises me is that the writing was in my father's hand and written in signs peculiar only to him."

I was struck by Velasquez's words, particularly the fact that he could not overcome his sleepiness. I suspected that he had been given a wine similar to the one my cousins prepared for me on our first meeting in the Venta or perhaps like that poison I had been made to drink in the underground caves and that was actually only a sleeping potion. The company now broke up, each going his own way. As I was getting ready for bed, I overheard more remarks that made me think that all my adventures could probably be explained by natural means. And with such thoughts I fell asleep.

The twenty-sixth day

The next twenty-four hours we spent resting. As the life our gypsy friends led and their smuggling, which was their chief means of livelihood, demanded a constant and tiring movement from place to place I was glad for once to spend the day in the same spot where we had halted for the night. Each of us devoted a little time to his own affairs. Rebecca added a few pieces of jewelry to her dress and it was easy to see that she was making an effort to attract the young Duke's attention. From that time on we called Velasquez "the Duke."

We all gathered together on the greensward that was shaded by beautiful chestnut trees and, after we had eaten a midday meal that was unusually delicious, Rebecca announced that, as the gypsy leader had less to do today than usual we should ask him to continue the story of his adventures. Pandesowna did not need much urging and he began with these words.

CONTINUATION OF THE STORY OF PANDESOWNA

Life in the seminary proved to be exactly what I had feared. The continual dependency in which our headmaster kept us seemed to be unbearable. I had grown accustomed to my aunt's caresses and her gentle indulgence. Moreover, I counted a great deal on hearing her say a hundred times a day what a good heart I had. Here at the seminary my good heart was good for nothing; if you did not keep a sharp lookout you were given a taste of the rod. I hated either one equally. The result was I developed a fundamental dislike for everyone who wore the black frock and I let them know it by playing all sorts of tricks on them. Among the Theatine priests Pater Sanudo the headmaster proved to be the strictest and most relentless of them all. This hardness did not come from his heart; on the contrary, that priest was by nature extraordinarily sensitive, but his secret inclinations were always at war with his duty. Sanudo had reached his thirtieth year without ever ceasing to fight and to win.

Pitiless towards himself, Sanudo had become inexorable towards others. The daily sacrifices he made to moral precepts were all the more meritorious as the contrast between the voice of Nature, on the one hand, and the demands of religion on the other, could not have been stronger with any man than with him. He was the handsomest man you could imagine and few women could meet him without admiring him. Sanudo, however, lowered his eyes, frowned and passed by as though he had not noticed them. That was Pater Sanudo, or rather that was what he had been for a long time.

But after so many victories his mind had relaxed, it no longer had the same energy. Constrained to fear women, in the end he had come to think of them only, and the enemy he had fought so long was constantly present in his dreams. Finally a serious illness, followed by a long convalescence, left him with an excessive sensitivity, which showed itself in constant impatience. Our slightest errors irritated him, but our apologies could move him to tears. He had become a dreamer and in his abstraction his eyes, even when turned on a nondescript object, often wore an expression of real tenderness and if anyone interrupted one of those ecstasies, his expression turned to one of pain, not severity. We were too much in the habit of watching our mentor for such a great change to escape our notice, but we did not know the cause. Then one day we had an opportunity to observe something that put us on the track. So that you will understand, I must go back a little in time. The two most aristocratic families of Burgos were the families of the Count de Lirias and the Marquisa de Fuen-Castilla. The Lirias even belonged to what is called, in Spain, *graviados,* that is, people who should have been made grandees. Moreover, the grandees addressed them with the familiar *"tu,"* as they did each other and the *graviados* were, to a certain extent, drawn into their circle.

The head of the house of Lirias was an elderly man of sixty, of an extremely noble character and the greatest kindness. His two daughters had died and all his possessions were to go to the young Countess Lirias, the daughter of his eldest son.

The old Count, who had been denied an heir, had promised the hand of his granddaughter to the heir of the Fuen-Castillos who, on marrying, was to take the name of Fuen de Lirias y Castillo. In every respect, even in regard to the age, appearance and characters of the two fiancés, this marriage was a fortunate choice. The young couple therefore loved each other with even greater passion and old Lirias rejoiced in their innocent love which reminded him of the sweetest period in his own life.

The future Countess de Fuen de Lirias lived in the convent of the Annunziata. But day after day she went to dine with her grandfather and to spend the evening in the company of her future husband. On those occasions she was always accompanied by a *dueña-mayor,* Doña Clara Mendoce, a woman of about thirty and extremely respectable but by no means sullen, for the old Count would not have tolerated such a person around him.

Every day the young Lirias and her chaperone drove past our seminary for that was the road that led to the old Count's; and as that always happened during our free period we often stood at the window or ran to it the moment we heard the sound of her carriage. The first one to reach the window would often hear la Mendoce say to her charge:

"Let us take a look at the handsome Theatine."

That was the name society women had given Pater Sanudo. As a matter of fact the *dueña* had eyes only for him. As for the young *señorita* she would let her eyes wander over all of us; perhaps our youth reminded her of her lover or perhaps she was looking for her two cousins who attended our seminary.

Sanudo hurried to the window just as the rest of us did; but as soon as the ladies caught sight of him, he put on a stern expression again and turned away in scorn. This contradiction surprised us. If he despises women, we said, then why does he come to the window? And if he is curious to see them, why does he turn away from them? To this a young student, named Veyras, said that Pater Sanudo was no longer an enemy of women as once he had been, and that he, Veyras, would find a way to prove it. Veyras was the best friend I had in the seminary; that is, he joined me in all the pranks which he himself often started.

Around this time a new novel had appeared entitled *Leonce in Love*. The author had painted love in such alluring colors that the reader was exposed to danger and our teacher had strictly forbidden us to read it. Veyras managed to get a copy of *Leonce* and stuck it in his pocket at the same time purposely allowing a piece of it to show. Sanudo noticed it and confiscated the book. He threatened Veyras with the most severe punishment if he ever did such a thing again. Then he pleaded illness and did not appear for the evening lecture. For our part we pretended great anxiety about our teacher's health and walked unannounced into his room. We found him absorbed in reading the dangerous *Leonce,* his eyes suffused with tears, clear proof of how fascinating he found this book. Sanudo seemed embarrassed but we pretended not to notice anything. Soon we had further proof of the great change that had come over this unfortunate priest.

The women in Spain fulfill their religious duties very frequently and each time they always ask for the same confessor. They call that; *buscar su padre.* That is why many a wicked joker, when he sees a child in church, asks whether it has come to *buscar su padre* (to look for its father). The ladies of Burgos would have been delighted to confess to Pater Sanudo, but the shy headmaster had declared that he would not accept penitents of the feminine sex for confession. The day after the fatal reading, however, one of the most beautiful women in the city asked for Pater Sanudo, and he immediately went into his confessional. For this he was paid compliments that had a double meaning. He replied with the greatest seriousness that he need no longer fear an enemy he had fought so often. The fathers may have believed that, but we pupils knew better.

With every day Sanudo seemed to be more interested in the secrets the beautiful woman revealed in confession. He became a cautious confessor; finishing off the old ladies in a hurry, and detaining the younger ones longer. He never failed to hurry to the window to see beautiful Señorita Lirias and the amiable Mendoce drive past and not until the carriage was out of sight did he raise his eyes to Heaven in disdain.

One day when we had done our lesson more carelessly than usual and had been given a taste of Sanudo's severity, Veyras drew me aside.

"It is time," he said, "to revenge ourselves on this cursed pedant who poisons the best days of our lives with penances and seems to take pleasure in meting out punishments to us. I've thought of a fine trick, but we have to find a young girl with a figure like Lirias's. Juanita, the gardener's daughter, is usually ready to play along with all our pranks but she hasn't the wit for this one."

"My dear Veyras," I replied, "even if we had a girl whose figure resembled young Lirias's, she still wouldn't have the lovely face the other one has."

"I'm not worried about that point," replied Veyras. "During Lent our ladies are in the habit of wearing veils which they call *catafalcos.* They're made of a sort of crepe material that falls in graduated folds one over the other, and hides their faces so well that even at a ball they could not be better masked. Juanita will be useful to us after all, if not to play the part of Lirias or Mendoce at least to provide clothes for the false Lirias and her *dueña*."

That day Veyras said nothing more. But one fine Sunday as Pater Sanudo seated himself in his confessional, he saw two women, shrouded in cloaks and veils, enter the church. One of them sat down on a mat on the floor as is the habit with the women in Spain. The other woman took her place as a penitent before the confessional. The latter, who appeared to be very young, burst into tears and was wracked with sobs. Sanudo did his best to calm her, but she kept on repeating;

"Father, I have committed a deadly sin."

Finally Sanudo told her she was not in any condition to confess to him and that she should come back the next day. The young sinner withdrew, threw herself down before the altar, prayed long and ardently and left the church with her companion.

The next day at the same hour the two sinners, for whom Sanudo had waited a long time, appeared again. The younger one went again to the confessional; she seemed to be more in control of herself. But this time, too, there was much weeping and sobbing. Finally in silvery tones she said:

"Father, not so long ago my heart seemed to walk steadily in unison with my duty on the path of virtue. A young and charming husband had been chosen for me and I thought I loved him."

Here she began to sob again. Sanudo, however, spoke to her with such holy fervor that he succeeded in calming the young girl who continued as follows:

"An unwise chaperone had too frequently called my attention to the charms of a man to whom I cannot belong, indeed of whom I dare not even dream. Nevertheless I cannot overcome this unrighteous passion."

The word "unrighteous" seemed to warn Sanudo that the man in question was a priest, perhaps even himself.

"My child," he said and his voice trembled, "you owe all your affection to the husband your parents have chosen for you."

"Oh, Father," replied the young girl. "Why is he not like

the man I love? Why does he not have the same tender yet stern expression, the same noble and beautiful features?"

"My child," said Sanudo, "this is not the way to confess."

"This is not a confession," replied the young girl. "It is an avowal."

As if ashamed of her admission, she rose, ordered her companion to get up and together they left the church. Sanudo followed them with his eyes. The rest of the day he appeared unusually thoughtful. All the next day he spent in the confessional, but no one came, nor on the day after that either.

On the third day the young girl returned with her *dueña,* went to the confessional and said to Sanudo:

"Father, last night I think I had a vision. I was overcome with shame and despair, my evil spirit induced me to tie one of my garters around my neck; I ceased to breathe. Suddenly I thought someone held my hand back, a strong light shone in my eyes, and I saw Saint Teresa, my patron, standing beside my bed. 'My daughter,' she said to me, 'confess tomorrow to Pater Sanudo and beg him to give you a lock of his hair. This you will carry over your heart and your heart will be filled with grace . . .' "

"Go, my child," said Sanudo. "Go to the steps of the altar and weep for this aberration. For my part I shall pray God to have mercy on you."

Sanudo rose, left the confessional and retired to the chapel. There he stayed until evening, praying with unusual fervor.

The next day the *dueña* appeared alone and went to the confessional.

"Oh, Father," she cried, "I have come here to implore your indulgence for a young sinner whose soul is threatened with corruption. The harshness with which you treated her yesterday threw her into despair. She says you refused to give her a holy reliquary which you possess. She is losing her mind, she is trying to kill herself. Go to her house, Father. Take her the reliquary she has asked for. Do not refuse her this kindness!"

Sanudo buried his face in his handkerchief, left the church and returned shortly afterwards. In his hand he held a little reliquary box which he handed to the *dueña.*

"Señora," he said, "what I am giving you is a piece of the skull of our holy founder. A bull of the Pope's connects innumerable indulgences with this reliquary. It is the most precious thing we have here. Your charge is to wear this holy remains on her heart and may Heaven come to her aid."

When the reliquary finally came into our hands, we opened the box in the hope of finding a few locks of hair—we found nothing. Of course Sanudo was soft, perhaps even a little vain, but he was virtuous and true to his principles. After the evening lecture Veyras asked him: "Father, why aren't priests allowed to marry?"

"To their misfortune in this world and perhaps to their damnation in the next," replied Sanudo. And he added even more sternly and emphatically:

"Veyras, never ask me such questions again."

The next day Sanudo did not appear in the confessional. The *dueña* asked for him, but another priest was there in his place.

We were about ready to give up all hope of pulling off our shameful trick when chance raised our hopes again.

At the very time the young Countess Lirias was to be married to Count de Fuen-Castillo, she was taken seriously ill with high fever accompanied by brain convulsions and delirium. All Burgos sympathized with the two aristocratic families and Señorita de Lirias's illness called forth widespread consternation. The Theatiner fathers were by no means the last to be informed and in the evening Sanudo received a letter that read as follows:

Father:
The holy Teresa is angry. She says you have deceived me. She also blames la Mendoce. Why did she let me drive day after day past the Theatine seminary? The holy Teresa loves me—you do not . . . I have terrible pains in my head . . . I am dying . . ."

This letter was written in a shaky hand and was almost illegible. At the bottom of the page another hand had added: "Father, she writes twenty letters like this a day. Now she is no longer able to write. Pray for us, Father! That is all I can say to you at the moment."

Poor Sanudo did not know what to think. He was so upset he was almost beside himself. He came, he went, he went away, he made inquiries and what was best of all for us, he did not give any more evening lectures or at least when he did they were so short that we could manage to endure them without being bored. In the end a fortunate crisis or some kind of a sudorific saved the life of the charming Countess Lirias. Her recovery was announced and Sanudo received the following letter:

Father:
At last the danger is past, but common sense has not returned. The young girl is constantly on the point of escaping from me. Would it not be possible, Father, for you to receive us in your cell? The convent is not closed until eleven o'clock. We could come at nightfall. Perhaps your exhortations will be more effective than your reliquaries. If this situation continues, I will lose my mind too. Father, in the name of Heaven, save the honor of two illustrious houses.

This letter made such an impression on Sanudo that he could scarcely find his way back to his cell. He locked himself in and we crowded against the door to hear what went on. At first we heard him sobbing and weeping and after that praying with great fervor. Then he sent for the house porter and said to him:

"Brother, if two women come and ask for me do not let them in under any circumstances."

Sanudo did not appear for the evening meal. He spent the evening in prayer. Toward eleven o'clock he heard a knock on his door. He opened it and a young person rushed into the room, thereby knocking over his lamp which immediately went out. At that moment the Father Prefect's voice was heard calling Sanudo. The latter had just time to lock his door and hurry off to the Prefect. I should be underestimating the listener's intelligence were I to assume that he had not already guessed that the false Mendoce was none other than Veyras and the beautiful Lirias the same person the Viceroy of Mexico had wanted to marry—in other words, myself. So there I was, locked in Sanudo's cell, without a light and uncertain how to carry on the comedy which had certainly not developed as we had intended. Though Sanudo was gullible, he was never weak or hypocritical. No doubt it would have been better to end our comedy at this point. To Sanudo, the marriage of Señorita Lirias, which took place a few days later, and the happiness of the newlywed couple remained an inexplicable mystery that worried him all his life. We, however, wanted to gloat over our mentor's bewilderment, and I wondered whether it would be better to end this last act with a great burst of laughter or with an ironical twist. I was still mulling over this spiteful plan when the door opened and Sanudo entered. His appearance made a deeper impression on me than I had expected. Wearing stole and surplice, he carried a candle in one hand and an ebony crucifix in the other. Setting his candle down on the table, he clasped the crucifix in both hands and turned to me.

"Señorita, you see me in these holy vestments which should remind you of the priesthood with which I am imbued heart and soul. As a priest of the Redeemer I cannot better fulfill my duty than to save you from the brink of an endless abyss. The demon of evil has distorted your mind that he might plunge you into an orgy of lusts. Turn back, Señorita, turn back to the path of virtue! For you it was strewn only with flowers. A young husband stretches out his hand to you. To him the virtuous old man, whose blood flows in your veins, has entrusted you. That old man's son was your father; he has gone before you both to the abode of pure souls from whence he shows you the way. Lift up your eyes to the heavenly light. Fear the demon of lies who blinds you and in that delusion has turned upon the servant of that God whose eternal foe he is."

Sanudo said many other beautiful things which would have converted me if I had been Señorita Lirias and in love with my confessor. But I was only a little scamp decked out in shawl and veil and I was anxious to know how it was all going to end. Sanudo took a deep breath.

"Come, Señorita," he said. "All arrangements have been made for you to leave the seminary. I will take you to the gardener's wife and they will call la Mendoce who will come and fetch you." As he spoke, Sanudo opened the door—and

I made ready to run for my life. At least that is what I should have done! But at that moment some evil spirit put it into my head to take off my veil and throw myself on the headmaster's neck.

"Cruel man," I cried. "Are you going to let the lovesick Lirias die?"

Sanudo recognized me—and stared at me in utter consternation. Then, tears poured down his face and, obviously in the greatest anguish, he repeated again and again:

"My God! Oh, my God! Have pity on me! Enlighten me! Take away my doubts! My God! Oh, my God! What shall I do?"

The poor headmaster roused my pity. I clasped his knees and begged him to forgive me. I swore that Veyras and I would keep his secret.

Sanudo raised me to my feet, bathed me with his tears and said:

"Unhappy child, how can you think that fear of appearing ridiculous could put me in such a state? Unhappy child, I weep for you. You have not hesitated to besmirch the holiest of holies; you have played tricks with the confessional. It is my duty to report you to the tribunal of the Inquisition; you will suffer the torment of prison." With this he embraced me and, with an expression of deepest sorrow, said:

"No, my child, do not despair. Perhaps I can manage to have your punishment left to us. It will be hard, but it will have no influence on your future life."

Sanudo then went out, double-locked the door and left me in a turmoil which I leave it to you to imagine. It had never occurred to me to think of our trick as a crime, and the foolish plot we had hatched had seemed only an impertinent jest. The punishment I faced depressed me to such an extent that I could not even cry. I don't know how long I remained in this condition. At last the door opened and the Prefect entered. He was followed by a confessor and two lay brothers who took me by the arms and led me along corridor after corridor to a distant room. There they shoved me inside, but did not follow and I heard several bolts shot to behind me.

I took a deep breath and looked around my prison. A full

moon, shining through the bars of my window, fell on dirty, blackened walls and in one corner a bundle of straw. The window looked out on a graveyard. Three corpses, wrapped in shrouds lay on three biers in a cloister. This sight filled me with such horror that I did not dare to look around in my room.

Soon I heard a noise in the graveyard and saw a Capuchin friar arrive, accompanied by three gravediggers. They went to the cloister and I heard the Capuchin say: "Here is the body of the Marquis de Valornez. You will take it to the embalming room. But as for these two Christians, they will be thrown into the new grave that was dug yesterday."

Scarcely had the friars stopped speaking than I heard a loud groan, and three hideous ghosts appeared over the top of the cemetery wall. This apparition and the groans that accompanied it so frightened the two gravediggers and the Capuchin friar, that they fled uttering loud cries. I was frightened too, but my fear had the opposite effect on me: unable to move, I stood at the window, numb with horror.

Then I saw two of the ghosts jump down from the wall into the graveyard and hold out their hands to the third ghost who seemed to have difficulty getting down. Thereupon more ghosts appeared and they too jumped down into the cemetery until there were ten or twelve of them there. At this the ghost who had helped the others over the wall strode to the cloister and examined the three corpses. Then he turned to the other ghosts.

"My friends," he said, "here is the body of the Marquis de Valornez. You saw how those dunderheads, my professional colleagues, treated him. They were completely wrong in diagnosing his illness as dropsy of the lungs. I, Dr. Sangro-Moreno, I was the only one to hit the mark when I pronounced it *angina polyposa* which has been so excellently described by the masters of our profession.

"Scarcely, however, had I uttered the word *angina polyposa* than those dunderheads in a lucrative position, my colleagues, shrugged their shoulders and turned their backs on me as if I were an unworthy member of their guild. Oh, no doubt, Dr. Sangro-Moreno does not belong among them. Donkey-drivers from Galizia and mule-drivers from Estramadura, those were the right people to lead them and bring them to their senses. But Heaven is just. Last year the brutes died like flies. If the plague continues this year, you can be sure that none of my colleagues will survive; then Dr. Sangro-Moreno will have the field to himself. And you, my dear pupils, will bear aloft the banner of medicine. You have seen how I, single-handed, saved young Señorita Lirias with a fortunate mixture of phosphate and antimony. The semi-metal and its scientifically tested compounds—those are the heroic remedies, the valiant cures that combat and conquer all diseases—not roots and herbs that are only fit for my honorable colleagues, those asses in a lucrative post, to graze on.

"My dear pupils, you witnessed my urgent pleas to the Marquesa de Valornez to permit me to insert even the tip of my knife in the nobel Marquis's windpipe. But goaded by my enemies, the Marchioness stubbornly refused her consent. Now at last I am in a position to produce the proof. If it were only possible for the noble Marquis himself to be present when his body is opened! With what pleasure I would show him the hydratic and polyp-like materials that have their roots in his bronchial tubes and whose branches reach to the top of the larynx. But what shall I say? Completely indifferent to the progress of science, the avaricious Castilian refuses us anything he himself cannot use. If the Marquis had been blessed with even the slightest feeling for medicine he would have left us his lungs, his liver and all his inner organs which can no longer be of any use to him. But no! At the risk of life and limb we are forced to desecrate the sanctuary of death and disturb the peace of graves. What does it matter, my dear pupils? The more obstacles we have to overcome, the greater will be our renown. So then courage! Let us carry out this great enterprise to the end! When you whistle three times, our good comrades on the other side of the wall will hand us a ladder and we shall promptly carry off the noble Marquis. He should consider himself fortunate to have died of such an unusual disease, but even more so to have fallen into the hands of such capable men who recognized the disease and called it by its correct name.

"Day after tomorrow we shall have the honor of fetching an illustrious person who died as the result of . . . But silence. One should not tell all."

When the doctor had finished speaking, one of his pupils whistled three times and I saw them pass the ladders over the wall. After that the Marquis's corpse was bound around with ropes and lifted over to the other side; the ghosts followed and the ladders were pulled up again. When there was nothing more to see, I laughed so much at the fright I had had, I could not stop laughing.

Here, however, I must tell you about a special sort of burial that is customary in a number of cloisters in Spain and Sicily. Dark, little vaults are built in which, however, air circulates freely by means of artificially created circulation. In these vaults are placed the dead who are to be preserved. The dark protects them from insects and the air dries them out. After six months the vault is opened. If the enterprise has been successful, the monks go in procession to congratulate the family. They they clothe the dead in a Capuchin robe and lay him in a vault that is reserved for presumably holy men or at least for such as have reached a certain degree of blessedness. In these cloisters the funeral procession accompanies the corpse only to the gates of the cemetery where lay brothers receive it on order of their superior and take charge of it. The dead are usually brought there in the evening. The superiors confiscate it and at night it is taken to its resting place. Some corpses can not be preserved.

The Capuchins wanted to let the Marquis's corpse dry out and they had just set to work on it when the ghosts put the gravediggers to flight. At the first sign of day they tiptoed hesitantly back, one huddled close against the other. They were terrified when they found that the Marquis's corpse had disappeared; they thought the devil had carried it off. Soon afterwards all the monks arrived, armed with aspergillums, sprinkling holy water, driving out the devil and shrieking at the top of their lungs. However, as I could not fight my weariness any longer, I flung myself down on the straw and fell sound asleep.

The next day my first thought was of the punishment that

threatened me, the second of a way to escape it. Veyras and I had plundered the larder so often that such housebreaking was mere child's play for us. We were also adept at loosening bars on windows and putting them back again so that no one could notice that they had been disturbed. Using a knife I had in my pocket, I pried a nail out of the wood in my window and with this nail worked the mounting of a rod. I worked steadily until noon.

Then the peephole in my door opened and I recognized the face of one of the lay brothers who was on duty in our dormitory. He shoved bread and a pitcher of water inside and asked me if he could do anything for me. I begged him to ask Pater Sanudo to have me given sheets and a clean cover, for it was right to punish me but not to subject me to dirt. This argument worked: they sent me what I asked for and even added a little meat for my nourishment. I learned from a roundabout source that Veyras was not worried and I was delighted to hear that the fathers were not looking for any accomplices. I asked when my punishment would begin. The lay brother told me he knew nothing about that, but that the Fathers usually took three days to think things over. That was enough to restore my calm in full.

The water they gave me I used to wet the grating I was trying to remove. The work went well. By the morning of the second day the window grating was completely free. Then I cut up my sheet and my cover, tied them together like a sort of rope ladder and waited for night to make my flight. It was high time, for the night porter informed me that the next day I was to be sentenced by a Junta of Theatiner monks under the chairmanship of a member of the Inquisition tribunal.

Towards evening a corpse, wrapped in a black cloth that was trimmed with heavy silver fringe, was brought in. I thought this must be the distinguished gentleman of whom Dr. Sangro-Moreno had spoken.

As the night was very dark and silent, I made fast my sheet-ladder and was just climbing down when the ghosts appeared on the wall again. They were, as you correctly suspect, the doctor's pupils. Going straight to the dead nobleman they carried him away, but left the black silver-fringed cloth behind.

When they had gone I opened my window and climbed down with the greatest of ease. Then I set about placing one of the biers against the wall to serve as a ladder. As I started to work I heard the cemetery gate open. I ran to hide, lay down on the bier and covered myself with the fringed cloth but held up one corner to see who the intruders were. At the head of a little procession strode a young squire clad all in black and carrying in one hand a torch and in the other a sword. He was followed by servants in mourning and last of all, swathed from head to foot in black veils came a lady of wondrous beauty. The beautiful mourner walked straight to my bier, fell to her knees and cried out in deep anguish:

"O adored remains of the most lovable husband! If, like a second Artemis, I could mingle your ashes in my wine you would revive a heart that has always beaten only for you. My religion does not permit me to be your living grave, nevertheless I shall rescue you from the dust of the dead. Day after day my tears will water the flowers on your grave where we shall soon be reunited."

The lady then turned to her squire and said:

"Don Diego, have your master's body taken away. Afterwards we shall bury him in the garden chapel."

Immediately four stalwart servants picked up the bier and if they thought they were carrying a dead man they were scarcely mistaken for I was almost dead from fright.

When the gypsy had come to this part of his adventure he was informed that business of the tribe demanded his attention. He left us and we did not see him again that day.

The twenty-seventh day

The next day we stayed in the same place. The gypsy had a little free time and Rebecca seized the first opportunity to ask him to go on with his story. The leader acquiesced cheerfully and began as follows:

CONTINUATION OF THE STORY OF PANDESOWNA

While the servants were carrying me on my bier, I peered through a mesh in the black cloth that covered me and saw that the lady was riding in a black sedan chair, the squire had mounted his horse and my bearers were taking turns carrying the bier, the faster to reach their destination. We had left Burgos through I don't know which gate and had been about an hour on the way, when we stopped in front of a garden. They entered and I was finally placed in a pavilion in the middle of a vast hall lined with black and faintly lighted by the glimmer of several lamps.

"Don Diego," said the lady to her squire, "you may withdraw. I wish to weep over these adored remains with which from very grief I shall soon be united."

When the lady was alone she sat down in front of me and said: "Barbarian! Now you see what your implacable rage has brought you to. How will you ever be able to answer before the terrible Last Judgment?"

At that moment another woman entered. She clutched a dagger in her hand and she looked like a fury.

"Where," she demanded, "are the shameful remains of that monster in human form? Now we shall see whether he had a heart in his body! I'll tear out that pitiless heart and cut it in little pieces; I'll crush it in my hands and satisfy my rage."

It now seemed to me high time to make myself known. Flinging aside my black cover, I clasped the lady with the dagger around the knees.

"Lady," I begged, "have pity on a poor schoolboy who hid under this cloth to escape a flogging."

"Miserable wight," she cried. "Where is the Duke of Sidonia's corpse?"

"In the hands of Dr. Sangro-Moreno," I said. "His pupils made off with it this very night."

"Just Heaven!" exclaimed the woman. "He was the only one who knew that the Duke died of poisoning. I am lost . . ."

"Never fear," I told her. "The doctor will never dare to admit that he robbed the Capuchin graveyard and those who think the devil carried off the corpse will take good care not to admit that Satan has so much power over their cloister."

At that the woman with the dagger looked at me sternly and said:

"And who will vouch for your silence?"

"Lady," I replied, "today a Council of the Theatine Fathers presided over by a member of the Inquisition will pass sentence on me. There is no doubt but that they will sentence me to a thousand lashes. I implore you to make sure of my silence by hiding me from all eyes."

Instead of answering, the lady opened a trapdoor in the hall and motioned me to climb through it. I obeyed and the trapdoor fell shut above me. I went down a very dark staircase that led to an equally gloomy subterranean vault, so dark that I ran against a post. My hands clutched chains, my feet struck against a gravestone above which rose a metal cross. Such gloomy objects did not invite sleep, but I was at the fortunate age in which one sleeps in spite of everything. I stretched out on the flat grave and the next moment I was sound asleep.

The following day the gleam of a lamp that had been lighted in another vault, separated from mine by bars, shone in my prison. Shortly afterwards the lady with the dagger appeared at the bars and set down in front of it a basket covered with a cloth. She tried to speak but tears choked her voice. Through signs she made me understand that this place awakened frightful memories in her. In the basket I found a generous supply of victuals and several books. I was saved from a flogging! I was also certain not to see any Theatiner monks and all these reflections had the effect of giving me a very pleasant day.

The next day, the young widow was the one who brought me food. She too tried to speak, but unable to utter a single word, she withdrew.

The following day she came again, this time with a basket on her arm which she handed to me over the bars. In the vault in which she stood, there was a large crucifix and, flinging herself on her knees before this image of our Redeemer, she prayed:

"Oh my God, beneath this grave rest the pitiful remains of a gentle and sensitive being who has certainly taken his place among the angels whose very image he was on earth. He is certainly pleading for mercy for his barbarous murderer, for the woman who revenged his death, and for the unhappy creature who, as an involuntary accomplice, became the victim of so much atrocity."

The lady continued her prayer in a lower voice but with

greater fervor. Finally she rose, came to the bars and said in a calmer voice: "Tell me if you need anything and what we can do for you."

"Madam," I replied, "I have an aunt named Dalanosa. She lives on the Río Theatine. I should like to let her know that I am alive and safe."

"Such an errand," said the lady, "could be dangerous for us. However, I promise you I shall find a way to reassure your aunt."

"Madam," I replied, "you are kindness itself and the husband who is responsible for your unhappiness must have been a monster."

"Oh!" cried the lady. "How mistaken you are! He was the best and most considerate of men."

The next day the woman with the dagger brought my food. She did not seem to be so excited or at least she was more in control of herself.

"My child," she said, "I myself went to see your aunt. She seems to love you like a mother, for without a doubt, you have no parents anymore."

I replied that it was true, I had lost my mother and that later I had had the bad luck to fall into my father's inkpot and in consequence he had banished me forever from his sight.

The lady asked me to explain and I told her my story which made her laugh.

"My child," she said, "do you realize that I laughed? That has not happened for a long, long time. I had a son who now lies beneath the marble gravestone on which you are sitting. I should like to find him in you again. I nursed the Duchess of Sidonia at my breast. I am only a woman of the people, but I have a heart that knows how to love and to hate. One should never look down upon people of my temperament."

I thanked the lady and assured her that I would always entertain the sentiments of a son for her. Several weeks passed in about the same way. The two ladies became daily more accustomed to me. The nurse treated me like a son and the Duchess was extraordinarily kind to me. She often spent several hours in the crypt.

One day when she seemed less sad than usual I ventured to ask her about her unhappiness. She hesitated a long time, but finally relented and told me the following story.

THE STORY OF THE DUCHESS OF MEDINA-SIDONIA

I am the only daughter of Don Emanuel de Val-Florida, Secretary of State, who died recently. His rulers mourned him and, so I was told, even the European Courts connected with our great monarchy observed mourning for him. I knew that distinguished man only in the last years of his life. In my youth I lived in Asturia with my mother who was separated from her husband. After the first year of marriage she left him and went to live with her father, the Marquis de Astorgas, whose sole heir she was. I do not know how much my mother was to blame for losing her husband's affection, but I do know that her lifelong suffering should have been enough to atone for the most serious failings. She was always melancholy, her eyes full of tears, her smile sad. Not even her sleep was untroubled; her sighs and groans often broke the silence of the night.

The separation was by no means complete; my mother received letters regularly from her husband and she answered them. On two occasions she journeyed to Madrid to see him, but her husband's heart was closed to her forever. The Marchioness had a loving and tender heart. She transferred all her affection to her father and this feeling, which became a real passion with her, somewhat sweetened the bitterness of her long suffering. As for me, I would be embarrassed if I tried to describe my mother's feeling for me. There is no doubt that she loved me, but she felt shy at interfering in my fate. Far from instructing me, she scarcely dared to give me any advice. For, to tell the truth, she probably did not feel worthy to train her daughter in virtues which she herself had violated. I was therefore left to grow up in a sort of neglect which might have robbed me of the advantages of a good upbringing had not Girona been with me, first as my nurse and then as my governess. You have met her. You know that her spirit is strong, her mind noble. She left nothing undone to make me the happiest of women.

But an inevitable fate won out in spite of all her care. Pedro Giron, my nurse's husband, was known as an enterprising, but by no means irreproachable, man. Compelled to leave Spain, he sailed for America and nothing more was heard of him. Girona had only one child by him, a son who was my foster-brother. That son was so extraordinarily handsome that he earned the nickname of "Hermosito" which followed him all through his short life. The same milk had nourished us both and we had often lain in the same cradle. But our intimacy lasted only till his seventh year. Then Girona thought it was time to tell her son about the difference in our rank and the great distance that Fate had placed between him and his young friend.

One day after we had had a little quarrel, as is usual among children, Girona called her son and in a very serious voice said to him: "Never forget that Señorita de Val-Florida is your mistress as well as mine and that we are only the head servants in the house."

Hermosito did his best: my wishes were his and it was a matter of pride with him to anticipate my desires. This utter devotion seemed to have a special charm for him and I greatly enjoyed finding him obedient to my every whim.

Girona soon recognized the danger of the new relationship that had grown up between us and decided to separate us as soon as we reached our thirteenth year. Having settled that point, she thought no more about it and turned her attention to other matters.

As I have already told you, Girona is an educated person. At the right time she gave us a number of Spanish authors to read and taught us a general outline of history. As she also wanted to develop our judgment, she allowed us time to reflect on our reading and showed us how it could be used to advantage in discussions. As a rule when children begin to study history, they are filled with enthusiasm for the grandest and most splendid personalities. In our case my hero was always the same as Hermosito's hero. And if I changed, he promptly took over my new fancy. I had become so accustomed to Hermosito's submission that the slightest opposition on his part would have greatly astonished me. There was no fear of that, however, and I myself felt bound to hold my power in check or at least to use it prudently. One day I wanted a glistening shell I saw at the bottom of clear, deep water: Hermosito immediately plunged in to get it and was almost drowned. Another time as he was climbing a tree to get a bird's nest for me, the branch broke under him and he was badly hurt. After that I was careful about expressing my wishes, but I found it very pleasant to know that I possessed such great power even if I did not make use of it. That, if I remember correctly, was my first sign of arrogance. In this way we reached our thirteenth year.

That day Hermosito's mother said to him:

"My son, today we have celebrated your thirteenth birthday. You are not a child anymore and you cannot live in such close contact with the Señorita as you have up to now. Tomorrow you will go to your grandfather in Navarro."

No sooner had Girona stopped speaking than Hermosito displayed the greatest despair: he wept, he fainted and when he recovered consciousness, he began to weep again. I comforted him though I did not share his suffering. To me he was a creature completely dependent on me, one who, so to speak, breathed only with my permission. I considered his despair altogether unnatural, and I did not think I owed it to him to share it. I was still too young and too accustomed to seeing him for his extraordinary beauty to make any impression on me.

Girona was not the woman to be moved by tears. Hermosito wept in vain, he had to leave. But two days later his muleteer, looking very worried, arrived to inform us that on the journey he had left *his* mule for a second and when he returned Hermosito was gone. The muleteer had called him and searched for him in the forest but to all appearances the wolves had eaten the boy. Girona was more surprised than worried.

"You will see," she said, "that stubborn little fellow will come back to us."

She was right. In a little while we saw the runaway coming home. He clasped his mother around the knees, crying:

"I was born to serve Señorita de Val-Florida and I will die if you send me out of the house."

A few days later Girona received a letter from her husband from whom she had not heard for a long time. He told her that he had made a fortune in Vera Cruz and expressed his longing to have his son with him. Girona, who was anxious to get Hermosito away at any cost, did not fail to take advantage of this opportunity.

Since his return Hermosito had not been living in the castle, but on a farm that belonged to us near the seashore. One morning his mother went to him and forced him to go aboard the boat of a fisherman who had offered to put him on a ship for America. That night Hermosito jumped into the sea and swam ashore. Again Girona forced him to go aboard the ship. Such sacrifices she made to her duty! It was easy to see how heavy her heart was. All these things I have told you, happened in quick succession; they were followed by very sad events. My grandfather fell ill. My mother, weakened by her long illness, died at the same time as the Marquis de Astorgas.

My father was expected daily in Asturia. But the King could not make up his mind to let him leave, for the political situation was such that his absence was not desirable. The Marquis de Val-Florida therefore wrote Girona a most touching letter and ordered her to bring me to Madrid with all haste. My father had taken into his service all the servants of the Marquis de Astorgas, whose sole heir I was. They accompanied me on the journey and formed a splendid body of retainers for me. However, the daughter of a secretary of state can always be certain of being well received from one end of Spain to the other. The honors paid me on that journey have, I believe, contributed to awakening the feeling of pride that has since determined my fate. As I approached Madrid, I discovered another sort of pride. I had seen how my mother, the Marchioness de Val-Florida loved and worshipped her father, how she lived and breathed only for him whereas, on the other hand, she treated me with a certain coldness and reserve. Now I would have a father of my own and I vowed to love him with all my heart and to make him happy. This hope made me very proud; I felt that I was quite grown up although I was still only fourteen years old.

These thoughts filled my mind as my carriage drove into the courtyard of our town palace. My father received me at the foot of the great staircase and embraced me a thousand times. Shortly after that a command from the King summoned him to Court. I retired to my suite of rooms, but I was so excited that I could not sleep that night.

The next morning my father sent for me. He was just drinking his chocolate and he allowed me to have breakfast with him. Then he said to me:

"My dear Eleonore, I am very sad and depressed; but now that you have been given back to me I hope for happier days in the future. My study door will always be open to you. Bring some handiwork with you. I have a secluded study for conferences and confidential business. I shall always have time in the midst of my work to chat with you and I hope to find, in these unconstrained talks, some of the family happiness of which I have been deprived for so long."

The Marquis then rang for his secretary who came in carrying two baskets, one of them containing the letters that had come that day, the other those still unanswered. I spent some time in the study and returned again at dinner time. There I found several friends of my father's who, like him, were entrusted with important matters of State. They talked quite openly in front of me. Now and then I ventured a few naïve remarks that seemed to amuse them. I thought I noticed that this interested my father and my courage rose.

The next morning I went to his study as soon as I learned he was there. He was drinking his chocolate and looking very pleased.

"Today is Friday," he said. "We shall have mail from Lisbon."

Whereupon he rang the bell and the secretary came in with the two baskets. Looking preoccupied, my father rummaged around in one of them and pulled out a two-page letter. One of the pages was in cipher and this one he handed to his secretary; the other, written by hand, he began to read with the greatest interest. While he was thus occupied, I picked up the envelope and carefully studied the seal: a ducal crown above a fleece. Alas! that gorgeous coat-of-arms was one day to be mine! The next day brought the mail from France and so, little by little, letters arrived from every land. But none of these letters interested my father so much as the one from Portugal.

A week later I said to him:

"Today is Friday. We shall have mail from Lisbon."

When the secretary came in, I ran to the basket and fumbled around in it; then I pulled out the favorite letter and handed it to my father who, as a reward, embraced me tenderly.

I repeated this procedure on several Fridays in succession, with the result that one Friday I ventured to ask my father what made this letter so special.

"This letter," he replied, "is from our ambassador in Lisbon, the Duke of Medina-Sidonia. He is my friend and protector and more than that, for I have good reason to believe that my life is closely bound up with his."

"In that case," I said, "it is my right to interest myself in this kind Duke and I must make an effort to get to know him. I don't ask to know what he sends you in cipher, but I beg you to read me the page he has written in long hand."

This suggestion seemed to irritate my father. He treated me like a spoiled, stubborn child; then he relented and not only read me the Duke of Sidonia's letter, but even allowed me to keep it. I still have it and will bring it to you the next time I come.

When the gypsy finished telling us this part of his adventure, he was informed that he was needed to settle some matters for the tribe. He therefore went off and that day we did not see him again.

The twenty-eighth day

We gathered fairly early for breakfast. When Rebecca saw that the leader was not too busy, she begged him to continue his story which he did in the following words:

CONTINUATION OF THE STORY OF PANDESOWNA

The Duchess actually brought me the letter of which she had spoken the day before. It ran as follows:

CONTINUATION OF THE STORY OF THE DUCHESS OF MEDINA-SIDONIA

The Duke of Medina-Sidonia to the Marquis de Val-Florida:
In the dispatch in cipher you will find, dear friend, the continu-

ation of our negotiations. Here I want to tell you more about the hypocritical, cynical Court at which I am forced to live. One of my people will take this letter to the frontier and I can therefore write to you quite frankly.

King Pedro is beginning to turn the convents into the settings for his love affairs. He has dismissed the Abbess of the Ursulines in favor of the Prioress of the Visitation. His Majesty insists that I accompany him on his beloved pilgrimages and for the sake of our affairs I am obliged to submit. The King stays with the Prioress from whom he is separated by a menacing barred door which, however, so they say, His Majesty's all-powerful hand can lower by means of a special mechanism.

We courtiers remain in the reception rooms where the young female anchorites do the honors. Portuguese men find a very special pleasure in talking with nuns whose conversation, however, has no more sense than the twittering of birds in a cage, of which the nuns, with the cloistered life they lead, remind you. However the touching pallor of these consecrated virgins, their pious sighs, their tender zeal which is expressed in the language of piety, their semi-naïveté and their vague desires all combine to enchant Portuguese gentlemen and give them something they could never find among the ladies of Lisbon.

Everything in these sanctuaries intoxicates the soul and the senses. The air one breathes is full of fragrance, there are masses of flowers before the pictures of saints. On the opposite side of the reception room the eye catches a hasty glimpse of the nuns' sleeping quarters which are equally flower-filled and perfumed. The strains of a worldly guitar mingle with the rich tones of organs and drown the sweet whisperings of two young lovers who press against the barred gate, one on each side of it.

I can lose myself completely for several moments in this tender madness, but then those flattering words of passion and love arouse memories of crime. And yet I have committed only one: I killed the friend who saved your life as well as mine. The gallant customs of our aristocratic world led to the accursed deed that has ruined my entire life. I was then in those adolescent years when the soul is as susceptible to happiness as to virtue. Undoubtedly my soul would have responded to love, but surrounded by such horrible examples as I was, that emotion had no chance to develop. When I heard people talk of love, I saw only my hands covered with blood.

And yet I wanted to love. This feeling that had developed into real love in my heart was transformed into a general feeling of goodwill for everyone and everything around me. I loved my country, above all I loved these good Spanish people who stood by their customs, their King and their word. The Spanish repaid love with love, and the Court found that I was too well loved. Since that time I have never been permitted to serve my country in honorable exile; I could do good to my vassals only from afar. Love of my country and of mankind has filled my life with the greatest happiness. As for that other love which should have embellished the springtime of my life, what benefit could I expect from it today? I am determined to remain the last of the Sidonias. I know that the daughters of grandees are eager to marry me. They do not know, however, that the hand I have to offer is a dangerous gift. My character is not suited to the customs of today. Our fathers looked upon their wives as trustees of their happiness and honor, and in old Castile unfaithfulness was punished by dagger and poison. I am far from censuring my forefathers, but I should not care to be obliged to follow their example. As I said, it is better for my family to die out with me . . .

When my father came to this part of the letter, he hesitated as if loath to continue reading, but I insisted that he go on and he read as follows:

I rejoice with you in the happiness you find in the company of lovely Eleonore. Good sense, at her age, must be enchanting. What you tell me proves to me that you are very happy, and that makes me happy too . . .

I did not want to hear anymore; I made my father happy, I was sure of that. Delirious with joy, I clasped my father around the knees. When at last I could speak, I asked how old the Duke of Sidonia was.

"Five years younger than I am," said my father. "In other words, thirty-five years old. But," he added, "he is one of those people who remain young a long time."

I was at the age when young girls are not yet interested in a man's age; a young man, who like myself had just turned fourteen, seemed to me a mere child and unworthy of my notice. I did not consider my father old and the Duke, who was younger than my father, seemed to me a young man. Those ideas were subsequently paramount in determining my fate.

I then asked about the murder of which the Duke had

spoken. At this my father looked very serious, thought for a while and then said:

"My dear Eleonore, that event is closely connected with the separation which, as you know, existed between your mother and me. Perhaps I should not speak of it to you, but sooner or later out of curiosity you would discover it for yourself, and rather than that, I prefer to tell you about it myself."

After that introduction, my father then told me the following story.

THE STORY OF THE MARQUIS DE VAL-FLORIDA

You know that your mother was the last of the Astorgas, and that the Astorgas and the Val-Florida were the oldest families in Asturia. Everyone in the province expected me, the heir to the Val-Floridas, to marry Señorita de Astorgas. As we became accustomed to this idea at an early age, our feelings for each other were such as tend to make a happy marriage. Various circumstances delayed our marriage, however, and I did not marry until I had passed my twenty-fifth year. Six weeks after our wedding, I explained to my wife that, as all my ancestors had served in the army, I felt in duty bound to follow their example; moreover there were many garrisons in Spain where we could pass the time more agreeably than in Austria. Señora de Val-Florida replied that in everything connected with my honor she would always agree with me. So it was decided that I should serve in the army. I wrote to the Court and was given a cavalry squadron in the Medina-Sidonia regiment; this regiment was in garrison in Barcelona, and there you were born.

At that time Portugal was still waging a long-drawn-out war. The Court at Madrid was too proud to recognize the Braganzas and too lazy to depose them. Don Luis de Haro was cleverer than his uncle Olivarez, but he also shared some of his faults. To be sure he was less negligent, less involved in Court intrigues, but his shilly-shallying often had unfortunate results. From time to time he sent a number of troops across the frontier into Portugal; but then thinking it would be better to engage them elsewhere, he withdrew part of his troops and soon the army was forced to evacuate Portuguese soil.

During one of these periods of activity a corps of twelve thousand men, to which our regiment belonged, was ordered to cross Portugal's border, another corps was sent to seize the provinces in the north and Walloon troops were ordered to plunder the little kingdom of Algarves. The Portuguese cleverly abandoned their frontiers to us and massed their forces against us. We pushed forward in the neighborhood of Bajados and marched on Elvas. Soon we came up against the Portuguese who were almost twenty thousand strong. Don Estevas Serra, our general, gave battle before he had ascertained the enemy's strength though he was cautious enough to call up a strong support of which our regiment was a part. At the end of the day fresh columns of Portuguese troops arrived and our men were put to rout. At that moment a hero appeared; a man in the flower of his youth, a shining figure in glittering accoutrement.

"Follow me," he cried. "I am your colonel, the Duke of Medina-Sidonia."

And truly he did well to give us his name for otherwise we might have taken him for the angel of battles or for some other prince of the heavenly host. He was like a young god. Our regiment was as if newly revived and our enthusiasm infected even the rear guard. In a headlong rush we drove back the enemy and put them to rout. The night covered their retreat but we remained victors on the battlefield.

I had reason to believe that, after the Duke, I was the officer who had fought the most valiantly. At least it was a highly flattering proof that my famous colonel did me the honor to ask for my friendship. Nor was that an idle compliment on his part. We became true friends with no hint of condescension on the Duke's part, nor of any of the junior officer's sense of inferiority on mine. We Spaniards are accused of being somewhat stiff in our manner. But only by avoiding familiarity can we be proud without haughtiness, dignified when respectful. That we held the battlefield all night and also the next day, did not improve our situation greatly. The enemy had formed at three places around Elvas and was making ready to attack us again. Our general took up a position on the heights of Borgo-Leon and the Portuguese decided to detach a number of troop units and send them to relieve their provinces in the north and in the south.

About this time revolt broke out in Catalonia and Don Sancho was ordered to advance with half of his corps. At the same time the King bestowed the rank of lieutenant-general on the Duke of Sidonia with orders to remain at any cost on Portuguese soil and to await relief. This plan looked like an effort to avoid the shame of a full-size retreat. Moreover, I have reason to believe that it was suggested by enemies of the House of Sidonia.

The Duke was well aware of the dangers involved. He had only five thousand men left with whom he took shelter as best he could. He appointed me his new quartermaster and I fulfilled my duties, if I may say so, with great zeal.

When the Portuguese learned that our forces had been weakened, they again surrounded us and hemmed us in so that we could not escape, but they did not dare to attack us.

Soon France came out openly in support of the unrest in Catalonia. Madrid decided to offer Portugal an armistice: But first they had to relieve the Duke. A Spanish courier, who had great difficulty in getting through to us, outlined the situation. Though we had permission to evacuate our position, that was not all by far. We had to withdraw through the midst of the Portuguese army who had torn up the roads, blocked the exit to the passes and armed the countryfolk for miles around. At that point we received help we had least expected.

After he had laid waste the kingdom of Algarves, Van Berg, colonel of the Walloon sharpshooters, drew back to Bajadoz. He learned of the Duke's predicament, made a forced march, broke through the Portuguese lines and won breathing space for us, at least on one side. This encouraged the Duke and the next day we lay before Bajadoz without having lost one gun, but with only three hundred men left. Van Berg's Walloons joined us. As soon as we had gone into quarters the Duke sought me out.

"My dear Val-Florida," he said. "It takes two to form a friendship as I know; one cannot overlook that fact without violating its sacred laws, but I think the outstanding service

Van Berg has done us justifies me in making an exception. We owe it to him, I think, to offer him your friendship, as well as mine and to make him the third in the tie that unites us."

I agreed with the Duke, who went to Van Berg and offered him our friendship with a ceremoniousness which showed the value he placed on the title of friend. Van Berg seemed surprised.

"Your Highness," he said, "Your Excellency does me great honor. But I am in the habit of getting drunk almost every day and if by chance I am not drunk, I gamble for the highest stakes possible. Should Your Excellencies not have the same habits I don't think our friendship would last very long."

This answer at first disconcerted the Duke, but then he had to laugh. He assured Van Berg that he had a high regard for him and promised to intervene at Court and see that he was handsomely rewarded. Van Berg wanted above all lucrative compensation. The Duke journeyed to Madrid where he received for our rescuer the baronetcy of Duelen in the district of Malinas; I was given the rank of lieutenant-colonel. In fact we were all rewarded, for the Duke, who had asked for the rank of colonel-general of Cavalry, was assured of it at a later date. As a result he decided to spend the winter in Bajadoz to train his future regiment and to study that arm of the service from the ground up. He turned over the command of his corps to the commandant of the province, a lieutenant-general older in rank.

Everyone therefore made ready to spend the winter in Bajadoz: Señora del Val-Florida came to join me. She loved society and I enjoyed receiving the higher-ranking officers of the army in my house. However, the Duke and I took little part in the social whirl. Occupations of a different sort demanded all our time. Manly virtue was young Sidonia's ideal, the commonweal his dream wish. We made a special study of the Spanish constitution and drew up many plans for Spain's future good. To make the Spaniards happy, we wanted first to make them love virtue, then to teach them to overcome their selfishness which we thought would be very easy. We also wanted to awaken the old spirit of knighthood. A Spaniard should be as true to his wife as to his King and every soldier should have a brother-in-arms. I was already the Duke's brother-in-arms. We were convinced that one day the world would speak of our friendship and that men of honor, following the example of our covenant, would in future find the path of virtue easier and steadier.

My dear Eleonore, I would be ashamed to tell you these foolish things but for a long time it has been generally believed that young men who in their enthusiasm have aspired too high would not become great and useful citizens. The contrary is true: young Catos grow colder with age and cannot rise above their own calculated egotism. Their physical being hampers their mind and makes them completely unable to develop the kind of thinking that constitutes the statesman or the man who helps his fellow-men. To this rule there are few exceptions. We gave free reign to our fantasy in this orgy of virtue and hoped to put into practice the rule of Saturn and Rhea in Spain. Meantime Van Berg brought the golden age back to the present. He had sold his baronial manor, Deulen, to an army contractor named Walser-Wandyk and had received in exchange one hundred and sixty thousand piastres in hard cash. He had then pledged his word of honor to spend not only all this money during the two months in our winter quarters, but also to make debts amounting to ten thousand piastres. Our extravagant Fleming discovered that he would have to spend about five thousand five hundred piastres a day in order to keep his word of honor, a feat which, in a city like Bajadoz, was not easy. He feared that in his recklessness he had gone too far. Someone suggested that he might spend part of his money in helping the needy and making them happy, but Van Berg rejected that advice. He said he had pledged himself to spend money and not to give it away and his delicacy of feeling would not allow him to divert any part of the money for charity. He would not even consider gambling for, on the one hand, he might win and, on the other hand, money lost was not money spent.

This dreadful predicament seemed to affect Van Berg deeply. For days he went around looking very thoughtful. Finally he found a way to save his honor; he gathered around him every cook, musician, comedian and other genial sage he could find. At midday he gave enormous dinners, in the evenings balls and plays and hilarious greased-pole contests at the gates of his palace but, in spite of all his efforts, he did not succeed in spending five thousand five hundred piastres. The rest of the money he ordered thrown out of the window, a procedure that, he said, was equivalent to an honorable extravagance. Having salved his conscience in this fashion, Van Berg became good-humored again. He had much natural wit with which he defended the crazy actions that aroused criticism on all sides. This defense in which he had had good practice lent his conversation a certain sparkle, and in this he differed from us Spaniards who are all very reserved and serious.

Van Berg often came to me as did all the other high-ranking officers, but he also came when I was not at home. I knew of this, but I was not suspicious. I thought that in his extreme self-confidence he felt that he was welcome any place and at any time. The public was clearer-sighted, and rumors damaging to my honor spread abroad. Of this, however, I knew nothing, but the Duke was informed. He knew how devoted I was to my wife and, because of his friendship for me, he suffered.

One morning the Duke went to Señora de Val-Florida, threw himself on his knees before her and implored her not to forget her duty and not to receive Van Berg when she was alone. I do not know what answer she made; in any case Van Berg called on her that same morning and was undoubtedly told of the admonition she had received.

The Duke went to Van Berg intending to speak to him in the same vein and to win him over to a more honorable point of view. Van Berg was not at home and the Duke went back after dinner. The room was full of people. Van Berg, however, was sitting alone at a gaming table, throwing dice. I was also present and was chatting with young Fonseque, the Duke's brother-in-law, the beloved husband of his favorite sister.

Sidonia spoke to Van Berg in the friendliest manner and, laughing, asked what was new in the matter of his expenditures.

Van Berg glared at him.

"I spend money to receive my friends," he said, "not gossip mongers who meddle in affairs that do not concern them."

"Are you calling me a gossip monger?" asked the Duke. "Take back those words."

"I take nothing back," said Van Berg.

"You have saved my honor and the honor of Spain," said the Duke; "I can't do it! My arm refuses to take your life."

Van Berg spat out the word: "Coward!"

The Duke flung his glove in his face and cried: "To the death!"

The room was full of Van Berg's friends; he had actually more than we did. There was a tremendous uproar. In those days it was the custom in dueling to have several seconds who for their part fought the two leading duelists or else they fought each other. Fonseque and I were the Duke's two seconds and each of us had two seconds. Van Berg chose six Flemings. We went to a plain on the banks of the Guadiana that was well adapted to this sort of fighting.

Van Berg was mortally wounded. Two Flemings wanted to avenge his death, but according to custom, they had to first put the Duke's two seconds, Fonseque and me, out of the fight. This they proceeded to do: Fonseque was killed and I was seriously wounded. Sidonia killed our opponents and came away with only a slight wound. The other seconds fought among themselves, but only one of them was still in condition to cross swords with the Duke who ran him through. One of the seconds was buried on the field, the wounded were carried to their beds. The Duke, the only one of us able to walk, was the most to be pitied: he had to face his favorite sister who blamed him for her husband's death; he saw me lying on my deathbed—and all to save my wife's good reputation which, however, was now lost forever.

Van Berg was dead and I lay dying. But, in spite of my serious wound I survived. While your mother nursed me, she shed many tears which I ascribed to her anxiety about my life. However, after I was well, her tears did not cease to flow and I could not understand the reason for them. I also had no idea what had caused the quarrel between Van Berg and the Duke and I asked all my friends about it. Finally someone took pity on me and told me the whole story which I would rather not have heard. I had convinced myself, I do not know with what justification, that my wife loved me only. And many difficult days passed before I was willing to admit that the opposite was true. Finally a couple of incidents threw a new light on the situation; I went to Señora de Val-Florida and said to her:

"Señora, I have received word that your father is ill. I consider it proper for you to be at his side. Moreover, your daughter needs your attention. From now on you will live in Asturia."

Señora de Val-Florida lowered her eyes and accepted her sentence. You know how we have lived since then. Your mother had a thousand estimable qualities which in all fairness I always acknowledged.

The war began again in the spring and as men of honor we took part in it, though no longer as wholeheartedly as before. For the first time we had met with misfortune. The Duke had had great respect for Van Berg's courage and military talents and he reproached himself for the exaggerated zeal with which he had tried to assure my peace which was now, nevertheless, gone. He had learned that it is not enough to do good: one must also know how to do it. As for me, I kept my sorrow to myself—and suffered all the more deeply. We no longer dreamed up plans for the good of Spain.

At last Don Luis de Haro signed the famous Pyrenees peace. The Duke decided to travel and together we visited Italy, France and England. On our return to Spain my noble friend became a member of the council of Castile and I was appointed Court scribe on the same council. The years and his travels had matured the Duke. He had not only got over his youthful and overzealous interest in virtue, he had also become much wiser. The commonweal was no longer his pet crotchet though it was still a passion with him; but he realized that one cannot accomplish everything at once, that one must prepare minds, must carefully conceal the means and the goal. So far did his caution go that it seemed in the council as though he never had an opinion of his own, but always followed the others. And yet the ideas they put forward were originally his. The care with which he tried to hide his talents let them appear all the more to his advantage. The Spaniards felt this and they loved him. The Court became jealous. When the Duke was offered the post of ambassador to Lisbon, he knew very well he would not be permitted to refuse. He accepted but with the proviso that I be made secretary of state. Since then I have never seen him again, but we have remained the closest of friends.

At this point in his story, the gypsy leader was summoned to attend to some tribal matters. After he had left, Velasquez took the floor.

"Although I have paid close attention to our leader's words, I fail to see any connection between them. I do not even know who is talking and who is listening. At one minute the Marquis de Val-Florida is telling his daughter the story of his adventures, the next moment the daughter tells these adventures to the gypsy leader and now the leader is telling us. The whole thing is a labyrinth. In my opinion novels and all similar works should be written like chronological tables in separate columns."

"You are right, Señor," replied Rebecca; "in that way you would read in the first column something like Señora de Val-Florida betrays her husband, in the second column we would learn what happens to him as the result of these events and that would undoubtedly throw a new light on the story."

"That was not what I meant," said Velasquez. "Take for instance, this Duke of Sidonia whose character I shall never fathom until I have seen him lying in his coffin. Would it not have been better to begin with the Portuguese war? Then in the second column I would see Dr. Sangro-Morena meditating on the art of medicine and I would not be surprised at his secretive actions."

"Of course," Rebecca interjected, "those constant surprises do not add to the interest of the story, for you can never see how one follows as the result of the other."

Whereupon I put in a word.

"My father," I said, "was very young at the time of the

Portuguese war, but we were always amazed at the superior wisdom he had shown in the matter of the Duke of Medina-Sidonia."

"There is no sense in talking about that," said Rebecca. "If your father had not dueled with the eleven officers it could have come to a battle, therefore he was right to forestall it."

It seemed to me that Rebecca was making fun of us all. There was something caustic and satirical in her character. I thought to myself, who knows whether she could not tell us quite different adventures from that of the heavenly twins, and I made up my mind to ask her about it at my leisure. Meanwhile the time to part had come and everyone went his own way.

The twenty-ninth day

We met again fairly early, and, as the gypsy was not busy, he went on with the story of his adventures.

CONTINUATION OF THE STORY OF PANDESOWNA

After the Duchess had told me her father's story, she did not appear for several days and Girona brought me my basket. She also informed me that the outlook for me had been improved, thanks to my great-uncle the Theatine, Fra Bartolommeo Santoz. The Inquisition had reprimanded me for heedlessness and had sentenced me to two years penance. They had referred to me only by the first two letters of my name. Girona also brought word from my Aunt Dalanosa that I must remain in hiding during those two years and that she was coming to Madrid to collect the income from the Quinta which would one day be mine. I asked Girona whether she thought I would have to spend those two years in the vault I was now in. She replied that this would be safer for me and that her own safety also depended upon those precautions.

The next day the Duchess came again and I was delighted for I liked her better than her former nurse. I was also eager to hear the rest of her story.

CONTINUATION OF THE STORY OF THE DUCHESS OF MEDINA-SIDONIA

I thanked my father for the trust he had shown in telling me the notable events of his life. The following Friday I again handed him a letter from the Duke of Sidonia. Though he did not read it to me, he often spoke of his friend and I noticed that no other subject of conversation seemed to interest him.

Some time later I received a visit from the widow of an officer. Her father was by birth a vassal of the Duke's and she claimed a fief held by the Duke of Sidonia. It had never occurred to me that I should deny her protection. The opportunity this offered me was flattering. I drew up a memorandum in which I explained the widow's rights clearly and in a businesslike manner. This I then showed my father who was delighted with it and, as I expected, sent it to the Duke. The Duke granted the widow's request and wrote me a letter complimenting me on my intelligence which was far in excess of my years. It was true that I never lost an opportunity to increase my intelligence and enrich my mind and in this respect Girona's knowledge, of which she possessed so much, was very useful to me. Thus two years went by.

One day, when I was sixteen years old, as I was sitting with my father, I heard a confused uproar that sounded like the acclamations of a great crowd. Running to the window I saw an excited and happy throng accompanying as in a triumphal march a golden coach on which I recognized the arms of the Sidonias. Countless *hidalgos* and pages surrounded the doors of the coach from which stepped an extraordinarily handsome man. He wore the Castilian apparel which our Court had recently adopted: the ruff, the short cloak, the plume and, what particularly enhanced the costume, the diamond-studded fleece that glittered on his chest.

"It's the Duke!" cried my father. "I knew he would come!"

I withdrew to my room and did not meet the Duke till the next day. But after that I saw him daily for he did not leave my father's house.

The Duke had been summoned on an extremely important matter connected with checking the violent unrest that had broken out in Aragon on the imposition of new taxes. This kingdom had special institutions, among others that of the *"ricos hombres"* (rich men), which was formerly analogous to what we in Castile call grandees. The Sidonias were the oldest of the *"ricos hombres"* which in itself would have been enough to procure great respect for the Duke who was moreover much loved for his personal qualities. The Duke went to Saragossa where he succeeded in reconciling the interests of the Court with those of the nation. When it was left to him to decide what he wished for a reward, he asked to be allowed to breathe the air of his homeland for a while.

The Duke, who had a very open nature, made no secret of the fact that he enjoyed talking with me and we were almost daily together while my father and his friends attended to the affairs of state. Sidonia confessed to me that he was inclined to be jealous and even sometimes violent. Most of the time he talked about himself or about me. And when once there have been conversations of this sort between a man and a girl, their relationship usually becomes more intimate. I was therefore not surprised when one day my father sent for me and informed me that the Duke wished to marry me. I did not have to ask for time to consider the matter for, anticipating that the Duke would show great interest in his friend's daughter, I had already weighed his character and the difference in our ages. However, the grandees of Spain usually married in their own class. How would they look upon our marriage? They might even refuse to address the Duke with the familiar *"tu"* which is usually the first sign of their displeasure.

"I have already put forward this objection to the Duke," my father replied. "He answered that he wanted only your consent and the rest would be his affair."

Sidonia was waiting nearby. He appeared, looking rather shy in direct contrast to his usually proud expression. I was touched and quickly gave my consent. And in so doing I made two men happy, for my father was more delighted than I can say. As for Girona, she was wild with joy.

The next day the Duke invited all the grandees in Madrid to dinner. When they had all assembled he asked them to be seated and proceeded to make the following speech:

"Alba, I appeal to you, for I consider you the noblest among us, not because your house is more famous than mine, but out of respect for the heroes whose name you bear.

"A prejudice which redounds to our credit requires us to choose our brides from among the daughters of grandees and I would certainly scorn any among us who, impelled by love of riches or dissolute tastes would marry beneath his station in life.

"The case I am about to lay before you has nothing to do with this. You know that the Asturians consider themselves as 'noble as the King if not more so.' Exaggerated as this saying may be, their aristocracy stems in great part from the reign of the Moors and they have the right to consider themselves as the finest aristocracy in Europe.

"Well then! The purest blood of the Asturians flows in the veins of Eleonore de Val-Florida, and in herself she combines the most unusual qualities. I maintain that such a union can only be an honor to the house of a Spanish grandee. If anyone has a different opinion, let him take up this gauntlet which I fling down here among the assembled company."

"I take it up," said the Duke of Alba, "but to give it back to you and to congratulate you on such a beautiful marriage." Whereupon he embraced the Duke of Sidonia and all the other grandees did the same. My father looked rather sad when he told me about this scene.

"That is my old Sidonia," he said, "with all his knightliness. Take care, Eleonore, not to hurt him."

I have already confessed that I was naturally inclined to

haughtiness, but my proud longing for greatness passed as soon as it was satisfied. I became the Duchess of Sidonia and my heart was filled with the tenderest emotions. The Duke was at heart the most loving of men for he was first and foremost a lover. He was kindness itself, a man of never-failing tenderness and his gentle spirit showed in all his features. But sometimes when he was in a gloomy mood, his face wore such a terrifying expression that I shuddered. But few things put Sidonia in a rage and everything about me made him happy. He liked to watch me when I was busy, and even before I spoke he could guess my slightest thought. He could scarcely have loved me more, but the birth of our daughter increased his love for me and brought our happiness to the full.

Soon after my child was born, Girona said to me:

"My dear Eleonore, you are now a wife and a happy mother. You do not need me anymore. Moreover, my duty calls me to America."

I did not want to let her go.

"No," she said, "my presence there is necessary."

Girona left me and with her went all the happiness I had known. I have described that brief period, which could not last, for obviously so much happiness is not made for this world. Today I have not the strength to tell you about all the sorrow that followed. Good-bye, my young friend. You will see me again tomorrow.

The young Duchess's story had interested me greatly. I was eager to hear the rest of it, to understand how so much happiness could change into such horrible unhappiness. I also thought about the conversation with Girona who said I would have to spend two years in this mausoleum. That was by no means my intention and I began to prepare my escape. The Duchess brought me my provisions. Her eyes were red, she had apparently wept a great deal. Nevertheless, she said she felt strong enough to tell me the story of her tragedy.

I have told you that Girona was my chaperone, my *dueña-mayor*. In her place there now came a certain Doña Menzia, a woman of thirty and still very pretty whose mind was not uncultivated and who was therefore qualified to be admitted to our company. On such occasions she acted as though she were in love with my husband. I merely laughed about it and he paid no attention to it on the whole. La Menzia tried to work her way into my good graces, but above all to get to know me. She frequently introduced amusing incidents into the conversation or recounted the latest gossip from the city so that more than once I was obliged to ask her to be quiet. I had nursed my daughter but fortunately I had weaned her before the event happened about which I shall now tell you. My first sorrow was the death of my father. Stricken by a mortal illness, he blessed me and died in my arms without foreseeing what lay ahead for us all.

Trouble broke out in Biscaya, and the Duke was sent there. I accompanied him as far as Burgos. We had estates in every province in Spain and houses in almost all the cities. In Burgos, however, the Sidonias had only a country house a mile from the city, the same in which you now are. The Duke left me there with all his retainers and went on to his destination. One day when I returned home, I heard a great noise in the court. I was told that the servants had caught a thief and that, in the struggle, he had been hit on the head with a stone. He was, however, a young man of such beauty as one had never seen. Several servants dragged him before me and I recognized Hermosito.

"Heavens!" I cried. "This is no thief. This is a young man from Astorgas who grew up in my grandfather's house." I then turned to the majordomo and ordered him to take Hermosito with him and to see that he was given good care. I even think I said the young man was Girona's son, but I cannot quite remember.

The next day la Menzia told me the young man had a fever, that in his delirium he talked of me constantly and passionately. I told la Menzia that if she came to me again with such nonsense, I would dismiss her from my service.

"We shall see about that," she answered.

I ordered her not to appear before me again. The next day she came back, begged my pardon, flung herself at my feet and I forgave her. Eight days later la Menzia came into my room as I sat alone; with her was Hermosito who was apparently so weak that she had to hold him upright.

"You sent for me," he said in a faint voice.

I looked in astonishment at la Menzia, but as I did not want to worry Girona's son, I let him sit down in a chair a few feet away from me.

"My dear Hermosito," I said to him. "Your mother has never mentioned your name to me. I should like to know what has happened to you since I saw you last."

It was difficult for Hermosito to speak, but with a great effort he pulled himself together.

THE STORY OF HERMOSITO

When I saw that our ship had hoisted sail, I lost all hope of reaching the shores of my homeland again. I was in despair at my mother's stern decree that had banished me before I could even grasp her motives. She had told me I was your servant and I served you with all the zeal of which I was capable. Never had I disobeyed you. Why, I asked myself, do they drive me away as though I had committed the worst crimes? The more I thought about it the less I understood.

On the fifth day of our voyage we met the squadron of Don Fernando Arudez. They shouted to us to come alongside the stern of the Admiral's ship, a gilded frigate decorated with multi-colored flags. I caught sight of Fernando who was wearing a whole row of medals. The officers stood respectfully around him in a circle. He held a megaphone in his hand, asked us several questions, also what ships we had met at sea and then ordered us to continue on our course. As we sailed past his ship, the captain said:

"A Marquis! And yet he began like this ship's boy who sweeps out our cabins."

When Hermosito came to this part of his story, he cast despairing glances at la Menzia. I thought I understood that he was embarrassed to speak before her and tried to get the woman to leave. In so doing I had only my friendship for Girona in mind and the thought that I might put myself in a false position never entered my mind. As soon as la Menzia had left the room, Hermosito went on with his story:

I, who suckled my first milk at the same source as you, Madam, believe that we are kindred souls. I can think only of you and through you and can share all my experiences with you. The captain told me that Don Fernando was made a Marquis, although he began as a ship's boy. I remembered that you were a Marquise and I thought there could be nothing more beautiful than to be a Marquis. I asked how Don Fernando had brought it to pass. The captain explained that he had risen from rank to rank as a reward for his brilliant deeds. From that moment I decided to become a sailor and practiced climbing the rigging. The captain who had taken an interest in me was opposed to this, but I held out and by the time we arrived in Vera Cruz I was already a very good seaman.

My father's house was on the seashore. We went there in a launch. My father received me surrounded by his flock of young mulatto girls, whom he allowed me to embrace one after the other. They danced, they teased me in every possible way and the evening passed in all sorts of gaiety and foolishness.

The next day the *corregidor* sent word to my father that a man who ran such a house as his could not be allowed to keep his son with him and that he should send me to the high school run by the Theatine fathers. My father agreed, though regretfully. In the school I found a Pater headmaster who told us that the Marquis de Campo-Salez, the assistant Secretary of State, had begun as a poor student and that he owed his fortune to his industry. When I realized that one could become a Marquis by this means too, I studied for two years with the greatest assiduity.

The *corregidor* of Vera Cruz was dismissed and as his successor was not so strict, my father thought he could venture to take me back home again. So once more I found myself at the mercy of the young mulattos whom my father encouraged in a thousand ways. Their jokes were far from pleasing to me. But from them I learned much I had not known before and at last I understood why I had been sent away from Astorgas.

At that time the most troublesome changes took place in

me. New emotions developed in my heart arousing memories of games I used to play in my early years, reminding me of the happiness I had lost, of the gardens of Astorgas that I had wandered through with you and of the many proofs of your kindness. Too many enemies attacked my poor head at the same time: it could not withstand them, nor could my health. The doctors said I had a low fever, but I did not feel sick. However, my emotions became so confused that I often thought I saw things that were not actually there and that had no reality. It was you, Madam, whom my rambling fantasies continually saw in a vision, not as you are today, but as you were when I left you. One night I suddenly sat up straight. I saw you come towards me, shining, out of the shadows. When I went out of doors every sound in Nature seemed to echo your name: sometimes I thought I saw you in flesh and blood, walking through the countryside. And if then I raised my eyes to Heaven to implore Him to end my tortures, I saw you silhouetted against the sky.

I had noticed that I suffered less in a church and that prayer eased my torment. In the end I spent whole days in those sanctuaries of devotion. One day the priest, who had grown gray hearing confessions, spoke to me.

"My son!" he said, "your soul is full of an endless love that is scarcely made for this world. Come to my cell, I shall show you the way to Paradise." I followed him and saw in his cell hairshirts and many other instruments of martyrdom. They did not frighten me: my suffering was an even greater torture. The priest read aloud several pages from the lives of the saints: I asked permission to take the book with me, and I read all night long. My head was filled with completely new thoughts. I saw in dreams the heavens open and I saw angels who, to tell the truth, all looked a little like you.

At that time we heard, in Vera Cruz, of your marriage to the Duke of Sidonia. For a long time I had been toying with the thought of devoting my life to religion. My greatest joy was to pray day and night for your happiness in this world and for your soul in the next. My pious teacher told me there was much indolence in American monasteries and advised me to enter a monastery in Madrid as novice.

I informed my father of my decision. He had always regarded my piety with displeasure, but he dared not dissuade me openly. He merely asked me to wait for my mother who would arrive shortly. I told him I no longer had any parents on earth and that heaven was my family. When I arrived in Bilboa, I learned that my mother had sailed for America. My letter of obedience was made out for Madrid and I set out on my way. In passing through Burgos, I learned that you were living in the environs of the city and I wanted to see you once again, before I took leave of the world. I thought that when I had seen you I would be able to pray with greater fervor for the salvation of your soul.

I therefore set out on the road to your country house. Entering the first courtyard, I looked about for some of the servants who had been in your service in Astorgas, for I knew they had come here with you. I intended to make myself known to the first one I met and to ask him to hide me some place in the house where I could see you when you entered your coach; for I wanted to see you without being seen.

The servants that went past were all strangers to me and I did not know what to do. I went into a completely empty room but, thinking I saw someone I knew pass by, I stepped out and was knocked down by a stone . . . But I see, Señora, that my story has made a deep impression on you.

"I can assure you," the Duchess told me, "that Hermosito's religious delusions aroused only pity in me." And she continued:

As he talked of the garden at Astorgas, of our childhood games, memories of times past filled my heart with a sweet and melancholy emotion, perhaps because I was thinking of my present happiness or because I was suddenly worried about the future, and I realized that I was bathed in tears.

Hermosito rose and I think he intended to kiss the hem of my gown. His knees buckled, his head drooped and his arms clasped me in a strong embrace. At that moment I saw in the mirror la Menzia with the Duke whose face was contorted with such terrifying rage that he was scarcely recognizable. The blood froze in my veins. I looked up at the mirror again and saw nothing there. Freeing myself from Hermosito's arms, I called; la Menzia appeared. I commanded her to take care of the young man, and I went into the adjoining room. The vision I had had upset me greatly, though my people assured me that the Duke was not at home.

The next day I inquired after Hermosito and was told that he was no longer with us. Three days later, as I was about to take a rest, la Menzia brought me a letter from the Duke. It contained the following words:

> Do whatever Doña Menzia dictates. As your husband and your judge I command you to do this.

La Menzia tied a handkerchief over my eyes. I felt someone grasp me by the arms and I was led to this sepulchral vault.

I heard the rattle of chains. The bandage was removed from my eyes and I saw Hermosito. His neck was chained to the posts on which you are leaning, his gaze was empty and he was as pale as a corpse.

"Is it really you?" he asked in a dying voice. "It is difficult for me to speak. They do not give me any water, my tongue clings to the roof of my mouth. But my martyrdom will soon be over; when I get to Heaven I shall bear witness for you there."

As Hermosito was speaking a shot came from the slit you see here in the wall and shattered his arm. He cried out:

"My God! Forgive my torturers!"

A second shot followed the first. I do not know what effect it had for at that moment I lost consciousness.

When I came to myself, I was surrounded by my women who apparently did not know what had happened. They told me only that la Menzia had left the house. The next morning a squire, sent by my husband, appeared. He told me that the Duke had gone on a secret mission to France and would not return for several months. I was therefore left to my own devices. I laid my problems before the Highest Judge and devoted myself to bringing up my daughter.

Three months later Girona arrived. She had come back from America and had gone to see her son in the monastery in Madrid where he was to make his novitiate. Not finding him there she went to Bilboa and from there traced Hermosito as far as Burgos. As I feared the worst for her, I told her only part of the truth, but she managed to get the rest out of me.

You know how hard and violent that woman's temperament is. Rage, fury, all the dreadful emotions that can tear one asunder flooded her heart. I myself was far too unhappy to comfort her.

One day as Girona was cleaning her room, she discovered a door, covered by an arras, that led to the vault. She recognized the stake I had told her about—it was still stained with blood—and she came to me in a condition bordering on madness. After that she frequently shut herself up in her room, or rather I believe that she went down into that accursed tomb and brooded over her revenge.

One month later the Duke's arrival was announced. He came in looking calm and controlled, embraced my daughter several times, then asked me to sit down and took a seat beside me.

"Señora," he said to me, "I have given much thought to the attitude I am obliged to take towards you and from which I shall not swerve. In the house you will be treated with the same respect as before and outside I shall show you the same deference until the day your daughter is sixteen years old."

"And when my daughter is sixteen, what will happen to me?" I asked the Duke.

At that moment Girona brought in chocolate. For a moment the thought occurred to me that it might be poisoned, but the Duke went on talking.

"The day your daughter is sixteen years old, I shall tell her: 'My daughter, you resemble a woman whose story I shall now tell you. She was very beautiful and her soul seemed to be even more beautiful. But her virtues were all sham. By bending every effort to appear virtuous she succeeded in making the best marriage in Spain. One day her husband was obliged to be away from her for several weeks and at once she sent for a little ragamuffin from her province. The two remembered their former love and fell into each other's arms. My daughter, this despicable hypocrite stands here before you; she is your mother.' Then I shall banish you from my presence and you may shed your tears on the grave of a mother who was no better than you are yourself."

Injustice had so hardened my heart that this cruel speech did not even make a great impression on me. I took my daughter in my arms and went into the next room. Unfortunately I forgot the chocolate. Later I learned that the Duke had not eaten for two days. The cup stood there before him and he emptied it to the last drop. After that he went to his room. Half an hour later he ordered his servants to send for Dr. Sangro-Moreno and not to admit anyone but the doctor to his room. The servants went to the doctor's house—he had gone to a country house where he was in the habit of dissecting. They hurried to that house—he was not there. They called on all his patients in their search for him. Three hours later he appeared: the Duke was no longer alive.

Sangro-Moreno examined the body with the greatest care. He tested the nails, the eyes, the tongue, he even sent to his own house for a number of bottles which he used for I know not what purpose. Then he came to me.

"Señora," he said, "you can be sure that the Duke died of an atrocious mixture of narcotic resin and corrosive metal prepared with diabolical cunning. It is not my duty to search for the guilty person. I leave it to the great Judge up above to solve the crime. I shall announce publicly that the Duke died of an apoplectic stroke."

Then other physicians came and agreed with Sangro-Moreno's diagnosis.

I sent for Girona and told her what the doctor had said. Her confusion betrayed her.

"You have poisoned my husband," I said to her. "How can a Christian woman be guilty of such a crime?"

"I am a Christian," she replied, "but I am also a mother. If someone had murdered your child, perhaps you would have been even fiercer than a raging lion."

I did not know what to answer, so I merely reminded her that she might have poisoned me too.

"No," she said. "I was watching through the keyhole and if you had touched the cup I would have come into the room at once."

Then the Capuchin monks appeared to take charge of the Duke's body and, as they had been sent by the Archbishop, I could not refuse.

Girona, who up to then had shown such an undaunted spirit, now suddenly seemed worried and upset. She feared that when the corpse was embalmed, traces of the poison would be discovered. And so haunted was she by this idea that I almost feared she would lose her mind. Her urgent pleas compelled me to have the corpse removed, and as a result we have had the honor of sheltering you in our house. The speech I made at the cemetery was intended to deceive my people. When we saw you were the one they had brought us, we had to deceive them again and bury another corpse in the garden chapel.

In spite of all these precautions Girona is not reassured. She talks of going back to America and will stay here only until she has made up her mind. As for me I have no fear. Should I ever be interrogated, I shall tell the whole truth. I have made Girona understand this. The Duke's injustice and his cruelty have killed my love for him and I could never have made up my mind to live by his side again. My entire happiness now lies in my daughter and I am not worried about her future. The dignity of twenty grandees of our lineage rests on her head; that is enough to assure her of a good reception in every family in Europe.

That, my young friend, is the story you wanted to hear. Girona knows that I am telling you everything and she agrees that you should be told. But the air in this vault is stifling: I shall breathe freer up above.

After the Duchess had gone I looked around me and I discovered that there really was something oppressive about this place. The young martyr's grave and the stake to which he had been bound seemed to me more than tragic. I had been comfortable in this prison so long as I was afraid of the

Theatine Council. Now that my affairs were in order, I found it very unpleasant. I laughed at Girona's trust—she had expected to keep me here for two long years! The two ladies were certainly not fitted to be prison matrons. They left the door of the vault open, perhaps in the belief that the grating that separated me from them was an impassable barrier. Meanwhile I had not only made plans to escape, but also about my situation during the two years of my penance. I will tell you what I was contemplating. While I was at the Theatine seminary I had frequently meditated on the luck of a number of little beggars who stood at the portals of our church. They seemed to me to be far better off than I was. And truly, while I grew paler and paler over my books, without ever satisfying my teacher, those fortunate children of poverty strolled freely about the streets and played cards on the marble steps using chestnuts instead of money to pay their debts. They scuffled and fought and nobody separated them; they were dirty and nobody forced them to wash; they took off their clothes on the street and washed their shirts in the gutter. Could one possibly spend the time more pleasantly?

The thought of the happiness those young street urchins enjoyed occurred to me again in my prison and, as I speculated on what pursuit would be the most suitable for me in future, it seemed best to choose the life of a beggar for the duration of my penance. To be sure I had enjoyed an upbringing that distinguished me by my educated speech from my future colleagues, but I hoped gradually to take on their tone and their ways and to revert to my own later. This was a rather strange solution but it was the best choice I could make in my position.

The decision once made, I broke a knife blade in half and began to work on the window bars. It took me five days to pry them apart. Taking great care I collected the little pieces of stone and put them back together around the bars so that you could not see I had worked on them.

The day I finished, Girona brought me my basket. I asked her whether she was not afraid someone might discover that she was feeding a young man in the vault.

"No," she replied, "the trap-door through which I came

down here leads to a remote pavilion, the same one to which the gravediggers carried you that time. On the pretext that it reminded the Duchess of sad events I had the door walled up. The passage we use ends in my bedroom; the door is hidden by a tapestry."

"I hope," I said, "it is a strong iron door."

"No," she replied. "It is fairly light, but extremely well hidden. Moreover I always lock my bedroom door." And with this, Girona made ready to leave me.

"Why are you leaving so soon?" I asked.

"Because the Duchess is going out. Today marks the end of her first six weeks of mourning and she wishes to take a drive."

By that time I had learned everything I wanted to know and I did not detain Girona any longer. On leaving the vault she neglected to lock the door. I hastily wrote a note to the Duchess thanking her and asking her forgiveness and laid it on the grating. Then I loosened the bars and stepped into the ladies' vault and from there into a dark passageway that ended at a locked door. Hearing the rumble of a carriage and the clatter of horses' hoofs, I concluded that the Duchess had driven out and that the nurse was not in her room.

I promptly set to work to unfasten the door which was half-rusted and gave at my first pressure. I now found myself in the nurse's room, and as I knew she was in the habit of carefully locking her door, I thought there would be no danger in staying there.

Catching a glimpse of myself in a mirror I decided that my appearance was too great a contrast to the young beggars' with whom I wanted to associate. So, with a bit of charcoal I toned down my high coloring, then I tore my shirt and my clothes and went to the window. It looked out on an open garden once well tended by its owners but now completely wild. Opening the window, I peered out, but could not see any other windows on this side. Moreover it was no distance at all to the ground and I could have jumped down into the garden, but I chose instead to fasten one of Girona's sheets to the ledge and slide down. The skeleton of an old tree branch made it easy for me to climb onto the garden wall from which I leapt down into the fields. I was delighted to breathe country air again and even more delighted to be rid of Theatines, Inquisitions, Duchesses and nurses.

Away off in the distance I saw the city of Burgos, but I took the opposite direction and soon came to a gloomy inn. Showing the innkeeper's wife a twenty-*reales* gold piece that I had carefully wrapped in paper I told her I intended to spend all the money I had with me in her house. She laughed and offered me bread and onions for double that sum. I had some more money but I was afraid to let her see it, so I went into the stable and slept there as well as in any bed.

On my journey to Madrid I had no adventures worth recounting. Twilight was falling as I entered the city. I knew the way to my aunt's house, and I leave it to you to picture her joy on seeing me again. However I did not tarry there for I was afraid of betraying myself. After wandering all around Madrid, I came to the Prado, where I lay down on the ground and fell fast asleep.

As soon as day dawned I ran about the city's streets and squares looking for one where I could practice my new profession. On my way through the Calle di Toledo, I met a maidservant carrying a bottle of ink. I asked her whether she came from Señor Avadoro.

"No," she replied. "I come from Don Felipe Tintero Largo."

Thus I learned that my father was still known by this nickname and was as interested now as before in the same business. As the day wore on I was obliged to think about a place to sleep. Under the porch of the St. Rochus church I saw a number of street urchins of my own age. I liked their looks so I went up to them and introduced myself as a boy from the provinces. I said I had come to Madrid to ask the help of charitable people, that I had only a handful of *reales* left, but if they had a common till I would gladly contribute to it.

This introduction pleased them. They told me they really did have a common till which they had entrusted to the care of the woman who sold chestnuts at the end of the street.

After they had taken me to her, we came back to the porch and began to play tarots. We were deep in this game which requires quite a bit of concentration when a well-dressed man appeared and looked us over carefully one by one. Then, after he had obviously chosen me, he called me to him, ordered me to follow him and led me into a side street.

"My boy," he said, " I have chosen you over your comrades because you look more intelligent and that is needed for the task I have in mind. Now, listen to me. A great many women will pass by here all wearing black velvet skirts and black lace mantillas, which hide their faces so well that it is impossible to recognize them. Fortunately, however, there are different patterns of velvet and lace and it is therefore possible to follow the trail of these beautiful unknowns. I am the fortunate lover of a young girl who is, I fear, rather inclined to be fickle and I wish to know if this is true. Here are two samples of velvet and two of lace. If you see two women pass by wearing gowns that correspond to these samples, you are to notice whether they enter the church or whether they go into the house opposite, that belongs to the Knight of Toledo. You will then come to the tavern at the end of the street and report to me. Here is a gold piece for you. You shall have a second piece if you carry out my instructions satisfactorily."

While the man was speaking, I studied his face with the greatest care. He did not look like a lover to me, but much more like a husband. The Duke of Sidonia's terrible rage came to my mind and, as I object to sacrificing Amor's interests to the suspicions of Hymen, I made up my mind to carry out only half of my task. Should the ladies go into the church I would then so inform the jealous man, but should they go somewhere else, I would on the contrary warn them of the danger threatening them. I went back to my comrades, told them to go on playing and to pay no attention to me. Then I lay down behind them, with the two samples of velvet and lace before my eyes.

Soon a great many women appeared, always walking in pairs; and two of the ladies actually wore the same material as my sample. The two women seemed to be on their way to the church; but at the door they stopped and looked all around. Seeing that no one was following them, they then hurried quickly across the street and disappeared into the house opposite.

When the gypsy reached this part of his tale, he was obliged to leave us. Velasquez promptly seized the floor.

"I am worried about this story," he said. "All of the gypsy's adventures begin simply and the listener thinks he can guess the end, but he is mistaken. One story leads to another, out of which a third develops like those Chinese boxes that in certain cases can be divided endlessly. But there is a way to put an end to progression, whereas here, as the sum of all the gypsy tells us, I get only an incomprehensible hodgepodge."

"And yet," said Rebecca, "you, Señor, take great pleasure in listening to him for, as I recall, you had intended to go directly to Madrid and now cannot bring yourself to leave us."

"Two reasons compel me to remain in this region," Velasquez replied. "First, I have started work on some important mathematical calculations which I expect to finish here; and secondly, Señorita, I must confess that the company of other women has never given me such pleasure as does yours. To speak more plainly, you are the only woman with whom I enjoy conversing."

"Honored Duke," retorted the young Jewess, "I would be happy if the second reason were some day to become the first."

"It certainly means little to you, Señorita, whether you or geometry come first in my thoughts. Another matter worries me. So far I do not know your name and so am obliged to designate it by the letter X or Y, with which in algebra we indicate an unknown quantity."

"My name," said the Jewess, "is a secret I would gladly entrust to your judgment if I did not fear the results of your absent-mindedness."

"You need fear nothing, Madam, thanks to alphabetical symbols often used in calculations. I have accustomed myself to denominate a given value in always the same way. Therefore if I have once designated you by a name, you will no longer be able to change it even should you wish to."

"Very well," said Rebecca, "then call me Laura Uzeda."

"With pleasure," said Velasquez, "or also the beautiful Laura, the erudite Laura, the bewitching Laura, for all those are universal exponents of your total personality."

While they were talking together, I remembered the promise I had given the robber to meet him at a certain spot, four hundred paces westward from the camp. I buckled on my sword and when I had reached the appointed distance, I heard a pistol shot. Directing my steps towards the forest from which the shot came, I found there the same people with whom I had dealt before. Their leader said to me:

"Greetings, Señor caballero, I see you are a man of your word and I have no doubt you are as brave as you are trustworthy. Do you see this opening in the rock? It leads into an underground area where you are awaited with the greatest impatience. I hope you will not disappoint the trust placed in you."

I climbed down into the earth leaving behind the stranger, who did not follow me. After I had gone a few steps I heard a great rumbling behind me and saw that gigantic stones, propelled by some mysterious mechanism, had blocked the entrance. A faint gleam of light shining through a cleft in the rock was lost in the dark corridor. In spite of the darkness I walked forward easily for the ground was smooth with only a slight declivity. I was not in the least tired. But I think many a man in my place would have been afraid if he had been forced to descend into the bowels of the earth without knowing where he was going. I walked for a good two hours. In one hand I held my sword, the other I stretched out before me to protect myself from running into some object. Suddenly the air vibrated near me and a soft, harmonious voice whispered in my ear:

"With what right does a mortal dare to enter the kingdom of gnomes?"

Another voice, equally soft, continued:

"If he would throw away his sword, we could come close to him."

"Bewitching gnomes," I cried, "if I am not mistaken I know you from your voices. I am not allowed to throw my sword away, but I have thrust the point in the ground and you may come close to me without fear."

The underground goddesses took me in their arms and I sensed instinctively that they were my cousins and the bright light that suddenly streamed from all sides showed me that I was not mistaken. They led me into a cave that was covered with carpets and lined with costly opal-colored stones that shimmered in a thousand reflections.

"Well," said Emina. "Are you glad to see us? But you are now living in the company of the young Israelite whose cleverness equals her charms."

"I can assure you," I replied, "that Rebecca has made no impression on me. But when I see you two, I am always afraid I may not see you again. They have tried to persuade me that you are impure spirits, but I have never believed them. Some inner voice assured me that you are beings of flesh and blood like me and made for love. It is generally believed a man can love only one woman—that is without any doubt a mistake, for I love you both. In my heart I can never separate you one from the other; you both reign there together."

"Ah," cried Emina, "the blood of the Abenceragas speaks through you since you are able to love two women at the same time. Accept the holy faith that permits a plurality of wives!"

"In that case," Zibeddé added, "it might be possible for you to attain the throne of Tunisia. If you could see that magic land, the seraglios of Bardo and Manubo, the gardens and fountains, the gushing wells, the marvelous baths and the thousand young slave-girls, all of them much prettier than we are!"

"Let us not talk of kingdoms on which the sun shines," I said, "so long as we are in these subterranean regions which are, moreover, completely unknown to me. But even should they border on hell, we can nevertheless enjoy delights here which, as we say, the prophet promises only to his chosen ones."

Emina smiled yearningly and gazed at me with tender eyes, while Zibeddé flung her arms around my neck.

The thirtieth day

When I awoke, my cousins had disappeared. I felt uneasy but after looking around on all sides I finally descried a long lighted passageway which I took to be the path I should follow. I dressed quickly and after walking for half an hour I came to a spiral staircase which could be used either to mount to the surface of the earth or to descend into its bowels. I chose the latter direction which led me to an underground tomb where I saw a white marble gravestone illumined by four lamps and before it an old dervish who was chanting prayers.

The old man turned to me and said in a soft voice:

"We welcome you, Señor Alfonso. We have been expecting you for a long time."

I asked him whether this was by chance the underground realm of Kasar-Gomelez.

"You are not mistaken, noble Nazarene," replied the dervish. "This grave shelters the famous secret of the Gomelez. But before I come to that important matter allow me to offer you a light refreshment. Today you will need all the strength of your mind and body, and it could be," he added maliciously, "that the latter requires rest."

The old man then led me into an adjoining cave where I found a spotlessly served breakfast. After I had fortified myself he asked me to listen carefully to what he had to say.

"Señor Alfonso, it is not unknown to me that your beautiful cousins have told you the story of their ancestors and have given you to understand what the secret of Kasar-Gomelez means to them. In fact, nothing in the world could be of greater significance. It would be easy for men who possess our secret to compel entire nations to obedience and perhaps even to establish an all-encompassing monarchy. But these powerful and dangerous means could also fall into the hands of an irresponsible man who would destroy all order based on obedience. Laws that have held sway for centuries decree that the secret may be revealed only to men who have Gomelez blood and then only if they have passed convincing proofs of the stability and honesty of their mode of thought. Moreover, we require of a man a solemn oath which must be fortified with all the power of religious forms. However, as we know your character, we shall be satisfied with your word of honor. I therefore take the liberty of asking you to give me your word of honor that you will never reveal to any human being whatever you will see and hear in this place."

At first it seemed to me that, as I was in the service of the Spanish King, I dared not pledge my word of honor until I had learned whether there were things to be seen in hell that were not incompatible with that honor. I mentioned these doubts of mine to the dervish.

"Your caution, Señor, is justified," replied the old man. "Your arm belongs to the King you serve. But here you are in a subterranean domain to which his might has never penetrated. The blood from which you spring also places duties on you and finally the pledge I ask of you is only the result of the one you have given your cousins."

I had to be satisfied with this reasoning, though I found it somewhat amazing, and I gave the desired word of honor.

Whereupon the dervish pushed aside a wall in the tomb revealing a flight of stairs that led down into even greater depths.

"Go down here," he said to me. "I do not need to accompany you, but this evening I shall return and fetch you."

I therefore went down the stairs and I saw things I would tell you about with the greatest pleasure if the man to whom I gave my word of honor had not sworn me to secrecy.

That evening, true to his promise, the dervish came to fetch me. We went into another cave in which a supper was laid. The table stood under a golden tree depicting the genealogy of the Gomelez. It spread out in two large branches of which the Mohammedan Gomelez was apparently a bloom with a strong growth while the other, the Christian Gomelez, was visibly withered, its long sharp thorns reaching out menacingly. After the evening meal the dervish said to me:

"Do not be surprised at the difference you notice between the two main branches. The Gomelez, loyal to the laws of the Prophet, received crowns as a reward while the others vegetated unknown and held only a few unimportant positions. None of them has been admitted to our secret and if they make an exception of you, you owe it to the special regard you have earned thanks to the goodwill of the two princesses. Nevertheless, so far you could have only a faint idea of our policy. If you wished to go over to the other branch, which blooms and will bloom more profusely with every day, you would have everything you needed to satisfy your egotism and to bring great things to pass."

I was about to reply, but the dervish did not give me time.

"Nevertheless, a share of your family's possessions comes to you and a certain reward for the trouble you have taken to reach this underground region. Here is a check on Estaban Moro, the richest banker in Madrid. To all appearances the sum amounts to only a thousand *reales,* but a secret stroke of the pen makes it limitless, and on your signature you will be given any sum you ask for. Now follow this spiral staircase. After you have counted three thousand five hundred steps you will come to a very low vault where you will be obliged to crawl on your stomach for fifty steps to reach the inner sanctum on the Alcazar, in other words, of the Kasar-Gomelez. You will do well to spend the night there. The next morning you will easily find the gypsy camp at the foot of the mountain. Farewell, dear Alfonso, may our holy Prophet enlighten you and show you the way to truth."

The dervish embraced me, bade me farewell and closed the door behind me. I followed his various instructions literally. As I climbed up again, I stopped frequently to catch my breath; and at last I perceived the starry skies above me. I lay down under a rocky arch and fell asleep.

The thirty-first day

When I awoke I saw the gypsy camp in the valley and noticed that they were preparing to set out on their wanderings again. I hastened to join them, and though I expected sundry questions about my absence during the past two nights, no one spoke to me. They were all too busy making ready for their departure.

When we had mounted our horses, the cabalist said to me:

"I can assure you that today we can enjoy a conversation with the Wandering Jew whenever we so desire. I have not lost my power as that impudent fellow dared to suggest. He was already in the neighborhood of Tarudant when I forced him to turn back. Of course he is fighting against it, but I have the means to hasten his steps."

With this he pulled a book out of his pocket, read aloud a

number of barbaric formulas and soon we saw the old wanderer on the top of the mountain.

"Look at him!" shouted Uzeda. "The rascal! The lazy bones! Just wait till you hear what I'm going to say to him!"

Rebecca interceded for the culprit, the cabalist's anger seemed to cool, and when the Jew caught up with us, he was let off with a few sharp remarks from the cabalist in a language I did not understand. He then ordered the Wandering Jew to walk beside my horse and to resume the story of his adventures at the point where he had left off. The unfortunate wanderer bowed his head and began as follows:

CONTINUATION OF THE STORY OF THE WANDERING JEW

I have told you that in Jerusalem there was a sect known as the Herodiades, which claimed that Herod was the Messiah. In addition I promised to explain the secret meaning Jews connect with this word. Know then that the Hebraic word Messiah, the Anointed, means he who is anointed with oil, and that Christos (Christ) is the Greek translation of this word. When Jacob awoke from his famous dream, he poured oil on the stone on which his head had rested and named the place Bethel or the house of God. You can see for yourself in Sanchuniathon that shame entered the Bethelites, that is, the living stones. In those days it was believed that the Holy Ghost immediately entered into anything that was consecrated by anointing. Since then kings are anointed, and since then Messiah means the same as king. When David speaks of the Messiah, he means himself as we can see from his Twenty-second Psalm. But when the Jewish kingdom, first split apart and then occupied, became the plaything of neighboring powers, and especially when the people were made prisoners, their prophets comforted them with the hope that the day would come when, from the line of David, a prophet would be born who would humble the pride of Babylon and lead the Jews in triumph out of captivity. The most marvelous castles in the air sprang up inspired by these prophets. They did not fail to depict a future Jerusalem, worthy to receive such a great king within its walls or to erect within them a temple in which there would be nothing lacking to encourage veneration for faith among the people. Although the Jews attributed little importance to the words of the prophets, they liked to listen to them. Why should they also have been inspired by events that the great grandchildren of their great grandchildren were to witness?

It seems that under the rule of the Macedonians the prophets were somewhat forgotten. Therefore none of the Maccabees were looked upon as the Messiah although they had freed the land from enemy rule. Nor were any of their descendants who bore the title of king, proclaimed by the prophets as the Messiah.

It was different in the reign of old Herod. That ruler's courtiers who, in the course of forty years had exhausted all the flattering speeches that could please him, finally persuaded him that he was the Messiah whom the prophets had heralded. Herod, who had lost all liking for anything except the highest sovereignty over which he watched more jealously every day, saw in this belief a means of discovering which of his subjects were really loyal to him. His friends therefore founded the sect of Herodias whose leader was the swindler, Sedekias, my grandmother's younger brother. You will understand that neither my grandfather nor Dellius gave any further thought to moving to Jerusalem. They had a brass casket made and enclosed in it the sales contract of Hillel's house and his note for over thirty thousand darics together with a transcription which Dellius had drawn up in favor of my father, Mordecai. They then sealed the little casket and agreed to forget all about it until their situation had taken a more cheerful turn.

Herod died and Judea fell victim to the most deplorable division. Thirty tribal leaders had themselves anointed, and each claimed to be the Messiah. A few years later Mordecai married the daughter of one of his neighbors and I, sole fruit of that union, came into the world in the last year of the reign of Augustus. My grandfather wanted to take over the feast of the circumcision himself and to this end he ordered a magnificent banquet prepared. But as he was so accustomed to solitude, he fell ill as the result of his exertions and no doubt also of his extreme age which, a few weeks later, brought him to the grave. He breathed his last in Dellius's arms, enjoining him to preserve the brass casket for us and not to allow the swindler Sedekias to enjoy the fruits of his misdeeds. My mother, who had not recovered from the effects of my birth, outlived her father-in-law by only a few months.

In those days the Jews were in the habit of adopting Greek or Persian names. I was named Ahasver. Under this name I introduced myself to Anton Colterus in Lubeck in 1603 as may be verified in the works of Dudulens. I also bore the same name in 1710 in Cambridge as is shown in the works of Tenzelius.

"Señor Ahasver," said Velasquez, "you are also mentioned in the Theatrum Europaeum."

"That is possible," replied the Jew, "for I am only too well known ever since the cabalists had the idea of calling me out of the depths of the African desert."

I then asked the Jew just why he liked that deserted region.

"Because there I do not meet any human being," he replied. "But if I come upon a wanderer who has lost his way or a Kaffir family, I lead them to a nursing lioness whose lair I know and watch with delight as she tears them to pieces before my eyes."

"Señor Ahasver," Velasquez interjected, "you seem to me to have extremely insane views."

"Didn't I tell you so?" cried the cabalist. "He is the greatest blackguard in the world."

"If you had lived as I have more than eighteen centuries," retorted the Wanderer, "you would certainly be no better."

"I hope to live longer and to be more esteemed than you," said the cabalist. "But enough of these ugly insinuations. Get on with the rest of your story."

Ignoring the cabalist, the Jew continued as follows:

Old Dellius remained with my father who was crushed by so many blows. They therefore lived quietly in our place of refuge, while Sedekias, deprived of Herod's protection through the latter's death, was making anxious inquiries about us. Constantly tormented by fear of our arrival in Jerusalem, he finally determined to sacrifice us for the sake of his peace of mind. Everything seemed to favor his purpose for Dellius became blind and my father, who was genuinely devoted to him, led a more secluded life than ever. In this way six years passed.

One day we were told that Jews from Jerusalem had bought the house next to ours and that it was filled with people who looked like thieves. My father, who liked solitude, found in this circumstance a fresh reason not to leave our house anymore.

A great clamor in the caravan interrupted the Wandering Jew's story and he seized this opportunity to disappear. Soon thereafter we reached our night quarters where we found our supper already on the table. We ate heartily as travelers should and when the tablecloth had been removed, Rebecca turned to the gypsy.

"If I am not mistaken, you said before we were interrupted that after the two women had made sure no one was watching them, they hurried across the street and entered the Knight of Toledo's house."

When the gypsy saw how eager we were to hear the rest of his adventure, he began in the following words:

CONTINUATION OF THE STORY OF PANDESOWNA

I overtook them while they were still on the steps, showed them the samples and told them about my mission. Then I said to them:

"Ladies, you had better go into the church. I will bring the alleged lover, who is doubtless the husband of one of you ladies. He will probably leave as soon as he has seen you, then you can go wherever you think best."

The two ladies approved of this advice. I went to the tavern and told my employer that the two ladies had really gone into the church, and we went back there together. I showed him the lace sample, but he still seemed doubtful. Then one of the ladies turned and casually raised her veil. At once an expression of husbandly pleasure spread over the jealous man's face; he vanished into the crowd and left the church. I caught up with him on the street. He thanked me and gave me another gold piece. It is true I had a few twinges of conscience about accepting it, but I was afraid of betraying myself.

After watching him out of sight, I went to look for the two ladies and accompanied them as far as the knight's house. The prettier woman wanted to give me a gold piece.

"No, Señora, I betrayed your supposed lover because I recognized the husband in him. Though my conscience forced me to this step, it is too sensitive to permit me to accept payment from both sides."

I then returned to the door of St. Rochus church and showed my comrades my two gold pieces. They were dumbfounded. They had often undertaken similar errands, but never had they been so richly remunerated. I went off to put this money in the common till and my comrades followed me to witness the tradeswoman's astonishment. She was in fact fascinated by the sight of the gold and declared she would not only give us as many chestnuts as we wanted, but she would also supply us with little sausages and whatever we needed for roasting them. The prospect of such a savory meal aroused great joy among our group, but I held aloof and made up my mind to find a better kitchen. Meanwhile we filled our pockets with chestnuts and returned to the door of St. Rochus. After we had eaten, we wrapped ourselves in our cloaks and fell asleep.

The next day one of the ladies I had seen the evening before came looking for me, gave me a letter and asked me to deliver it to the knight. I went to the knight's house and handed the letter to his manservant. The Knight of Toledo's appearance greatly impressed me in his favor and I could well understand that the ladies would not casually pass him by. He was a fine figure of a young man with a natural gaiety which, even when he was not laughing, showed in all his features. Moreover, in his every movement he was extraordinarily graceful, though in his manner one could detect something superficial that might have harmed him in his relations with women if they had not all been so sure of their ability to hold even the most irresponsible of men.

"My friend," said the knight, "I have already heard of your cleverness and your sensitive feelings. Would you care to enter my service?"

"I cannot do that," I told him. "I am a nobleman by birth and I cannot accept a position of servitude. I have become a beggar because that is a vocation in which one guards one's honor jealously."

"Bravo!" replied the knight. "Such views are worthy of a Castilian. But what can I do for you, my friend?"

"Señor knight," I replied, "I like my profession because it is honorable and because it keeps me alive, but the food is bad. I would be grateful if you would permit me to eat with your servants and to share the remains from your table."

"Gladly," said the knight. "On the days I expect ladies, I make it a point to send my servants away. If your noble background permits, it would please me if you were to attend me on those occasions."

"My lord," I said, "when you are in the company of your mistresses it will be an honor for me to attend you, for the pleasure of being useful to you will ennoble those deeds in my eyes."

I then took leave of the knight and went to the Calle di Toledo, where I asked to be directed to the house of Señor Avadoro. No one knew where it was; so I then asked for Don Felipe Tintero, and immediately I was shown a balcony on which I beheld a very important-looking gentleman who was smoking a cigar and apparently counting the tiles on the Palacio Alba. It gave me a strange feeling to think that Nature had supplied the father with so much importance, the son with so little. I thought it would have been better to give a little to each; but then I remembered that one should praise God for everything. I therefore went back to my comrades; we ate the tradeswoman's sausages and they tasted so good that I forgot all about the remains from the knight's table.

Towards evening I saw the two ladies go into his house where they stayed a long time. When I went there to find out whether I was needed, the ladies were just leaving. I paid the prettier lady a rather ambiguous compliment which she answered by rapping me on the cheek with her fan.

A moment later a young man, whose imposing appearance was further enhanced by a Maltese Cross embroidered on his cloak, spoke to me; from the rest of his clothing I took him to be a traveler. He asked me where the Knight of Toledo lived and I offered to lead him there. As there was no one in the entrance hall, I opened a door and entered the room with him. The Knight of Toledo was overcome with surprise.

"What do I see?" he cried. "You, my dear Aguilar, in Madrid? How happy I am! What is going on in Malta? What are the Grand Master, the Grand Commander, the Master of Novices doing? Let me embrace you!"

The Knight of Aguilar responded to all these greetings just as warmly, but much more solemnly.

I took it for granted the two friends would like to dine together, and finding in the entrance hall what I needed to set a table I then went off to fetch the dinner. As it was being served, the Knight of Toledo sent me to his wine merchant for several bottles of champagne. I brought them back and popped the corks. In the meantime the two friends had told each other all their news and had exchanged many memories. Toledo now held the floor.

"My friend," he said, "I don't understand how we, with such opposite characters, can love each other so deeply. You have all the virtues. Well! I love you as much as if you were the worst ne'er-do-well! That is so true that I have formed no ties here in Madrid and you are still my only friend. But to tell the truth, in love I am not so constant."

"Have you," asked Aguilar, "still the same principles where women are concerned?"

"The same principles? No, not quite. Formerly I had one mistress after the other as quickly as I could, but I found that I wasted a lot of time that way. Now I begin a new affair before the last one is over, and I already have a third in view."

"In other words, don't you ever expect to give up your loose living?"

"On my honor, no! I am much more afraid it will be the one to give me up some day."

"Ours is a military order; it is also a religious order. We take vows like monks and priests."

"And undoubtedly like women when they promise to be true to their husbands."

"Perhaps they will be punished in another world."

"My friend, I have all the belief a Christian should have, but in that remark there are several inevitable discrepancies. How the devil can you hope that the wife of Governor Uscariz will burn in hell because of the one hour she usually spends with me?"

"Religion teaches us that there are degrees of sin."

"You mean Purgatory? Oh, as for that, I have already known Purgatory; for example, the time I loved that pest from Navarra, the most pretentious, conceited creature you can imagine. Since then I have given up ladies of the theatre. But, my friend, you are not eating, you are not drinking . . . I have emptied my bottle and your glass is still full. What are you thinking of?"

"I was thinking that today I have seen the sun."

"That I can easily believe for I too have seen it."

"I also thought I would like to see it tomorrow . . ."

"But you will see it, at least if there is no storm."

"That is not so certain. I might die tonight."

"I must say you bring us very cheering table talk from Malta."

"Oh! That we must die is certain: only the hour is uncertain."

"Now tell me who gave you that pleasant bit of news! He must be an extremely interesting mortal. Do you often invite him to supper?"

"By no means. My confessor said so to me this morning."

"What? You come to Madrid and confess the same day? Or have you come to fight?"

"Exactly that."

"Excellent. It's a long time since I rattled a sword. I shall be your second."

"That is impossible. You are the only man in the world I cannot have as a second."

"Great heavens! Have you started your damned quarrel with my brother again?"

"That is right. The Duke of Lerma would not give me the reparation of honor I demanded. We will fight tonight by torchlight on the banks of the Manzanares below the great bridge."

"Good God! Then must I lose a brother or a friend to-night?"

"Perhaps both. We will fight to the death with short spears instead of swords and with a dagger in our left hand. You know what cruel weapons they are."

Toledo's sensitive temperament reacted violently to all impressions; in one moment he passed from exuberant gaiety to the deepest despair.

"I knew this would be painful to you," Aguilar said, "and I did not want to come to you, but a voice from heaven commanded me to speak to you of punishments in the next world."

"Oh, my friend, give up trying to reform me!"

"I am only a soldier. I do not know how to preach, but I follow the voice of Heaven."

At that moment we heard the clock strike eleven. Aguilar embraced his friend.

"Toledo," he said, "listen to me. A premonition tells me I shall die. But I should like my death to be for the good of your spiritual welfare. Therefore be on the alert. If it is possible for the dead to communicate with the living, be assured that your friend will give you news from the other world. Above all keep a good watch around midnight; that is the hour when spirits appear."

Whereupon Aguilar embraced his friend and left. Toledo flung himself on his bed and wept bitterly. I withdrew to the anteroom, but left the door open so that I could see what happened at midnight.

Toledo got up, looked at his watch, went back to his bed and wept. The night was stormy; now and then a distant flash of lightning pierced the slats of our shutters. The thunder came nearer, the fear it inspired adding to our gloom.

The clock struck midnight and we heard three taps on our window.

Toledo opened the shutters and said: "Are you dead?"

"I am dead," replied a hollow voice.

"Is there a Purgatory?" cried Toledo.

"There is a Purgatory and I am already in it," replied the same voice.

Then we heard something like an anguished groan.

Toledo bowed his head reverently. Then he stood up, put on his cloak and went out. I followed him. We took the path that led to the Manzanares river, and we had not yet reached the great bridge when we saw a lot of people, some of whom carried torches. Toledo recognized his brother.

"Go no further," said the Duke of Lerma. "You will come upon the corpse of your friend."

Toledo fainted. I saw that he was surrounded by his servants, so I left him and set out on my way to the church porch. Arrived there I began to meditate on all I had seen and heard. Pater Sanudo had always told me there was a Purgatory so I was not very surprised to hear this confirmed; that whole scene had made little impression on me and I fell asleep as quickly as usual under the porch of St. Rochus.

The first person to enter the church the next day was the Knight of Toledo, but he looked so pale and so haggard I scarcely recognized him. He said a prayer and asked for a father-confessor.

At this point in his story the gypsy was interrupted and had to leave us. The rest of us separated, each going about his own business.

The thirty-second day

We made an early start and followed a road that led through the deepest valleys in the mountain chain. An hour later we met the Jew Ahasver who again took his place between Velasquez and me and went on with his story as follows:

CONTINUATION OF THE STORY OF THE WANDERING JEW

One day a Roman clerk of the Court was announced. He was shown in and we learned that my father was accused of high treason as well as of the intent to hand over Egypt to the Arabs. When the Roman had left, Dellius said to my father:

"My dear Mordecai, it is senseless to defend yourself for everyone knows you are innocent; this business will cost you half your fortune and all you can do is to give up voluntarily."

Dellius was right; this latest blow ate up half of our fortune. The following year as my father was about to leave the house one day, he found, lying at the door, a man who was apparently half dead. My father had him brought into the house and tried to revive him; but at that moment police magistrates forced their way into the house. With them came the people who lived in the neighboring house, eight all told, and every one of them swore he had seen my father murder this man. For six weeks my father was held in prison; nor was he released until he had sacrificed the remaining half of his fortune—in other words, everything he possessed. All he had left was his house. But scarcely had he returned home when fire broke out in his malicious neighbor's house. It was night. The neighbors broke into my father's house, pulled out everything they could carry with them and set the house on fire. By sunrise it was only a heap of ashes on which blind Dellius wandered about with my father, who held me in his arms and bewailed his misfortune.

When the shops opened, my father took me by the hand and led me to the baker who had always supplied us. That man seemed to be genuinely sorry for us and he gave us three loaves of bread. We then went back to Dellius who told us that, during our absence, a man he could not see, had said to him:

"Oh, Dellius, may your misfortune fall on the head of Sedekias! Forgive those who were his tools. We were paid to ruin you, but we spared your life. Take this, it will help you to get along for a while." Whereupon the man handed him a purse containing fifty gold pieces.

This unexpected windfall delighted my father. Spreading a partially burned carpet over the ashes, he laid the loaves of bread on it and brought water in a broken earthen vessel. I was then seven years old, but I distinctly remember sharing my father's high spirits and going with him to the well. I also partook of the feast.

We had scarcely begun to eat when a boy about my age came weeping and begging for a piece of bread.

"I am," he said, "the son of a Roman father and a Syrian mother who died in giving me birth. The soldier's women who belonged to the same cohort, the camp followers, took turns in giving me the breast. Obviously they must have added other nourishment for I am still alive; but my father who was sent to fight a tribe of shepherds, never came back and all his comrades have been killed. Yesterday I ate the last of the bread they left me. I tried to beg for some in the city, but I found only closed doors. However, as you have nothing left, neither doors nor house, I hope you will not turn me away."

Old Dellius, who never missed an opportunity to moralize, said: "No man is so miserable that he cannot do good to another, just as no man is so powerful that he does not need other men. Yes, my child, you are welcome! Share with us the bread of misery. What is your name?"

"My name is Germanus," said the child.

"May you live long!" replied Dellius—a blessing that proved to be a prophecy for the child lived a long, long time and still lives today in Venice where he is known as the Chevalier de Saint Germain.

"I know him," cried the cabalist. "He has some knowledge of cabalism."

Ignoring this interruption, the Jew went on with his story.

When we had eaten, Dellius asked my father whether the cellar door was broken in. My father replied that it was closed as before the fire, and that the flames had not touched the cellar roof.

"Well now," said Dellius, "take two gold pieces from the purse that was given me, engage workmen and build a shelter over the roof. They will certainly be able to use some of the débris from the old house."

In the end the workmen found a number of beams and planks that had escaped the fire, put them together as well as they could, laid palm branches between them, covered them with mats and we had a comfortable shelter. In our fortunate climate nothing more is necessary. Beneath a cloudless sky like ours, the slightest hint of a roof is enough and the lightest food is at the same time the healthiest. One can therefore truly say that even misery is not so terrible among us as it is in your latitude which you call the temperate zone.

While the men were working on our housing, Dellius carried a mat out to the street, sat down on it and played a tune on a Phoenician guitar, then he sang an aria he had once composed for Cleopatra. The voice of this man over seventy was still powerful enough to draw a large crowd, who listened in delight. When he finished his aria, he said:

"O citizens of Alexandria, give a slight donation to poor Dellius, the man your fathers knew as Cleopatra's first musician and Antony's favorite." Whereupon little Germanus went around with an earthen cup and everyone gave a contribution.

Dellius made it a rule to sing and beg only once a week. On those days all the people in the neighborhood gathered about and we were not allowed to go home without a generous supply of alms. For this we had not only Dellius's voice to thank, but even more his talks that were entertaining, instructive and full of witty anecdotes. Our situation was therefore quite bearable. However, my father whose health had been greatly undermined by the many successive blows he had suffered, went into a general decline which, by the end of the year, brought him to his grave. We were therefore again entrusted to Dellius's care and had nothing to live on but the alms his old, cracked voice earned. The next winter a severe cough, followed by loss of his voice, robbed us of even this source of income. However a relative, who had died in Pelusium, left me a small inheritance. The sum provided for five hundred gold pieces, though it actually did not amount to a third of what was due me. But, as Dellius said, the law was not made for the poor man; he must be satisfied with what he was given out of charity. Dellius therefore declared in my name that he was satisfied, and so well did he administer the money that it was enough to support me throughout my entire childhood.

Moreover, Dellius neglected neither my education nor that of young Germanus. Each in turn, one or the other of us was always with him. On those days when I was not on duty, I attended a little Jewish school in the neighborhood and on the days Germanus was free, he took lessons from a priest of Isis named Cheremon. In the course of time he became torch-bearer in the mysterious cult that honored the goddess and he often entertained me with descriptions of their ceremonies.

By the time the Wandering Jew had come to this part of his story, we halted for the night and the wanderer seized this opportunity to disappear among the hills. Toward evening we all gathered together again. The gypsy leader appeared to be in good spirits; and Rebecca cajoled him into continuing his story.

CONTINUATION OF THE STORY OF PANDESOWNA

The Knight of Toledo's conscience was apparently burdened with many sins, for he lingered long at the confessional. When he emerged his face was wet with tears and he showed every sign of complete repentance. Catching sight of me, he motioned me to follow him.

It was very early in the morning and the streets were still empty. The knight rented the first mule we saw and we rode out of the city. I suggested that his servants would be worried about his long absence.

"No," he replied, "they have been informed."

"Señor knight," I then said, "allow me to make an observation. The voice we heard yesterday told us something you could just as well have read in your catechism. You have confessed and no doubt you were not refused absolution. But in future be more circumspect in your life and for the present don't take this matter so much to heart."

"Oh, my friend," said the knight. "When once you have heard the voice of the dead, you have not much more time left among the living."

I then realized that my young patron believed he would soon die and this thought troubled him. I felt sorry for him and I made up my mind not to desert him.

We came to a road that was little traveled and that led

through a rather wild region to the gates of a Camaldolese monastery. After he had paid off his muledriver, the knight rang the bell and a monk appeared. Introducing himself the knight asked for permission to remain in the monastery several weeks. The monks led us to a hermitage at the end of the garden, and by signs made us understand that a bell would announce the refectory hour. As our cell was well supplied with devotional books, reading became the knight's sole occupation. For my part I found a Camaldolese who fished with an angling rod, and joining him in this sport was my only amusement.

The first day I did not mind so much the silence that is part of the rules of the Camaldolese order, but after the third day I found it unbearable. As for the knight, his melancholy deepened from hour to hour.

We had been in the monastery eight days when one of my comrades from St. Rochus porch arrived. He had seen us mount our rented mule, and later meeting the same muledriver, had learned from him the place of our retreat. Anxiety over my absence, he said, had broken up our little group and he himself had entered the service of a merchant from Cadiz who had fallen ill in Madrid. This young man had suffered an accident, had broken both arms and legs and needed people to work for him.

I told him I could not stand it any longer here among the Camaldolese and begged him to take my place with the knight for a few days. He replied that he would gladly do so, but he could not fail the merchant from Cadiz who had taken him into his service. The merchant had hired him in the St. Rochus porch and if he did not live up to his obligation he might make things difficult for the other lads who had been there with him.

I told him I would take his place beside the sick man. And as I had earned much prestige among my young comrades, Chiquito, too, felt he dared not refuse me. Taking him to the knight, I introduced him as the boy who was going to replace me for a few days. The knight did not speak, but signed to me that he consented to this arrangement.

I therefore went off to Madrid to the inn my comrade

had designated. There I learned that the sick man had moved to a doctor's in the calle de Alcantara where I had no trouble in finding him. I explained that I had come in place of my companion, Chiquito, that my name was Avarito and that I would give him the same service as had my friend.

I was told that my services would be accepted, but that first I must sleep for I would have to watch beside the sick man for several nights. I therefore went to sleep and reported for duty in the evening. I found the sick man in a helpless condition: he could use only his left hand and he suffered great pain in all the other limbs. I tried to make him forget his pain by keeping him occupied and distracting his attention, and so well did I succeed that he announced he was ready to tell me his story.

THE STORY OF LOPE SOAREZ

I am the only son of Gasparo Soarez, the richest man in Cadiz. My father, who was by nature unbending and puritanical, required me to work in the counting-house and did not permit me to indulge in any of the pleasures the sons of the best families in Cadiz enjoyed. As I desired to please him in all things I went to very few plays and did not attend on Sundays the brilliant parties that are so popular in commercial towns and that make one's visits there so delightful. The relaxation the mind needs from time to time, I found in reading those amusing but dangerous books called novels; in fact such pleasure did I take in them that they aroused in me a desire for love. However, as I went out seldom, and as few friends came to our house, I had little opportunity to lose my heart. It happened that my father had business at the law court and considered this a good opportunity for me to see Madrid. Far from wishing to oppose him, I was delighted to shake off the dust of the warehouse, to escape from the counting-house and to breathe a freer air. When all preparations for my journey had been made, my father summoned me to his office and made me the following speech:

"You will find yourself in a city where merchants do not play the leading role they do here in Cadiz. It is therefore important for you to conduct yourself with the most dignified circumspection so that you do not demean a position that redounds to your honor and contributes greatly to the wealth of your native land and to the real power of your sovereign.

"Here now are the three rules to which you must adhere strictly if you do not wish to arouse my wrath. First; I command you to avoid conversations with nobles. They think they do us an honor to address us or even to exchange a few words with us. But do not foster this mistaken idea in them, for our fame is not dependent on what they have to say to us.

"Secondly; I command you to call yourself simply Soarez and not Don Lope Soarez. Titles do not add to a merchant's good name which rests entirely on his cleverness, on his connections and on the foresight he employs in his enterprises.

"Thirdly; I forbid you ever to draw the sword. I permit you to wear one since such is the custom. But you must know that a merchant's honor depends solely on the scrupulousness with which he fulfills his obligations. That is why I never allowed you to take a single fencing lesson. Should you act contrary to any of these three rules, you will call down upon yourself my wrath. There is, however, a fourth rule that you must follow. Otherwise you can expect not only my wrath and my curse, but the curse of my father and of my grandfather, who was your great-grandfather and the founder of our fortune. This rule is that you must never enter into or so much as consider any association either direct or indirect with a member of the house of Moros Brothers, the Court bankers.

"The Moros Brothers enjoy, and rightly so, the reputation of being the most honest men in the world and I can understand my prohibition surprises you. But you will be less surprised when you hear of the shame they have brought upon your house. I shall therefore give you a brief outline of our history.

"The founder of our fortune was Inigo Soarez, who, after sailing the seas in his youth, took over a goodly share of the Potosi mines and founded a business in Cadiz. In the interests of this firm he sought the friendship of the most important merchants in Spain among whom the Moros played an important role. My grandfather informed the Moros of his intention to enter into a permanent association with them. They agreed to this arrangement and in order to do business with them, he deposited money in Antwerp which when needed he intended to draw from their bank in Madrid. How great, however, was his indignation when his draft was returned to him with a protest. To be sure by the next post he received a deeply apologetic letter in which Rodrigo Moro informed him that he had been absent in San Ildefonso with the Minister, the dispatch boat had been late and his chief counting-house clerk had not dared to depart from their business rule, but that he was ready to make everything good. However, the affront had occurred. Inigo Soarez severed all connections with the Moros and on his deathbed advised his son never to form any association with them.

"Ruiz Soarez, my father, obeyed this injunction for many years. Then a flurry of bankruptcies decreased the number of commercial houses and forced him to seek help from Moro. He had every reason to regret it. I have told you we owned a large share in the output of the Potosi mines. As a result we were entitled to many silver ingots, which we were accustomed to use in making payments and which were therefore not subject to fluctuations in the rate of exchange. For this purpose we used cedar packing cases; each case contained one hundred pounds in silver, that is, two thousand seven hundred and fifty-seven *piastres* and six *reales*. You can still see some of those cases in our warehouse. They were braced with iron bands and supplied with lead seals that bore the trademark of our house. Each case was numbered. They were sent to India, came back to Europe, went to America. No one thought of opening them at the borders and everyone was delighted to receive them in payment. They were known even in Madrid. But one day a man who had to make a payment to the Moros Brothers had four of the cases delivered to them, whereupon the office manager not only opened the cases but also had the silver tested. When word of this insulting action reached Cadiz, my father was furious. To be sure in the next mail he received a letter full of apologies from Antonio Moro, son of Rodrigo, explaining that he had been sent to Valladolid where the Court was in residence and on his return had roundly reprimanded his head clerk who, as a foreigner, was not conversant with Spanish customs. However, my father was not pacified by these excuses. He broke off all relations with the Moros and on his deathbed advised me never to enter into any association with them. For a long time I obeyed this injunction, but when, under special circumstances, I came in touch with the Moros again, I forgot my father's last recommendations, or at least they slipped my mind, and you will see what happened to me.

"Current business made it necessary for me to go to Madrid where I formed an acquaintance with a man named Livardez, a merchant who had retired from the business world and was living on his capital which was considerable. There was something about the man's temperament that corresponded to mine, and we were already on friendly terms when I learned that this Livardez was the uncle of Sancho Moro, the present head of the house.

"I should have broken off with Livardez at once, but I did not. Quite the contrary, my relations with him became even closer. One day Livardez told me—well knowing what a clever deal I had made with the Philippines—that he wished to invest a million with me, with title to a share in the company. I pointed out that as the uncle of the Moros Brothers he should invest his capital in their firm.

" 'No,' he replied, 'I do not like to do business with relatives.'

"In the end he managed to persuade me and all the more easily as in that deal I myself actually had no connection with the Moros Brothers. On my return to Cadiz I added a ship to the two others that I sent to the Philippines regularly every year and thought no more of the matter.

"The following year poor Livardez died. Sancho Moro wrote me that I should make over to him the million his uncle had invested with me. Perhaps I should have told him about the agreement concerning a share in the company, but I did not want to have any dealings with that accursed house and I promptly refunded the million. Two years later when my ships came home, my capital had trebled. That meant that I owed the dead Livardez two million. I was therefore obliged to enter into correspondence with the Moros. I wrote them that I was in duty bound to pay over two million to them. They replied that the capital had been collected two years before and they did not want to hear anymore about the matter. You can imagine, my son, how offended I was at such intolerable scorn, for this action meant nothing more than that they were making me a present of two million. I consulted several merchants from Cadiz. They told me the Moros were right and that it was illegal to share the profits of capital that had been drawn from the bank. I pointed out that Livardez' capital was really invested in the ships and that if the ships had sunk I would have had the right to demand reimbursement of the million. But I saw clearly that the name of Moro made an impression and that had I summoned a council of merchants, their *parere* would have gone against me.

"I sought the advice of a lawyer who told me the Moros could have withdrawn their late uncle's capital without permission. I, however, had employed it according to their uncle's wishes so that in reality the said capital was in my hands and the million the Moros had cashed was a completely different million that had nothing to do with Livardez' million. He advised me to sue the Moros in the Seville courts. I did so. For six long years I carried on a lawsuit that cost me six hundred thousand piastres and which nevertheless I lost. The two million remained in my hands.

"At first I was inclined to use it for a number of charitable purposes but I was afraid that the confounded Moros would get part of the credit. I still do not know what to do with this money. When I draw up my annual balance, I shall write two million less among my assets. You see therefore, my son, that I have good and sufficient reason to forbid you to have any dealings with the Moros."

When the gypsy had spoken those words, someone sent for him and we each went our own way.

The thirty-third day

Soon after we had started on our journey, the Wandering Jew joined us and went on with his story:

CONTINUATION OF THE STORY OF THE WANDERING JEW

We grew up, if not under the eyes of good Dellius who was blind, at least guarded by his wisdom and guided by his excellent advice. Eighteen centuries have gone by since then, and the years of my childhood are still the only period in my long life that I remember with any joy. I loved Dellius as though he were my father and I had become close friends with Germanus. True, we frequently quarreled and always over the same subject—religion. And as I was completely imbued with the intolerant principles of the synagogue I was constantly telling him:

"Your idols have ears, but they do not see; they have ears, but they do not hear. A goldsmith molded them. Mice build their nests in them."

Germanus often replied that one should not think of the idols as gods and that I had a false conception of the Egyptian religion. This statement, which he repeated so stubbornly, roused my curiosity. I begged him to ask the priest, Cheremon, to instruct me in his religion which, to be sure, could only be done in secret, for if this were known at the synagogue I would be ignominiously excommunicated. Germanus was a favorite of Cheremon's and the priest was therefore ready to grant my request. A few nights later I waited for him in a coppice near the Temple of Isis. Germanus introduced me to Cheremon who invited me to sit beside him. The priest folded his hands, collected his thoughts and said the following prayer in the language of the people of Lower Egypt which I understood perfectly.

Oh my God, All Father,
Holy God, Thou revealest Thyself to Thy people,
Thou art the Holy One who created all through the Word.
Thou art the Holy One whose image is Nature.
Thou art the Holy One who did not spring from Nature.
Thou art the Holy One more mighty than any might.
Thou art the Holy One more eminent than any eminence.
Thou art the Holy One to whom no praise reaches.
Receive graciously the sacrifice of my heart and my word
Thou art ineffable and Thy preaching is silence.
Thou hast canceled errors that are contrary to true knowledge.
Take me up, strengthen, and let this grace be shared by all who still abide in ignorance, as well as those who recognize Thee and are therefore my brethren and Thy children.
I believe in Thee, I acknowledge it aloud.
I soar to the life above like light
I would share in Thy holiness and it is Thou who kindles this longing in me.

After Cheremon had ended his prayer he turned to me.

"My child," he said, "you see that, like you, we acknowledge a God who created the world through the Word. The prayer you have just heard is taken from Pimander, a book we ascribe to the thrice great Thot whose works are carried in solemn procession on all our feast days. We have twenty-one thousand rolls which, we assume, were written by this philosopher who lived two thousand years ago. However, as only our Sahis are allowed to copy them, it is probable that they have made many additions to them. Moreover the writings of Thot are full of a mysterious and subtle metaphysics and as a result there have been many and varied interpretations. I shall therefore limit myself to instructing you in the general dogmas which are very much like those of the Chaldeans. Like everything else in this world, religions are subject to a constant silent force, with the result that their form and nature are always changing. After a few centuries a religion that one thinks is still the same offers an entirely new light on the things men believe—allegories, whose meanings men can no longer plumb, or dogmas, which they only half-believe.

"Therefore I cannot promise to instruct you in the old religion whose ceremonies you can still see depicted on the bas-reliefs of Osymandias. But I shall pass on to you the teachings of my masters exactly as I propound them to my pupils.

"First of all I advise you not to cling to either pictures or symbols but to seek to grasp the meaning of things. Thus, for example, slime is the symbol of all things material. A god, seated on a lotus leaf and floating over the slime, represents thought that is based on material but does not touch it. Our lawgiver proceeded from this symbol when he said that the spirit of God hovers over the waters. Moses is said to have been brought up by priests of the city On or Heliopolis and your rites are actually very much like ours. Like you we have families of priests, prophets, the rite of circumcision, an aversion to swine and many other similarities."

When Cheremon had come to this part of his discourse, a priest of the Temple of Isis announced the hour of midnight. Our master explained that religious duties called him to the Temple and that we should come back the beginning of the following night.

"But you," the Wandering Jew added, "will soon reach your camp. Allow me therefore to postpone the rest of my story until tomorrow."

After the Wandering Jew had left us, I began to think about his words. It seemed to me that they quite obviously sprang from a desire to undermine our belief in the principles of our religion and to reinforce the designs of those two women who kept insisting that I should change my faith. However, I knew what honor dictated in this respect and I was firmly convinced that all such efforts were hopeless. Meanwhile we had halted for the night and, after first fortifying ourselves with food as usual, we took advantage of the gypsy leader's leisure and urged him to continue his story.

CONTINUATION OF THE STORY OF PANDESOWNA

After young Soarez had told me his family history, he seemed to be very drowsy and, as I knew how badly he needed rest in order to regain his strength, I urged him to continue his story the following night. He slept soundly and the next night he seemed much stronger. As he was wakeful, he decided to tell me his story.

CONTINUATION OF THE STORY OF LOPE SOAREZ

I have said that my father forbade me to use the title of Don, to draw my sword and to consort with nobles, but above all to enter into any relations with the Moro family. I have also mentioned my insatiable craving for novels. Disregarding my father's warnings, I therefore visited all the booksellers in Cadiz and provided myself with novels from which I expected to derive the greatest pleasure on my journey.

I took passage on a *pink* and, sailing away from our dusty, barren island, we ran along the flower-laden banks of the Guadalquiver and landed in Seville where I tarried only long enough to engage a mule-driver. I found one who, instead of the usual coach, had a comfortable and rather elegant carriage, I promptly engaged him and, with my carriage crammed full of the novels I had bought in Cadiz, I set out for Madrid.

The beautiful landscape through which one drives on the way to Cordoba, the picturesque mountain chain of the Sierra Morena, the country customs of the *Manchegos* (inhabitants of La Mancha), all added to the romantic sensations aroused in me by my favorite reading. I was deeply moved and filled with great yearnings so that, by the time I arrived in Madrid, I was head over heels in love—though I had no idea with whom.

In the capital I put up at "The Maltese Cross." It was noon and my dinner was served promptly. After that, like all travelers when they move into a hotel room, I started to unpack; then I heard a sound at my door. Striding across the room, I flung open the door so violently that it struck against an obstacle and I thought I must have injured someone. And, in truth, I saw before me a well-dressed man who was rubbing a bruised nose.

"Noble Don Lope," said the stranger, "I learned at the inn that the son of the famous Don Gasparo Soarez had arrived and I have come to pay you my respects."

"My dear sir, if you had intended merely to enter my door, the opening of the door would have given you at the least a bump on your forehead, but as your nose is injured, I assume that you may have had an eye at the keyhole."

"Bravo! Your keen observation is amazing. You are right. Desirous of making your acquaintance, I wanted first to get an impression of you and I was delighted to see with what an aristocratic air you went back and forth in the room arranging your possessions." So saying, the stranger, still talking, walked into my room, though I had not invited him to enter. "Noble Don Lope," he went on, "in me you see the famous offspring of the Busqueros of Old Castile whom I beg you not to confuse with other Busqueros from Leon. The world knows me under the name of Don Rochus Busqueros, but from now on I shall be distinguished only by my devotion to your Excellency."

I remembered my father's instructions and said to this peculiar person:

"My dear Don Rochus, I think I shall have to acquaint you with one of our family customs. When I took leave of my father, Gasparo Soarez, he instructed me never to permit anyone to address me by the title Don. He has also forbidden me ever to associate with nobles; from which your Excellency will understand that it is impossible for me to accept your courteous proposal."

At this Busqueros looked very grave.

"Noble Don Lope—and not Lope Soarez," he said, "Your Excellency's words embarrass me greatly for when my father died in my arms he commanded me always to address famous merchants with Don and to seek their company, whereupon your Excellency will understand that you cannot follow your father's instructions without forcing me to act contrary to my father's last wishes; and no matter how much you try to avoid me, all the more often will I endeavor to be with you."

Busqueros's arguments dumbfounded me. Moreover, he looked very serious and as my father had forbidden me to draw my sword I had to do my best to avoid disputes.

In the meantime Don Rochus had discovered on my table two gold coins about the value of eight Dutch ducats.

"Noble Don Lope," he said to me, "I have a collection of coins like these, but these two are the very ones I lack to make a full thousand. You know what a collector's mania is and I am sure you will be delighted to have the opportunity of doing me a favor, should the occasion offer, for I possess coins similar to these from the year 1707, when they were first minted and these two here are the only ones still lacking."

I gave Don Rochus the two gold pieces and thought he would then go; this however was not his intention. Suddenly he looked very serious again and said:

"Noble Don Lope, I would consider it quite improper for us both to eat from the same plate or to be forced to hand each other first the spoon and then the fork. I shall therefore order a second service brought in." Busqueros proceeded forthwith to give his instructions. We were then served and I must admit that my importunate table-companion's conversation was most entertaining. Had it not been for my distress at disobeying my father I would have enjoyed having him as my table guest.

Busqueros left immediately after dinner. I, however,

waited until the great heat of the day was over and then had myself driven to the Prado. I admired the beauties of this promenade, but I was in a hurry to see the Buen-Retiro for that deserted garden plays a great role in our novels, and instinct told me that in that garden I would form a tender relationship. The sight of the Buen-Retiro delighted me more than I can say, and I would certainly have lingered there, lost in admiration, had I not been distracted by the sight of something shining in the grass. Picking up the object I saw that it was a portrait suspended on a gold chain. It was the likeness of a very handsome young man. The other side of the medallion contained a bit of hair drawn through a gold band and the inscription "All thine, my dearest Inez." I put the piece of jewelry in my pocket and went on with my walk.

As I came back to the same place, I noticed two women; one of them, as young as she was beautiful, was searching for something she had lost and looking very worried. It was not hard to guess that she was hunting for the portrait so, addressing her I said:

"Señora, I think I have found what you are looking for. However, to be on the safe side, I cannot let it out of my hand until you are kind enough to prove your right by giving me a description of it."

"Señor," replied the fair stranger, "I am looking for a portrait. It was on a chain of which I have only this little piece left."

"And did not the portrait have an inscription?" I asked.

"Yes," replied the stranger blushing. "You will have learned from it that my name is Inez and that the original of this portrait is very close to me. So then what is keeping you from giving it to me?"

"Señora, you have not told me what this fortunate mortal's relation is to you."

"Señor, I thought I had merely to allay your doubts, not to satisfy your curiosity. You have no right to ask me such a question."

"It would have been more correct," I replied, "to call it my interest rather than my curiosity. As for my right, I beg you to consider the following: the finder of a lost object is entitled to a proper reward. All I ask of you is merely to tell me something that will perhaps make me the unhappiest man in the world."

The beautiful stranger looked grave and said:

"You go too far on a first meeting; that is not always a sure way to lead to a second. However, I shall satisfy you on this point. The original of this portrait is . . ."

At that moment Busqueros suddenly came out of a nearby path and addressed us with the greatest self-assurance. "I congratulate you, Señora," he said. "You have made the acquaintance of the son of the richest merchant in Cadiz."

An expression of the greatest indignation appeared on the beautiful stranger's face.

"I do not know," she said, "what right you have to address me without knowing me." Then turning to me, "Señor, will you kindly give me the portrait you found." Whereupon she stepped into her carriage and was driven off. Busqueros too had disappeared or rather he had already reached the end of the path for he probably did not think it well to wait for my reproaches.

When the gypsy came to this part of his story, he was called away and was therefore obliged to postpone the rest of his story until the following morning. After he had gone the beautiful Jewess, whom from now on we called Laura, turned to Duke Velasquez and said:

"What do you make of young Soarez's passionate emotions? Have you ever in your life thought for even a second about what is called love?"

"My system," replied Velasquez, "comprises the whole of nature and must therefore include every emotion the heart of man has known. I have explored them all deeply and I have described them. I was especially successful with love for I discovered that it can be expressed with the help of algebra and, as you know, Señora, algebraic problems are solved in a way that leaves nothing to be desired. Take, for example, that Love is a plus value and is expressed by a plus sign; Hate, as the opposite of Love, by the minus sign; then Indifference, which is lack of feeling, will equal zero. If I multiply Love by Love, that is, if I say: I love Love or I love to love Love, then I always get a positive value—for plus times plus always gives plus. If on the other hand I hate Hate I am already making inroads into the feeling of Love and therefore this minus times minus gives a plus.

"On the other hand, if I hate the hatred of Hate I break into the opposite feeling to Love, that is, into the minus value, for the cube of minus gives minus. As for the results derived from multiplying Love with Hate or Hate with Love, they are always negative, for plus times minus or minus times plus always gives minus. For if I hate Love or love Hate my feeling is constantly the opposite to Love. Have you any objection to this argument, lovely Laura?"

"Not the slightest," replied Laura. "On the contrary, I am sure there is no woman alive who would not be convinced by these deductions."

"I would not like that at all," replied Velasquez, "for if women were so quickly convinced they would miss the results of my comparison, that is, the conclusions resulting from the principles.

"But I shall continue my demonstration. As Love and Hate are to each other like positive and negative, it follows that instead of Hate I can write minus Love. This can by no means be considered the same as Indifference which is equivalent to zero. Now let us consider the behavior of two lovers: they love each other, they hate each other, then they hate Hate, which they have felt for each other, and love each other more than ever as long as a negative factor does not change their Love into Hate. In these changes one cannot fail to detect the successively operative forces as well as the positive and negative forces. In the end you hear that the lover has murdered his sweetheart and you do not know what to make of it. Was it the result of Love or of Hate? The same thing occurs in algebra. You get the minus-plus, the cube of X whenever the indices are odd numbers.

"The proof of my demonstration is that love often begins with a sort of dislike, a slightly negative quantity, which we can denote by a minus B. This dislike leads to a quarrel which we will denote by a minus C. The product of these two numbers will be plus BC. That is, a positive quantity, in other words—the emotion of love."

Here the beautiful Jewess interrupted Velasquez:

"Your Highness, if I have understood you correctly, it would be better to express Love by the two powers A minus X, whereby you would assume X to be smaller than A."

"Charming Laura," said Velasquez. "You have read my thoughts. Yes indeed, my lovely lady, the binomial theory which Sir Isaac Newton discovered should be as much the point of departure in any research on the human heart as it is in all our calculations."

After these words, we separated. But it was obvious that the beautiful Jewess had made a deep impression on Velasquez's mind and heart. Like me, he sprang from the race of Gomelez who, I had no doubt, were using the lovely Laura's influence to convert Velasquez to the faith of the Prophet. What follows will show that I was not mistaken.

The thirty-fourth day

Early the next morning we mounted our horses, but the Wandering Jew who had not expected us to break camp so early was far away. We were therefore obliged to wait a long time for him. At last he appeared, took his place beside me and began as follows:

CONTINUATION OF THE STORY OF THE WANDERING JEW

Symbols, Cheremon said, have never prevented us from believing in one God who was greater than all the other gods. A text of Thot's leaves no doubt on this point. This is what he says:

God is One and unmoved in the remoteness of His unity.

Even Reason cannot combine with Him any more than anything else. He is His own father and He is His own son, the only God, the Father. He is Good, He is the source of all ideas and of all fundamental principles. This one God declares Himself because He is sufficient unto Himself. He is the primal cause, the God of gods, the monad of unity, the source of Being, and because He was before all Reason, he is called Noetarch.

You see therefore, my friends, Cheremon went on, that there is no more sublime concept of divinity than ours; but we believed we should deify a part of God's attributes and his connection with us to make an equal number of godheads or rather godlike qualities. So we call God's thought Emeph; and when God manifests himself through the Word we call it Thot (persuasion) or Ermeth (exegesis). When God's thought—and in His care the truth—descends to earth and becomes a generative force, it is called Amun. When thought is combined with art, it is called Phta or Vulcan. When thought becomes the best of good actions, it is called Osiris.

We consider God as One; but the great number of beneficent relations He deems us worthy of leads us to believe that it is not blasphemous for us to dare to look upon Him as multiple. For He is truly many-sided and the attributes we are able to perceive are infinitely varied.

As for demons, we think that each of us has two of them, a good demon and an evil demon. The souls of heroes are like the demons of the kingdom of the air, and the ordinary soul seems to have something earthy about it. Divine Providence we compare to the light that fills the whole world. According to ancient tradition we too speak of powerful beings, angels or heralds whose task it is to deliver God's commands and of a being of a still higher order whom the Greek Jews have called the Archonton or the Archangel.

Those among us who have been ordained priests consider ourselves empowered to call up the actual presence of gods, demons, angels, heroes and souls; but we cannot practice this invocation without disturbing the order of the universe a little. When the gods descend to earth the sun or the moon vanishes for a brief time from the sight of mortals.

The archangels are surrounded by a more brilliant light than the angels; the souls of heroes do not shine so brightly as those of angels, but brighter than the souls of plain mortals that are darkened by shadows.

The princes of the zodiac are known by their exceedingly majestic forms. Moreover, the manifestation of these various beings are accompanied by an infinite number of special conditions that serve to distinguish them one from the other. Thus, for example, evil demons are recognized by the wicked deeds that always follow on their heels.

As for idols, we believe a bit of divine being descends on them if they are made under a certain position of the stars and accompanied by certain ceremonies of invocation. But this art is so delusive and true knowledge of God so unworthy that in general we leave these matters to priests of a much lower rank than the one to which I have the honor of belonging.

When one of our priests calls upon the gods, he becomes to some extent a part of them. He does not cease to be a human being, but to a certain degree he is pervaded by the divine attribute. In a certain measure he becomes one with his god. In this condition it is easy for him to control the dark and earthbound demons and to force them to enter some body or other or to drive them out of it.

Now and then our priests fashion out of stones, medicinal herbs and animal matter, a mixture that would be worthy to receive divinity: but the true bond that unites the priest with his god is prayer. All these rites and dogmas which I have just explained to you, we do not ascribe to Thot or to Mercure the Third who lived in the days of Osymandias. In our opinion their real author is the prophet Bytis who lived two thousand years earlier and who has interpreted the concept of Mercure the First but time, as I have already said, has changed many things and added many others and I do not believe that this primitive religion has come down to us unalloyed.

And finally, our priests sometimes make so bold as to threaten the gods: during the sacrifice they will say something like this: "If you do not fulfill my request, I shall reveal what Isis hides from all eyes, I shall make known the secrets of the depths, I shall break open Osiris's Tomb and scatter his limbs to the four winds."

I must confess that I myself no longer employ these formulas and that the Chaldeans refrain from using them altogether.

"As Cheremon came to this part of his lesson," said the Wandering Jew, "the Temple priest announced midnight: and as you are approaching your camp, allow me to postpone the continuation of my story until tomorrow."

After the Wandering Jew had left us, Velasquez declared that he had learned nothing new from him and that everything he had told us could be found in the Book of Jamblichos. "That," he added, "is a work I read with great attention and I could never understand why the critics who recognize as authentic Porphyrios's letter to the Egyptian Anebon, thought that the Egyptian Abammon's reply was merely an invention of Porphyrios. On the contrary, it seems to me that what Porphyrios did in his work was to shore up Abammon's answer by adding a treatise on the Chaldean philosophers."

"Whatever that may be about Anebon and Abammon," said Uzeda the cabalist, "I assure you that the Wandering Jew has told you nothing but the truth."

We halted for the night and after the evening meal the gypsy, who was free for a while, took up his story again.

CONTINUATION OF THE STORY OF PANDESOWNA

After young Soarez had told me how his meeting in the Buen-Retiro ended, he was unable to fight off the sleep he so badly needed. And soon he was fast asleep. The following night, however, he went on with his story.

CONTINUATION OF THE STORY OF LOPE SOAREZ

As the next day was Sunday I was sure, if I visited every church, of meeting the beautiful Inez. I entered three of them in vain, but in the fourth I found her. She recognized me, and when Mass was over she left the church. As she passed me she deliberately leaned close to me and said in a low voice:

"That was a portrait of my brother."

Then she was gone and I stood glued to the spot, delighted by the words I had heard. For truly the trouble she had taken to calm my fears seemed to indicate a budding interest in me.

Returning to my hotel, I ordered my dinner and hoped I would not see Busqueros. However, he arrived with the soup. "Noble Don Lope," he said, "I have refused twenty invitations for, as I have already told you, I am your Excellency's devoted servant."

I was greatly tempted to tell his Excellency Don Rochus a few friendly things but remembered that my father had forbidden me to draw my sword and I therefore had to avoid quarrels. Busqueros ordered a serving for himself, sat down and turned to me with an extremely self-satisfied expression on his face.

"Admit, noble Don Lope," he said, "that I did you a very good turn yesterday by casually letting the lady know that you are the son of a rich merchant. To be sure she appeared to be highly indignant but that was only to show you that she was not attracted by the lure of money. Do not believe that, noble Don Lope! You are young, full of life and you have a good figure, but if someone falls in love with you your money will always play an important part. In my case I do not have to fear that; if I am loved, I shall be loved for myself and I have never inspired a love based on avarice." All through the meal Busqueros talked this sort of nonsense and as soon as he had dined, he left.

That evening I went to the Buen-Retiro although I felt sure I would not see the beautiful Inez. And truly she did not appear, but Busqueros did, nor did he leave my side the whole evening. The importunate fellow came back the next day to dine with me and, as he was leaving, remarked that he would meet me again in Buen-Retiro. I told him I was not going for a walk, but I knew he did not believe me. Toward late afternoon I took up my post in a shop on the way to the Buen-Retiro. Scarcely had I arrived when I saw Busqueros: he was on his way to the Buen-Retiro and when he did not find me there, he looked for me in the Prado.

I therefore set out for the Buen-Retiro where, after strolling back and forth a few times, I saw the beautiful Inez enter. I approached her most respectfully which did not seem to displease her; but I did not know whether I should thank her for the words she had said to me in the church. Fortunately she herself came to my aid by saying with a laugh:

"You maintain that a man is entitled to a decent reward when he finds a lost object and as the finder of the portrait, you asked about my connection with the original. Now you know what it is. So do not ask anything more unless you should find something else that belongs to me in which case you would undoubtedly be entitled to a new reward. However, it is not seemly for us to be seen often together. Farewell, I do not forbid you to address me when you have anything to say."

Inez went off, giving me a charming nod which I answered with a deep bow. Then I turned into a side path, but I kept looking back at her. She walked about for a while; then as she was getting into her coach she gave me one last glance which seemed to me to indicate a kindly feeling.

I was still puzzling over Inez' attitude the next morning. I felt that I had made some progress and considered the moment not far off when the beautiful Inez would permit me to write to her. But because I had never written a love letter, I thought it would be a good idea to practice the correct style. I therefore took my pen in hand and wrote the following letter:

Lope Soarez to Inez . . .
Consistent with a feeling of shyness, my trembling hand hesitates to write these lines. And truly, what can they express? What mortal could write at the dictate of love? The pen cannot follow fast enough. If only I could collect my thoughts on this paper, but they escape me. They roam among the boscage of the Buen-Retiro; they linger on the sand that bears the imprints of your footsteps, from which they cannot bear to part. Is this garden of our kings really so beautiful as it seems to me? No, undoubtedly it is so charming only in my eyes, for would it be so empty if others saw in it the beauty I discover there?

In this garden the grass is fresher, the jasmine sends forth its perfume to the last drop and the little woods, through which you walked, protect more vigilantly its shadows intoxicated with love and shades them more jealously against the burning light of day. The little woods you only passed through, but what will you do to a heart in which you have taken up your abode?

After I had finished the letter I read it over and found it too gushing. I therefore had no desre to deliver it or to send it off. But to give myself a pleasant illusion, I sealed it and wrote on it: To the beautiful Inez. Then tossing it into a drawer I went out. As I strolled about the streets of Madrid I came to "The White Lion" inn and I thought it would be a good idea to dine there and avoid that confounded Busqueros. So this I did and then returned to my hotel.

When I opened the drawer in which I had placed the love letter, it was not there. On questioning my servants I learned that no one had come, except Busqueros. I had not the slightest doubt that he had taken the letter and I was extremely worried as to what he would do with it. That afternoon I did not go directly to the Buen-Retiro, but remained in the shop where I had been the previous day and kept a sharp lookout. Soon the beautiful Inez' carriage appeared with Busqueros running after it and waving a letter he held in his hand. Shouting and gesturing he managed to stop the carriage and place the letter in the hand for which it was intended. Thereupon the carriage went on its way to the Buen-Retiro and Busqueros disappeared in another direction.

As I had no idea what the result of this scene would be, I went slowly on my way to the garden. There I found the beautiful Inez with her companion, seated on a bench beside a clump of wild roses. She motioned me to come nearer, made room for me beside her and spoke as follows:

"My dear sir, I must speak frankly to you. First, I must ask you to tell me why you wrote all these foolish things and why you entrusted the letter to that man whose impertinence I find offensive."

"Señora," I replied, "it is indeed true that I wrote you that letter, but it was not my intention to have it delivered to you. I wrote it to please myself and then tossed it in a drawer. That abominable Busqueros, this man who has been my misfortune ever since I came to Madrid, stole it."

Inez began to laugh. She reread my letter—with evident pleasure—and then said to me:

"So your name is Don Lope Soarez? Are you related to the famous, rich Soarez, the merchant from Cadiz?"

I replied that I was his only son.

Inez then spoke of unimportant matters and walked to her carriage. But before getting into it she said to me:

"It is not proper for me to keep this foolish letter. I shall return it to you, but do not lose it. Perhaps I shall ask you for it later on."

She gave me the letter and clasped my hand. It was the first time a woman had ever shaken hands with me. I had read about such things in novels: but had never been able to imagine the pleasure it would give me. This way of expressing one's feeling I found quite enchanting and I returned to my hotel the happiest man in the world.

The next day Busqueros again did me the honor of dining with me.

"Well," he said to me, "did the letter reach its destination? I see by the mood you are in that it made a good impression."

I could not help telling him that I owed him a certain measure of thanks. Towards evening I went to the Buen-Retiro and no sooner had I entered than I saw Inez walking a few feet ahead of me. She did not have her companion with her but was followed at a distance by only a footman. She turned around, then went on her way and dropped her fan. I took it to her and she received it very graciously.

"I promised you," she said, "a suitable reward should you ever return an object I had lost. Let me sit down on this bench and talk this serious matter over." She led me to the same bench on which we had sat the day before. "Well now? When you returned the portrait you learned that it was a portrait of my brother. What else do you want to know?"

"Oh, Señora," I replied, "I should like to know who you are, what your name is and on whom you are dependent."

"Listen to me," said Inez. "Perhaps you thought your

wealth had dazzled me but you will change your mind when you know that I am the daughter of a man who is just as rich as your father. He is the banker Moro."

"Great Heaven!" I cried, "do I hear correctly? Oh, Señora, I am the most unhappy man in the world. I cannot think of you without bringing down upon my head the curse of my father, of my grandfather and of my great-grandfather, Inigo Soarez who, after crossing all the seas, owned a portion of the output of the Potosi mines and founded a business firm in Cadiz."

At that moment Don Busqueros stuck his head through the clump of wild roses, beside our bench, and pushed himself between Inez and me.

"Do not believe him, Señora," he said. "That is his usual way of getting rid of a person. Because he was not interested in knowing me, he pretended that his father had forbidden him to frequent nobles. Now he is afraid of angering his great-grandfather, Inigo Soarez, who sailed across the seven seas and owned part of the output of the Potosi mines. Do not be discouraged, Señora. These little Croesuses are always afraid of falling into a trap, but into it he has to go."

Looking very indignant, Inez rose and went to her carriage.

At this point in his story the gypsy was interrupted and we did not see him for the rest of that day.

The thirty-fifth day

We mounted our horses again and rode slowly through the mountains. When we had been about an hour on the way, the Wandering Jew appeared and, taking his customary place between Velasquez and me, went on with his story as follows:

CONTINUATION OF THE STORY OF THE WANDERING JEW

The following night the honorable Cheremon received us with his usual kindness and said to us:

The rich store of subjects we touched on yesterday did not give me an opportunity to mention a dogma that is generally acknowledged among us, but which enjoys even greater fame among the Greeks, thanks to the prestige Plato has given it. I mean belief in the Word or the divine wisdom which we sometimes call Mander, sometimes Meth and sometimes Thot or persuasion.

There is still another dogma I want to mention. It was founded by one of the three Thot who was called Trismegistos or the Thrice Great, because he pictured the Divinity as having three times more power than God Himself, whom he called Father, or than the Word or than the Holy Ghost. Those, therefore, are our dogmas. As for the commandments, they are equally simple and pure, above all the precepts for us priests.

The vegetarian diet to which we are committed keeps the blood in our veins from becoming overheated and it is not so difficult for us to subdue our passions. The priests of Apis refrain from commerce with women. That therefore is our religion today. It has departed from the original religion on a number of important points, among others on the transmigration of souls which has few devotees today although it was in high repute when Pythagoras visited our land over seven hundred years ago. Our ancient mythology has also much to say about the gods of the planets, who were called Regents; but today this doctrine is left to the makers of horoscopes. As I have already told you, religions change like everything else in the world.

There are only the holy mysteries left for me to speak of and I shall tell you everything that is important for you to know. Above all be assured that even as initiates you would not learn any more about the origin of our mythology. Turn to the historian Herodotus.

He was an initiate and boasts of it on every page; and yet he probed the origin of the Greek gods like a man who knew no more than the uninitiated.

What he calls the ordination speech, does not accord in any way with history. In reality it was what the Romans call "turpiloquens" or defamation. Every initiate was told a story which offended against the usual notion of decency: in Eleusis the story of Baubo whom Ceres received in her house, in Phrygia the love affairs of Bacchus. In Egypt we consider depravity a symbol that reveals how base the intrinsic property of matter is in itself and more than what we do not know. A famous consul named Cicero has recently published a book on the nature of the gods. He admits that he does not know the origin of the religious cult of Italy and yet he was augur and therefore initiated into all the mysteries of the Etruscan religion. The uncertainty found in all the works of the initiated shows us that even initiation fails to uncover the origins of our religion. This all goes very far back. As early as on the bas-relief of Osymandias you see an Osiris Procession, and the cult of Apis and Mnevis was introduced into Egypt by Bacchus more than three thousand years ago.

Initiation therefore clarifies neither the origin of religious cults nor the history of the gods, nor the meaning of our symbols; nevertheless the preparation for the mysteries is of great use to mankind. A man who must reproach himself for great failures or whose hands are flecked with blood, goes to the priests of mysteries, confesses his sins and is absolved by baptism. In the days before this merciful institution, many men were driven out of the community because they had forfeited their right to go to the altar and they became robbers.

In the mysteries of Mithras, the initiated are handed bread and wine and this is called the Feast of the Eucharist; the sinner who partakes of it is reconciled with God and begins a new and blameless life.

Here I interrupted the Wandering Jew by calling his attention to the fact that the Eucharist belongs exclusively to the Christian religion. Whereupon Velasquez broke into the conversation:

"Excuse me," he said, "what he pointed out in this respect agrees perfectly with what I have read in Justinian the Martyr who, moreover, has written that we can recognize the malicious cunning of demons by the fact that they acted in advance as later on a Christ would have been obliged to act. But continue your story, my dear sir."

The Jew took up the thread of his story as follows:

Among the mysteries, said Cheremon, is one ceremony that is common to all religions. A god dies, is buried, the people mourn him several days, then follows the resurrection of the god and his reunion with the community. Many people say this ceremony symbolizes the course of the sun, but most people believe it refers to the seeds buried in the ground that spring up again.

This, my young Israelite, the priest added, is about all I have to tell you about our dogmas and rites. You see that we are not idolators as your prophets have so often accused us of being. But as I must admit, the people are beginning to be less and less satisfied with both your religion and mine. Wherever we look, we see unrest and the desire for something new. In Palestine the people go in masses on pilgrimages into the desert to hear that new prophet who baptizes in the river Jordan! Here you see the therapeutist or healer, the wizard, who mingles the cult of the Persians with ours, young Apollonius who flaunts his blonde mane in city after city, and as Pythagoras would like to put it: mountebanks pose as priests of Isis, and the old cult of the goddess is abandoned: her temples are deserted, incense no longer rises on the altars.

When the Wandering Jew came to this part of his story, he noticed that we were getting near the camp and he disappeared into the valley. I drew Duke Velasquez aside.

"Allow me to ask you what you think of the things the Wandering Jew has told us," I said. "It seems to me we should not have listened to all of it, for the greatest part of his argument is contrary to the belief we profess."

"Señor Alfonso," replied Velasquez, "your piety does you honor in the eyes of every thinking man. My belief, I dare say, is more liberal, but no less passionate and pure than yours. The best proof of this is my system which I have many times brought into our conversation and which contains a great number of observations about divinity and its eternal wisdom. Therefore, Señor Alfonso, I think that what I listen to in all peace, you, too, can hear with a clear conscience."

This answer calmed me and dispelled my anxiety. The gypsy, who was free that evening, took up the story of his adventures as follows:

CONTINUATION OF THE STORY OF PANDESOWNA

After young Soarez had told me his sad adventure in the Buen-Retiro garden, he was overcome with sleep and I left him to his rest. When I went to him again the following night, I urged him to satisfy my curiosity about the further events in his story. Stretched out on his sickbed and able to use only his tongue, the young merchant was still outraged at the thought of Busqueros's intolerable conduct.

CONTINUATION OF THE STORY OF LOPE SOAREZ

Would you believe it possible that this disgusting fellow had the effrontery to appear in my room the next day just as the soup was being served? When he had satisfied his hunger, he said to me:

"Noble Don Lope, I can understand that, at your age, you have no desire to marry; that is a folly one always commits too soon. But to excuse oneself to a young girl by telling her about the animosity of your great-grandfather Inigo Soarez, who crossed the seas and took over a large share of the output of the Potosi mines, is a disgusting disaster. You may be glad that I have partially fixed the matter up again."

"Noble Don Rochus," I replied, "have the kindness to add one more to the many services you have already done for me and do not go to the Buen-Retiro this afternoon. To be sure I do not think the lovely Inez will be there, and even should she come, she will not deign to speak to me. But I shall go to that same bench on which I sat with her yesterday, there to bewail my misfortune and to sigh to my heart's content."

Don Rochus looked very serious.

"Noble Don Lope," he said, "your Excellency's words are extremely insulting. They give the impression that my devotion is not agreeable to you. As a matter of fact, I could let you sigh and bemoan your bad luck undisturbed, but if the beautiful Inez should come to the garden and I were not present, who would be there to make amends for your awkwardness? No, no, dear Don Lope, I am too devoted to you to obey you."

Don Rochus withdrew immediately after dinner, I waited until the worst heat was past, then I set out on my way to the Buen- Retiro, but did not fail to hide in the usual shop. Soon I saw Busqueros go past. He went into the Beuen-Retiro and, not finding me there, turned around and took the road to the Prado—or so I thought. I then promptly left my hiding place and went to the bench where I had recently known both joy and sorrow.

Suddenly I felt a tap on my shoulder. I thought it was Busqueros and swung around in a rage—and there stood Inez smiling sweetly at me. She sat down beside me, ordered her companion to withdraw a little and then turned to me.

"My dear Soarez," she said, "I was very angry with you yesterday because I could not understand why you made that speech about your grandfather and your great-grandfather. But I have made inquiries and I have learned that for centuries your house has not wished to have any relations with ours and this because of some sort of trouble which, they say, is of little importance. But if you are facing difficulties, so am I. My father decided upon my future long ago. He was afraid I might take it into my head to make a different marriage from the one that suited him. He does not like me to go out often and will not allow me to go to the Prado or to attend the theatre. Only the greatest need for a breath of fresh air gives me an opportunity to come here with my *dueña.* As these paths are not much frequented my father thinks it is safe enough for me here. My future husband is a Neapolitan noble, the Duke di Santa-Maura. I think he is marrying me only for my fortune with which he hopes to restore his own. I have always felt a strong aversion to this marriage, but my father is a very stubborn man. Fortunately, Señora d' Avoloz, his younger sister, has a great influence over him. This dear aunt is very friendly to me and she feels equally unfriendly towards the Neapolitan Duke. I have told her about you and she wishes to meet you. Come with me to our carriage. At the garden gate you will find one of Señora d' Avoloz's servants who will take you to her."

Those words of the adorable Inez filled my heart with joy. I followed her to her carriage and then went to meet her aunt whom I had the good luck to please. In the days that followed I called on Señora d' Avoloz always at the same hour and I always met her niece there. My happiness lasted six days; on the seventh day I was told that the Duke di Santa-Maura had arrived. Señora d' Avoloz urged me not to lose courage and one of her house servants brought me the following letter:

Inez Moro to Lope Soarez:
The hateful man to whom I am pledged is in Madrid. Our house is filled with his entourage. I have received permission to withdraw to a wing of the house where a window looks out on the calle Augustina. The window is not very high and we could easily converse there for a few moments. I must tell you about plans of greater importance. Come to the Buen-Retiro as soon as the sun sets, to the bench we sat on the last time. The man who took you to my aunt will fetch you.

By the time I received this letter it was seven o'clock in the evening, and as the sun set at eight, I had no time to lose. I therefore hurried to the Buen-Retiro where I indulged in sweet dreams in which frankly a little self-reproach was mingled, because I was not obeying my father's orders. But love fills us with flattering hopes and I yielded to its spell.

Then I saw Busqueros approaching. My first reaction was to climb a knotty oak tree nearby but I was not clever enough so I climbed down again, sat down on the bench and stoically waited for my enemy.

Busqueros approached me with his customary self-assurance.

"Well, Don Lope," he said, "I think the beautiful Inez will end by softening the heart of your great-grandfather Inigo Soarez who sailed the seven seas and owned part of the output of the Potosi mines . . . But you do not answer, noble Don Lope? . . . Aren't you going to answer me? Bravo! As long as you won't answer me, I shall sit down on this bench and tell you the story of my life. You will find much in it that can be instructive to you."

I made up my mind to endure it all until sunset and Busqueros began as follows:

I am the only son of Don Blasius Busqueros, who was the younger son of the youngest brother of another Busqueros. My father had the honor to serve the King for thirty years as an *alferez,* that is, an ensign in an infantry regiment. When he saw that all his endurance did not help him to rise above the rank of second lieutenant he resigned from the service and settled in the market-town of Alazzuelos where he married a young lady from the nobility on whom an uncle had settled an income of six hundred piastres. I was the only fruit of this marriage which lasted only a short time for my father died before I was eight years old.

I was left in the care of my mother who paid little attention to me. She allowed me to wander around the streets from morning till night and did not worry too much about my activities. As the other children in the town were not at liberty to go out when they wished, I was therefore the one to visit them. Their parents, accustomed to my visits, did not bother me and I was privileged to enter any house in the market-town at any hour.

Gifted with a good mind and keen observation I noticed everything that went on in the families I visited and reported it faithfully to my mother who took great pleasure in tales. I must even admit that I have to thank her wise guidance for this fortunate talent of mine for mixing into the affairs of others—though more to her advantage than to my own.

For a time I imagined I would please my mother by telling the neighbors what went on in our house. She received no visitors, held no conversations, no matter how secret, that the entire neighborhood did not hear about at once. These revelations, however, were not of the sort to please her and a fairly severe punishment made it clear to me that it was all right to bring home news from the outside, but all wrong to talk about our own affairs.

Soon I realized that in every house people were avoiding me. I was hurt. But though they made more and more strenuous efforts to thwart my curiosity, I discovered a thousand ways to peer into their rooms, and the light construction of the houses in our village favored these maneuvers. The ceilings were made only of planks laid one alongside the other. At night I used to climb up on the roofs and bore holes in the planks. Soon I knew all the family secrets in the village. These I shared with my mother who relayed them to all the inhabitants of Alazzuelos or rather to each one individually. They probably realized that my mother got her information from me and their hatred of me grew from day to day. Though all the houses were closed to me, the holes in the roofs were still open. Crouched in their storerooms I was in the midst of my fellow citizens without their knowing it; they sheltered me against their will; I lived in their houses as unwelcome as the rats. And like those animals I had the same habit of getting into their pantries whenever I could and nibbling their food.

When I reached my eighteenth year, my mother thought it was time for me to choose a profession. But I had long ago made my choice: I wanted money, I intended to do nothing at all, to attach myself to the house of some great lord, to give myself up to slothfulness and the pleasure of raising the devil. For the sake of form, however, I had to spend several years in the university. I therefore went to Salamanca and registered as a law student.

What a difference between a great city and the wretched little market-town in which I was born! But also how many new obstacles! The houses were several stories high, they were properly locked at night and as if to annoy me even more the dwellers on the second and third floors left their windows open to get the fresh air. I saw at first glance that I could do nothing by myself: I would have to make the sort of friends who would help me in a number of enterprises.

I therefore attended my law courses and studied the characters of my fellow-students for I dared not place my trust too lightly. Finally I found four young men who seemed to have the necessary qualifications and I began to roam around with them at night and to shout and brawl on the streets. As soon as I thought they were well enough prepared I spoke to them as follows:

"My friends, are you not surprised that the citizens of Salamanca have the courage to leave their windows open the whole night? Now I ask you! Because they are twenty feet above the ground, they claim the right to defy us students. Sleep is libelous to us, their quiet disquiets me. I have decided first to find out what goes on in their houses and then to show you what we can do about it."

This speech met with approval, but the young men still did not know what I was after. I came to the point. "My dear friends," I said to them. "First of all we need a very light fifteen-foot ladder. Wrapped in your cloaks three of you can carry it easily. At the most it will look as if you were marching goose-step, especially if you are careful to keep to the poorly lighted side of the street. Of course, you will place the ladder against the wall. If then we use it, we will place it against a window and while one of us climbs to the top of the building which he will watch, the others will keep at a certain distance to watch over the safety of us all. As soon as we have learned what goes on above the ground floor, we shall decide what to do next."

This plan was accepted and I had a light but strong ladder built. I picked out a very nice-looking house with windows that were not too high. Then, leaning my ladder against it, I climbed up so that from inside the house only my head was visible.

Although the interior of the room was bright with moonlight, at first I could not distinguish anything. Then I saw a man in a bed: he was staring at me in the greatest alarm. In fact, fear seemed to have robbed him of speech. He quickly recovered it.

"You dreadful bloody head," he cried, "stop following me and blaming me for a crime I never meant to commit!"

When Don Rochus reached this part of his story, I thought the sun looked very low in the sky. As I had not brought my watch with me, I turned to the narrator and asked him what time it was. This simple question appeared to offend him.

"Noble Don Lope," he said in annoyance, "when a nobleman has the honor to tell you his story and when you interrupt him at the most interesting point to ask the time, you make him think that he is what we call in Spain *pesade,* in other words, boring. I do not believe I can be accused of that and secure in this conviction I shall continue my story."

When I saw that the man mistook me for a bloody head I put on the requisite fearsome expression or, to use a local expression, I made a horrible face. Unable to bear the sight of that terrible countenance, the man jumped out of bed and ran from the room. However, he had not been alone in that bed: a young woman woke, stretched two round arms out of the covers and curved them over her head the way one does when one wakes from a sound sleep. The young lady caught sight of me but she did not seem to be surprised by this apparition. Getting up, she locked the door through which her husband had fled, then, by signs, made me understand that I could come in. My ladder was somewhat short, but I helped myself by holding on one of the fancy scrolls on the wall; I then put my foot on it and leapt into the room. When she saw me at close quarters the lady apparently realized her mistake and I understood that I was not the man she had expected. However, she asked me to sit down, went off to put on a dress, and returning, sat down a few feet away from me.

"Sir," she said, "I was expecting a relative who sometimes comes to talk over family matters with me and you can imagine that he does not come by way of the window without good reason. As for you, sir, I do not have the honor of knowing you, nor do I know why you choose to call on me at such an unusual hour."

"Madam," I replied, "it was not my purpose to call on you, but only to look in your window to see what went on in this room."

Hoping that she might help me in my enterprise I promptly seized this opportunity to tell the young lady about my inclinations and my activities during my childhood, as well as the relations I had formed with the four young men.

The lady listened attentively. "Sir," she said, "what you have just told me fills me with respect for you. You are quite right; there is nothing pleasanter in the world than to learn what other people are doing, and on this point I share your views. I cannot let you stay here any longer, but we shall see each other again."

"Madam, before you woke, your husband did my head the honor to mistake it for a horrible, bloody head that had come to reproach him for an unwanted crime. Be so kind as to tell me more of the details."

"I approve of your curiosity. Come to the municipal park tomorrow; for this evening, good-bye."

The lady very courteously accompanied me to the window. I climbed down the ladder, joined my comrades and told them what had happened. The next day punctually at five o'clock I went to the municipal park.

When Busqueros had come to this place in his story I looked at the sun and saw that the lowest part of the disk had almost touched the horizon. I therefore turned to Busqueros and said to him most humbly:

"Noble sir, I assure you that a matter of greatest importance obliges me to leave you. It will not be difficult for you to take up the thread of your story again the next time you do me the honor of dining with me."

Busqueros looked very grave. "Don Lope Soarez," he said, "it is plain to me that you are trying to insult me. If this is so, you would do better to tell me frankly that you think me an impudent gossip and a great bore. But no, noble Don Lope, I cannot believe that you think that of me and I shall take up the thread of my story again . . ."

I met the lady in question in the municipal garden, with her friend, a tall, well-built girl who might have been the same age as herself. We sat down on a bench and as the lady wanted me to know her better she began to tell me the story of her life.

THE STORY OF FRASQUETA SALERO

I am the oldest daughter of a brave officer, who arranged that, on his death, his full pay should revert as a pension to his widow. My mother, who was born in Salamanca, retired there with my sister, Dorothea, and me, whom they called Frasqueta. The house she owned was in a very lonely quarter, but she had it renovated; we moved in and lived very simply as became the modest appearance of the house. My mother did not allow us to go to the theatre or to bullfights. She herself paid visits and received callers, but as I had no other pleasure I stood at the window almost all day long.

As I am naturally inclined to be extremely curious, I followed every well-dressed passer-by with my eyes, looking at him in such a way that he must have been convinced he had made a good impression on me. Nor were those passers-by insensitive to the impression they made on me; many of them bowed to me, others came back frequently to our street just to see me again. When my mother discovered my little dodge, she did not fail to say to me:

"Frasqueta, Frasqueta, what are you doing? Be modest and serious like your sister or you will never get a husband."

My mother was mistaken, for my sister is still unmarried and I have been married for over a year. Our street was very lonely and I seldom had a chance to see a man whose appearance deserved my attention. One circumstance, however, was in my favor. Not far from our window was a large tree and beneath it a stone bench where anyone could sit without arousing suspicion or being seen. One day a very elegantly dressed young man sat down on the bench, took a book out of his pocket and began to read. However, as soon as he caught sight of me he lost interest in his reading and never took his eyes from mine. The next day the young man came back again.

Once he came close to my window, pretending he was looking for something. "Did you drop something, Señorita?" he asked.

I said I had not.

"Too bad," he said. "If, for example, you had dropped the little cross you wear around your neck, I would have picked it up. And if I had something that belonged to you, I could imagine that you are not altogether indifferent to me or that you have marked me out from all the others who come to sit on this bench. The feeling you inspire in me deserves perhaps . . ."

At that moment my mother entered the room and I could not answer the young man, but I quickly unfastened my cross and tossed it out on the street.

Late that afternoon I saw two ladies coming along the street followed by a footman in handsome livery. They sat down on the bench and flung back their mantillas. Then one of them pulled a crumpled paper from her pocket, unfolded it and took out a little gold cross; at the same time giving me a mocking glance. I was convinced that the young man had given this first token of my affection to this lady and I was so furious that I could not shut an eye all night. The next day my faithless suitor sat on the bench again and I was very surprised to see him take a crumpled piece of paper out of his pocket, unfold it, take out my cross and kiss it passionately.

That evening two footmen in the same livery as yesterday brought a table and proceeded to set it. Then they went away and returned with ices, chocolate, orangeade, cakes and similar confections. Soon the two ladies of the day before appeared. They sat down on the bench and began to eat.

My mother and my sister, who never stand at the window, could not control themselves at the sound of clinking glasses and bottles. One of the ladies noticed them and, finding their appearance attractive, invited them to share their meal and to bring a chair with them. My mother accepted with alacrity. We put on a little more jewelry and went out to keep the ladies company. As I approached the lady who had invited us, I noticed that she bore a strong resemblance to my young man. I imagined she might be his sister and I decided that he had told her about me and had given her my cross the evening before and that she had come here to look me over.

Soon we noticed that there were not enough spoons and my sister went to fetch some of ours. Then we noticed that napkins were lacking. My mother told me to go and get some, but the lady motioned to me and I replied that I could never find them, whereupon my mother went to get the napkins. No sooner had she gone than I said to the lady:

"It seems to me, Señora, that you have a brother who looks very like you."

"No, Señorita," I was told, "I am the brother of whom

you speak. But I have a brother, the Duke de San-Lugar and I myself will soon be the Duke d'Arcos because I shall marry the heiress of that name. It is true that I detest my future wife, but if I were to refuse to marry her there would be ghastly scenes and I do not like scenes. As I cannot follow my desire and am not free to marry as I choose, I have decided to at least keep my heart for a girl who is more adorable than the young Arcos. Far be it from me to speak of matters that touch your honor closely; but as you remain in Spain and I shall too, chance could bring us together. Should it not, then I myself will make an opportunity to see you again. Your mother will soon come back. Here is a ring with a very valuable solitaire. I have chosen such a costly one to prove to you that what I have told you about my background is not empty talk. I implore you to accept this memento which will remind you of me."

I had been brought up very strictly by my mother and I knew very well that the proper thing was for me to return this gift. But certain considerations, which I no longer recall, impelled me to accept it. My mother came back with napkins, my sister with spoons. The strange lady was very charming all evening and when we parted we were all extremely pleased. However, the charming young man did not appear beneath my window again. No doubt he married the Arcos heiress.

The next Sunday it occurred to me that sooner or later someone would discover the ring. Therefore, while I was in church, I pretended to find it at my feet and I showed it to my mother. She thought it was only a piece of glass though it had a beautiful setting. Near us lived a jeweler to whom my mother showed the ring which he appraised at eight thousand pistoles. My mother was delighted. She thought the proper thing would be to sacrifice it to Saint Anthony of Padua, the patron saint of our family. Should they sell the ring, however, it would bring a handsome dowry for my sister and me.

"Excuse me, Mamma," I said, "I think it only right to let it be known that we have found the ring and not to mention its value. If the real owner turns up, we will return his ring but should he not, my sister has not the slightest right to it. Nor does Saint Anthony of Padua for unquestionably the ring belongs to the person who found it."

My mother did not know what to answer. We let it be known in Salamanca that we had found a ring but kept its value secret and as you correctly surmise no one came to claim it.

The young man to whom I owed this valuable present had made such a deep impression on my heart that no one saw me at the window for eight whole days; then however my curiosity won out, I went to the window as always and spent all my time there.

The stone bench on which the young Duke had sat was now occupied only by a fat gentleman who seemed to have a very calm and thoughtful temperament. He noticed me at the window but my presence obviously annoyed him for he turned his back on me. It was plain, however, that I disturbed him even when he did not see me, for he kept turning around restlessly from time to time. Soon he went away, still glaring at me with obvious annoyance. The next day, however, he came again and repeated the same scene. Finally he turned around so often that, two months later he asked me to marry him. My mother said it was not easy to find a good match every day and commanded me to accept him. So I changed the name of Frasqueta Salero for that of Francesca Cabronez and lived in the house you saw yesterday. When I became the wife of Don Cabronez I concentrated all my thoughts and actions on making him happy. In this I succeeded only too well for after three months I found him looking happier than I liked, and what was even more annoying, he fancied he was making me completely happy too. This expression of utter self-satisfaction was not becoming to him; it displeased me more every day and made me more and more impatient. Fortunately this state of bliss did not last long.

One morning as Don Cabronez was going out of the house he saw a young boy, holding a letter in his hand and looking very embarrassed. Taking the letter from the boy he noticed that it was addressed to "The Adorable Frasqueta." Cabronez looked so furious that the little messenger fled in fright. Cabronez then took the valuable document with him and read the following:

If my wealth, my name are not known to you, I am ready to do anything, to give anything, to undertake anything, if only you will notice me. Those friends who offered to help me have undoubtedly betrayed me as I have not had any sign from you. But I am bold and nothing can stop me when it comes to declaring a passion that, from the first, has known no restraint.

Count de Penna-Flor

On reading this letter, all the happiness Cabronez had known vanished. He became restless, suspicious and no longer permitted me to go out except when accompanied by a neighbor about whom he knew little but whom he admired for her great piety. Cabronez did not care to mention his anxiety to me for he did not know how involved I was with the Count de Penna-Flor nor even whether I was aware of his love. But a thousand incidents increased the poor man's unrest. Once he found a ladder leaning against the garden wall; another time a stranger had apparently hidden in the house. Moreover, we frequently heard serenades, a music all jealous husbands detest. At last the Count de Penna-Flor's temerity exceeded all bounds. One day when I was walking with my pious neighbor along a path in the Prado where we were almost alone, the Count approached and declared his love for me. He was determined, he said, to dare all to capture my heart. The foolhardy man seized my hand forcibly and I do not know what he would have done had we not broken into loud cries.

We went home in a terrible state of confusion. The pious neighbor told my husband she would not go out with me again. It was too bad, she said, that I had no brother to put the fear of God into the Count as my husband was so unsuccessful in making me respected. Religion, she added, forbade revenge, but the honor of a loving and faithful wife deserved more protection, and it was plain that the Count de Penna-Flor had dared to go so far only because he was aware of Cabronez' weak nature.

The following night as my husband was coming home along a narrow street he habitually used, he saw two men blocking his path. One of the men was furiously stabbing a long dagger into a wall while the other man cried: "Bravo, Don Ramiro, if you use these tactics on the notorious Count de Penna-Flor, he will not be the terror of brothers and husbands much longer."

"My dear friend," said the man with the big dagger, "I am not interested in putting an end to the Count de Penna-Flor's luck in love, nor do I want to kill him, but only to give him a good lesson that will keep him from coming back again. It is no accident that Ramiro Carmanza is counted the best swordsman in Spain; only the consequences of a duel are holding me back. If I had a hundred doubloons I would take refuge in the Canary Islands for a while."

The two friends were about to move away when my husband, who had hidden in a porch, addressed them. "Gentlemen," he said, "I am one of the husbands whose peace the Count de Penna-Flor is disturbing. Had it been your intention to kill him, I would not have intervened, but as you merely wish to teach him a lesson I shall be delighted to offer you the hundred doubloons you need to go to the islands. Stay here, and I will fetch the money."

He went home and returned with the hundred doubloons which he handed over to the terrible Caramanza. The next night we heard a peremptory knock on the door and an *alcalde* with two *alguaciles* appeared. The officer said to my husband:

"Out of consideration for you we have come at night, so that our presence here will not reflect on you in any way. We are here to question you about the Count de Penna-Flor who was murdered yesterday. A letter that apparently fell out of the pocket of one of the murderers led us to suspect that you gave them one hundred doubloons to encourage them in this crime and to facilitate their flight."

With unusual presence of mind my husband replied:

"I have never seen the Count de Penna-Flor. Yesterday two men I know presented me with a draft for one hundred doubloons which I had drawn last year in Madrid, and I paid the sum. If you wish I will fetch the bill."

The law officer pulled a piece of paper from his pocket and said: "Here it says: 'We are going to the islands with the hundred doubloons from good old Cabronez.' "

"Right!" said my husband. "Those are the hundred doubloons from the draft. It was due and I did not have the right to postpone payment."

"I am from the criminal court," replied the law officer "and business matters are not in my department. Good-bye, Señor Cabronez. Pardon us for troubling you."

When the danger was partially over I asked my dear Cabronez whether it was true that he had really had the Count murdered. At first he would not answer, but finally he admitted that he had given the swordsman Caramanza one hundred doubloons, not to kill the Count, but to teach him to give up his wild ways.

"My dear Frasqueta," he added, "although I most certainly did not desire this murder, it weighs on my conscience. It horrifies me and if I were a believer I would immediately go to Saint James of Compostella and perhaps even farther, to seek and obtain indulgence."

My husband's admission was the prelude to the strangest of incidents. Each night brought new and more frightful visions that only added to the confusion of an already tormented conscience—visions that almost always were concerned with the hundred doubloons. Sometimes we heard a voice in the dark saying: "I will pay you back the hundred doubloons." At other times we heard how the money would be paid.

One evening, one of the maids saw in the corner a dish filled with doubloons. She started to pick it up , but grasped only dry leaves and brought them to us in the dish. The next day Don Cabronez was absent-minded, pensive and worried. In the evening as he was passing through a room that was faintly illumined by moonlight, he thought he saw a platter with a human head on it and he hurried to me in a terrible state to tell me about it. I went into the room and I saw the wig-block that had been accidentally left in his shaving-basin. I did not like to contradict my husband; indeed, I was even eager to nourish his fear. I therefore gave a loud shriek and insisted that I had seen a horrible head covered with blood. After that the same head was seen by almost all the servants. Cabronez took it so much to heart that we even feared for his sanity. There was, however, as I must tell you, nothing at all to these visions. Count de Penna-Flor was only an ideal, an imaginary being, invented to worry my husband and to rob him of his contentment. The law officers and the bullies were servants of the Duke d'Arcos, for this charming gentleman had returned to Salamanca immediately after his marriage.

During this past night I had intended to give my husband a real fright, get him out of the bedroom and send him to his study where he has holy water and several pictures of saints. I then planned to lock the bedroom door for the Duke expected to come to me through the window. There was no danger of my husband seeing the Duke as he climbed up or of his finding the ladder, for the house is carefully locked every night and I keep the key under my pillow. Then, all of a sudden your head appeared at the window, my husband thought it was the head of Penna-Flor, who had come to accuse him of the hundred doubloons.

Now I must tell you about this very pious, very model neighbor in whom my husband put so much trust. This lady was the Duke himself and it is he whom you see sitting here beside me. Don't you think women's clothes are becoming to him? I am still faithful to my obligations, but I cannot make up my mind to send that lovable Duke away as I am not sure that I will always be so virtuous, and if I decide to take the step, I should like to have Arcos at hand.

When Frasqueta ended her story, the Duke d'Arcos then said to me:

"The reason we have confided in you is because we want you to help us hasten the good Carbronez' journey. We even hope he will not go on an ordinary pilgrimage, but that he will decide to do penance in a monastery. To bring this about, we need your creative mind."

When Busqueros came to this part of his story I noticed that the sun's disk was now really touching the horizon and this story of Frasqueta which commenced with her birth was beginning to get on my nerves. I therefore interrupted the narrator and urged him to postpone the rest of the story till the next day. Busqueros answered with his usual impertinence. At that I lost my temper.

"Outrageous Busqueros!" I cried. "Very well then, either take my life which you are poisoning for me anyway, or defend your own." At the same time I drew my sword and forced him to do the same. To begin with I swung my sword around in a circle, which seemed to astonish my opponent. But then he made some sort of a feint and ran me through the arm. The tip of his sword even touched my shoulder and in a trice I was covered with blood. But worst of all—and this was enough to drive me mad—I missed my rendezvous and could not learn what Inez had intended to tell me.

When the gypsy came to this part of his story, he was called away on a matter concerning the tribe. After he had gone, Velasquez said sadly:

"I foresaw that the gypsy leader's stories would develop one out of the other. Frasqueta Salero told her story to Busqueros, Busqueros told it to Lope Soarez, who told it to the gypsy. I only hope he will finally tell us what happened to the beautiful Inez. If he begins again with a new story I shall be as angry with him as he himself was with Busqueros. But I do not think our narrator will return to us today."

And in truth the gypsy did not appear again and soon we all went to our rest.

The thirty-sixth day

Later on, as we started out on our journey, the Wandering Jew joined us and took up his story again.

CONTINUATION OF THE STORY OF THE WANDERING JEW

The teachings of the learned Cheremon were far more comprehensive than the brief outline I have given you. They all rested on the fact that in his works a prophet named Bytis had proved the existence of God and the angels and that another prophet named Thot had veiled Bytis's ideas in an extremely involved metaphysics through which they appeared to have gained greater sublimity. In this theology God, who was called the Father, was praised only through silence. When, however, they wanted to show that He was sufficient unto Himself, they said, He is His own father, He is His own son. When He was thought of as the son, He was called God's power of understanding or Thot which, in Egyptian, means persuasion. And, finally when they thought they perceived spirit and matter in Nature, the spirit was considered an emanation of God and He was depicted as floating over the slime, as I have already said. The discoverer of this metaphysic was called Thrice Great. Plato, who spent eighteen years in Egypt, brought the doctrine of the Word to the Greeks and thereby earned the surname of the Divine. Cheremon contended that all this did not quite measure up to the original Egyptian religion which had changed as all religions must. His opinion was soon vindicated by an incident in the synagogue at Alexandria. I was not the only Jew who studied Egyptian theology; others too had formed a liking for it. They were particularly attracted by the spirit of mystery that prevails throughout all Egyptian literature and that probably had its origin in the Egyptian command not to cling to the symbol but to seek the hidden meaning.

Our rabbis in Alexandria also wanted to have their secrets; they liked to assume that Moses's writings, though they presented a factual account, were written with such divine art that in addition to the historical there was an allegorical and a hidden meaning in them. Many of our scholars have extracted this hidden meaning with a subtlety that to this day has brought them great honor; but among all the rabbis none was so outstanding as Philo. A prolonged study of Plato had schooled him in cloaking false ideas in the obscurities of metaphysics with the result that he was called the Plato of the synagogue.

Philo's first work treated of the creation of the world, but above all of the peculiarities of the number seven. In this work God is called the Father, which corresponds to the Egyptian theology, but not to the style of the Bible. Here we read that the story of the serpent is an allegory of passion and the creation of woman out of man's rib is likewise allegorical.

This same Philo wrote a book on dreams in which he said

that God had two temples: one of the temples was the world and the high priests of this temple were the Word of God; the other temple was the pure and rational soul and man its high priest. In his book on dreams, Philo expresses himself even more in the vein of the Egyptian when he says:

"He, whom our holy scriptures call The Being or He Who Is, He is the Father of all; from both sides he is defined by the oldest and most immovable powers of the highest entity; the Creative Power and the Ruling Power. The one is called God and the other Master, in such a way that the highest entity which is inseparable from its two powers, appears now as single, now as threefold: as indivisible when the completely purified soul rises above all numbers, even above dualism which is so close to unity, and arrives at the abstract, sublime and simple idea; the highest manifestation of the soul that is not yet initiated into the mysteries, appears as threefold."

This Philo, who thus practiced Platonism to the destruction of true insight and reason, is the same man who was later sent to Emperor Claudius. He enjoyed a great reputation in Alexandria; the beauty of his style and the love all men feel for something new led to almost all Greek Jews accepting his interpretations—and from then on they were Jews in name only. For them the books of Moses were now merely a sort of rough draft in which they could scribble their allegories and mysteries at will, above all the mystery of the Trinity.

At that time the Essenes had already developed their wonderful community; they had no wives and their possessions were shared by all. At length new religions began springing up everywhere, mixtures of Hebrewism and magic, of Sabaism and Platonism and above all a great deal of astrology. And meanwhile all around us the old religions were dying.

By the time the Wandering Jew came to this part in his narrative, we had almost reached the camp and the unfortunate wanderer left us to disappear among the hills. As the gypsy leader had a little free time, he went on with his story that evening.

CONTINUATION OF THE STORY OF PANDESOWNA

After young Soarez had told the story of his duel with Busqueros, he was overcome with sleep and I left him to rest. But the next day when I asked him about his further adventures, he continued his story as follows:

CONTINUATION OF THE STORY OF LOPE SOAREZ

After Busqueros had wounded me in the arm he declared that he was delighted to have found another reason to prove his devotion to me. He slit my shirt, wrapped up my arm, covered me with a cloak and took me to a physician. The latter put the first bandage on my wound, then I sent for my carriage and drove home. Busqueros ordered a bed set up in my entrance hall. I would gladly have objected, but I was completely discouraged.

The next day I had fever, as is usual with a wound. Busqueros was constantly at my side and did not leave me even on the following day. On the fourth day I got out of bed and carried my arm in a sling.

On the fifth day the man who led me to Señora d'Avoloz brought me a letter which Busqueros promptly seized and read aloud:

Inez Moro to Lope Soarez

I am told that you have fought a duel and have been wounded in the arm; the man who was to bring you to my window saw you from a distance. Since then he has inquired for you daily and I hear that you have recovered. We must now summon all our courage and act boldly. I want my father to discover you at my window. The plan is rash, but my Aunt Avoloz will protect us. Trust yourself to the man who brings you this letter.

"Noble Don Lope," that disgusting Busqueros then said, "you cannot get on without me now, for at least you must admit that an adventure of this sort is right in my field. I have always thought it was your good fortune to have me for a friend, but on this occasion you are to be specially congratulated. By Saint Rochus, my patron saint, if you had only let me tell you the story of Frasqueta Salero and what I did for her and her lover; but instead you rudely had to interrupt me. I have no regrets about what followed, for the sword thrust I gave you furnished me with an opportunity to prove my devotion.

"For the present, noble Don Lope, I ask nothing but a single favor in return for all I have done so far for you. What I ask of you, noble Don Lope, is that you do not worry about anything, not the slightest question, not the lightest word. Let come what may, noble Don Lope, let come what may!"

After this speech Busqueros went into the next room with Señorita Moro's trusted servant where they held a long conversation. Busqueros came back alone holding in his hand a sort of diagram on which the rio Augustino was drawn.

"Here," he said to me, "is the end of the street that leads to the Dominicans. The man who has just left us will wait there with two other men for whom he vouches. I shall post myself at the opposite end with the élite of my friends who are also your friends, noble Don Lope. No, no, I am wrong. At this point there will be only two of us, but the rest will lurk at this back door to hold off Santa-Maura and his Neapolitans."

I felt that his explanations gave me the right to say a few words and to find out what I myself should be doing all this time, but Busqueros broke in imperiously.

"No questions, noble Don Lope," he cried. "Not a word! This is our business and should you have forgotten it—*I* have not."

The rest of the day Busqueros spent constantly coming and going and he did the same that evening. At one moment he protested that the adjoining house was too brilliantly lighted, at another that there were suspicious-looking people on the street, or the signal they had agreed on had not yet been given. Sometimes he appeared in person, at other times he sent me reports by one of his accomplices. But at last he came to fetch me and I made ready to follow him. You can imagine how my heart was pounding. I was greatly distressed at the thought of disobeying my father, but love was stronger than any other emotion.

In the rio Augustino, Busqueros pointed out the friends he had chosen to stand guard and he gave the password. "If anyone passes by," he said, "my friends will pretend to be quarreling and the passer-by will quickly turn into another street. Now," he added, "here we are and here is the ladder you must climb. You see it is quite solidly placed against the wall. I shall be under this arch playing the guitar and as soon as I get the signal I shall play a *glissando* with the back of my hand. Then you climb up and when you come to the shutters, knock three times."

Who will believe that, in spite of all these preparations, Busqueros had made a mistake in the window and even in the house? But that is just what happened and I shall now tell you what followed.

Though my right arm was in a sling, I climbed smartly up the ladder, helping myself with one arm, when I heard the signal from the guitar. When I reached the top and was ready to knock on the shutters, I found that I could hold on only with my feet. Then I knocked.

A man flung open the shutters with such force that I was struck, thrown off balance and fell down the ladder to the stones below. I broke my wounded arm in two places, one leg that was caught in the ladder was also broken and the other leg sprained. From my neck to my hips I was a mass of black and blue bruises. The man who had opened the shutters, no doubt with the intention of killing me, shouted: "Are you dead?"

I was afraid he wanted to finish me off so I shouted back: "Yes indeed, I am dead."

Whereupon the man asked:

"Is there a Purgatory?"

I was in terrible pain. "Of course there is a Purgatory," I cried, "and I am in it." Then I fainted.

Here I interrupted Soarez and asked him whether there had been a thunderstorm that night.

"Of course," he replied, "it thundered and lightened and that is perhaps why Busqueros mistook the house."

"Ah!" I cried. "Poor noble Don Lope! There can be no doubt about it. The house you climbed into belonged to the Knight of Toledo. We were expecting a visit from the soul of the Knight of Aguilar, who had been killed in a duel. When you knocked on the shutters we thought you were the inhabitant of another world and that is why we were anxious to hear your report about Purgatory."

But Lope Soarez did not hear my words. Exhausted by the long story he had told me, he had fallen into a deep sleep. When day dawned, I roused the sick man's servant and ran off to engage a mule. I rented two and hurried to the Camaldalese monastery where I found the Knight of Toledo praying before the picture of a saint. Kneeling beside him, I put my mouth close to his ear and told him in a few words the story I had heard from Soarez. At first this seemed to have no effect on him, but then I saw the old expression of gaiety come over the knight's face. Leaning towards me, he whispered:

"My dear Avarito, do you think the judge-advocate's wife has remained true to me?"

"Bravo!" I cried. "But let us not make any trouble for these honest recluses. Go on with your prayers as usual; I will inform them that the period of our retreat is over."

When the prior learned that the knight intended to return to the world, he praised his piety and gave us his blessing. As soon as we were out of the monastery the knight completely regained his gay spirits. I told him about Busqueros; he said he knew him, that he was a nobleman who had attached himself to the Duke d'Arcos and that all Madrid considered him an impossible fellow.

When the gypsy had said this, one of his people came to make the daily report. He went off with the man and we did not see him again that day.

The thirty-seventh day

The next day was devoted to rest. Breakfast was more lavish and better prepared than usual and the whole company was on hand to partake of it. The beautiful Jewess appeared to have dressed with greater care than usual. If she was trying to please Duke Velasquez, her efforts were superfluous for it was not her face or her figure that fascinated him. Velasquez saw in Rebecca a woman distinguished by depth of thought and a cultivated mind that was well trained in the exact sciences.

For some time Rebecca had been eager to learn the Duke's opinion of religion. I had long suspected that she was in sympathy with those two beautiful conspirators who were trying to convert us to the faith of the Prophet. She therefore asked the Duke half in earnest, half in jest, whether he had found a special equation to symbolize his religion too. At the reference to religion Velasquez's brow darkened and when he realized that the question had been put half in jest he thought for a while—and the expression on his face was far from pleasant. At last he said:

"Señora, I see what you are getting at. But as you ask me a geometrical question, I shall answer it by reviewing the laws of that illustrious science from the beginning.

"To denote the infinite I write the symbol for infinity and divide it by one. When on the contrary, I want to denote the infinitesimal I write a one and divide it by the symbol for infinity. But these two signs used in calculations give me no notion of what I want to express. The infinite is the starry heavens raised to the infinite power. The infinitesimal is the smallest part of the atom. I can therefore denote the infinite, but I do not understand it.

"If then I can neither understand nor express, indeed scarcely even denote, but at the most, point to the infinite and the infinitesimal from a distance, how then could I express what is at once infinitely large, infinitely wise, infinitely good and the creator of all infinities?

"Here the Church comes to the aid of my geometry. She shows me the presentation of three persons in one, whereby the one still remains one. What objection can I raise to that, which is beyond my power of comprehension? I must surrender.

"Science never leads to disbelief, but instead it is lack of education that lets us relapse into it. An uneducated man who sees a thing daily thinks he already knows it; the true natural scientist moves constantly among puzzles. Though he keeps delving deeper and deeper, he always only half understands them. At length he learns to believe what he does not understand and in so doing he approaches the temple of faith. Newton and Leibnitz were both professing Christians, and even theologians, and both accepted the mystery of numbers although they could not understand it.

"Had they been born in our faith they would also have accepted the second mystery, namely the possibility of a closer tie between man and his Creator. No facts, only a lot of unknown quantities, argue in favor of this theory. But the acceptance of this tie convinces us of the fundamental difference between men and other material beings. On the other hand, if man is really a unique creature on this earth, if we are convinced by proofs that he is indeed different from the whole animal world, then we can more easily accept the tie with God.

"After these considerations let us look for a moment at the perceptive faculty peculiar to animals. The animal will remember, will hesitate, will draw conclusions and will proceed to act. The animal thinks, but by no means with his own thoughts, that is, with a perceptive faculty of a lower order. The animal does not say: I am a thinking being. The abstract is so inaccessible to him that no one has ever seen an animal who had even the slightest idea of numbers. But numbers present the simplest form of the abstract. The magpie does not leave her nest until she is sure there is no one nearby. We put her to the test. Five hunters disappeared into a covert and came out one after the other. The magpie did not leave her nest until she saw the fifth man come out. But when the hunters came by sixes and sevens, the magpie could not count and flew off after the fifth had appeared. From that they concluded that she could count only to five. They were wrong. The magpie had retained a group picture of five men, but she had not counted them. Counting is determining the number of objects. We often see charlatans bring out little ponies who stamp out the number of hearts and diamonds they see on the playing cards. But we do not notice the signs from their master that guide them. Accordingly, animals have not the slightest notion of numbers and this simplest of all abstractions can be taken as the limit of their perceptive faculties.

"Nevertheless, there is no doubt that the perceptive powers of animals often closely resemble ours. The dog easily recognizes the master of the house and differentiates between his friends and strangers; the former he is fond of, the latter he can barely tolerate. He hates men with evil looks, they confuse him, he wriggles around and around, he is restless. When he is caught doing something forbidden, he expects punishment and is ashamed. Pliny tells about several elephants that had once been taught to dance and were seen to repeat the lesson by moonlight.

"We marvel at the intelligence of animals, but it remains limited to particular cases. Animals follow the commands they have given themselves, but avoid everything that causes them pain. Nevertheless, they have no general abstract idea of a good deed nor a separate notion of any definite act. They cannot divide actions into good and bad, for this abstraction is much more complicated than numbers. As it is impossible for them to master the easier action, there is no ground for believing they are capable of the more difficult one. Knowledge is partly the work of man for what in one country is considered good, in another is considered bad. In general, knowledge, or rather conscience, warns against what the process of abstraction has, in one way or another, established as evil. Animals are incapable of grasping such an abstraction; in other words, they have no knowledge, they cannot follow its impulse and they therefore deserve neither the praise nor the punishment which we—for our own good, never for theirs—deal out to them. From this we see that man is unique on earth where everything else has its place in a general system. Only man is able to think his own thoughts, to be abstract and to embrace many attributes within a general concept. By this alone is he capable of acting worthily or ignobly; for the process of generalizing and distinguishing between good and evil has developed a conscience in him.

"But why does man possess characteristics that differentiate him from the animals? Here through analogy we come to the assumption that if everything in the world has a definite purpose, man's conscience was not given him in vain.

"In this way reflection brings us to primordial naturalism, and does not this lead us to the same goal as a revealed religion, in other words, to a future reward or punishment? Whenever ideas are the same, the hypotheses cannot be dissimilar.

"However, demonstration, on which naturalism rests, is often a dangerous weapon that can transform the person who avails himself of it. What virtues has one not tried to discredit with the help of a syllogism, what vices to excuse on a logical basis? Did Divine Providence wish to expose the fate of moral society to this danger, to leave it to the mercy or the destruction of sophistry! Undoubtedly not. Faith, which is founded on habits familiar to us from childhood—on the love of children for their parents, on all the needs of the heart—gives mankind a far firmer foundation than reasoning. To be true we even have doubts about conscience, the most important difference between us and the animals. Skeptics have tried to make a mere game of it, to persuade us that man is no different from the other material and reasoning creatures that people the earth. But in spite of the skeptics man is aware of conscience in himself and the priest tells him at ordination: 'God, the Only One, descends to this altar and is united with you.' Then man remembers that he does not belong to the animal world, communes with himself and discovers his conscience.

"In spite of all this, you will tell me there could be no question here of proving that naturalism and revealed religion lead to the same goal. If you are a Christian you must profess the latter and believe in the miracles of which they tell you. But first we must settle the difference between naturalism and revealed religion.

"For the theologian as for the philosopher, God is the creator of the Christian religion, since everything that happens springs from God's will. The theologian, however, leans heavily on miracles and, as these form an exception in the general laws of Nature, they are not to the taste of the philosopher. The latter, as a natural scientist, believes that God, the Creator, established the Christian religion only through general laws of Nature and thereby did not depart from the already established laws ruling the moral and the material world.

Up to this point the difference is not very great. But the philosopher wishes to differ from the theologian much more decisively. Therefore he says to him:

"Those who have seen miracles with their own eyes, can easily believe in them. The merit of belief belongs to you who were born eighteen centuries later. If belief is a virtue, then you have proved yours sufficiently and it is therefore of no concern whether these miracles actually were performed or whether you learned of them only through hallowed tradition. For when the pattern of faith is the same, the merit must also be the same."

Here the theologian begins to defend himself and speaks to the natural scientist:

"But who revealed the laws of Nature to you? How do you know that miracles, instead of being exceptions, are not expressions of phenomena unknown to you? You cannot boast of really knowing how decisive natural laws are. You have examined refracted rays of light according to the laws of optics, but why do those rays invert when they come in contact with a looking-glass as if they had brushed against a feathered body? Sounds break too; the echo is a kind of mirrored reflection that can be compared with laws pertaining to optics, although they are actually waves, whereas rays seem to be only physical entities. To these questions, however, you know no answers, and that means you do not know anything at all."

The natural scientist has to admit that he knows nothing, but he replies:

"If I am not in a position to explain a miracle, neither have you, Señor Theologian, the right to reject the testimonies of the Church Fathers who admit that the dogmas and mysteries of our faith may already have existed in pre-Christian religions. As, however, they were not made manifest in those religions, you have to come closer to my opinion and admit that one could then also accept the existence of those dogmas even if they were not corroborated by a miracle. My final opinion about the beginning of Christendom," the scientist continued, "is the following: The ancient temples were nothing but slaughter-houses and their gods shameless libertines." But a number of truly educated men had much purer principles, and the sacrifices they offered were not revolting. Greek philosophers described divinity by the word Theos, without mentioning Jupiter or Saturn by name. Then Rome conquered the world and made it a partner in its infamous deeds. The divine Master appeared in Palestine and taught brotherly love, disdain for riches, forgiveness of sins, submission to the will of the Father who is in Heaven. Simple men surrounded him during his earthly life. After his death they joined with other enlightened men who selected from heathenish customs those that could best be combined with the new faith. In the end, the Church Fathers preached from their pulpits brilliant sermons which were much more convincing than anything people had had an opportunity to hear from other platforms. In this way Christendom developed, apparently with the help of human means, from that which had been purest in heathen religions and in the Jewish faith.

"Thus was fulfilled the decree of Divine Providence. The Creator of the world could undoubtedly have written His holy laws in letters of fire in the starry heavens, but He did not do so. In the ancient mysteries He concealed the seeds of the perfect religion just as He hides in the oak the forest that one day will shade our descendants. We ourselves live, without knowing it, among causes whose effects will astonish the world to come. That is why we call God the Divine Providence, for otherwise we could call him the Power Above. In this way the opinion of the philosopher and the opinion of the theologian, like lines known under the name asymptote, can come closer and closer without ever meeting until the distance between them is smaller than any we can imagine, that is, the difference between them will be smaller than any difference that can still be defined, and smaller than the smallest number that can still be estimated. As, however, I am not in a position to define that difference, by what right would I dare to set up my opinion against the conviction of my brother and of the Church? Dare I spread doubt within the faith to which you adhere and which you have accepted as the foundation of your morale? That right I do not have and so I humble myself heart and soul. As I have already said, Newton and Leibnitz were Christians and even theologians; indeed, Leibnitz had long been concerned with the union of churches. As for me, after these great men I should not waste any words on myself, I who only explore theology in the works of creation to find new reasons for worshipping the Creator."

So saying, Velasquez removed his hat, looked very thoughtful, and lapsed into a meditation that one might have thought was ascetic rapture. Rebecca was rather embarrassed but I realized that those women, who wished to weaken our religious principles and persuade us to come over to the faith of the Prophet, would not only find it as difficult with Velasquez as they had with me, but that with him it would be utterly impossible.

The thirty-eighth day

The rest we had enjoyed over the past days had been good for us and now, with fresh courage, we set out on our way. The Wandering Jew had not appeared the day before since, as he was doomed to be constantly moving, he could not tell us his story as long as we ourselves were not on the march. However, we had not been gone a quarter of an hour before he appeared, took his usual place between Velasquez and me and began as follows:

CONTINUATION OF THE STORY OF THE WANDERING JEW

Dellius had grown old and, as he felt his end approaching, he sent for Germanus and me and ordered us to dig in the cellar alongside the door; there we would find a tin box which we should bring to him. We did as he said, found the box and brought it to him. Dellius took a key from his breast, opened the box and said:

"Here are two legal documents, complete with signatures and seals. One of them assures my dear son possession of the finest house in Jerusalem. The other is a draft for three thousand darics with interest and compound interest." Hereupon he told me the whole story of my grandfather Hiskia and my great-uncle Sedekias and added: "This unjust and avaricious man is still alive, which is proof that conscience does not kill. My children, when I am no longer alive, you are to go to Jerusalem; once there, do not make yourselves known before you have a protector, and perhaps it would be better to wait for Sedekias's death which, considering his advanced age, cannot be too far off. During this period of waiting you can live on your five hundred darics. You will find them sewed into this pillowcase I always keep beside me. I can give you only one piece of advice: lead a blameless life and you will find your reward in the serenity a good conscience will bring you in the evening of your life. As for me, I shall die as I have lived—singing. The song I shall now sing will be my swan-song. Homer, who was blind like me, dedicated a hymn to Apollo, the sun he did not see and which I shall not see much longer. I once set this hymn to music. I shall begin to sing it, but truly I fear I shall not reach the end."

Dellius sang the hymn that begins with the words: "Hail to thee, blessed Latona," but when he came to the words: "Delos, if thou desirest my son to choose Thee as his residence . . ." Dellius's voice failed; he slipped down against my shoulder and gave up the ghost.

Germanus and I mourned our old friend a long time, then we set out for Palestine and, on the twelfth day after leaving Alexandria, we arrived in Jerusalem. To be on the safe side we took other names. I called myself Antipas, Germanus gave his name as Glasphyras. At first we stayed in a tavern outside the city gates; when we asked our way to Sedekias's dwelling, we were promptly directed there for his was the finest house in Jerusalem, a real palace, worthy of a king's son. We rented a miserable room from a shoemaker who lived opposite. I seldom went out; Germanus ran about the city and gathered information.

After several days he said to me:

"My friend, I have made a good discovery. The rushing torrent Kedron forms a marvelous pond behind Sedekias's house and there the old man spends every evening in a jasmine arbor. He is there now: I will show you your persecutor."

I followed Germanus and we came to the banks of the torrent opposite a beautiful garden in which I saw an old man asleep. I sat down and studied him carefully. How different his sleep was from Dellius's! Bad dreams seemed to trouble him and cause him to shudder every now and then.

"O Dellius!" I cried. "How right you were to recommend a blameless life!" Germanus agreed with me. We were still thinking about the old man when we noticed something that promptly made us forget our meditations. She was a wondrously beautiful young girl of sixteen or seventeen and she was wearing the most costly jewels. Her neck and legs were wound about with pearls and chains of precious stones; otherwise she wore nothing but a linen tunique interwoven with gold.

"Venus in person!" exclaimed Germanus.

Obeying an involuntary impulse I flung myself down before her. The young beauty noticed us and looked somewhat perturbed; then however she pulled herself together, unfurled a peacock-feather fan and fanned the old man's head to refresh him and prolong his sleep.

Germanus quickly took out a book and pretended to read; and I pretended to be listening to him. But the only thing that held our attention was what went on in the garden.

The old man awoke; several questions he asked the young girl showed us that his eyes were very weak and that he could not see us. That greatly pleased us for we had already made up our minds to come here often.

Sedekias went off leaning on the young girl and we returned to our lodging. As we had nothing better to do, we inveigled our host, the shoemaker, into talking and learned from him that none of Sedekias's sons was alive and that his fortune would fall to the daughter of one of those sons. This girl was named Sara and she was her grandfather's favorite. When we had retired to our room, Germanus said:

"My dear friend, I see a chance to get even with your great uncle—you must marry his granddaughter! But to do that would of course take a lot of cunning."

This idea greatly pleased me; we talked it over a long time and that night I dreamed of it. The next day I went back to the torrent and I also went there the day after that. In short, I could not stay away: I had to see my young cousin, alone or with her grandfather. And though I did not say a word to her the young beauty was well aware that I went there solely on her account.

By the time the Wandering Jew had come to this part of his story, we had arrived at the camp and our luckless vagabond disappeared into the hills.

Rebecca did not pursue the subject of religion, but as she was eager to know more of what she called the Duke's system, she seized on the first opportunity to ply him with questions.

"Señora," said Velasquez, "we are like blind men who recognize the end of a certain street by touching the houses they pass, but whom, for that reason, we dare not ask to give us the plan of the city. However since you urge me, I shall try to give you an idea of what you call my system, but what I myself consider merely a definite method of speculation.

"Everything our eye embraces, not only in this valley here, but in all of Nature, everything our senses can perceive, can be divided into dead matter and organic matter. Organic matter differs from dead matter in that it possesses organs, but in a deeper sense the former is contained in the latter, for it is composed of the same elements. Thus we could find in these rocks or in this plot of grass the same elements out of which you, Señora, are made. You have chalk in your bones, flint in your body, alkali in your bile, iron in your blood, salt in your tears. Your muscles are a mixture of combustible stuff and a certain element of air. Were you to be put in a chemical retort, Señora, you could be changed into the same material that goes into a decanter. But were we to add metallic lime, the resulting material would make an excellent telescope.

"You draw a fascinating picture of me, your Highness," said Rebecca. "Please go on."

Velasquez thought he must have paid the beautiful Jewess a compliment—though he really did not know when. He took off his hat with a flourish and continued his explanation.

"In the elements of lifeless matter we find an irresistible impulse, if not to the organic, at least to a combination. The elements join and separate again to connect with other elements. They take on definite shapes and one could think they were made for an organic existence. But they cannot of themselves become organic and without the life-giving spark they are unable to merge with any combination whose final product is life.

"We become aware of life, like an electric current, only in the manifestation of its results. The first of these manifestations of life is the checking of inner decay in the organic body, that is, of the decomposition that first sets in after life has left the organic body. Life may be preserved a long time in a liquid, as for example, in egg, or even in a solid matter, and can develop only under favorable conditions. Life circulates through all parts of the body, even in a fluid like blood, that deteriorates when removed from our veins. It is in the blood vessels of the stomach and protects them from the action of the gastric juices which dissolves the dead substances that enter the stomach. It even remains for some time in limbs that have been severed from the body. But above all, life makes use of its creative qualities and this process which we call the secret of conception is as incomprehensible as almost everything else in Nature.

"Organic beings are divided into two great classes. The first is more easily combustible and produces solid alkalis; the second is rich in fluid alkalis. Plants are included in the first, animals in the second.

"There are animals that, according to their organic structure, seem to be lower than many plants, as for instance, the mollusks in the sea or the coenure that bores into the sheep's brain. There are other animals of a much higher organism in which it is impossible to recognize clearly the thing we call the will. When, for example, the coral opens its feelers to swallow the tiny creatures on which it feeds, we think this movement is the result of its organic action just as we see flowers that close at night and turn to the sun by day.

"We may compare the will of a polyp, that stretches out its tentacles, to the will of a newborn babe, that already wants something though it still does not think. With children desire comes before thought and is the direct result of need or pain.

"In fact, a part of our body that is pinched immediately recovers its normal shape. The stomach often rebels against the food we expect it to digest. When we see a favorite dish the saliva begins to flow so that it is often difficult for us to control ourselves. Notice a man who has not eaten or drunk for a long time and lies there with cramped limbs. In a word, a man who has not performed an organic function for some time and we discover that various parts of his body urge various desires on him.

"In a fully developed polyp we can already see the desire that springs directly from need. It is the first pledge of a higher will that has developed according to the mandates of the organism. With newborn babes, as we have said, desire precedes thought, but the distance between is slight, for even thought has its primary elements of which I shall speak another time."

When Velasquez had developed his theories to this point, he was interrupted. Rebecca told the Duke how pleased she had been to listen to him, and the rest of the lecture—which had also interested me—was postponed till the next day.

The thirty-ninth day

Soon after we set out on our journey the Wandering Jew joined us and resumed the thread of his story.

CONTINUATION OF THE STORY OF THE WANDERING JEW

While I was absorbed in the beautiful Sara, Germanus, who was not so interested in her, spent several days listening to the teachings of a master named Joshua who later became so famous under the name of Jesus; for Jesus in Greek is the same as Jehosophat in Hebrew as one can learn from the version of the Septuaginta. Germanus even wanted to follow his teacher to Galilee; but the thought that he might be helpful to me, kept him in Jerusalem.

One evening Sara took off her veil and was about to fasten it on the branches of a pine tree when the wind seized the light gossamer, whirled it here and there and then blew it towards the Kedron. I leapt into the rushing torrent, seized the veil and tied it to a branch beneath the terrace. Unfastening a gold chain from her neck Sara flung it to me. I kissed it and swam back through the torrent.

The disturbance had roused old Sedekias. He wanted to know what had happened; and Sara told him. He thought he was standing near a balustrade, but was actually standing on a rock so thickly surrounded by bushes that any idea of putting up a balustrade had been abandoned. The old man's foot slipped, the bushes gave way—and he rolled into the water. I sprang in after him, managed to reach him and brought him to the bank. This was all the work of a moment.

Sedekias recovered consciousness, discovered that he was lying in my arms and realized that he had me to thank for his life. He asked who I was; I replied that I was a Jew from Alexandria, named Antipas, and as I had neither parents nor property I had come to Jerusalem to make my fortune.

"I will be a father to you," said Sedekias. "You will live here with me."

I accepted the invitation without mentioning Germanus, who did not find anything wrong with that and went on living at the shoemaker's. Thus I was settled in my archenemy's house and day by day I rose in the respect of a man who would have had me murdered had he known that I was the legitimate heir to the bulk of his fortune. And with every day Sara, too, was more pleased to see me.

In those days money-changing was carried on in Jerusalem exactly as it is today throughout all the Orient. If you come to Cairo or Bagdad, you will see at the gates of the mosques men squatting on the ground and holding on their knees a little tablet with a groove at one end through which the money that has been counted can roll. Beside the men lie sacks filled with gold and silver with which, when needed, they can serve their customers. Today these money-changers are called "Sarrafs." Your evangelists call them trapezoid men because of the little tablets I mentioned.

Almost all the money-changers in Jerusalem worked for Sedekias who, in agreement with the Roman lease-holders and customs officers forced the rate of exchange up or down as they pleased. I therefore followed the rise and fall of the exchange very closely and I had such success with it that after two months Sedekias never entered into any financial transaction without first asking my advice.

At this time there was a report that Tiberius had ordered a general reform of currency throughout the empire whereby all silver coins would be withdrawn from circulation and melted down to ingots to establish the prince's Crown Treasure. I was not responsible for starting this rumor, but I felt justified in spreading it and you can imagine the effect it had on the money-changers. Even Sedekias did not know what to think of it and could not come to any decision.

I have already said that throughout all the Orient one still sees money-changers before the gates of the mosques. In Jerusalem we sat in the temple itself; it was very spacious, and in the corner we had taken possession of, we did not disturb the worshippers. However for several days we had not seen a single money-changer, for the unrest was general. Sedekias did not ask my opinion, but he seemed to be trying to read it in my eyes. At length I considered silver sufficiently discredited and informed my uncle of my plan: he listened to me attentively and for a time seemed uncertain and thoughtful. Finally he said:

"My dear Antipas, in my cellar I have two million gold sesterces. If your speculations are successful, you may ask for Sara's hand."

The hope of possessing the beautiful Sara and the prospect of money, which is always tempting to a Jew, delighted me so much that the only way I could control myself was to go through the city and bring even further discredit to silver. In this effort Germanus helped me to the best of his ability. I interested several traders who refused to buy silver money. Finally things went so far that the citizens of Jerusalem accepted silver money only with a mixture of disgust and fright. After we thought this feeling had gone far enough, we set out to put our plan in action.

When day dawned I had my entire fortune carried to the Temple in closed bronze receptacles. I announced that Sedekias had to make a payment in silver, and had therefore decided to buy two hundred thousand sesterces and give one ounce in gold for twenty-five ounces of silver. This meant for him a gain of more than one hundred percent. The willingness of the public to profit from this good deal was so great that I had soon changed half of my gold. Our porters were kept so busy carrying our silver out that people took for granted that I had bought twenty-five thousand or thirty thousand sesterces in this way. All went well from there on and I was on the point of doubling Sedekias's fortune when a Pharisee came to us and said . . .

When the Wandering Jew came to this part of his story, he turned to Uzeda and said: "A mightier cabalist than you compels me to leave you."

"Indeed," said the cabalist. "You merely do not want to tell us about the uproar that broke out in the temple and about the beating you were given."

"The old man from the mountains of Lebanon calls me," said the Jew and disappeared from our sight.

I must admit that I was not sorry. I did not want him to come back, for I realized that this man was a swindler who happened to be also an excellent raconteur. Under pretext of telling us his own adventures, he talked of things to which we, as believing Christians, had no business to listen.

In the meantime we came to a resting place and Rebecca again urged the Duke to explain his system. Velasquez thought for a while, then he began with these words:

Yesterday I tried to explain the intrinsic property of the will. I said that will precedes thought. After that we decided to speak of the primordial existence of thought. One of the greatest philosophers of antiquity has shown us the right path to follow in such metaphysical researches. Those who think they have added anything new to his researches have not, in my opinion, made a single step forward. Even long before Aristotle, the expressions "concept" and "idea" meant to the Greeks the same as "picture." Aristotle went to the root of these concepts and recognized that they actually go back to the "picture," that is, to the expression of an impression. In this we see the reason why even genius is incapable of creating anything. Mythologists have added to man's body a horse's rump and to woman's body a fish tail; they robbed Cyclops of one eye and they gave Briarius a hundred arms, but they have not made anything new, for creation is not within the power of man. From Aristotle we took over in general the principle that only what is in our thoughts has first passed through the senses.

But in our day philosophers appeared who considered themselves greater than Aristotle and they said; "We admit that of itself the mind cannot perfect any new faculties without the intervention of the senses, but when once certain faculties have developed in it the mind comprehends abstractions that have no connection with the senses as, for example, space, eternity or mathematical truths. I must confess that I by no means support these new theories. Abstraction seems to me to be dragged in by the hair. If you want to be abstract, you must first subtract. If therefore in my mind, I take everything out of my room, including the air, I have pure space left. If I take away beginning and end from Time, I get the concept of eternity. If I take his body away from a thinking being, I get the concept of angels. If I mentally subtract the width of two lines merely to reflect on their length and their surface, I get the first axiom of Euclid. If I remove a man's eye and add to his height, I get a Cyclopean figure. These are all metaphors produced with the help of the senses. If the new wise men could show me an abstraction that did not refer to a subtraction, I would promptly become their pupil. Until then, however, I shall cling to old Aristotle. The words "concept," "idea" and "picture" are not dependent on the impressions we gain through visual means. A note strikes our ear and gives us the concept that belongs to our sense of hearing. Our teeth grit against each other when we eat a lemon and in this way we get the notion of sourness. Observe, moreover, that an impression can affect our senses even if the actual object is not before our eyes. When we are reminded of biting into a lemon, saliva begins to flow in our mouth and we notice a bitter taste on our tongue. Shrill music rings in our ears a long time after the sound has ended. In the present state of physiology we cannot sufficiently explain our sleep and our dreams, but we can conjecture that, independently of our will, certain movements put our organs in the same condition in which they were during the impression received by the senses, that is, when the idea rose.

It therefore follows that, without going further into the science of physiology, we can consider impressions made on our brain theoretically as concepts—that is, impressions received by the organs whether the object is present or not. Notice also: if we think of an object and do not see it, the impression is less vivid; on the other hand, during fever, the impression can be as strong as the first impression received through the senses.

Animals related to men through their type of organism, who show a certain imaginative faculty, all have—so far as I can judge—an organ which we call the brain. On the other hand among animals related by their organism to plants, this organ is lacking.

Plants live, many of them even move. Among animals there are some which, like plants, cannot move from the spot. I have seen others, and what is more, even marine animals, who always move rhythmically, like our lungs, as if they had no will at all. Animals that are better equipped organically have a will and a certain imaginative faculty, but only man has the power of abstraction.

However, not all men have this power. Impairment of the thyroid gland robs the mountain dweller suffering from goiter of this faculty. Moreover the failure of one or two senses weakens the faculty of abstraction extraordinarily. Deaf-mutes who, through their inability to speak are like animals, have difficulty in grasping abstract ideas. But if you show them five or ten fingers, though this has nothing to do with the fingers themselves, it gives them an idea of counting. They see people praying, bowing—and they get an idea of divinity.

The blind offer fewer difficulties in this respect, for they have the gift of speech, that great instrument of human communication and they also grasp abstract ideas quickly. Moreover, the blind are not distracted by things or people about them and therefore are far more capable of putting two and two together.

Imagine a newborn babe, completely blind and deaf and dumb: you know it is incapable of understanding abstract ideas. The only notions it will be able to grasp are those conveyed through smell, taste and touch. Such a child will even be able to dream of those notions. When he eats something that hurts him, he will, if his memory does not fail him, refuse to eat that particular food the next time. Nevertheless I cannot assume that it would be possible to instill the abstract idea of evil in his mind. He will therefore have no conscience, no knowledge and consequently deserves neither reward nor punishment. Should he, when a grown man, commit murder, no one would have a right to punish him. There are therefore two kinds of spirits, two aspects of the divine breath. But why such a great difference between them, although it is a question only of the lack of two senses?

There is a much smaller, but also much more important difference between an Eskimo, a Hottentot and an educated man. Now what is that difference? It lies not in the lack of one or more senses, but in a different number of ideas and combinations. A man who has seen the whole world through the eyes of a traveller and has absorbed all the important events of history, carries in his head a multitude of pictures that a peasant does not have. If, in addition, the traveler arranges, compares and combines his ideas then we say he had intelligence and knowledge.

It was Newton's habit constantly to combine concepts and among the extraordinarily great wealth of combinations he gathered were also the concept of the falling apple and the concept of the moon bound in its orbit to the earth. From this I have concluded that the difference between the various kinds of understanding depends on the number of pictures an intelligence can grasp and on its ability to combine, or better still, it rests on the relationship between the number of pictures and the ease in combining them one with the other.

Animals with an undifferentiated organism have presumably neither will nor ideas. Like the mimosa, the sensitive plant, their movements are unconscious.

But for all this we can assume that when the freshwater polyp puts out its feelers to swallow a worm and makes a point of swallowing the one that tastes better to him than the others, he has some notion of what good, bad, or better are. But when he has the ability to discard bad worms, then we must assume that he is not lacking in will. His will originates first of all from his need that forces him to stretch out his feelers. Then swallowing the little creature gives him two or three notions and finally, the act of tossing aside one of the worms and swallowing the other signifies a free choice which has arisen out of one or several notions.

If we apply the same reasoning to a child, we shall see that even with him will springs first from need. This will compels the child to put his mouth to his mother's breast and as soon as it has tasted the nourishment, the idea is already present. His senses receive other impressions too and in this way the child becomes the possessor of one, two, three or more ideas. Hence one can count ideas exactly as one can combine them. That is why calculation or even more the principles of combination, can be used on ideas. We call combination associating ideas and not classifying them. Thus for example AB is the same combination as BA. Two letters can therefore be put together only in one way. Three letters, each taken by twos, can be put together or combined in three ways and in a fourth way if we put all three together. Four letters, each taken by twos, give six combinations, each by threes—four, by fours—one and all combinations together, eleven.

Thus:

5 letters together give	26 combinations
6 letters together give	57 combinations
7 letters together give	120 combinations
8 letters together give	247 combinations
9 letters together give	502 combinations
10 letters together give	1013 combinations
11 letters together give	2036 combinations

We see therefore that each new idea increases the number of combinations by a multiple. Therefore, for example, the combinations of five ideas are to the combination of ten ideas as 26 is to 1013 or as approximately 1 to 39.

It is not my purpose to assess intelligence with the help of these material calculations. I merely wished to point out the general principles of combination by a suitable example. We have seen that the difference between the kinds of intelligence rests on the relationship of the number of ideas and the ease with which they are combined.

According to this we can imagine a scale of all these diverse ways of understanding. Let us put at the top of that scale Isaac Newton, whose perception we shall designate by a hundred million at its lowest end, and an Alpine peasant, whose perception will be designated by a hundred thousand. Between these two figures we can put the infinity of the mean proportional, which those ways of understanding that are higher than the peasant's, but lower than the brilliant Newton's would indicate.

Within this scale my understanding and yours too, Madam, would also lie. Now only the method of understanding that stands at the top, has the possibility of adding new discoveries to Newton's discoveries, of grasping them and at least partially understanding them and of mastering the art of combining them.

In the same way we can represent the descending scale. It would begin with the peasant's hundred thousand we noted, then pass on to the ways of perception that are designated by twenty-six, eleven, five; then come to beings who have at their disposal four concepts and eleven combinations and end with those beings who have only three ideas and four combinations.

The child that has four ideas and eleven combinations is not yet in a position to think abstract thoughts. But between this number and one hundred thousand a perception can appear in which a certain number of ideas are put together in such combinations that abstract ideas could result.

Few animals or deaf and blind children ever attain this composite perception; the former for lack of impressions, the latter for lack of combinations. The idea of numbers is the simplest of all abstract ideas. It is based on separating things from their numerical attributes. As long as a child does not grasp this idea it is not yet capable of thinking abstract ideas, but merely has the ability to subtract by analyzing possession—which moreover also leads to a kind of abstract idea. The child comes to it slowly and only after it has completed the first abstraction does it progress to a combination of ideas.

The list of idea-forming forces, from the smallest to the largest, is therefore always composed of units of the same kind, that is, of homogeneous values which are arranged according to the number of ideas and the corresponding number of combinations. The elements are always the same. Therefore one can describe the various idea-forming forces —even when they are of different grades—as belonging to one and the same kind. Just as calculation that is completely erroneous is nothing but a row of additions and subtractions and the same can be said of any mathematical problem.

Velasquez added a few more comparisons of this sort but as Rebecca had apparently already grasped his thesis they separated, both of them well pleased.

The fortieth day

I awoke early and, stepping out in front of the tent to cool off in the fresh morning air, I found that Velasquez and Rebecca had had the same idea. We turned our steps towards the highroad to see whether any travelers were passing. When we came to a gully that wandered between two rocks, we decided to rest. Soon we saw a caravan approaching the gully as if it would pass fifty feet below the rocks on which we were sitting. The nearer the travelers came, the greater our curiosity grew. The procession was headed by four Indians whose only garment was a long lace-trimmed shirt. On their heads they wore straw hats bedecked with feather brushes, and all four were armed with long muskets. After them trotted a herd of llamas with a monkey riding on the back of each animal. They were followed by a well-armed group of Negroes mounted on excellent horses and behind them rode two elderly gentlemen on magnificent Andalusian steeds. The two gentlemen were wrapped in white velvet cloaks on which, even at a distance, the Calatrava Cross was visible. They were followed by eight Malaysians carrying a Chinese palanquin in which sat a young woman wearing a rich Spanish gown. A young man galloped his proud horse gaily beside her. Then we saw a young girl lying unconscious on a stretcher, while beside her on a mule rode a priest, sprinkling her face with holy water and obviously exorcising evil spirits. At the end of the procession marched men of all colors, from the black of ebony to skins of olive. Only white was missing.

As long as the caravan was passing by we did not have time to wonder who these men were, but when they had passed, Rebecca said:

"It would cetrainly be interesting to learn who these people are!"

As Rebecca made this remark, I caught sight of a man who belonged to the caravan but had lingered behind. I decided to climb down the rock and run after the tardy fellow. The latter, trembling in every limb, fell on his knees before me and stammered:

"O good bandit, have pity and do not kill a nobleman who, though born in the midst of gold mines, has not a single farthing with him."

I told him I was no bandit, that I only wanted to know the names of the distinguished persons who had just passed by.

"If that is all you want," said the American getting to his feet, "I shall gladly satisfy your curiosity. But let us climb up on these high rocks from where we can overlook the whole caravan. Do you see, Señor, those strangely dressed people at the head of the procession? They are mountain folk from Cuzco and Quito and guardians of the fine llamas my lord wishes to present to the most glorious King of Spain and the Indies.

"The Negroes are slaves of my lord, that is, they were; for Spain tolerates neither slavery nor lack of freedom and from the moment the Negroes stepped on Spanish soil, they have enjoyed the same freedom as you and I. The gentleman of advanced age whom you see on the right, Señor, is Count de Penna-Velez, brother-in-law of the famous Viceroy of the same name and a grandee of the first rank. The gentleman beside him, who is older, is the Marquis de Torres-Rovellas, son of the Marquis de Torres and the husband of the last heiress of the Rovellas family. The two gentlemen have always been the closest of friends and through the marriage of the only daughter of the Marquis de Torres-Rovellas and young Penna-Velez the friendship is even more closely united.

"You can see the charming couple from here. The young man strokes his prancing horse, the fiancée sits in the palanquin that years ago the King of Borneo presented to the late Viceroy de Penna-Velez. But of the girl, lying on the stretcher, over whom the priest is saying prayers I know as little as you, Señor. Yesterday, with rash curiosity, I went up to a gallows that stood on the side of the highroad. There I found this young girl lying between the corpses of two hanged men and promptly called the rest of the company to show them this strange sight. When the Count, my protector, saw that the girl was still breathing, he ordered her to be brought to our resting place for the night and even decided to wait there a day to nurse her back to health. The young stranger deserves all these attentions, for she is incredibly beautiful. Today they ventured to put her on a stretcher, but every second the poor girl's mind wanders and she faints. The courtier walking behind the stretcher is Don Alvar Massa-Gorda, the First Kitchen Master or actually the Marshal of the Count's Court. Beside him you see the pastry cook Lemada and the confectioner Zurgana."

"I thank you, Señor. You have told me far more than I could have wished to know."

"And last of all," added the man, "there is the man who brings up the end of the procession and who has the honor to talk with you—Don Gonzalez de Hierro-Sangre, a Peruvian nobleman descended from Pizarro and Almagar and heir to their courage."

I thanked the good Peruvian and joined my friends to

whom I related the above information. We returned to the camp and told the gypsy leader we had met his little Lonreto and the daughter of that beautiful Elvira whose place he had once taken. The gypsy said he had known that for some time she had intended to leave America, that she had landed the month before in Cadiz, had left there last week and that she had spent two nights on the banks of the Guadalquiver, nor far from the gallows of the Brothers Zoto, where they had found the young girl between two hanged men. Then he added:

"I don't think there is any connection between this girl and the Gomelez; in any case I know nothing of it."

"What!" I cried in astonishment. "This girl is supposed to be the tool of the Gomelez and yet she is found under the gallows? Have the mad deeds of the spirits of Hell come true?"

"Who knows? Perhaps you are right," replied the gypsy.

"We must manage to detain these travelers for several days," Rebecca decided.

"I have already thought of that," said the gypsy. "This very night I shall have half of their llamas stolen."

The forty-first day

This struck me as a very strange way to detain travelers and I intended to give the leader my opinion about it. But the chief ordered us to strike camp at sunrise and I recognized in the voice with which he gave his command that my advice would be useless. This time we went forward only a short distance to a place where there must have been an earthquake, for we saw a gigantic rock that had been split in half to almost its full height. We ate at noon and after that everyone went to his own tent.

Towards evening, hearing an unusual commotion in the chief's tent, I went there to investigate. Two Americans and the descendant of Pizarro were arguing violently that the chief must give them back the llamas. The chief listened to them patiently but this humility only drove Señor de Hierro-Sangre to shout louder and louder and to call the gypsy names—scoundrel, thief, robber and the like. Suddenly the chief gave a piercing whistle and in a second the tent was filled with armed gypsies. At this unexpected sight, Señor de Hierro-Sangre lowered his voice which now trembled so much that we could scarcely make out his words. When the chief saw that the Peruvian had calmed down, he shook hands with him in a friendly manner and said:

"Forgive me, brave Peruvian. Appearances are against me: I fully understand your justified anger. But first go to the Marquis de Torres-Rovellas and ask him whether he remembers a certain Doña Dalanosa whose nephew, out of sheer courtesy, once decided to become Vicereine of Mexico in the place of Señorita Rovellas. If he has not forgotten him, then please beg him to honor us with his visit."

Don Gonzalez de Hierro-Sangre was delighted that the adventure, which had begun to worry him greatly, had not turned out any worse. He promised to carry out the mission promptly. After he had left, the gypsy said to me:

"In earlier days the Marquis de Torres-Rovellas had a taste for the romantic; so now we shall receive him in a place as romantic as he could desire."

Passing through a crevice in the rocks that was thickly shadowed with bushes on both sides I suddenly saw before me a landscape different from any I had ever seen before and I was greatly affected by the sight. Precipitous rocks with, between them, flower-covered hills, encircled a lake whose waters were deep green and crystal clear. There on all sides where the rocks came down to the water, narrow paths carved in the stone wound their way from hill to hill. In many places the water flowed into caves similar to those that once adorned the isle of Calypso. They were enchanting, mysterious places to which the heat never penetrated and where a refreshing bath lured the wanderer. Deep silence prevailed, evidenced that for a long, long time, no man's foot had trod this ground.

"This," said the chief, "is a little province of my kingdom. Here I have spent several years of my life that were, if not the happiest, at least not the stormiest. But soon the two

Americans will arrive. We must look for a sheltered spot where we shall await them with pleasure."

We then entered the most enchanting of caves and shortly afterward we saw the two old gentlemen approaching.

"Is it possible," said one of the old men, "that after so many years I am to meet again a man who in my youth did me such an important service? Again and again I have asked after you, even sent you news of me, while you were still with the Knight of Toledo, but since then . . ."

"Yes," the old chief broke in, "since then it has been harder to find me, but today now that we are together again, I hope, Señor, that you will do me the honor to spend a few days in this sanctuary. After the fatigue of such a strenuous journey, I think a little rest might be profitable . . ."

"Yes, truly," said the Marquis and added: "This is a devilish region."

"At least it is so considered," replied the gypsy. "At the time of the Arabian rule this region was called 'Afrit hamanik' that is, Devil's Bath; today it is known as La Frita. The inhabitants of the Sierra Morena are afraid even to come near it. At nightfall they tell each other a thousand terrifying tales that are supposed to have happened here—and I saw no reason to disabuse them. I should even like to ask you to leave the greater part of your retinue outside of the valley at the place where I have pitched my camp."

"With the greatest pleasure," replied the Marquis. "But allow me to exclude my daughter and my future son-in-law from this arrangement."

In answer the chief made a low bow and promptly dispatched his men to bring back the Marquis's family and several of his servants.

While the gypsy was showing his guests around the valley, Velasquez picked up a little stone from the ground.

"No doubt," he said, "one could melt this stone in any of our glassworks without adding even a single foreign particle to it. We are in the crater of a volcano that has long been extinct. From the inside of this inverted funnel we can measure its depth and calculate the force that was necessary to extinguish it. This subject is worth deeper reflection."

Velasquez thought for a while, pulled out his tablet and began to scribble on it. Then he said:

"My father had an unusually clear picture of volcanoes. In his opinion the centrifugal force in the center of the volcano is much greater than the power of steam or combustible niter and from that he concluded that men would some day come to know fluids, the results of which would help to explain most of our natural phenomena."

"Do you think, Señor," asked Rebecca, "that this lake was formed by the volcano?"

"Yes," Valesquez replied. "A comparison of this stone and the shape of the lake gives us sufficient proof of that. To judge from the size of the object I see on the opposite shore, the diameter of the lake must be three hundred meters and as the inward slant of the volcanic cone is about seventy degrees, I assume that the center lay at a depth of four hundred and thirteen fathoms. From that it follows that the matter that filled it amounts to seven times thirty-four thousand, three hundred and fifty-five fathoms. But as I have already said we know today that the forces of Nature, no matter how compressed, could not have produced such an action."

Rebecca started to refute this argument but just then the Marquis and his family arrived. This conversation, however, would not have been equally interesting to all, and to cut short Velasquez's mathematical investigation, the gypsy said to his guest:

"When I knew you, Señor, you were as beautiful as an angel and as sensitive as a young girl. Your marriage to Elvira must have been one long incredible rapture. Your life has been a bed of roses without any thorns."

"It is not quite like that," said the Marquis. "To be sure tender emotions have filled perhaps too great a part of my life, but on the other hand as I have never neglected any of the duties a self-respecting man is in duty bound to fulfill, I have no hesitation in admitting my weaknesses. This is an extraordinarily suitable spot for a romantic story; if you wish, I shall tell you the story of my life."

The whole company greeted the Marquis's suggestion with enthusiasm and he began with the following words:

When you entered the Theatine monastery, we were living, as you know, not far from your aunt Dalanosa. My mother often visited her niece Elvira, but she did not take me with her. As Elvira had entered a convent it was not proper for her to receive visits from a young man. We were therefore forced to endure all the torments of separation which, however, we softened as much as possible by writing countless letters. My mother generally forwarded them, though she always protested, for she thought it would not be so easy to get a dispensation in Rome and not until we had received it should we have the privilege of corresponding. However, despite this scruple, she continued to carry letters back and forth . . . As for Elvira's fortune, no one dared to touch it; should she take the veil the fortune would revert to a collateral branch of the Rovellas family.

Your aunt talked to my mother about your uncle, the Theatine friar, describing him as an experienced and sensible man who could give her good advice about a dispensation. My mother thanked your aunt profusely and wrote to Pater Santez. That good man considered this matter so important that he came to Burgos in person accompanied by one of the Nuncio's advisers, the latter under an assumed name to preserve the secrecy which had to surround the whole matter. It was decided that Elvira should remain in the convent for six months as a novice. Should it then appear that she no longer felt the call to become a nun, she should continue to live in the convent as a person of high rank, surrounded by a suitable retinue of ladies who were to share her convent life. In addition she should have, outside of the convent, her own richly furnished house, run by a staff of servants exactly as though she were living in it herself. For my mother, who would soon move into this house, and for several lawyers who had to attend to various details of the guardianship, special rooms had already been prepared. Meanwhile I was to go to Rome with my tutor and the adviser would follow shortly. This last plan could not be realized immediately, for I was considered still too young to apply for a dispensation. Thus two years passed before I left Burgos.

During those two years I saw Elvira only behind a grating. The rest of the time I devoted to writing letters to her or to reading novels from which I generally drew inspiration for my declarations of love. Elvira read the same books and answered my letters in the same spirit. I admit that, in general, our correspondence was noted for many original thoughts, but our sentiments were genuine and a strong attraction bound us. The grating that separated us only served to enflame our love, our blood burned with the fires of youth, in a word, we were both madly in love.

When the time for my departure came, the parting was terrible indeed. Our suffering was very real. Elvira in particular was in a dreadful state—there was even fear for her health. I bore my suffering with greater courage, and all the more so as the distractions of the journey helped in various ways. I also had much to thank my tutor for. There was nothing of the dusty, schoolmasterish pedant about him; on the contrary he was a former officer and had lived for some time at the Spanish Court. His name was Diego Santez and he was closely related to the Theatine monk of the same name.

This man, as keen of mind as he was sophisticated, tried in various ways to lead my thoughts along the paths of truth, but his efforts unfortunately met with little success. On our arrival in Rome, the first thing we did was to call on Monsignor Ricardi, a member of the Rota. He was a proud, dignified man whose imposing presence was enhanced by a large cross of diamonds that sparkled on his breast. Ricardi told us that he was informed about our affairs, that we must keep very quiet and appear in society as little as possible. "However," he added, "you will do well to come to see me frequently. The interest I show in you will call attention to you and the less you are seen in other places, the more that will work to your advantage. I shall consult the Sacred College and hear what they have to say about your affairs."

We followed Ricardi's advice. I spent the forenoons visiting Roman antiquities and in the evening went to the Monsignor's villa which was near the Barberini villa. The Marchesa Paduli received Monsignor Ricardi's guests. She was a widow and lived with Ricardi because she had no closer relatives—or so people said. But, in reality, no one knew anything, for Ricardi was a Genoese and the alleged Marquis Paduli had died abroad in the foreign service.

The young widow had all the requisites of a charming hostess: tremendous amiability and the most exquisite courtesy combined with reserve and dignity. For all that, I thought I noticed that she had taken a definite fancy to me, indeed even an affection which betrayed itself on every occasion, but so subtly that no one present could notice. I recognized that secret sympathy of which all novels speak and I regretted that la Paduli should entertain such feelings for a man who was unable to reciprocate them. I therefore made a point of talking with the Marchesa and easily turned the conversation on my favorite subject: love and the various ways of loving, the difference between tender love and passionate love, between faithfulness and constancy. While I was discussing these dangerous subjects with the beautiful Italian, it never occurred to me that I could be untrue to Elvira, and my letters to Burgos were as fervid as ever.

One day I was in the villa without my tutor. Ricardi was not at home. I went for a walk in the garden, stepped into a summer-house and there I found la Paduli lost in deep dreams from which she was roused by the slight noise I made on entering. Her tremendous surprise when she saw me almost made me think I had been the object of her dreams. She even had the frightened expression of a person who is trying to escape from danger. Nevertheless she pulled herself together, invited me to sit down and addressed me in the polite phrases customary in Italy:

"*Lei ha girato questa mattina?* Did you go for a walk this morning?"

I told her I had been on the Corso and had seen many women there but that the Marchesa Lepri was the prettiest.

"Don't you know any prettier women?" la Paduli asked me.

"Yes, indeed," I replied. "I know a young girl in Spain who is far more beautiful."

This answer appeared to disturb Signora Paduli. She sank

again into her reveries, lowered her pretty eyelids and stared at the ground with a sorrowful expression.

To distract her I started a conversation on the subject of tenderness. Thereupon she turned her languishing eyes on me and said:

"Have you ever experienced these emotions you describe so well?"

"But of course," I answered, "and a thousand times more vividly and a thousand times more fondly and for the same young girl whose beauty is unsurpassed."

Scarcely had I spoken when a deathly pallor spread over la Paduli's face. She fell to the ground as stiff and motionless as if she were dead. I had never seen a woman in this state and had absolutely no idea what to do with her. Fortunately I saw two of the chambermaids walking in the garden, so I ran after them and told them they must come and help their mistress. I then left the garden and, reflecting on the occurrence, I was astounded at the power of love and how a spark dropped in the heart could cause such havoc there. I pitied la Paduli and I reproached myself for having caused her unhappiness, but I could not imagine being untrue to Elvira, either for la Paduli or for any other woman in the world.

The next day I went to the Villa Ricardi, but they were not receiving. Signora Paduli was ill. The following day all Rome was talking about her illness, from which I inferred that it must be serious. I suffered as many twinges of conscience as though I had done something wrong. On the fifth day of the Marchesa's illness, a young girl, her faced covered with a black veil, entered my room.

"Signore forestiere," she said to me, "a dying woman wishes to see you. Follow me."

I realized that the woman in question was Signora Paduli, but I thought I dared not oppose a dying woman's wish. A carriage waited for me at the end of the street. I got into it with the veiled girl. We reached the villa through the garden from the rear, entered a dark vestibule, passing from there into a corridor, then through several darkened rooms and finally came to Signora Paduli's bedroom. She lay in bed and held out her hand to me; it was burning hot, which

I took for the result of fever. I looked at the sick woman—and saw that she was almost naked. So far all I had known of women were their hands and faces. My eyes blurred, my knees became weak. I was untrue to Elvira . . .

"God of Love!" cried the Italian woman. "Here is one of your marvels! The man I loved has given me back my life."

From a state of complete innocence, I suddenly knew the most marvelous experiences of sensual pleasure. Four hours passed; finally the lady's maid appeared to warn that it was time to part. I went back to the carriage again—though with some difficulty for I had to lean on the arm of the young maid servant, who laughed at me. Before she left me, she threw her arms around my neck, crying:

"It's my turn next!"

Scarcely was I in my carriage when the thought of the pleasures I had enjoyed caused me the most lamentable remorse.

"Elvira, Elvira," I cried, "I have been untrue to you! Elvira, Elvira, I am not worthy of you! Elvira, Elvira, Elvira . . ."

Then I said all those things men are in the habit of saying at such times and sat back, firmly determined never to return to the Marchesa again.

When our guest had finished speaking, some of the gypsies came to take their leader's orders. The latter asked his old friend to postpone the continuation of his story and went off.

The forty-second day

The next morning we all gathered in the same cave, and the Marquis, noticing our impatience to learn the rest of his story, began with these words.

CONTINUATION OF THE STORY OF THE MARQUIS DE TORRES-ROVELLAS

I was sure that the Signora Paduli's maid would come the next day to take me to her mistress's bed, and I determined to receive her most ungraciously. But Sylvia did not come the next day, nor even the day after that, which somewhat surprised me. In fact, she did not come till a week later. This time she had obviously dressed with great care which was not at all necessary for she was much prettier than her mistress.

"Sylvia," I said to her, "go away! You have made me untrue to the most adorable of women. You deceived me. I thought I was being taken to a dying woman, but you led me to a woman who lives only for lust. My heart is innocent, though now I myself am not."

"Yes, you are," replied Sylvia, "very innocent. Don't worry about that. But I haven't come to take you to the Marchesa who at this moment is lying in Ricardi's arms."

"Her uncle?"

"Not at all. Ricardi is not her uncle. Come with me, I shall explain it all to you."

Out of sheer curiosity I followed Sylvia. We got into the carriage, we came to the villa, we went through the garden. Then the pretty messenger took me up to her room, a wretched servant's hovel. It seemed to be full of jars of face cream, combs and all sorts of geegaws with, in addition, a little snow-white bed and under the bed two noticeably elegant little slippers. Sylvia removed her gloves, her veil and then the kerchief she wore around her bosom.

"Stop!" I cried. "Don't go any farther. This is the way your mistress caused me to be unfaithful."

"My mistress," answered Sylvia, "employs extreme means —which I do not need."

At the same time she opened a cupboard from which she took fruit, pastry and a bottle of wine. All this she put on a table which she pushed up to the bed.

"Now, my fascinating Spaniard," she said, "the servants' quarters are poorly furnished. There was one chair here but they took it away this morning. Sit down on the bed beside me and don't scorn this light repast which I admit is not much, but which is a gift from the heart."

How could I refuse such a friendly offer! I therefore sat down beside Sylvia, ate some of her fruit, drank some of her wine, and urged her to tell me the story of her mistress, which she began as follows:

THE STORY OF MONSIGNORE RICARDI AND OF LAURA CERELLA, SURNAMED MARCHESA PADULI

Ricardi, son of a distinguished Genoese family, became, at an early age, a member of the regular clergy and soon after that a prelate. A good figure and violet stockings were in those days effective recommendations among the fair sex in Rome. Ricardi made use of his advantages and, like all his colleagues among the young prelates, even abused them. At the age of thirty he discovered that pleasures bored him and that he wanted to play a role in public life.

He had no intention of giving up women altogether: what he wanted was an arrangement that would offer him only pleasure but he did not know how to obtain it. True, he was *cavaliere servente* to the most beautiful princesses in Rome, but after a while the beautiful princesses began to prefer younger prelates. Moreover, he was tired of the constant courting that put him through the usual agonies and, in the end, becomes unbearable. Moreover, even women have their drawbacks, for they are ignorant of the social world and a man does not know what to talk to them about.

In the midst of his doubts Ricardi hit upon a scheme that many men before him and after him have been trapped into: namely to choose a young girl and mold her so completely to his taste that she would make him happy. What a pleasure it was to see both beauty of mind and figure unfold in a lovely young girl, to show her the world and society, to enjoy her wonder, to observe the first awakening of love and to make her wholly his own! And then, what can one do with this charming little creature? Many men marry them. Ricardi could not. His interest in these ambitious plans did not prevent our prelate from keeping an eye on his own promotion. An uncle of his, a member of the Rota, had been promised a cardinal's hat as well as the privilege of having his nephew step into his present position. But all this was still four or five years off. Ricardi thought he could venture to visit his home in the meantime and even to travel.

One day as Ricardi was walking along a street in Genoa, he was addressed by a thirteen-year-old girl who was carrying a basket of oranges. With bewitching grace she offered him one. Ricardi ran his hand sensuously over the uncombed hair that fell over the girl's face, pushed it back and discovered features that promised to be incredibly beautiful. He asked the orange-seller who her parents were. She replied that she had only a mother who was very poor and a widow. Her name was Bastiana Cerella. Ricardi told the girl to take him to the mother to whom he promptly introduced himself. Then he told Bastiana that he had a relative, a very charitable woman, whose pleasure it was to bring up young girls and give them a dowry. He would take little Laura to her.

The mother smiled and said:

"I do not know your relative who must surely be a very worthy woman, but your charity towards young girls is well known and you can take this one with you. I do not know whether you will bring her up to be virtuous, but at least you are rescuing her from a poverty that is worse than any vice."

Ricardi made ready to close a deal with the mother.

"No," she told him. "I won't sell my daughter. But I will accept the present you send me. To live is the first rule and my poor health often prevents me from working."

That same day little Laura was sent to board with a client of Ricardi's. They rubbed her hands with almond cream, put curlpapers in her hair, pearls around her neck, lace across her breast. The young girl looked in the mirror and did not recognize herself. She understood, however, from the first moment, why she had been brought here and she managed to adapt herself to her new situation.

However, the young girl had companions from her childhood who did not know what had become of her and were very worried about her. The one who had the greatest interest in finding her was Ceco Boscone. He was a young boy of fourteen, the son of a porter and already completely on his own. He had fallen in love with the little orange-girl whom he often saw either on the street or at our house, for he was distantly related to us. I say "us" because my name is Cerella too and I have the honor to be first cousin to my mistress.

We were all the more worried about my cousin because no one ever spoke of her in front of us and we were even forbidden to mention her name. My usual work was doing laundry and my cousin was busy at the harbor where he waited to be given bales to carry. On days when I had had a good day's work, I would meet him in the vestibule of a church and we would shed many tears over my cousin's fate. One evening Ceco said to me:

"I have an idea. For days it has been raining buckets and Signora Cerella could not go out. But on the first fine day she won't be able to resist visiting her daughter—that is if Laura is still in Genoa. All we have to do is to follow her and we'll find out where Laura is hidden."

I was delighted with this idea. The next day was beautiful. I went to Signora Cerella and saw her take out of an old box an even older veil. I chatted with her a little while and then ran off to give Ceco the news. We lay in wait and when we saw Signora Cerella leave the house, we followed her to a distant quarter where she went into a house. We hid again, waited until she left the house. As soon as she was out of sight, we rushed to the house, climbed the stairs or rather leapt up the steps and opened the door of an aristocratic dwelling . . . There I see Laura and throw myself in her arms. Ceco pulls her away from me and fastens his lips on hers. Then another door opens and Ricardi appears, boxes my ears twenty times and gives Ceco as many kicks. His servants seize us and, before we know it, we are out on the street again, our ears boxed, soundly trounced and thoroughly convinced that we dare not make any further researches about our cousin. Ceco sailed aboard a Maltese pirate ship as cabin boy, and I have never heard of him again.

However, I had not lost my desire to find my cousin; in fact one might say that desire grew with me. I went into service in numerous houses, at the last in the house of the Marquis Ricardi, our prelate's elder brother. There was much talk about Signora Paduli and they could not understand where the prelate had found this new relative. For the moment this mystery eluded all the researches of the family. Nothing, however, escapes the curiosity of servants. We traced the matter on our own initiative and soon knew that the so-called Marchesa was no other than Laura Cerella. The Marquis asked us to keep the secret and I was sent as quickly as possible to his brother to warn him that he must redouble his precautions if he would not ruin himself. But I do not want to tell you my story and here I am not saying a word about the Marchesa Paduli whom we left as little

Laura with the prelate's client. However, she did not stay there long. She was sent to a little town on the coast near Genoa where she disappeared again. Monsignor visited her every so often, and every time he returned he was more pleased with his handiwork.

At the end of two years Ricardi went to London. He traveled under an assumed name giving himself out as an Italian merchant. Laura accompanied him and was introduced as his wife. He took her to Paris and to other large cities where it was easier to preserve his incognito. Laura became more charming from day to day, she adored her benefactor and she made him the happiest of men. Three years passed on wings. Ricardi's uncle was about to be given the cardinal's hat and urged him to return to Rome.

Ricardi took his mistress to a family estate he owned in the neighborhood of Görz. The day after they arrived he said to her:

"Signora, I must give you some news that will please you. You are the widow of the Marquis Paduli who has just died in the service of the Emperor. Here are all the papers to confirm it. Paduli was a relative of ours and you will certainly not refuse to belong to my family."

The new Marchesa began to consider seriously Ricardi's character, her relations with him and the advantages she could derive from it. Three months later she was summoned to her so-called uncle and found him in the full glory of the position he now graces. Part of this glory fell on her and she received much homage. Ricardi let his family know that he had taken the Marchesa Paduli, widow of his cousin on his mother's side, into his house. His brother, the Marquis Ricardi, who had never heard that Paduli was married, investigated the matter as I have already said and sent me to the new Marchesa to urge her to display the greatest discretion.

I made the journey by sea, landed in Civita Vecchia from where I went to Rome and presented myself to the new Marchesa. She dismissed her servants and threw herself into my arms. We talked of our childhood, of my mother, of her mother, of the chestnuts we used to eat together. Nor was little Ceco forgotten. I explained that he had sailed on a pirate vessel and that since then nothing had been heard from him. Laura, who was easily moved, burst into tears and could not calm herself. She begged me not to tell the prelate who I was, but to pass myself off as her lady's maid. As my Genoese accent might betray me she advised me to say I had been born in the country near Genoa, not in the city.

Laura had her plans. For two weeks she displayed a gay, even temper, but at the end of that time she seemed to become serious, moody and bored with everything. Ricardi tried in vain to please her; he could not bring back the charming, sunny girl she had been before.

"My dear Laura," he said to her one day. "What is the matter with you? Just compare your present position with the one from which I freed you."

"And why did you do it?" Laura replied violently. "It is my poverty I miss. What am I doing among all these princesses? Their double-edged courtesies, their bitter insults. Oh, how I weep for my rags! My black bread, my chestnuts! It breaks my heart just to think about them! Oh! my little Ceco! You should have married me as soon as you were strong enough to be a porter! With you I would have known great privation but no black moods and even the princesses would have envied me my lot."

"Laura, Laura," cried Ricardi, "what sort of talk is that?"

"It is the language of nature," Laura responded. "It makes young girls become wives and mothers in the class in which they were born and not the nieces of dissolute priests." Then Laura went into the next room and locked the door behind her.

Ricardi was deeply embarrassed. He had introduced la Paduli as his niece and if that reckless girl disclosed the truth, he was lost and his career ruined. Moreover, he loved the little devil and he was jealous. All this contributed to making him very unhappy.

The next day Ricardi knocked timidly on Laura's door and was pleasantly surprised to receive the tenderest of receptions.

"Forgive me, dear uncle!" she said. "Dear benefactor! I am an ungrateful wretch and not fit to see the light of day. I am the work of your hands. You have formed my mind, I have you to thank for everything. Forgive a mood in which my heart had no share."

Peace was soon restored.

Several days later Laura said to Ricardi:

"I cannot be happy with you. You are too much the lord and master. Everything here belongs to you and I find myself completely dependent. That young lord who comes to see us has presented his mistress with the best land in the Duchy of Urbino. That's what I call a lover! Were I to ask you for even the barony in which I spent three months, you would refuse me although it is a legacy from your uncle Camiasi and you have the right to do with it as you please."

"You want to be independent only to get rid of me," said Ricardi.

"To love you even more," replied Laura.

Ricardi did not know whether to yield or to refuse. He was in love and jealous. He was afraid of losing some of his dignity and he also feared that he himself might become dependent on his mistress.

Laura could read his inmost thoughts and would gladly have forced him to the limit. But Ricardi had great power in Rome; a word from him and four policemen would have seized his niece and dragged her off to a convent where she would have been forced to undergo a long penance. This consideration deterred Laura and at last she decided to play sick in order to bring Ricardi to the point where she wanted to have him. This is the plan she was mulling over when she stepped into the summer-house.

"So I wasn't the one she was thinking about?" I exclaimed in great surprise.

"No, my dear," said Sylvia. "She was thinking of a fine barony with an income of four thousand scudi. Suddenly she had the idea of pretending to be sick, even dead. She had already practiced imitating the actresses she had seen in London and she wanted to find out where she could deceive you. You see therefore, my little Spaniard, that up to then she had taken you for a fool. But you have no right to complain of later developments, nor does my mistress complain of you. As for me, I found you completely charming as, in your weakened condition, you reached for my arm to support yourself. That was when I swore that I too would have my turn."

Thus spoke the lady's maid.

What shall I tell you? I was crushed by what I had heard; I had been robbed of my illusions and I no longer knew where I stood. Sylvia took advantage of my bewilderment to trouble my senses. It was not difficult for her to attain her object and to use her superior strength—and to misuse it. When at last she put me in my carriage, I did not know whether I ought to feel remorse again or whether I should not think about my unfaithfulness anymore.

When the Marquis came to this part of his report, the gypsy, who had important matters to attend to, urged him to postpone the rest of his story until the following day.

The forty-third day

We assembled as usual and when the Marquis saw that we were all waiting in silence, he went on with his story as follows:

CONTINUATION OF THE STORY OF THE MARQUIS DE TORRES-ROVELLAS

I have told you that I was unfaithful to Elvira twice, that the first time I suffered dreadful remorse, but the second time I did not know whether to be remorseful or simply not to think any more about it. Moreover, I can assure you that I still loved my cousin just as dearly as before and still wrote her just as passionate letters. My tutor, who wished to cure me of my romantic exuberance, occasionally used means that overstepped his authority. By pretending not to know anything, he put temptations in my way that I found hard to withstand. Nevertheless, my love for Elvira was still the same and I waited impatiently for the Apostolic Chancellery to grant the dispensation for our marriage. At last one day Ricardi sent for me and Santez. His manner was solemn, but his voice lightened as, with a gentle smile, he said:

"Your affairs have been settled, though not without great difficulty. It is true that we frequently grant permission to members of Catholic countries to marry, but as regards Spain where the faith is purer and its principles more closely adhered to, we take a different attitude. Nevertheless, in consideration of the numerous religious donations the Rovellas family has made in America and realizing that the error the two children made was the result of family misfortune and not of a careless upbringing, His Holiness has, I repeat, severed the ties of relationship that bound you, ties that will also remain severed in heaven. Therefore, so that youth may not be encouraged by this example to fall into similar error and that there may be sufficient penance in accordance with the holy laws, His Holiness commands you to wear around your neck a rosary made of a hundred pearls and to tell this rosary daily for three long years. In addition you are to have a church built for the Theatine monks in Vera Cruz. Moreover, I have the honor to transmit to you and to the future Marquesa best wishes for your well-being and your happiness."

You can imagine my joy! In the greatest haste I rushed to fetch the brief from His Holiness and two days later we left Rome, traveling day and night until we reached Burgos. I saw Elvira who, in the meantime, had become more beautiful than ever. We still had to ask the Court for consent to our marriage, but as Elvira was already in possession of her fortune we did not lack friends and we received the desired permission. At the same time the Court confirmed my title of Marquis de Torres-Rovellas. From then on we were occupied solely with clothes, finery, jewels and similar cares, so delightful to a young girl who is about to be married. Gentle Elvira bothered very little about these preparations, but devoted herself entirely to making her fiancé happy. At last came the moment of our wedding. The day seemed endlessly long to me for the ceremony was not to be held until evening in the chapel of the country estate we owned near Burgos.

I paced around the garden to quell the restlessness that consumed me. Then I sat down on a bench and began to think about my conduct, so unworthy of this angel with whom I was about to be united for eternity. I thought about the times I had been untrue to her and I counted twelve of them. Grief overwhelmed me and I burst into bitter lamentations:

"Wretched ingrate, did you not think of the treasure that was intended for you, the divine creature who sighed for you alone and who has certainly never spoken to another man?" While I was talking so passionately to myself, two of Elvira's maids sat down on a bench on the other side of the arbor in which I was seated and began a lively conversation. Their first words gripped my attention.

"Don't you think, Manuela," said one of the maids, "that our mistress must be glad to really love and give proofs of love at last instead of those little favors she granted so generously from behind the grating?"

"Do you mean," said the other girl, "the guitar teacher who kissed her hand secretly when he was showing her the proper movements of the fingers?"

"Oh no," said the first girl, "I'm talking about the dozen or so little love affairs, all innocent ones to be sure, in which our mistress indulged and which in her way she encouraged. First of all, there was the little academician, a geography teacher—oh, he was madly in love with her—to whom she gave almost a bushel of her hair so that when I went to dress her hair I hardly knew where to put the braid. The next one was that gossip of a superintendent who always talked to her about the state of her fortune and wanted to give her all the details. Not for nothing did he sit so close to our mistress, showering her with praise and turning her head with flattery; she gave him her portrait and several times she reached her hand through the bars for him to kiss. And what about all those flowers and bouquets they sent each other!"

I do not remember any more of the conversation, but I can assure you that not one of the dozen suitors was left out! I was filled with despair. I myself had received very innocent tokens of love from Elvira, which I might just as well describe as childish trifles. Elvira, at least the Elvira I had pictured, would not have dared to give the faintest appearance of unfaithfulness. Today I grant that my demands were extremely unreasonable. Even in her early youth Elvira talked only of love and I should have realized that she, who delighted in talking of her favorite theme, would not have spoken of it only with me. Never had I thought such behavior possible, but now that my own ears had convinced me of it, I was lost in grief and despair.

At that moment I received word that everything was ready. I entered the chapel with such a pale and worried face that my mother was astounded, my bride dismayed. Even the priest hesitated, uncertain whether he should pronounce the blessing. In the end he performed the ceremony. However, without exaggeration, I can say that never did a day so longed-for live up so little to the hopes placed in it.

The sight of the bewitching Elvira gradually dissipated the clouds of gloom that enveloped me. My young wife was so beautiful and looked at me so lovingly that I soon forgot my worries and gave myself up heart and soul to my newfound happiness.

The next morning we were both merry, I especially did not let the slightest shadow of worry oppress my heart. Men who know life understand that there is no happier moment than the one in which you are given a young and loving wife. Even today I would gladly exchange fame, distinctions and position for the return of those days. But man is young only once.

Our friends left us to our happiness. But after the first period of bliss had passed, they returned to spur us on to desire high honors. Count Rovellas had once hoped to obtain the title of grandee and our friends thought we should carry out his intention. They pointed out that while we were not in duty bound to do so for ourselves, we owed it to the children Heaven would some day bestow on us. Later on we might perhaps regret having neglected to do this and it was always better to spare oneself reproaches in time. We were at an age when one is inclined to follow the advice of those about us, and we therefore allowed our friends to take us to Madrid.

When the Viceroy learned of our plan he sent us a letter of warm welcome. In the beginning it looked as though our project could not fail to succeed; but that was only an appearance, clothed in the misleading glamour of courtly promises, and it never materialized.

Our friends took our disappointed hopes ill and so too, unfortunately, did my mother, who would have given anything to see her little Lonreto a Spanish grandee. Soon the poor lady fell ill with a consuming fever. Realizing that she had not long to live, she began to think of her spiritual welfare and she longed to show her gratitude to the inhabitants of the little town of Villaca who had so lovingly stood by us when we were in need. In particular she wanted to do something for the *alcade* and the priest. My mother had no money, but Elvira who was ready and willing to carry out her noble intentions, sent them gifts that far exceeded my mother's modest wishes.

When our former friends from Villaca learned what happiness was coming to them, they journeyed to Madrid and stood around their benefactress's sickbed. My mother left us at a time when we were happy and rich and still loved each other. She drifted quietly away into the eternal sleep which, because of her virtues and especially because of her great kindness, she so richly deserved.

Misfortune now befell us. After a brief illness, the two sons Elvira had given me were taken from this life. The title of grandee therefore no longer held any interest for us: we gave up our efforts and decided to go to Mexico where business affairs required our presence. The Marquesa's health was poor and the doctors thought a sea voyage would restore her strength. We therefore sailed for America and after a voyage of seven weeks which actually had a restorative influence on the Marquesa's health, we landed in Vera Cruz. Elvira arrived in America completely restored in health and more beautiful than ever.

In Vera Cruz we were met by the Viceroy's first officer who

had been sent to Mexico to welcome us and help us get settled; this man told us much about Count Penna-Velez's grandeur and about the practices of love prevalent at his Court. Some of them we already knew through our connections in America. When, for instance, the Viceroy had satisfied his pride, he yielded to his passionate fondness for women and as he had not been able to find happiness in marriage, he sought consolation in that charming and gallant relation with ladies in which years ago the Spanish Court excelled.

We did not remain long in Vera Cruz, but traveled with all the imaginable comfort I could provide to Mexico City. As you know, this capital lies in the midst of a lake. Night had already fallen when we reached the shore. Soon we saw hundreds of boats illuminated with torches. The most magnificent boat moved ahead of the others, came alongside, and we saw the Viceroy come toward us and address my wife:

"Daughter of the incomparable woman whom, till now, I have never ceased to worship! I thought Heaven had torn you from my heart but a merciful God has been graciously pleased to leave the world its most beautiful jewel for which I lay my heartfelt thanks at His feet. Come, beautiful Elvira, adorn our lands that, from now on, need no longer envy proud Europe!" The Viceroy also remarked that Elvira was so changed he would not have known her.

"To be sure I remember you when you were much younger and you need not be surprised that a short-sighted mortal fails to recognize the little bud in the rose."

He then honored me with an embrace and led us both to his gondola. After half an hour's journey on the lake we came to a floating island which, thanks to the ingenuity of art, looked like a real island. Although a grove of orange trees and countless other trees had been planted on it, it floated serenely above water. It could be steered to all parts of the lake so that from it one could observe and enjoy every aspect of this beautiful region.

In the middle of the island was a brightly lighted rotunda from which, even at a distance, the clangor of loud music reached our ears. Soon we could make out the initials of Elvira's name outlined in lights. As we approached the shore we saw two groups of men and women wearing gorgeous garments and very unusual jewelry in which the vivid colors of various types of feathers vied with the brilliance of costly precious stones.

"Madam," said the Viceroy, "one of those groups is Mexican. The beautiful woman at their head is the Marquesa de Montezuma, the last of this great name which was borne by the rulers of this land. The policy of the Council in Madrid no longer permits her to enjoy rights which many Mexicans still consider perfectly legitimate. We console her for this disfavor by proclaiming her queen of our festivals. The men and women in the other group call themselves Incas from Peru. They have heard that a daughter of the Sun has landed in Mexico and have come to pay homage to her."

While the Viceroy was paying my wife these compliments, I kept my eyes fixed on her and I saw in her eyes a wavering fire flare up, born perhaps from a spark of that self-love which had found no time to develop in the seven years of our marriage; for in spite of our wealth we had by no means played a leading role in Madrid. Elvira's life had been filled with my mother, with her children, with her own health. She had had little time to shine. Now, however, that the journey had restored her full beauty and she had become the leading lady on a new stage, she seemed inclined to yield to exaggerated ideas about herself and to attract everyone's attention.

The Viceroy installed Elvira as Queen of the Peruvians and then said to me:

"You are undoubtedly the first subject of this daughter of the Sun, but as we are all masked I must ask you to obey the commands of another ruler till the ball is over." At the same time he introduced me to the Marquesa de Montezuma and placed her hand in mine.

We mingled with the throng of merrymakers. The two groups danced, now separately, now together, and their competition lent life and movement to the ball. It was decided to continue the masquerade until the end of the season. I therefore remained the subject of the Pretender to the throne of Mexico while my wife ruled her subjects with an arrogance and condescension that did not escape me.

But I must draw you a picture of the daughter of the Cacique, or at least let you guess at her face, for it is impossible to describe the violent changes in her features that mirrored every mention of her passionate soul.

Tlascala de Montezuma was born in the mountainous portion of Mexico and she did not have the sunburnt skin of the dwellers on the plains. Though not blonde, her coloring was light and her eyes, like jewels, only emphasized its sheen. Her features, less pronounced than the facial features of Europeans, were not as flattened as those usually seen among the American races; in fact the only reminders of her race were her rather full lips and a smile that lent them a fleeting charm. Of her body I cannot tell you anything; I leave that to your imagination or to the imagination of the artist who would paint an Atalanta or a Diana. There was something special about the way she carried herself. In her movements one could divine a primitive surge of passion, tempered, however, by great self-control. Even her repose was full of emotion.

Too often the blood of the Montezumas reminded her that she was born to rule over a far-flung region of the world. When you approached her, the first thing you felt was the proud bearing of an insulted queen, but even before she spoke, you were captivated by the sweetest and most bewitching glance that would accompany her reply. When she entered the Viceroy's salon, you thought you detected a certain vexation at finding herself less in rank than her equals, but in a short time that had vanished. Hearts that are made to love recognized her as the ruler and competed for her favor. Tlascala was no longer the Queen but all woman, and she rejoiced that men paid homage to her.

Even at the first ball I was aware of her proud spirit. I thought I should pay her a few compliments on the unusualness of her costume and also mention my role as her first subject, which the Viceroy had delegated to me. I stirred up a veritable hornet's nest.

"My dear sir," she said, "to be queen of a ball may be flattering to those who are not born to the throne." At the same time she glanced hastily at my wife.

At that moment Elvira was surrounded by Peruvians, all

serving her on bended knee. Her obviously arrogant delight verged on ecstasy, and I was almost ashamed for her. That same evening I spoke to her about it. She listened absent-mindedly to my warning, received my advice coldly. Self-love held sway in her heart and had driven love out of it. Intoxication called forth by the incense of flattery dies slowly, but Elvira's intoxication only increased. . . . All Mexico was divided between admiration for Elvira's consummate beauty and Tlascala's incomparable charms. Elvira spent her days enjoying in retrospect the successes of the day before and preparing for the successes of the day to follow. Inclined to be thoughtless and frivolous, she was drawn to all sorts of pleasures. I tried to restrain her, but in vain. I myself was carried along with her, though in another direction, far from the flowery path, where all pleasures sprang up under my wife's feet.

I was not yet thirty years old, and still at an age when emotions have all the freshness of youth, and passions all the strength of a mature man. My love, sprung from Elvira's cradle, had never gone beyond that stage, and Elvira's mind, which had drawn its first nourishment from romantic legends, was still immature. My own mind was not much more mature than hers, but I had enough common sense to realize that Elvira's thoughts revolved around the most trivial matters, around rivalries, and often around petty backbiting, a *circulor vitiosus,* a vicious circle to which women are held fast more through a limitation of character than of the mind. In that sex there are seldom exceptions, and I personally was convinced that there was not a single one. But how delighted I was, when I learned to know Tlascala to find that I was wrong. Jealousy was completely foreign to her nature. She felt kindly towards her sex as a whole and women who were an honor to their sex because of their beauty, their charm or their sympathy, aroused her particular interest. She liked to have them around her, to win their trust, to gain their friendship. As for men, she spoke of them seldom, but always with reserve, unless there were noble and magnificent deeds to praise. Then she expressed her admiration freely, indeed even with warmth. Otherwise her conversation turned on general subjects and first became lively when it was a question of the welfare of the New World and the happiness of its inhabitants, a favorite subject to which she always returned when she felt she could do so without embarrassment. Many men seem destined through the influence of their star—and doubtless of their character—to be ruled all their lives by women who rule all those they cannot reduce to subjection. I unquestionably am one of those men. I had been Elvira's humble adorer and afterwards a fairly obedient husband. Elvira herself had made this bond all the stronger because it seemed to matter so little to her.

One masquerade followed the other and it so happened that in the course of this social life I accompanied the Marquesa de Montezuma wherever she went. However, for my heart the result was far more serious. The first change I noted in myself was that my thoughts went winging on high. My soul expanded, my character became firmer, my will more decided. I felt the need to express my feelings in acts and to influence my fellow-men. I aimed for a star—and won.

Through the position with which I was entrusted many provinces came under my dominion. I witnessed the oppression of the native by the people of the conqueror, and I undertook to defend them. I made powerful enemies and fell into disgrace with the Minister, even the Court seemed to threaten me; I fought back valiantly. But I won the love of the Mexican, the respect of the Spaniard, and what in my eyes had the greatest value, the keen interest of the woman to whom I was already wholeheartedly devoted. It is true that Tlascala treated me with the same reserve she showed all men, but her eyes sought mine, lingered tenderly and turned restlessly away. She had little to say to me, not even about what I had done for the Americans, but when she addressed me her heart beat faster, she caught her breath, and her soft, shy voice lent a note of incipient intimacy to the most ordinary conversation. Tlascala believed that in me she had found a kindred spirit . . . She was wrong. Her soul had passed into mine. She roused my enthusiasm and forced me to action. I was mistaken about the strength of my character. My fantasies became deliberations, my thoughts about the welfare of America developed into daring plans. My amusements took on a somewhat heroic note. I hunted the jaguar and the puma in the forests and even attacked these wild animals. But most often I pressed on into uninhabited valleys where the lonely echo was the only confidante of a love I was afraid to confess to her who had inspired it.

However, Tlascala had seen through me. I too had gained a clearer knowledge of her feelings and we could easily have betrayed ourselves to a sharp-sighted public. Fortunately we escaped their attention. The Viceroy had important business that interfered with the brilliant festivals that had such a strong attraction for him and that, for the social world of Mexico, had become a regular passion. But now, for all of us a less distracting life began. Tlascala withdrew to a house she owned in the northern part of the lake. At first I visited her fairly often, finally going to see her every day. It is difficult for me to describe the tenor of our meetings. For my part it was a cult that bordered on fanaticism, on hers it was like a sacred fire, whose flame she nourished passionately and devoutly. It was always on the tip of our tongue to confess our feelings but we dared not. We lived in a state of sheerest joy whose sweetness we savoured and which we feared to change in any way.

When the Marquis had come to this place in his story, the gypsy was called away to attend to the business of the tribe and our curiosity about the end of the story could not be satisfied until the next day.

The forty-fourth day

We gathered in silence. The Marquis sat down and began his story as follows:

CONTINUATION OF THE STORY OF THE MARQUIS DE TORRES-ROVELLAS

Tlascala was convinced of the truths of our holy religion, but at the same time she was filled with pious reverence for the memory of her forefathers. In her gentle faith she had reserved a special paradise for them that lay not in heaven but in some middle region. To a certain extent she shared the superstitions of her fellow-countrymen. She believed that the illustrious shades of the Kings of her line were in the habit of descending in the dark of night to visit an old cemetery in the mountains. Nothing in the world could have made Tlascala go there at night. By day, however, we went there many times and stayed for hours. She explained the hieroglyphics engraved on the tombstones of her forefathers and illustrated them with tales of surrender in which she was well versed. We already knew most of the inscriptions, but pressed our researches farther and farther and came at last to gravestones which we freed from the moss and bramble bushes that covered them. One day Tlascala showed me clusters of a thorny undergrowth. It was, she thought, no accident that we had found it in this region for, whoever had planted it had done so to direct the vengeance of heaven on the spirits of their enemies. She told me I would do well to destroy this unholy bush. Taking an axe that belonged to a Mexican, I cut down those shadows of evil intent and in so doing laid bare a stone that was covered with more hieroglyphics than any we had seen so far.

"This," said Tlascala, "was written after the capture. In those days Mexicans mixed their hieroglyphics with several letters of the alphabet they had learned from the Spaniards. The inscriptions from those days are the easiest to read."

Tlascala began to read; but the farther she read, the more suffering showed in her face. Suddenly she fainted across the stone that had hidden for two hundred years the cause of her sudden fright. We took Tlascala home and she recovered consciousness, but only to stammer incoherent words. I went home in the greatest anxiety, and the next day I received the following letter:

"Alonzo, I have summoned all my thoughts, all my strength to write you a few lines. Old Xoax, my teacher of our ancient language will deliver this to you. Take him to the stone we uncovered so that he may translate the inscription. I cannot see clearly, a heavy mist hovers before my eyes. Alonzo, I shall not see you again . . ."

I went to the cemetery with Xoax and showed him the fateful stone. He made a transcript and took the copy with him. I went to Tlascala, but she was delirious and did not know me. By evening the fever had abated, but the physician sent word for me not to come. The next day Xoax brought me the translation of the Mexican inscription. It read as follows:

I, Coatril, son of Montezuma, have brought here the dishonorable body of Marina who prostituted her heart and her country to abominable Cortez, leader of the pirates of the sea. Spirits of my ancestors who return here, endow these lifeless remains for a few moments with life so that she may know the agony of dying and death. Spirits of my ancestors, hear my voice, hear my curse which I speak in the name of the human sacrifices with which my hands reek.

I, Coatril, son of Montezuma, am a father. My daughters wander on the peaks of icy mountains, but beauty is the inheritance of our illustrious blood. Spirits of my ancestors, if ever a daughter of Coatril's or the daughter of her daughters and her sons, if ever a daughter of our blood should give her heart and her charms to the vile race of pirates, if among the daughters of my race there should be a Marina, spirits of my ancestors, you who return here on dark nights, punish her with the most terrible tortures. Come back on dark nights in the form of flaming vipers, tear her body to pieces, scatter it in the bosom of the earth and may every limb you have torn from her suffer pain, death agony and death. Come back on dark nights in the form of vultures, with beaks like red hot irons and tear her body to pieces, scatter it in the air and may every torn limb you have pulled out suffer pain, death agony and death. Spirits of my ancestors, if you hesitate to do this, I call down on you the spirits of the gods of vengeance, drenched in the blood of human sacrifices. May they cause you to suffer the same tortures!

I carve this curse in the stone, I, Coatril, son of Montezuma.

It would not have taken much for this inscription to have the same effect on me as on Tlascala. I tried to persuade Xoax that the Mexican superstition was sheer nonsense, but I soon realized that I must not attack him from this side and he himself showed me another way to comfort Tlascala.

"Your Lordship," said Xoax, "one cannot deny that the spirits of the Kings come back to the cemetery and that they have the power to torture the living and the dead especially when they are urged to it by curses like those you have seen on the stone. There are, however, various circumstances that tend to weaken their terrible effect. First of all you have destroyed the evil bush that had been planted with forethought on this grave; and besides, what connection have you with Cortez and his terrible companions? Continue to be the protector of the Mexican and believe me that we are not totally unversed in placating the spirits of Kings, even those terrible gods we once worshipped in Mexico, and which your priests call demons."

I advised Xoax not to make known his religious opinions and offered to take every opportunity to help the natives of Mexico. These opportunities did not fail to arise. In the provinces captured by the Viceroy, revolt broke out. It was actually only a justified revolt against oppression and completely contrary to the intentions of the Court, but the stern Viceroy who had been prejudiced by false information paid no attention to that difference. Putting himself at the head of an army, he invaded New Mexico, drove out the rebels and carried off two Caciques whom he condemned to die on the scaffold in the capitol of New Mexico. Just as their sentence was about to be announced I entered the council room and cried out: *"Los toque por parte de el Rey"*—I touch you in the name of the King." This old and well-worn formula of Spanish law is still so powerful that no one would dare to oppose it, and it suspended execution of the sentence. However, he who makes use of it pledges himself to stand as guarantee. The Viceroy had the right to treat me as one of the rebels he wanted to condemn. He used that right to the full. He had me thrown into a dark prison hole and there I experienced the sweetest moment in my life.

One night—and in that darkness it was always night—I noticed at the end of a long passageway a pale glimmer of light coming towards me and I saw Tlascala's face. This sight alone would have been enough to make my prison a paradise. But not satisfied with embellishing it by her presence, she had prepared the sweetest of all surprises for me, the admission of a passion that equaled mine.

"Alonzo," she said to me, "brave Alonzo, you have won. The *Manes* of my fathers are appeased. This heart that no mortal should have possessed, is yours—the reward for the sacrifice you have made to aid my unfortunate fellow-countrymen."

Scarcely had Tlascala said this when she fell unconscious

and almost lifeless into my arms. I ascribed this attack to the shock she had experienced but oh! unfortunately the cause lay deeper and was much more dangerous. The horror that had seized her at the cemetery and the resulting fever-delirium had shattered her health. Meantime Tlascala's eyes opened in all their glory and a heavenly light seemed to transform my dark prison into a radiantly shining abode. Amor, divine Amor, never has thy might, neither in Knidos nor in Paphos, shone more radiantly than in the prisons of the New World! My prison became my temple, the block thy altar, the chains thy garlands. That enchantment has not faded yet; it lives on in my heart where, through the years passion has cooled; but always when my mind, excited by my memories, delves back deep into those years of past illusions, it seeks neither Elvira's marriage-bed nor Laura's lustful couch but the walls of a prison.

I have told you the Viceroy was very angry with me. His violent temper had triumphed over all his principles of justice, even over the friendship he felt for me. He sent a swift ship to Europe and in his report described me as the accomplice of the rebels. But scarcely had the ship hoisted sail when the Viceroy's kindness, his innate decency gained the upper hand. He now saw the matter in an entirely different light. Had he not feared to compromise himself, he would have sent a second report to contradict the first. However he dispatched a second ship carrying documents drawn in such a way that they could not fail to soften the effect of the first report.

The Council in Madrid, which is slow in all its decisions, gave itself enough time to receive the second report. Its reply was a long time coming, but it was worded, as we had hoped, with the greatest prudence. The Council's decision was, to all appearances, unusually severe: it pronounced the death sentence, not only for the rebels but also for their accomplice. However if one held literally to the wording of the sentence, it was difficult to discover the guilty parties and the Viceroy received secret instructions forbidding him to look for them.

Unfortunately the official part of the sentence was made known first and this added the final blow to Tlascala's failing health. A hemorrhage—a fever, at first light, then low, then raging and impossible to cure.

The sensitive old man could not go on. Sobs choked his voice and he walked away from us to hide his tears. We all waited in solemn silence, each of us secretly deploring the fate of the beautiful Mexican.

The forty-fifth day

We gathered together again at the usual hour and begged the Marquis to continue his story which he did as follows:

CONCLUSION OF THE STORY OF THE MARQUIS DE TORRES-ROVELLAS

As I have already told you, I was in disgrace, but I did not mention my wife's attitude at that time. Elvira had clothes made of some dark material and went into a convent whose seclusion was promptly changed into a reception salon. In any case my wife always appeared with a handkerchief in her hand and her hair loosened. This proof of an unalterable devotion touched me deeply. I was declared not guilty but because of certain legal formalities and the usual Spanish procrastination I had to spend four months more in prison. As soon as I was freed I hastened to Elvira's convent and brought her home where her return was celebrated by a magnificent ball.

Tlascala was no longer there! Even the most uninterested persons remembered her with tears in their eyes. You can imagine my grief; I was almost out of my mind and completely unaware of the people around me. Fortunately a new emotion that stirred precious hopes roused me from this pitiful condition. When a young man is endowed with fortunate inclinations, he seeks success, then later on respect and prestige. I have received all three; but perhaps I would never have attained any ot them had it been known how greatly love had helped me. People traced my deeds to certain virtues that can only be found in an outstanding character. In addition there was the enthusiasm which is always lavished on the man who has won a place in the limelight at the cost of his own safety. My popularity in Mexico made me aware of the high opinion people had of me there and their flattering acclamations roused me from the deep despair into which I had sunk. I felt, however, that I had not earned this general respect, and I determined to prove myself worthy of it in the future. Thus it sometimes happens that when we are exhausted by grief and can see only a gloomy future ahead, Divine Providence unexpectedly lets a light shine before us.

I wanted to deserve in my own eyes the respect others felt for me. Part of the management of the country was turned over to me and I carried out my duties with impartial justice. But fundamentally I was made for love. Tlascala lived in my heart; in my life she had left a painful void. I made up my mind to fill it.

When a man has passed his thirtieth year, he can experience a strong infatuation or even arouse one, but woe to the man who tries to indulge in amorous dalliance. His lips no longer smile, his eyes no longer sparkle with tender joy, his words are no longer tuned to fond nothings. He tries in every way to please, but although he is adept at all the moves, although he understands love and is well versed in its expressions—fickle and malicious youth flees before him and seeks younger company.

To tell the truth, I did not lack mistresses who returned

my feelings, but their tendernesses generally had other ends in view and often, as you may imagine, they left me for a younger man. Such conduct sometimes angered me; it never caused me grief. I flitted from one light attachment to another equally light and I must frankly admit that in these relationships I have known more joy than sorrow.

My wife was at the beginning of her fortieth year. Homage was still paid her, but more as a sign of deference than of adulation. Friends and admirers crowded around her to talk with her, but the talk was no longer of herself. The world had not yet left her, but for her it had lost all stimulus.

Then the Viceroy died. My wife, who was in the habit of receiving guests in his house now wished to see guests in her own house. At that time I was still very fond of the company of ladies and the thought that I could go down only one floor to find them always there thoroughly delighted me. The Marquesa became like a new acquaintance for me, I discovered new facets of her character and once again a ray of happiness brightened my life.

Elvira was pregnant and in time presented me with the beloved child who is with me on this journey. Unfortunately, the late birth had a bad effect on my wife's health. She became ill with a high fever that soon carried her to the grave. This blow of fate plunged me into the deepest grief. The Marquesa had been my first love and my last friend. Ties of blood had united us: I owed my success, my entire fortune to her—reason enough to mourn her loss. When I lost Tlascala I was still surrounded by the illusions of life; the Marquesa, however, left me alone without anyone to comfort me and in a depressed state from which nothing could rouse me. It is true, time healed my wounds a little. I traveled around my various estates and lived with one of my people whose daughter, really too young to pay attention to an old man, brightened the autumn of my days with a last ray of happiness.

At last age has stilled the demands of my senses, and there is only tenderness left in my heart. My devotion to my daughter moves me more than all my former passions. My one and only desire is to see her happy and to die in her arms. I cannot complain of her, the dear child responds genuinely to my feelings. Her lot in life is assured, and conditions, I believe, are favorable for her future as far as that is possible on earth. Peacefully, though not without regret, I shall leave this world in which, like every man, I have known much sorrow, but also much happiness.

That is the story of my life. I fear it has bored you, and all the more so as I see that for some time this gentleman here has preferred to devote himself to some sort of calculations.

And in fact Velasquez had taken out his tablet and was busily calculating.

"Pardon me, Señor," replied our mathematician. "Your story interested me extremely and my attention did not wander for even a minute. I followed you along your life's way and saw that, with every step you took, the same passion determined the cycle of your fate from youth to old age. I saw in my mind a curve which, running around your axis according to the given law, hovered a second at the vortex and finally gravitated downwards in the same relation to the force with which it rose."

"Truly," said the Marquis, "I thought one could draw a lesson in morals from my adventures, but it would never have occurred to me that they could be represented by an algebraic equation." The mathematician went on:

This is not a question here of a mere adventure, Señor, but of human life on the whole, of physical and psychic capacity which grows with increasing age, remains static for a brief period and then declines.

In this way life is identical with other forces, and is subject to the same laws, that is: it is determined by the relation between the number of years and the degree of capacity the character attains. Let me explain that more carefully. Take, for instance, the span of life as stretched over the great axis of an ellipse. The great axis may be divided into ninety years of life, the small axis may be so interpreted that, when it lies at a definite distance from 45, it does not cross the interval between 40 to 50 by two-tenths. Now notice that the division of the small axis which represents the degree of capacity does not denote a value of the same kind as that of the great axis which denotes the years, but only elements. According to the nature of the ellipse we get a curve that rises swiftly, remains stationary for almost a moment and finally falls down again the same way it rose.

Take the moment of birth as the beginning of the ordinate where X and Y are still equal to zero. You were born, Señor, and after one year your ordinate amounts to 31/10 of the dimension used for the great axis. After that the ordinates will not have an increase of more than 31. That is why the difference between zero and a creature who is just beginning to stutter the most elementary ideas, is much greater than any later difference. Man in his second, third, fourth, fifth, sixth, seventh year has in values of his capacity 47/10 then 57/10, 65/10, 73/10, 79/10, 85/10 whose differences are 16, 10, 8, 8, 6, 6.

The ordinate of the fourteenth year of life is 115/10 and the sum of the differences from the seventh year of life to the fourteenth is only 30. In the fourteenth year of life man first begins to be a youth and so he is still in his twenty-first year. The sum of the differences in these seven years is only 19, but from his twenty-first to his twenty-eighth year it is 14. I would like to remind you that my curve represents the life only of those people whose passions are moderate and who are most capable after they have passed their fortieth year and are approaching their forty-fifth year. For you, Señor, in whose life love was the paramount, the highest ordinate must be placed at least ten years earlier, somewhere between the thirtieth and thirty-fifth year. Therefore it must have risen relatively faster. In fact your highest ordinate falls on the thirty-fifth year and tallies 17 divisions of the great axis. Therefore the ordinate of the fourteenth year, which in a moderate man amounts to 115/10, is with you 127; with you the ordinate of the twenty-first year, instead of 134, came to 144. In general at the age of forty-four the temperate man increases his capacity, yours, Señor, was already declining.

Now kindly give me your attention another minute. At the age of fourteen you love a young girl; after passing your twenty-first year you became the best of husbands. At the age of twenty-eight you are definitely unfaithful for the first time, but the woman who loves you has a lofty soul, she embraces yours by her enthusiasm and at thirty-five you step forward honorably on the social scene. Soon, however, lust drives you to affairs which you already had enjoyed at the age of twenty-eight and here your ordinate again equals the ordinate 42.

In the course of time you will again be as good a husband as you were at twenty-one whose ordinate equals 49. Finally you go to one of your vassals where you fall in love with a young girl, who is somewhat like the girl you loved when you were fourteen whose ordinate corresponds to the ordinate 56. Do not think, however, my dear Marquis, that when I divide the great axis of your ellipse into only seventy slices that your life is therefore restricted to that number of years. On the contrary you could easily live to be ninety and even more; but in that case the ordinates will conform to the theory about curves, which is called a chain-theory.

While he was lecturing, Velasquez got up, waved his arms wildly, grabbed his sword and began to trace lines in the sand; he would certainly have explained the whole theory of curves, known as chain-lines, had not the Marquis and also the rest of the company, who had little interest in the mathematician's lectures, asked permission to retire. Only Rebecca remained. Velasquez paid not the slightest attention to the departing guests, the beautiful Jewess was enough for him and he therefore began to explain his system to her. I listened for a while until, exhausted by the many scientific and mathematical terms in which I had never taken any particular interest, I could keep awake no longer and went off to bed. Velasquez kept right on holding forth!

The forty-sixth day

The Mexicans, who had tarried with us longer than they had intended, decided at last to go on their way. The Marquis did his best to persuade the gypsy leader to come with him to Madrid, there to lead a life commensurate with his birth and position. But the gypsy would not listen to this suggestion. He even begged the Marquis not to speak of him to anyone and not to destroy the secrecy with which he had surrounded his life. The travelers expressed their great admiration for him and did me the honor to ask for my friendship.

We escorted them to the end of the valley and stood there for a long time watching them as they disappeared from sight. Suddenly it occurred to me that some member of their caravan was missing. I thought of the girl who had been found under the fatal gallows of Los Hermanos and I asked the gypsy leader what had become of her and whether this was really a new and extraordinary adventure or another trick of the cursed denizens of Hell who had given us so much trouble. The gypsy smiled mockingly and said:

"This time you are mistaken, Señor Alfonso, but human nature is so made that when it has once experienced wonders and has taken a liking to them, it has to explain even the simplest events in life by magic."

"You are right," Velasquez interjected. "One can just as well apply to these ideas the theory of geometric progression whose lowest rung would denote a dull, superstitious man, the highest rung an alchemist or an astrologer. Between the two rungs there is much room for all the superstitions with which mankind is burdened."

"I have nothing against this argument," I said, "but it does not explain to me who this unknown girl is."

"I sent one of my men," the gypsy said, "to gather information about her. He brought me word that she was a poor orphan who went mad after the death of her lover. As she can find no sanctuary anywhere, she lives on the charity of travelers and the pity of shepherds. Always alone, she wanders around the hills and sleeps wherever night finds her. That is probably the way she came to be lying under the gallows of Los Hermanos where she fell asleep peacefully unaware of the horror of the place. Pity impelled the Marquis to take care of her, but the mad girl escaped from those who were guarding her and was lost in the mountains. I am surprised that we have not met her somewhere. The poor girl will end by falling off a rock and killing herself. I must admit I thought it senseless to feel pity for such a wretched life. At night sometimes, when the shepherds make a fire, they see the girl hovering near them. Then Dolorita, for that is her name, sits down calmly beside them, stares with a piercing glance at one of them, suddenly flings her arms around his neck and calls him by the name of her dead lover. At first the shepherds fled from her, but now they have become accustomed to her and they let her wander around, unharmed, wherever she pleases—they even share their food with her."

While the gypsy was talking, Velasquez was busy formulating a theory about two mutually destructive forces, one of which, passion, after a long battle with reason, will finally conquer and, replete with foolscap and bells, hold sole sway in the mind. As for me, I was much surprised by the gypsy's words; I had been sure he would not miss the opportunity to give us an excellent chapter. But possibly the reason for cutting short Dolorita's story was the arrival of the Wandering Jew who came running swiftly along a mountain path. The cabalist promptly began to utter terrible exorcisms, but the Jew paid no attention.

"Your rule is at an end," he said to Uzeda. "You have lost the power of which you have shown yourself unworthy. A horrible future lies ahead of you."

The cabalist laughed boisterously, but the laughter did not seem to come from his heart, for he spoke to the Jew in a strange language and there was an almost pleading note in his voice.

"Good," Ahasver finally said. "For today then. Today for the last time! From now on, you will not see me again."

"That's not so sure," said Uzeda. "We shall see what happens later. But go on with your story, you old boor. We'll show you whether the Sheik of Taradant has more power than I have. Moreover, I know the reasons why you are avoiding us and you can be sure I shall divulge every one of them."

The unfortunate wanderer flung the cabalist a glance that could have killed, but when he saw that he could not get the better of him, he took his place as usual between Velasquez and me and after a momentary silence began to speak.

CONTINUATION OF THE STORY OF THE WANDERING JEW

I have already told you that at the moment I was about to achieve my most ardent desires an uproar occurred in the Temple, and that a Pharisee rushed at us and called me a swindler. As one does in such cases, I called him a liar and said if he didn't leave at once I would have my people throw him out of the door.

"Enough!" cried the Pharisee, then turning to the bystanders, "This unworthy Sadduccee is cheating you. He has spread a false report to enrich himself at your expense; he is taking advantage of your credulity. But now it is time to show him up for the swindler he is. To prove the truth of my words I offer each one of you double the money he offers for one ounce of silver." By this move the Pharisee still made twenty-five percent, but the people, carried away by lust for profit, crowded around him and called him the benefactor of the city, whereas they were not sparing of the sharp epithets they hurled at me. Gradually, as heads became heated from the angry words, a hand-to-hand fight ensued and in no time at all there was such an uproar in the Temple that a man could not even hear what his neighbor was saying to him. When I saw that real trouble was brewing, I had my men carry as much gold and silver as possible back to our house. But before the servants could take it all away, the angry mob rushed at the tables and swept up all the money that remained. In vain I tried to put up a good fight; the enemy was considerably stronger. In a second the Temple became a battlefield. I do not know how the fight would have ended—perhaps I would even have lost my life, for blood was already streaming from my head—when suddenly the Prophet from Nazareth entered with his followers.

Never will I forget that solemn thundering voice that calmed the tumult immediately. We waited to hear which side he would take. The Pharisee was sure he would win, but the Prophet rebuked both sides, accused them of robbing the Temple and of irreverence for the House of God and spoke of the Creator's scorn for the devil's property, money. His words made a deep impression on all present; the Temple gradually filled with people, among them many followers of the new doctrine. Both sides realized that, because of the Prophet's interference, they could only expect the worst—and they were not mistaken. As though from one breast rose the cry: "Drive them out of the Temple!" This time the people did not wait to gather their winnings, but, seized with fanatical enthusiasm, began to overturn the tables and to push us out of the door.

Crowds gathered in the streets but their attention was on the Prophet, more than on us. I took advantage of the general confusion to reach the house through back streets and byways and arrived just in time to catch the servants who were making off with the money I had rescued. A quick glance in the bags assured me that even though all hope of increasing our wealth was gone, at least there was no loss. At that thought I sighed with relief.

Sedekias already knew what had happened and Sara had awaited my return in great anxiety. When she saw me covered with blood, she turned pale and flung herself into my arms. The old man watched us in silence a long time, shook his head as if he were trying to collect his thoughts, and finally said:

"I promised that Sara would be yours when you had doubled the money I entrusted to you. What have you done with it?"

"It was not my fault," I replied, "if an unforeseen occurrence spoiled my plans. I risked my life to defend your property. You can count the money. You have lost nothing. There is even a little gain, but it is scarcely worth mentioning compared to what you expected." Then suddenly I had a bright idea. I decided to risk everything on one throw.

"But if you wanted this to be a day of winning, I can make good the loss in another way."

"How is that?" asked Sedekias. "It is sure to be another enterprise that will have as little chance of succeeding as the first one."

"By no means," I retorted. "You can see for yourself whether the value I shall now offer you is a real value or not."

With these words I hurried off and came back after a while with my tin box under my arm. Sedekias watched me attentively, and a hopeful smile appeared fleetingly on Sara's lips. I opened the box, took out the papers it held, tore them in half and handed the torn papers to the old man. Sedekias immediately recognized what they were, clutched the papers greedily, and a look of indescribable rage passed over his face. He rose, tried to say something, but the words stuck in his throat. Determined to force a decision, I fell at the old man's feet and washed them with hot tears. At that moment Sara knelt beside me and, sobbing, kissed her grandfather's hands. The old man's head sank on his breast: a thousand thoughts went through his mind. In silence he shredded the papers into tiny pieces, then with a violent gesture he stood up and left the room hastily. I must admit that I had lost all hope. After what had happened I considered it impossible to remain any longer in Sedekias's house. I took one last look at Sara's tear-stained face and was about to leave when I noticed at the entrance a great turmoil. I asked what it was all about and was told, smiling, that I, less than any other, should ask such a question.

"Sedekias has made known," someone added, "his intention to give his granddaughter Sara to you in marriage. He has commanded us to prepare as quickly as possible for a magnificent wedding."

You can imagine that my despair was immediately transformed into unspeakable joy. Two weeks later Sara became my wife. Only the friend, who should have taken part in such a brilliant change in my life, was missing. But Germanus had followed the teaching of the Prophet of Nazareth; he was one of those who had thrown us out of the Temple. So, in spite of the friendship I felt for him, I was obliged to break off all relations with him and I have never seen him again.

After the many vicissitudes I had to suffer, it now seemed that I could enjoy a quiet life and all the more as I gave up money-changing, a profession that had become dangerous for me. I wanted to live on my wealth. But in order not to waste time, I decided to lend money. As there was no end of requests, I realized a very good profit out of this business and from day to day Sara made my life more enjoyable. Then an unexpected event suddenly changed everything.

"But the sun is already setting," said the Wandering Jew, "you are getting near your resting-place. I, however, am called by a powerful conjuration I cannot withstand. Strange feelings penetrate my soul—can it be that the end of my sufferings is drawing near? Farewell!"

With these words the Wanderer disappeared into the nearest ravine. His last words surprised me and I asked the cabalist what they meant.

"I doubt," replied Uzeda, "that we shall get to hear the rest of the Wandering Jew's story. As often as he comes to this part of it where, because of the Prophet's curse, he was condemned to wander forever, he disappears, the scoundrel, and no power on earth can call him back. His last words do not surprise me. For some time now I have noticed that the Wanderer has aged greatly, but that does not mean he is going to die, for if he did, what would become of your Biblical legend?"

Noticing that the cabalist was about to speak of things it is not proper for a practicing Catholic to hear, I broke off the conversation abruptly, walked away from the company, and went back to my tent alone.

The forty-seventh day

The next morning the gypsy told us that, as he was waiting for new goods, it was better for safety's sake not to leave this particular spot. We welcomed this news for in the whole Sierra Morena one could not have found a more enchanting hiding place. That same morning I went hunting in the mountains with several of the gypsies, but when I returned I joined the company and listened to the leader who resumed his story in the following words:

CONTINUATION OF THE STORY OF PANDESOWNA

The Knight of Toledo, now completely reassured about the ghost, had only one thought in his head—to see Señora Uscariz again. We therefore hurried back to Madrid. The little beggar boy, whose place I had taken with Soarez, returned with us and I promptly sent him to the young invalid. I accompanied the Knight to his house and left him in the hands of his servants who were delighted to see him again. Then I went to the entrance of St. Rochus Church and gathered my little group around me; a deputation was sent to the market-woman, our usual source of provisions, and returned armed with a sausage and chestnuts. We ate gaily and congratulated ourselves on being together again. But scarcely had we finished this light repast, when a man stopped before us and studied us carefully as if he were about to make a choice. This man was not unknown to me: I had seen him coming and going almost every day and always as if he were in a great hurry. It dawned on me that it might be Busqueros. So I went over and asked him whether he was not that wise and clever friend whose advice had been so useful to Lope Soarez.

"In person," replied that eccentric gentleman. "And I would have arranged his marriage had not thunder and lightning interfered so that I mistook the house of the Knight of Toledo for the house of the banker Moro. But have patience! The Duke di Santa-Maura is not yet the beautiful Inez's husband and he never will be as long as my name is Don Rochus. Listen, my boy! I have been standing here trying to pick out an intelligent lad among you who can do the job I have in mind and, as you already know about the situation, you are the one I shall engage. Thank the Lord who has opened the way to your good fortune in such a fashion! At first what you will earn will not seem very brilliant to you, for I shall neither pay you a salary nor shall I clothe you; and, as for your food, how could I bother about that without insulting Divine Providence which feeds the raven's young as well as the proudest eagle?"

"In that case, noble Don Busqueros," I told him, "it is not very clear to me what advantage it would be to enter your service and attend to your business!"

"The advantages," replied this eccentric, "lie in the unusually great number of tasks I shall give you daily and which you will carry out in the antichambers of important persons who, one day, might become your protectors. Moreover, in the time between tasks, I do not forbid you to beg. So then, thank God for your luck and follow me to the barber shop where I shall rest a little and chat with you."

As soon as we were at the barber's, Busqueros laid before me the long list of his commands.

"My friend, I noticed that, as you came away from the card game, you stuck several half *reales* in your pocket. Take two of your coins and buy a pint bottle. You will then take it to Don Felipe Tintero on the Calle de Toledo and tell him that Busqueros asks him for some ink for a poet who is a friend of his. As soon as he has filled the bottle you will go to the Plaza Cevada, to the grocer on the corner. You will climb up to the attic room where you will find Don Ramuz Agudez whom you will recognize because he wears one black sock and one white sock, one red slipper and one green slipper, and perhaps even his trousers instead of a cap on his head. You will give him the bottle of ink and in my name make him swear to give you the satire dedicated to great gentlemen who marry beneath their station in life and which must be written both in Spanish and Italian. From there you will go back to the Calle de Toledo and enter the house next to Don Tintero's which is separated from the latter only by a narrow alleyway. You will then find out whether the occupants are still there and whether they are making plans to move out, for I have rented this house and I wish to put in it a relative of mine, who will perhaps free Don Tintero from his eternal inkpot. Then you will go to the banker Moro; go up to the *cuarto principal,* that is, to the reception rooms and ask for the Duke di Santa-Maura's chamberlain and give him this letter which contains a rosette. Then you will go to the Maltese Cross to inquire whether they have reserved a room for Gaspar Soarez, the merchant from Cadiz, then . . ."

"Have pity!" I cried. "Noble Don Busqueros! Do you realize you have given me tasks enough for a whole week! Don't begin by putting my zeal and my legs to such hard tests!"

"Well, all right!" said Don Busqueros. "I really intended to give you several more errands, but those you can do tomorrow morning. What I wanted to say: if they ask you at the Duke di Santa-Maura's who you are, say that you run errands for the Palais Avila."

"But, noble Don Busqueros," I protested, "won't that make trouble if you use such a prominent name?"

"No doubt," replied my new master. "No doubt you run the risk of a flogging but nothing ventured, nothing gained, and the advantages I am offering you outweigh the unpleasantness. Come, come, my friend, don't waste time reasoning, off now!"

Perhaps I should have declined the honor of serving Don Busqueros had not my curiosity been aroused to an extreme by the reference to my father and the lady who would free him from his inkpot. I also wanted to learn what Busqueros intended to do to prevent Santa-Maura from marrying the beaitiful Inez. I therefore bought a pint bottle and turned my steps towards the Calle de Toledo. As I stood in front of my father's house, I trembled in every limb and I could not make up my mind to go any further. My father appeared on the balcony and when he saw a bottle in my hand, he motioned to me to come in. As I climbed the stairs my heart beat faster with every step. At last I opened the door and stood face to face with my father. At that moment I wanted to throw myself on my knees before him. But my good angel saved me from doing so, for my agitated expression seemed to disturb him enough. He took the bottle, filled it with ink without even asking for whom it was intended and opened the door for me in a manner that warned me not to linger. I took one look at the wardrobe from which I had fallen into the ink.[1] I saw the sadiron my aunt had used to smash the receptacle and save my life. My excitement rose to the highest pitch, I seized my father's hand and kissed it. He was greatly startled, pushed me out of the door and locked it behind me.

Busqueros had ordered me to take the bottle to the poet Agudez and then to go back to the Calle de Toledo to see what my father's neighbors were doing. I thought it would be all right for me to change the order of his errands and went first to the neighbor. I saw that they had moved out

[1] This happened when Avadoro, as a small boy, was visiting his father.

and I made up my mind to keep a close watch on the future owner's actions.

Then I went to the Plaza Cevada where I had no trouble in finding the grocer's house. However, it was not so easy to reach the poet. I lost my way under roof tiles, slabs of slate and rain-gutters. At last I came to a garret window and, looking through it, saw a figure that was even more grotesque than Busquero's description. Agudez seemed to be filled with divine inspiration and, as soon as he saw me, he addressed me in the following lines:

O mortal, on your airy path you brush against
The sharp ridge of light red brick
And dark blue slate: from heavens of sapphire
Say what brings you earthward on wings of zephyr?
Speak, what is your desire?

I answered him:

I tell you without subterfuge,
I am an ink-fish and I bring you fresh ink.

Whereupon the poet said:

Then give me the fluid
That borrows the color and strength of flowing steel mixed with gall
From the source of Muses. With pride
My poet's heart swells, in waves, as black as ebony.

"Señor Agudez," I replied, "that is a description of ink that would delight the noble Señor Tintero, the maker of this ink which I bring you. But tell me, isn't it possible for you to talk in prose, for that is the language to which I am accustomed?"

"And I, my friend," said the poet, "will never become accustomed to it. Indeed, I even avoid associating with men because of their stupid, banal speech. When I want to write good verse it is important for me first to nourish my soul a long while with poetic thoughts and talk to myself only in mellifluous words. If they are not mellifluous in themselves, they will become so by the way I put them together and transform them into spiritual music. Through this artistry I have succeeded in producing an entirely new form of poetry. So far the language of poetry has been confined to certain expressions termed poetic. I, however, have introduced *all* words of the language into it. In the verses I have just written, I use words like goat, slate, gall."

"I can well imagine that you use all words as you please and no one could prevent you, but are your verses the better for it?"

"My verses are as good as verses can be and they can be used for anything. Out of poetry I have made a sort of universal tool, in particular, out of descriptive poetry which I have, so to speak, created and through which I can describe things that were formerly not worth so much trouble."

"Describe, Señor Agudez, describe, as much as you please! But tell me whether you have finished that satire you promised Don Busqueros."

"I do not compose satires as long as the weather is fine! When you see stormy days, rainy days, dark gloomy days, then come back and fetch the satire!"

The grief of Nature oppresses my soul
Grips my heart and mind and flows into my songs.
I hate myself and see in men like me
The pattern of dark moods and signs of all evil.
Dipped in night, my brush at such times paints
The grimace of decay, depravity's wry face,
But when through the blue ether blond Phoebus floats
The rushing flood of his light traversing the space of the world,
In the same rhythm my heart turns back to God
Flees from earth and rises up towards heaven.

"That last line," the poet added, "is not very good but it may go in an ex-tempore poem."

"I assure you, I have nothing against it. However, I shall tell Don Busqueros that you write satires only on rainy days. But when I come to fetch ours, how shall I ever reach you? The stairs I came up are the only ones in the house and they do not lead to you."

"My friend, behind, in the courtyard, is a ladder on

which you can climb to a haymow where a mule driver in the neighborhood stores his hay and provisions; from there you can come to me, at least if the haymow is not too full, for on such days you can't get in here at all and my food is brought to me by way of the scuttle through which you see me."

"You must be very unhappy in accommodations like that."

"Me—unhappy? How could I be unhappy when my verses cause the greatest rapture at Court and in the city, and people talk of nothing else?"

"I think, however, that each man talks only of his own interests."

"That is understandable, but my poems are not only the heart of that conversation, people refer to them again and again; by reciting several of my verses they acquire new and winged words. From here you can see the shop of the bookseller Moreno: people go in there only to buy my works."

"May your good luck continue! I suspect, however, that on the days when you write satires it is not too dry in your house."

"When it rains on one side, I move over to the other and often I don't even notice it at all. But now leave me: talking prose disturbs me."

I left the poet and went to the banker Moro. Going up to the state reception rooms I asked for the Duke di Santa-Maura's chamberlain. At first I was allowed to speak only to a young boy about my own age who served the servants of the head-servant. He let me speak to a lackey who let me speak to a valet, who let me speak to the chamberlain. And shortly after that, to my great surprise, I was led before the Duke, who was just getting dressed. I saw him through a cloud of powder; he was looking at himself in a mirror and before him lay rosettes of all different colors.

"Boy," he said rudely, "you will be given a touch of the birch if you do not tell me where you come from and who gave you this letter you brought me."

I let him press me a little, but finally admitted that I was a messenger from the Palais Avila and was fed with the kitchen boys. The Duke gave his chamberlain a meaningful look and then sent me away, at the same time tossing me several coins.

Now I had to go only to the Maltese Cross. Soarez, the father, had arrived and had been told about his son's duel: that his son had fought with a nobleman, with whom he dined daily, that this nobleman had then come to live with him, had made him acquainted with notorious women and that one of them had had him thrown out of the window of her apartment.

This information, half true, half false, was a stab in the heart for Soarez. He locked himself in his room and ordered that no one, no matter who it was, should be admitted. Members of his firm who were in touch with him came to offer their services—but they were not received.

I went to meet Busqueros who had given me a rendezvous in a pub opposite the barber's. He asked me how I happened to know about the Soarez's adventures. I explained that young Soarez had told me about them himself, and I proceeded to relate the whole story about the Soarez family and their enmity with the bankers Moro. Busqueros had had only a faint suspicion of all this and he listened to me attentively.

"I must draw up a new plan," he said, "it falls into two strictly separate actions. First, we have to make Santa-Maura quarrel with the Moros, then reconcile the latter with Soarez. As for the first part of my plan, it has already made good progress. Before I tell you about this, I must acquaint you with several situations in the Avila family . . .

"The present Duke was the most brilliant man in all the Court and enjoyed the honor, the favor and the trust of his monarch. It is seldom that young men do not boast about the advantages they are able to win and the Duke was no exception to the general rule. He considered himself greater than the great with whom he was of equal rank and made up his mind to marry into the royal family."

Here Bosqueros interrupted himself and said to me:

"You little scamp, what is there about you to make you worthy of such confidences, to share things which the common people from which you come should always be kept in ignorance and of which only a very small circle of nobles has any knowledge?"

"My dear maestro," I replied, "I did not know that one had to pass a test to gain the honor of your confidence, but without boasting about my ancestral tree, I can easily prove that I have enjoyed an upbringing which is given only to young men of the highest birth. From that you can understand that fate, rather than my background, is to blame if I am dependent on begging."

"Bravo," said Busqueros, "then that's why you don't speak the language of the common people. But do tell me who you are! Come now, tell me!"

I looked very serious, even worried.

"You are my master," I said, "and can force me to speak if you wish. However there is a tribunal that is as strict as it is holy and dedicated and . . ."

"I don't want to know any more," said Busqueros, "nor do I want to have anything to do with the tribunal of which you are speaking. All right! I shall tell you everything I know about the house of Avila. As you have your own secrets, you will know how to keep mine."

Proud of his success and the favor he enjoyed, the fortunate Avila was also eager to bind himself to his ruler through marriage. At that time the Infanta Beatrice stood out among her sisters for her charming demeanor and her lovely eyes that held a strong hint of tenderness. Avila was influential enough to place close to the Infanta a relative who was completely devoted to him. The young courtier's bold plan was to make a secret marriage and to wait for the most propitious moment to announce it. It is not known how far Avila was successful. For two years his secret was preserved and during this time he made every effort to overthrow Olivarez. He did not succeed. On the contrary, it was the Minister, who at least partly saw through his puzzling behavior. Avila was arrested, brought to the castle at Segovia and soon thereafter sent into exile. He was offered clemency if he would make any marriage whatever—he refused. The natural conclusion was that he was married to the Infanta Beatrice. There was some talk of arresting the first lady-in-waiting, Avila's relative, but there was also fear of causing a scandal that, in a certain measure, might besmirch the honor of the royal house.

The Infanta died of a broken heart. Avila was approached with new proposals and, to put an end to his exile, he decided to marry the young de Scar, niece of the Duke of Olivarez. A daughter was born to him and he dared to call her Beatrice, which was a bit too clear a reminder of the adventure with the Infanta Beatrice, but this audacity was soothing to his pride. Meanwhile he seemed actually to fear that his adventure might be forgotten. In the end, Don Luis de Haro, successor to the Duke d'Olivarez, came to believe that a secret marriage had taken place. Though efforts were made to discover the truth, they were unsuccessful.

The Duchess d'Avila died. The Duke sent his daughter to a convent in Brussels, where she was entrusted to the care of an aunt, the Duchess de Beaufort. Her upbringing was highly original and would have been more useful to one of our sex than to hers.

Beatrice has been here in Madrid for six months. She is extraordinarily beautiful, but very proud and she seems to have an aversion to marriage. She maintains that a crown princess is not in duty bound to take a husband and that she has the right to live independently. Her father supports her in these ideas. The old courtiers, on the other hand, who remember past stories, assume that the Duke was married to the Infanta, that he had a son by her and that he hopes to obtain recognition for him. But on this subject everyone preserves a discreet silence. If I know anything about it, it is because I have certain connections with the private life of that family.

The Duchess Beatrice d'Avila will not marry. She is extraordinarily proud, and I do not think anyone in Spain will dare to ask for her hand. I am counting, however, on Santa-Maura's tremendous egotism and hope to convince him that *la* d'Avila is head over heels in love with him.

Listen to what I intend to do next. You know that the present fashion is to wear ribands in the hair, on the arms and on dresses. Our great ladies import them from Paris, Naples or Florence and watch jealously to see that other women do not have ribands of the same pattern. Last Sunday the Duke di Santa-Maura was presented at Court. In the evening there was a Court ball. The Duke has a good figure, he dances gracefully; he is a foreigner and above all he attracts the attention of beautiful women. Each lady seemed to expect him to pay her homage. But the first to whom the Duke paid homage was proud Beatrice who responded with cold indifference. The Duke complained about this to several courtiers and permitted himself to jest about the pride of Spanish women.

In the course of the evening, under cover of offering the Duke a lemonade, a page handed him a note that contained only the words: "Do not be discouraged!" The note was not signed, but in it was a piece of a green and lavender rosette which on that evening was the color of Beatrice's riband. Meanwhile that lady had been told that the Neapolitan gentleman had complained about her slight. She feared she had overstepped the bounds of courtesy and made a point of being polite to him. From then on Santa-Maura had no doubt that the rosette was meant as the signature of the note. He went home highly pleased with himself; his future wife, Inez Moro, had lost value in his eyes, though on his arrival she had seemed very beautiful to him.

The next day when Santa-Maura ate with the banker Moro, his future father-in-law, at noon, he asked him questions about the Duchess d'Avila. Moro told him that, on account of her upbringing in Flanders, the Duchess had a certain dislike for Spain and Spaniards, at least so he explained to himself her unprecedented pride and her publicly announced decision not to marry. Moro thought, however, that the Duchess Beatrice could be persuaded to choose some foreign nobleman. In saying this the honorable banker was unconsciously working against his daughter's marriage which was so dear to his heart. Santa-Maura actually thought he had sufficient proof that Beatrice preferred foreigners to Spaniards!

That same forenoon Santa-Maura received a paper folded like a note, which contained only a piece of an orange and violet rosette. He went to the opera and saw that the Duchess was wearing ribands of the same colors.

"I take it, you rascal," Busqueros added, "that you have sense enough to guess how the knot of this intrigue is tied. You assume—and rightly so—that the Duchess's first lady-in-waiting is devoted to me and that every day she gives me a sample of the ribbon her mistress will wear on that day. The note you delivered contains a rosette and the suggestion for a rendezvous at the "tertuliar," the reception at the French Ambassador's. The Duke will be shown a certain amount of attention for, in a letter Beatrice received this morning from the Duchess of Osuna, the daughter of the King of Naples, there is much talk of him. It is impossible that there should not be a conversation between them and nothing they say will escape me, for the French ambassador has permitted me to attend all his receptions. To tell the truth I do not play any leading role there, thank God, but my ear is so perfectly trained that I can hear what is being said even at the other end of the room. But enough for today! You must be hungry: I won't keep you from getting yourself a meal."

As a matter of fact I went to the Knight of Toledo who was looking forward to a dinner with his beloved Señora Uscariz. He sent his servants away and I attended him. When the ladies had left, I told him about the intrigue Busqueros had woven and his plan to cause a split between Santa-Maura and the Moros. He was highly amused and promised to help us. Such an ally assured us of success.

The Knight of Toledo was one of the first guests to appear at the French Ambassador's reception and he promptly began a conversation with proud Beatrice. At first she treated him with her usual haughtiness, but the Knight's charm was irresistible; it was impossible not to laugh with him. Then he talked to her about Santa-Maura. Beatrice expressed a desire to meet the man her friend had described in her letter; she became more animated than usual, and this did not pass unnoticed. Two noblemen spoke to Santa-Maura and congratulated him on such a difficult conquest. That was the last straw. He was almost beside himself with delight, even hinting that he and Beatrice were married. On his return home he calculated how much greater the entire inheritance of the Duchess d'Avila was than Inez Moro's dowry, and after that he treated the Moro family with marked disdain.

The next day the Knight of Toledo sent for Busqueros, who felt very honored to be introduced to him. They decided to write a letter in Beatrice's name and, as the signature would be only a piece of ribbon, they considered this falsification unimportant. The letter was extremely puzzling: they only hinted at things, referring vaguely to difficulties and finally suggesting a rendezvous at the Duke d'Incaz's. Santa-Maura's reply was not lacking in wit and, as was to be expected, he arrived punctually at the rendezvous. This time Beatrice was as proud as ever—a situation that bade fair to spoil our plans, but the Knight of Toledo drew Santa-Maura aside and told him confidentially that Beatrice had had a violent disagreement with her father because he was determined to force her to marry a Spaniard. From that moment Santa-Maura believed that Beatrice loved him and his confident joy, that nothing could shake, was obvious to all.

We continued our exchange of letters with the credulous Neapolitan. Beatrice's letters (those she was supposed to write) became daily more significant, even going so far as to hint that a decision would soon be reached. However she expressed her astonishment that Santa-Maura was still living in the Moro house; he himself wanted to make a change, but did not know how to bring it about.

One day, instead of the usual letter, Santa-Maura received a work entitled "A satire on Great Lords who make Mésalliances." It began in the following way:

Insect brood, fed on the slime of Paculas!
Scum of the earth that swarms up even into the kingdom of Aeolus!
Do you think to climb to the highest heaven
And mingle your blood with the blood of the gods?
Remember the king who desiring to be like the gods
Toyed with the thunder, boldly rolling it through the clouds,
Playing Jupiter with false flashes of lightning,
While from the bronze car Salmoneus fell into the void.

As you can see, the satire inveighed less against great lords who married beneath them than against rich men who tried to climb the social ladder. This product of Aguzar was, like all his others, neither good nor bad. In this case, however, it brought the desired result.

As a joke, Santa-Maura read it to the Moros at dessert. When the entire company had risen from the table and gone into another room, the Duke, wasting no time in explanations, sent for his horses and moved into a hotel. The next day the entire city knew what had happened. The supposed Beatrice wrote a letter which was far more tender than any before, authorizing Santa-Maura to make his proposal in due form. He did so and was rejected by Beatrice's father who never even told his daughter about it. Consequently the Neapolitan did not consider this a disgrace and was not too sorry to be sent back to Inez again.

There was now nothing left but to reconcile the Soarez family with the Moros. This was done as follows: The elder Soarez, who had turned against his son and shut himself up in his hotel, finally decided to go out, and, to amuse himself, he went into a taproom. Whenever he saw people talking together, he would sit down at a table near them and pass the time listening to them without entering into their conversation, which moreover would not have been seemly, as he did not know anyone in Madrid. One day Soarez sat down near two men, one of whom was saying to the other:

"I can assure you, sir, that no commercial house in Spain can compare to the Brothers Moro and I know what I am saying for since the year 1580 I have examined their debit and credit and know the balance sheet of all the business they have transacted for a hundred years back."

"Sir," replied the other man, "you must admit that Cadiz is a city of far greater importance than Madrid and that the commerce of two worlds is a business of a much higher order than the miserable turnover in money that is transacted in the capital. It therefore follows that the House of Soarez, the leading house in Cadiz, is more important than the House of Moro, the leading house in Madrid."

As the man spoke in a very loud voice, a number of idlers gathered around and sat down at the same table with the two speakers. Soarez, waiting eagerly to hear what else they would say, pressed back against the wall the better to hear and not be seen.

One of the two men, raising his voice still louder, said:

"Sir, I have the honor to inform you that I have had the privilege of examining the Moros' books since 1580 and that I also know about the Soarez affair. After Inigo Soarez crossed the sea and established a house in Cadiz in the year 1602, he had the effrontery to offer the Moros a bank draft without indicating his security. Such an irregularity could have ruined this young house if the Moros had not been so broadminded as to hush up the whole matter."

By this time Soarez was on the verge of exploding, but the speaker was still talking.

"In the year 1612 and in the following years the Soarez had put into circulation ingots of very unequal value; but had declared that they were all of equal value. The Moros had an official test made and again could have ruined the Soarez but were so generous as to keep the matter quiet."

Soarez now had the greatest difficulty in controlling himself. The speaker went on.

"Finally Gaspar Soarez, who was doing business with the Philippines without sufficient capital, succeeded in interesting an uncle of the Moros, who lent him a million. To get back that disastrous million the Moros had to bring a lawsuit which is perhaps still dragging on."

At this point Gaspar Soarez could no longer control his rage, and he would undoubtedly have given full vent to his anger had not a man he did not know attacked the Moros' defender.

"Sir," said the stranger, "I declare herewith that not a word you have said is true. When Inigo Soarez arranged a bank draft on the Moros he actually had the capital in Antwerp. The Moros had no right to let the bank draft go to protest and their letter of apology is now in the Soarez office, as well as a second letter of apology dealing with the matter of the ingots. As for the lawsuit of which you spoke, without knowing anything about it, that was brought not to keep the Moros from taking back one million, but to force them to accept two million clear profit realized on the last expedition to the Philippines. The gentleman was therefore right when he told you the Soarez were the leading merchants in Spain. It is equally certain, that you, sir, are one of those braggarts who do not know what they are saying."

The man who had spoken in praise of the Moros was

embarrassed and left the taproom. Gaspar Soarez felt it his duty to make himself known to his defender. He therefore addressed him civilly and suggested a stroll in the Prado, which the stranger accepted. They sat down on a bench and Soarez said to his new acquaintance:

"What you said just now has put me greatly in your debt, as I am sure you will understand when I tell you that I am Gaspar Soarez, sole head of the house you have so generously defended against a base calumniator. I see that you know the business world of Cadiz well, and especially of my house. You are undoubtedly an experienced merchant. Would you be so kind as to tell me your name?"

The man to whom Soarez spoke was none other than Busqueros who felt it was wiser not to mention his name. He said he was Rochus Moraredo.

"Señor Moraredo," Soarez went on, "your name does not seem to be very well known in the business world, if I may say so. You have probably not had the opportunity to transact business commensurate to your talent and your desserts. I invite you to share in some of my interests and to prove my sincerity I shall tell you about the psychic state I am in and what I plan to do. I have only one son, in whom I had placed all my hopes. I sent him to Madrid and at the same time recommended three things to him: not to call himself Don Soarez, but simply Soarez, not to consort with the nobility and not to draw his sword. Well and good! Would you think it possible that in the hotel my son was known only as Don Lope Soarez? That his only acquaintance in Madrid was a nobleman named Busqueros? And what is worse, my son was thrown out of a window, a scandal no Soarez has ever suffered! To punish this ungrateful and disobedient son I intend to marry—and the sooner the better. That is settled. I am not yet forty years old and no one can criticize me if I think of marriage. I ask no more of my future wife than that she be the daughter of an honorable merchant and above reproach. You know Madrid. May I hope that you will guide me in my search for a bride?"

"Sir," replied Busqueros, "I know the daughter of a very honorable businessman who has just refused the hand of a distinguished nobleman because she is determined to remain true to her class. Her father is very angry and insists that she must choose a husband within a week and leave his house immediately. You say you are forty, but you look scarcely thirty. Go to the Theatre de la Cruz, see the first two acts of *The Siege of Granada* and when the third act begins I will come and fetch you."

Gaspar Soarez therefore saw the first two acts of *The Siege of Granada* and when the second act was almost over, his new friend arrived. He took Soarez out of the theatre and led him all about through streets and alleys as though he were trying to make him lose his way. Soarez asked him the name of the young girl, but his new friend gave him to understand that the question was indiscreet and that the young girl was particularly anxious to keep the whole adventure secret in case the marriage should not take place. Soarez agreed. They came out behind a large house, went through a stable, climbed a dark staircase and stepped into an unfurnished room lighted only by a few lamps. A few minutes later two veiled ladies entered. One of them said:

"Noble Señor Soarez, the step I have decided to take is not motivated by boldness, which is foreign to my character, but it is forced on me by the vain ambition of my father who wishes to marry me to a nobleman. Without a doubt great ladies are suitably reared for the world in which they must live, but I—what is there in that world for me? Its brilliance would probably dazzle the weak light of my reason. I could find no happiness in that world and would only risk my salvation in the next. I would like to marry a merchant; I respect the name of Soarez and I wanted to know you."

As she spoke, the lady raised her veil. Soarez, overcome by her beauty, knelt before her, drew from his finger a ring of great value and, without a word, held it out to her. At that moment a side door opened with a great clatter. A young man, sword in hand, rushed in, followed by servants bearing torches.

"Señor Soarez, do you consider this proper conduct for a man who wants to marry the daughter of the House of Moro?"

"Moro!" shouted Soarez. "I do not want to marry a Moro!"

"Go, sister," the young man then said. "As for you, Señor Soarez, who dare to approach a daughter of the House of

Moro without intending to marry her, I have every right to have you thrown out of the window! But I wish to respect my own house. I shall send my servants away and I myself will attend to teaching you a lesson."

The young man's servants left the room and the young man said to Soarez:

"Señor, now there are three of us here and as Señor Busqueros came with you, you cannot refuse to have him as your second."

"Who is Busqueros?" replied Soarez. "This man's name is Moraredo."

"That makes no difference," said young Moro. "Draw your sword. To be sure, you are older than I am, but as you were young enough to kneel at my sister's feet, you are young enough to fight me. Draw your sword, or jump out of the window!"

One can understand that Soarez wanted to appear brave, but as he knew no more about the art of fencing than his son did, his arm was soon pierced through. As soon as young Moro saw blood flow, he drew back and Busqueros bound the wounded man's arm with a handkerchief. He then took Soarez to a physician who bandaged his arm, and then saw him to his hotel.

There Soarez found his son who had been brought on a stretcher. This sight moved him to tears, but to hide his emotion he went to the opposite extreme and began to reproach him.

"Lope," he said to him, "I forbade you to consort with nobles."

"Oh, father," young Lope replied, "I have known only one, the same nobleman I see with you now. Moreover, I can assure you that my acquaintance with him was not of my choosing."

"At least," said the father, "you should not have fought with him. I forbade you to draw your sword."

"Señor," said Busqueros, "don't forget that you too have a wounded arm."

"I would have forgiven you everything," the elder Soarez went on, "but how can a man put himself in a position to be thrown out of a window?"

"Sir," interjected Busqueros, "the same unpleasantness could have happened to you a quarter of an hour ago."

The father was greatly embarrassed. At that moment a letter with the following contents was handed to him:

My dear Señor Gaspar Soarez:
I am addressing the following to you in the name of my son, Estaban Moro who, finding you with his sister, Inez, in our stable-boy's room, thought he had to show his resentment, and most humbly asks to beg your pardon.

Your son, Lope Soarez, had already tried to climb in her window; but made a mistake in the house, fell off the ladder and broke his leg.

Incidents such as these could lead us to assume that it is the purpose of your house to dishonor ours and I could have you brought before the courts for this, but instead I choose to make you the following proposition: We are involved in a lawsuit for two million piastres which you are trying to force me to accept. I therefore accept them on condition that I may add two more million to them and offer the full amount, along with the hand of my daughter, Inez, to your son.

Your son has done me a very great favor by preventing my daughter from marrying a nobleman to whom I, in my overweening ambition, was about to sacrifice her.

Noble Señor Gaspar Soarez, we are always punished for the errors we commit. Your son's courtship of my daughter can only do us extraordinary honor and if he tried to enter Inez's room through the window, that is doubtless the result of the hatred you have nourished against us for almost half a century though it was caused only by the mistakes of clerks, mistakes which we rectified as far as we could.

Cast aside, noble Don Gaspar, those feelings so contrary to the Christian love of one's neighbor; they do harm in this world as well as in the next. Have the kindness to consider as your son's father-in-law, the man who has the honor of signing himself

Your humble servant,
Moro

Soarez, who had read this letter aloud, sank down into a chair and gave himself up to conflicting emotions. The son realized what his father was going through: rolling off his stretcher he dragged himself over to his father and clasped his knees.

"Lope," the father cried, "did you have to love a Moro?"

"Don't forget," said Busqueros, "that you too knelt at her feet."

"I forgive you, my son," said Gaspar.

The end of the story is not hard to guess. That same evening Lope Soarez was carried to his future father-in-law's house and the care Inez gave him added not a little to his speedy recovery. Gaspar Soarez could not be completely cured of his prejudice against the Moros, and he returned to Cadiz immediately after his son's marriage.

For two weeks Lope Soarez had been the fortunate husband of the lovely Inez and was making ready to take her to Cadiz where Gaspara Soarez awaited them.

Busqueros, the instigator and, one might say, the producer of this romance, was already busy working on another marriage that was much more to his liking. He wanted to persuade my father to marry his relative. That pretty girl was already living in the house across the little alley-way from my father's house. This marriage, however, I made up my mind to prevent.

First of all, I talked with my uncle, the honorable Theatine monk, Fra Heronymo Santez, but that good priest refused categorically to have anything to do with a matter that smacked too much of worldly intrigue. He never bothered about family matters, he said, except to bring about a reconciliation or to prevent a scandal and things of that sort were not in his province. As I was now thrown on my own resources, I would gladly have had Toledo's help, but then I would have had to tell him who I was and that I dared not do. So for the present I contented myself with bringing Busqueros and the Knight together, but first I warned the Knight that Busqueros was a very importunate fellow. However Don Rochus could be tactful when he chose. The Knight had permitted him to call and pay his respects and he realized that if he would preserve this privilege he dared not abuse it.

While the gypsy leader was speaking, one of his men appeared to report on the day's work. The leader went off and we did not see him again that day.

The forty-eighth day

When we gathered together the following morning, the gypsy yielded to our insistence and went on with his story.

CONTINUATION OF THE STORY OF PANDESOWNA

One day the Knight asked Busqueros about the affair the Duke d'Arcos had been carrying on so many years and whether the woman, who had been able to hold him so long, was really so seductive.

"The fact that your Excellency has asked me about my lord's secrets shows that Your Excellency is confident of my devotion. On the other hand, fortunately, I understand your Excellency well enough to know that a certain indifference which is obvious in Your Excellency's manner has never resulted in unpleasantness even with women who, in this respect, are inclined to be indulgent, and that it would never compromise your servant."

"Señor Busqueros," said the Knight, "what I wanted to hear from you was not a eulogy of myself."

"I know that," said Busqueros, "but eulogies of your nobility force themselves to the lips of anyone who has the honor of knowing you. However, the story Your Excellency wishes to hear from me I had already begun to tell the young merchant who has just married."

"Up to that point I know it too," said the Knight. "Lope Soarez told it to young Avarito who repeated it to me. You, Señor Busqueros, climbed up to an apartment on the second floor where a man, terrified by your appearance, cried out: 'Dreadful bloody head! Why do you come to reproach me for an involuntary crime?' And you did not budge from the spot in the city park where Frasqueta told her story. The Duke d'Arcos, who was impersonating her woman companion, approached you and declared that he was anxious to hasten Cabronez's journey and, moreover, in such a way that the latter would not be satisfied with an ordinary pilgrimage but would go to a monastery to do penance for a long time."

"Your Excellency," said Busqueros, "has an extraordinary memory. Those are the very words the Duke said to me. But, as Your Excellency already knows the story of the married woman, to keep things straight, I must tell you the story of the husband and explain how the latter made the acquaintance of the terrible pilgrim, Hervas."

Toledo sat down, adding that he envied the Duke a mistress like Frasqueta; he had always liked pert, saucy women and in that respect this one far exceeded any he had ever heard of before. Busqueros smiled knowingly and began as follows:

THE STORY OF CABRONEZ

Frasqueta's husband, whose name (*cabron* in Spanish—cuckold) could be considered a significant emblem, is the son of a citizen of Salamanca. For a long time he held a humble position in the Municipal Council; he worked in wholesale and retail, supplying a number of retail shopkeepers. Later he inherited a considerable amount of money and, like many Spaniards, promptly decided to do nothing more—except go to church and smoke cigarettes.

You may object that Cabronez, who wanted only to have peace and quiet in life, should not have married the first little hussy who gazed amorously out of the window. It is, however, the great mystery of the human heart that no one ever does what he should. One man sees happiness only in marriage, wastes his whole life trying to make a choice and dies a bachelor. Another man swears he will never have a wife—and marries again and again. Cabronez therefore married. At first he congratulated himself, then he regretted it. When he saw that he had not only a Count de Penna-Flora around his neck, but also that his soul, which he thought had gone to hell, was torturing him, he became despondent and drew into himself. At last he had his bed moved into the study where there was a rosary and holy water. For days on end he seldom saw his wife and he spent more time in church than usual.

One day a pilgrim stood beside him. The man looked at him so strangely that Cabronez was disturbed and felt impelled to leave the church. Evenings when he went for a walk he met the same man and soon everywhere he went the pilgrim's stern, piercing glance caused him unspeakable fear. In the end, Cabronez overcame his natural shyness and addressed the stranger.

"Sir, I shall report you to the *alcalde* if you do not stop following me."

"Following you! Following you!" said the pilgrim in a hollow, sepulchral voice. "Yes, you will be followed and to the limit—one hundred doubloons, a head, a murdered man who died before he could take communion . . . Have I guessed it?"

"Who are you?" cried Cabronez in fear.

"I am a condemned man, but I still hope for divine mercy. Have you ever heard of the scholar Hervas?"

"I know his story in general. He had the misfortune to be an atheist and came to a bad end."

"Exactly. I am his son. I was born with the mark of Cain, but it has been granted me to recognize the stigma on sinners' foreheads and to lead them back to the path of salvation. The first time I saw you, I recognized the sign of the damned on your forehead and your whole story was revealed to me. Count de Penna-Flora actually intended to seduce and possess all women, but instead he did not seduce or possess a single one. As he never went beyond sinning in his thoughts, his soul was not in danger. However, he had neglected his religious duties for two years and as he was about to fulfill them, you had him murdered or at least you contributed to his murder. Those are the reasons for your obsession. There is only one way to rid yourself of them, and that is to follow the example of the Commander de Toralva,[1] I shall be your guide; you understand that I undertake this role for the sake of my own salvation too."

Cabronez allowed himself to be persuaded. He visited the places of pilgrimage in Spain and Italy, remaining for two long years on this pilgrimage. Señora Cabronez spent this time in Madrid where she had established her mother and sister.

When Cabronez returned to Salamanca, he found his house in the finest order and his wife more beautiful, gentle and charming than ever. After two months she went back to Madrid again to see her mother and sister, then she returned to Salamanca and remained there permanently—the Duke d'Arcos had been called to the embassy in London.

At this point the Knight of Toledo interrupted Busqueros.

"My dear Busqueros, I can't let you off now. I want to hear the rest of the story and what has become of Señora Cabronez."

"She became a widow," Busqueros replied. "Then she married again and since then she has enjoyed a spotless reputation. But what do I see? Here she comes and, if I am not mistaken, she is going straight to your house."

"What are you saying?" cried Toledo. "But that is Señora

[1] Commander de Toralva was freed of satanic obsessions by visiting holy places for which he received general absolution.

Uscariz! Why! the deceitful hussy! And she vowed I was her first lover! I'll make her pay dearly for this!"

As the Knight wanted to be alone with his mistress, he therefore left us in all haste.[1]

[1] The Days from forty-nine to fifty-three, inclusive, are found in the first volume, *The Saragossa Manuscript*.

The fifty-fourth day

The following day we gathered at the usual hour and begged the gypsy chief to continue the story of his adventures, which he did in the following words:

CONTINUATION OF THE STORY OF PANDESOWNA

Toledo, who now knew Señora Uscariz's true story, amused himself for a time by talking to her about Frasqueta Cabronez, an enchanting woman, the only one who could make him happy, the only woman who could hold him and make him settle down for good and all. In the end, however, all love affairs began to bore him, Señora Uscariz included.

The priory of Castile had become vacant and, as the

Knight of Toledo was being considered for it, the latter hurried off to Malta. So for a time I lost my protector who would have been in a position to spoil the plans Busqueros was plotting against my father's huge inkpot. As it turned out, I was merely an onlooker at the whole intrigue, and unable to prevent it. This is what happened.

THE STORY OF DON FELIPE TINTERO LARGO

I told you, at the beginning of my story,[1] that to get the air my father was in the habit of going out on a balcony from which one looked down on the Calle de Toledo, that he then went to another balcony that opened onto a little alley-way and that as soon as he caught sight of neighbors opposite he greeted them with an 'Agur!' He did not like to go back into the house until he had greeted the man. And the neighbors hastened to return his greeting in order not to keep him waiting. Aside from that, he had no further relations with them. These good neighbors moved away and their place was taken by the Cimiento ladies, two distant cousins of Don Rochus Busqueros. Señora Cimiento, the aunt, a woman of forty was a gentle, retiring person with a bright healthy complexion. Señorita Cimiento, the niece, was tall and well built with very pretty eyes and beautiful arms. As soon as the apartment was empty, the two ladies moved in and the next day when my father came out on his balcony overlooking the little alley-way he was delighted to see them on the opposite balcony. They returned his greeting most charmingly. But though he was pleasantly surprised, he nevertheless went back into his apartment and the ladies withdrew into theirs.

For eight days this exchange of courtesies continued. At the end of that time, my father discovered in Señorita Cimiento's room an object that roused his curiosity. It was a little glass case full of carafes and crystal bottles; one of them seemed to contain a bright-colored liquid such as one uses in dyeing, others contained gold, silver and azure sand and still others held golden varnishes. The glass case stood near the window. Señorita Cimiento, wearing only a bodice, came and went, fetching now one bottle, now the other.

[1] This tale was told in *The Saragossa Manuscript*.

What was she doing with them? My father could not imagine, and as it was not his way to ask questions, he preferred to know nothing about the matter.

One day, however, Señorita Cimiento sat quite close to the window. She was writing, but her ink was too thick; she poured a little water into it and thinned it so much she could not use it. My father felt compelled out of courtesy to fill a bottle with ink and send it to her. The maid returned, bringing him effusive thanks from her mistress and a paper bag containing twelve sticks of sealing wax, all of as many different colors. They were stamped with artistically wrought decorations and mottoes.

Now at last my father knew what Señorita Cimiento did and that her work was the counterpart of his. Filled with admiration he folded an envelope, wrote an address on it with his beautiful ink and pressed his seal on it with his new sealing wax. He laid the envelope on his table and never tired of looking at it. In the evening he went to the bookseller, Moreno. A man he did not know brought in a bag like his, which also contained the same number of sealing wax sticks. My father thought about it the whole evening and that night he dreamed of sealing wax.

The next morning my father greeted the ladies as usual. He even opened his mouth to speak but closed it again without saying a word and retreated into his apartment. He was careful, however, to choose a well-placed chair from which he could see what went on in Señorita Cimiento's apartment. That beautiful girl was looking through a magnifying glass at her furniture which the maid was dusting, and when she discovered even a speck of dust she ordered the maid to dust it again. My father was very particular about cleanliness too, and he held his neighbor in the highest respect. I have already said that my father's chief occupation was smoking cigarettes and counting the passers-by or the tiles on the Palais Alba. Now, however, he had no time left for that, scarcely even a few minutes, for an irresistible force drew him constantly to the balcony overlooking the little alley-way. Señora Cimiento paid no call and received no visitors. For his part, my father left his apartment less and less. It was not easy for him to change the schedule of his days and to forgo the theatre, but the slightest case of sniffles served him as an excuse to stay home. On those days he never left his place overlooking the alley and spent hours watching Señorita Cimiento arrange her little bottles and her sealing wax. Her beautiful arms, which she constantly showed to advantage, gripped his imagination and he could think of nothing else.

A new object began to rouse his curiosity; this was an earthen jug somewhat like the one that held his ink only much smaller; it stood on an iron tripod and was heated by lamps beneath it. Soon two other jugs, like this one, were placed beside it. The next morning when my father went out on his balcony, he said "Agur!" and opened his mouth to ask what the jugs were for, but as he was not used to speaking, he said not a word and went back into his apartment.

Tortured by curiosity he made up his mind to send Señorita Cimiento another bottle of ink; whereupon he received in return three little crystal bottles filled with red, green and blue ink respectively. The next day my father was in the shop of the bookseller Moreno when an employee of the treasury department came in. Under his arm the man carried a flat case, something like a writing tablet. On it were several columns written in red ink, the heading in blue ink and the lines in green ink. The treasury employee declared that he alone knew the composition of those inks and he challenged anyone to show him anything like them.

Someone my father did not know turned to him and said: "Señor Avadoro, would you, who are so adept at making black ink, be able to make colored inks like these?"

My father disliked being questioned: it always embarrassed him. However, he opened his mouth to answer the question, but then did not say a word and chose instead to go home and fetch the three bottles. The contents were greatly admired, and the treasury employee asked permission to take specimens of the inks with him. My father, who was overwhelmed with praise, silently gave the credit to Señorita Cimiento whose name he still did not know. Home again, he took out a recipe book and found in it three recipes for green ink, seven for red and two for blue. All this confused him very much. In his mind's eye he could see Señorita Cimiento's beautiful white arms and his repressed senses began to stir.

The next morning when my father greeted the beautiful señorita, he felt at last an uncontrollable desire to know her name. He opened his mouth to ask her what it was, but said not a word and went back into his apartment.

He then went out on the balcony overlooking the Calle de Toledo where he saw a well-dressed man carrying a bottle in his hand. He thought the man had come to ask him for ink and he began to stir the contents of his huge earthen receptacle around and around, for he wanted to give him a good quality ink. The cock of the enormous jug was at a third of the height so that there was never any danger of stirring up the dregs. The stranger walked in and my father filled his bottle. Then the man sat down and asked permission to smoke a cigar. My father wanted to answer, but said nothing. The stranger took a cigar from his case and lighted it at a little lamp that stood on the table.

The stranger was, of course, none other than the inevitable Busqueros.

"Noble Señor Avadoro," he said to my father. "You are making a fluid that has brought great trouble to the world. How many plots! How much treachery! How many intrigues! And how many bad books! And all that has flowed from ink—not to mention the love letters and all the little conspiracies against the happiness and honor of husbands. What do you say to that, Señor Avadoro? You say nothing, as usual, you say nothing. Never mind, I shall talk for two as is my habit. Listen to me, Señor Avadoro! Sit down there on that chair and I shall tell you what I am thinking. I maintain that ink will flow from this bottle . . ."

As he said this, Busqueros gave the bottle a shove and ink spurted out onto my father's knee and he left the room hastily to wipe it off and change his clothes. When he came back he met Busqueros who was waiting, hat in hand, to take leave of him. Delighted that the fellow was leaving, my father opened the door. Busqueros actually did go out, but he immediately came back in again.

"That's a fine business," he said, "Señor Avadoro, we forgot to fill the bottle, but don't bother, I'll fill it myself."

Busqueros took a funnel, stuck it in the neck of the bottle and opened the cock. As soon as the bottle was filled, my father again went to the door to open it and Busqueros hurried out. Suddenly my father discovered that the cock was still open and the ink was running all over the room. As he ran to turn off the cock, the door opened and Busqueros came in again. Pretending not to notice the disaster for which he was to blame, he put his ink bottle down on the table, sat down in the same chair he had sat in before and lighted a cigar.

"Listen to me, Señor Avadoro," he said to my father. "I am told you had a son who was drowned in that receptacle. My word, if he had known how to swim he could have been saved. But where did you get this jug? I suspect from Toboso; the clay there is excellent; receptacles like this one are used for making saltpeter; they are as hard as stone. Allow me to test it with this sadiron."

My father started forward to stop him, but too late! Busqueros smashed the receptacle and the ink gushed like a waterfall over my father and everything in the room, Busqueros included.

My father who seldom opened his mouth, opened it now, however, and shouted with all his might. The neighbors rushed out on their balcony.

"Oh, ladies!" cried Busqueros. "A terrible accident has happened! The enormous jug has broken, the room is swimming in ink and the noble Señor Tintero does not know whether he is coming or going! Perform an act of Christian charity and receive us in your rooms."

The ladies seemed only too delighted and in spite of the tragedy my father felt a little glow of pleasure when he heard that he was being taken to the charming young lady who seemed to open her beautiful arms to him and give him the most enchanting smile.

Throwing a coat around my father's shoulders Busqueros took him to the house of the ladies Cimiento. But scarcely was my father there than he received a very unpleasant piece of news; a draper whose shop was below my father's apartment informed him that the ink had poured down into his shop and that he had sent for the police to determine the extent of the damages. At the same time my father's landlord sent him word that he would not have him in his house any longer. Driven out of his home and befouled by ink, my father was the saddest sight in the world.

"Don't worry, Señor Avadoro," said Busqueros. "These ladies own a furnished apartment at the back overlooking the court which you can use. I'll have all your possesssions brought over here. You will be very comfortable; you will find red, green and blue ink here which is at least as good as your black ink. I advise you, however, not to go out too soon, for if you go to the bookseller Moreno everyone will want to hear the story of the broken jug and you are not so very fond of talking. And let me tell you something else, all the jackanapes in the neighborhood have rushed to your apartment to see the flood. Tomorrow all over Madrid people will talk of nothing else."

My father was very upset, but a loving glance from Señorita Cimiento gave him fresh courage and he went off to take possesssion of his new apartment. He did not stay there long. Señora Cimiento came to him; she had talked things over with her niece, she said, and they had decided to turn over the apartment facing the street to him. My father was delighted with this change. They asked his permission to leave the inks and colors where they were. He nodded his head in assent.

The earthen jugs were in the middle drawingroom. Señorita Cimiento came and went, chose colors and did not say a word. Complete silence reigned in the house. Never had my father felt so happy and in this way eight days passed. On the ninth Don Busqueros paid him a visit.

"My dear sir," he said, "I bring you news of a happiness for which you are secretly yearning without daring to declare yourself. You have won the heart of Señorita Cimiento. She consents to give you her hand in marriage and I have brought with me a little paper that must be signed if you want the banns to be published on Sunday."

My father stared at him in stunned amazement. He tried to answer. Busqueros gave him no time.

"My dear Señor Avadoro," he said, "your approaching marriage is no longer a secret. Everyone in Madrid knows about it. Should you intend to postpone it, Señorita Cimiento's relatives will meet at my house and you will also come there and explain to them the reasons for the delay. This is a consideration you cannot overlook."

My father was very upset at the thought of having to give an account of himself before a family council. He tried to speak, but Busqueros gave him no time.

"I know how it is. I understand you all too well. You want to hear your good fortune from Señorita Cimiento herself. But here she comes and I will leave you alone with her."

Señorita Cimiento entered the room, looking very embarrassed. She did not dare to meet my father's eyes. In silence she took several colors and mixed them. Her shyness gave my father courage. He looked at her and could not take his eyes from her.

Busqueros had left the announcement of the banns on the table. Hesitantly Señorita Cimiento went over to the table, picked up the announcement and read it. Then she covered her eyes with her hand and shed a few tears. Since the death of his wife my father had never wept and even less had he given anyone else cause to weep. Those tears touched him, all the more as he could not understand the reason for her embarrassment. Was Señorita Cimiento weeping over the publishing of the banns or because he had not signed the paper? Did she want to marry him or didn't she? It seemed that she could not stop weeping. To let her go on weeping was horrible; to make her talk would have led to a conversation! My father hastily seized a pen and signed the document. Señorita Cimiento kissed his hand, took the paper and left the room. At the usual hour she came back to the drawing-room, kissed my father's hand without saying a word and began to work with the sealing wax. My father smoked cigars and counted the tiles on the Palacio Alba.

Towards midday Fra Bartolommeo, my great uncle, arrived bringing a marriage contract that also protected my interests. My father signed it, Señorita Cimiento signed it, kissed my father's hand and went back to her work on the sealing wax. Ever since his gigantic inkwell had been destroyed my father had not dared to show himself at the theatre or at the bookseller Moreno's. This seclusion was beginning to tell on him. Three days after the signing of the banns, Don Busqueros invited my father to take a drive and my father accepted the invitation. They drove to the opposite bank of the Manzanares and when they came to the little church of St. Francis, Busqueros asked my father to get out. They entered the church where they met Señorita Cimiento who was waiting for them at the door. My father opened his mouth to say that he had thought they were simply taking a little drive. But he did not dare. Instead he took Señorita Cimiento's hand and led her to the altar.

When the newlyweds left the church, they entered a fine carriage, drove back to Madrid and went to a beautiful house where a ball was being given. Señora Avadoro opened the ball with a handsome young man: they danced a fandango and received great applause. My father tried in vain to find in his wife the calm, gentle person who had obediently kissed his hand. On the contrary he saw a noisy, lively, frivolous woman. As for him, he spoke to no one. And no one spoke to him, and this way of being alone, he did not find at all unpleasant.

As soon as refreshments had been served, my father, who was overcome with weariness, asked whether it was not time to go home. He was told that he was already at home, that this house belonged to him. My father naturally thought that the house was part of his wife's dowry. He was shown to a bedroom and went to bed. The next morning Señor and Señora Avadoro were awakened by Busqueros.

"My dear sir and cousin," Busquero said to my father. "I call you that because the Señora, your wife, is the nearest relative I have in the world. Her mother is a Busqueros from León and therefore belongs to another branch of my family. I have not wanted to discuss business matters with you so far, but am counting in future on interesting myself in your affairs even more than in my own, which is all the easier for me as I have practically no business at all. But as for you, Señor Avadoro, I have taken great care to inform myself about your income and also about the use you have made of it in the last sixteen years. Here are all the documents concerning this matter. At the time of your first marriage you had an income of four thousand *pistoles* which you, by the way, did not know how to spend. You used for yourself only six hundred *pistoles* and two hundred for your son's education. You therefore had three thousand two hundred *pistoles* which you placed in the Union Bank. You gave the interest to the Theatine Fra Heronymo to use for charitable purposes. I do not blame you for that but, my word! I do feel sorry for the poor people who can no longer count on that income! We shall certainly be able to spend the four thousand *pistoles* in one year and as for the fifty-one thousand two hundred you placed in the Union Bank we shall use them as follows: eighteen thousand *pistoles* for this house; I admit that's a lot but the seller is related to me and my relatives are your relatives, my dear Señor Avadoro. The necklace and earrings you saw on Señora Avadoro cost six thousand *pistoles.* We will put ten on account, the reasons for this I will tell you in a few days. That makes twenty-three thousand two hundred *pistoles* left. That devilish Theatine friar has carved out fifteen thousand two hundred for your ne'er-do-well son in case he ever turns up. Five thousand you need to furnish your house—that is not too much for between us, your wife's trousseau consists of six shifts and as many pairs of stockings. You will perhaps realize that in this way you have three thousand pistoles left with which you do not know what to do. Well, I am ready to help you out of that difficulty and to accept them as a loan at an interest to be agreed upon. Here, my dear Señor Avadoro, is a power of attorney: please sign it."

My father could not get over the dismayed confusion into which Busqueros's speech had thrown him. He opened his mouth to answer, but as he did not know how to begin, he turned over in bed and pulled his nightcap down over his eyes.

"Now this I won't put up with!" cried Busqueros. "You aren't the first man to think he could get rid of me by grabbing his nightcap and announcing that he has to sleep over the matter. I'm accustomed to such behavior and I always carry a nightcap in my pocket. I shall therefore lie down on this couch and after we had a little snooze we'll come back to the power of attorney or, if you prefer, we can call your relatives and mine together and then we'll see what is to be done."

My father, who had buried his head in his pillow,

thought the situation over seriously, pondering a way to get out of it peacefully . . . He assumed that if he gave his wife complete freedom he would be permitted to live as he pleased, to go to the theatre, to the bookseller Moreno and even to make ink. Somewhat comforted, he opened his eyes and by signs made Busqueros understand that he was ready to put his signature to the power of attorney. He then signed it and started to get out of bed.

"Wait, Señor Avadoro," Busqueros said to him. "It would be a good idea for me to tell you how we have planned the day before you get up. I think it will not displease you to learn that today and all the days to follow are merely a chain of pleasures and just as gay and lively as they are full of variety. Now I'll bring you a pair of beautiful embroidered gaiters and a complete riding outfit, a very pretty palfrey waits before your door and we will go for a little gallop in the Prado. Your wife will drive there in a two-wheeled carriage. You will see that she has many aristocratic friends who will also be your friends, Señor Avadoro. To tell the truth, Society has rather turned a cold shoulder on her, but when they see that she is married to a man of your merit, they will change their opinion. The leading nobles of the Court will seek you out, they will come to meet you, they will embrace you—what am I saying—they will smother you in embraces."

At this point my father fainted or rather he became so numb that it was almost like a loss of consciousness. Busqueros did not notice this and went gaily on:

"Several of these noblemen will invite themselves to dine with you. Yes indeed, Señor Avadoro, they will do you this honor and you can be prepared for something. You will see how well your wife does the honors. Oh, upon my word, you will not recognize the little sealing wax girl. You do not say anything, Señor Avadoro, you are right to let me talk. Very well! You enjoy Spanish comedy but perhaps you have never been to the Italian opera which the Court enjoys to the full. Very well then! This evening you will go to the opera and just guess in whose loge! In the loge of the Duke d'Ihar, who is no less than the Lord Grand Master of the Horse! From there we will go on to his Highness's *tertulia*.

You will see the whole Court, yes, the whole world will talk with you; prepare yourself to answer."

My father had regained consciousness but now cold sweat broke out on him from every pore. His arms became stiff, his neck cramped, his head sank back, his pupils grew abnormally large, deep sighs were forced from his breast; he was seized with spasms. Noticing his condition at last Busqueros called for help and then ran to the Prado where he met my step-mother.

My father had fallen into a sort of coma. When at last he roused from it, he did not recognize anyone but his wife and Busqueros. As soon as he saw them, his face became distorted with rage. Otherwise he was quiet, did not speak and refused to leave his bed. And when necessity forced him to leave it, he caught a chill and shook for half an hour. Soon the symptoms became aggravated. The patient could take nourishment only in very small quantities. Spasms closed his throat, his tongue was stiff and swollen, his eyes dim and troubled, his skin yellowish brown and dotted with little white pustules.

I had forced my way into the house as a servant and followed anxiously the development of his illness. My aunt Dalanosa was my only confidante and watched at the sick man's bedside many nights. My father apparently did not recognize her. It was obvious, however, that the presence of my step-mother was harmful to him, and finally Fra Heronymo persuaded her to go to the country where Busqueros followed her.

I devised a last means of freeing my poor father from his hypochondria and actually met with temporary success. One day my father saw through the half opened door, an earthen jug exactly like the one in which he had formerly mixed his ink. Beside it stood a table on which were various ingredients and scales for weighing them. A shimmer of glee swept over my father's face. He got up, went over to the table and asked for an armchair. As he was still very weak, we did the work for him and he watched the proceedings. The next day he was able to take part in the work himself and the day after that he was even better. But several days later he came down with a fever that seemed to have nothing to do with his former illness. The symptoms were not so serious but the sick man was too weak to fight off even the mildest attack. He slept away without ever having recognized me though we tried so hard to tell him who I was. Thus ended the life of a man whose physical and mental strength had not been sufficient to give him even a moderate amount of energy. A kind of instinct had made him choose a way of life suited to his temperament. When they tried to force him into an active life, they killed him.

It is time to tell you what happened to me. My two years of penance were almost at an end. Out of consideration for Fra Heronymo, the Inquisition permitted me to take back my own name, provided I made a pilgrimage on the galleys of Malta which I joyfully agreed to do, for I hoped to meet the Knight of Toledo again and this time not as a servant but as almost his equal. Thoroughly tired of wearing rags, I provided myself with a fine wardrobe and tried on all my new clothes at my aunt Dalanosa's, who was almost beside herself with delight. To hide my transformation from overly curious folk I departed early the next morning. I boarded ship in Barcelona and after a short crossing arrived in Malta. The Knight assured me he had never been deceived by my masquerade and had always counted on having me for a friend as soon as I resumed my real status. He commanded the Admiral's galley and he took me on board. Four long months we sailed the seas without managing to do any harm to the Berbers who had no trouble in slipping away from us in their fast light boats.

Here ends the story of my childhood. I have told it to you in full detail just as I have retained it in my memory. I can still see before my eyes, the cell of the Headmaster of the Theatines in Burgos and the face of Pater Sanudo. I can still see myself eating chestnuts in front of the St. Rochus Church and holding out my hands to the noble Toledo.

However, I shall not be able to tell you the adventures of my youth in the same detail. For as often as I go back in memory to those glamorous years of my life, I see only the confusion of passionate love affairs and the surge of their storms. To be sure, here and there through the mist of the past I get a glimpse of a love that was reciprocated, but the women who loved me blend into one another, and I see only pictures of beautiful women and young girls flinging their snow-white arms around my neck. Indeed I can even see their stern duennas, deeply moved at that sight, bringing together the lovers they should have kept apart. I see the lighted lamp shining through the window, the signal, so passionately desired, the secret stairs that led me to the forbidden door. At such moments ecstasy reaches its zenith. The clock strikes four; dawn is already breaking, we must part—but even parting is so sweet!

Love stories are, I think, the same from one end of the world to the other. Mine would scarcely be of interest to you, but, perhaps you would like to hear the story of my first emotions. The details are surprising enough, in fact they could even be called miraculous.

But today it is too late, I must attend to the business of the tribe. Allow me therefore to postpone the continuation of the story till the following morning.[1]

[1] The fifty-fith and fifty-sixth Days are found in the first volume, *The Saragossa Manuscript.*

The fifty-seventh day

We were expecting word of important events. The gypsy had sent out messengers in all directions and was now waiting impatiently for their return. To our questions as to when we would break camp, he shook his head: he could not say definitely. I was already beginning to be bored with our stay in the mountains and would gladly have pushed forward with all speed to rejoin my regiment but, despite this pressing desire, I was obliged to wait a while longer. The days passed for us fairly monotonously, whereas the evenings were made much more enjoyable by the presence of the gypsy leader in whom I was constantly discovering new facets. As I was curious about his further adventures I urged him, for my sake, to satisfy our curiosity and to continue his story, which he did in the following words.

CONTINUATION OF THE STORY OF PANDESOWNA

You remember I told you about my dinner with the Duchess d'Avila,[1] the Duchess of Sidonia and my friend Toledo, also that I learned then for the first time that the proud Beatrice was my wife. The carriages waited for us and we drove to Castle Soriente. There another surprise lay in store for me. The same *dueña* who had served the false Leonore in the rio de Retirada introduced me to little Manuela.[2] The duenna's name was Doña Rosalba and the child thought she was her mother.

Soriente lay on the banks of the Tajo in one of the most enchanting regions in the world. And yet the beauties of nature held me but briefly. Fatherly emotions, love, friendship, sweet trust, a general inward urbanity, all added up to make a most pleasant day. What we in this short life call happiness filled my every moment. This condition lasted six weeks. After that we had to return to Madrid where we arrived late in the evening. I escorted the Duchess to the steps of her palace. She was greatly moved.

"Don Juan," she said to me, "in Soriente you were Beatrice's husband, in Madrid you are still Leonore's widower."

No sooner had she spoken these words than I saw a shadow glide past behind the balustrade. I grabbed the shadow by the collar and dragged him to the lantern—and recognized Don Busqueros. I was about to make him pay dearly for his spying, but a look from the Duchess restrained me. That look did not escape Busqueros's attention.

"My lady," he said, as impudently as ever, "I could not resist the temptation to admire the splendor of your person and certainly no one would have discovered me in my hiding place had not the radiance of your beauty, like the sun, illumined these stairs." Don Busqueros then made a deep bow and went off.

"I am afraid," said the Duchess, "that awful creature overheard my words. Go after him, Don Juan, talk with him and try to drive unnecessary suspicions out of his mind."

1 See "Story of Leonora and the Duchess d'Avila," *The Saragossa Manuscript*, p. 216 ff.

2 Daughter of Avadoro and the Duchess d'Avila.

This incident appeared to upset the Duchess greatly. I hurried after Busqueros and caught up with him on the street.

"Honorable stepson," he said to me, "you almost beat me with your stick and that would have been very wrong on your part. To begin with, you would have been lacking respect to me, the husband of the woman who was your stepmother; and then you must learn that I am no longer the humble messenger you once knew. Since those days I have come far. The Ministry, even the Court, have recognized my capabilities. The Duke d'Arcos returned from London and is now in high favor. Señora Uscariz, his former mistress, is a widow and a close friend of my wife's. We are proud of our name and fear no one.

"But, my dear stepson, do tell me what the Duchess said to you! You were both so afraid I might overhear you. I must tell you, that we are not very fond of *la* d'Avila, nor *la* Sidonia either and not even your pampered Toledo. Señora Uscariz cannot forgive him for deserting her. I don't understand why you all went to Soriente; but during your absence we have been very much worried about you. You know nothing about it, you are as innocent as newborn babes. The Marquis Medina, whose family really stems from the House of Sidonia, is asking for the title of prince and the hand of the young Duchess of Sidonia for his son. To be sure her little Highness is only eleven years old, but that makes no difference. The Marquis has long been a friend of the Duke d'Arcos, who is a favorite of Cardinal Portocarrero's. The latter is all-powerful at Court wherefore the marriage is certain to take place. You can reassure the Duchess about that. But wait a bit, honored stepson! Don't think I didn't recognize you in the little beggar on the steps of St. Rochus church. At that time there was some difficulty between you and the holy Inquisition, but I am not interested in matters that have anything to do with that tribunal. Farewell! *Au revoir!*"

Busqueros hurried off and I realized that he was the same old Paul Pry and just as importunate as ever, with the sole difference that now he could use his talents in higher circles.

The next day I dined with Beatrice, the Duchess of Sidonia and Toledo. I related my conversation with Busqueros, which made a stronger impression on them than I had expected. Toledo, who was not so handsome as he used to be and no longer felt much desire to make love, now longed for higher honors; but unfortunately the Minister, Prince Oropesa, on whom he had counted, had retired. He was therefore thinking of new paths. He was not at all pleased by the return of the Duke d'Arcos and the favor the latter enjoyed at the hands of the Cardinal. The Duchess of Sidonia seemed to await with horror the moment when she would be dependent solely on her income. And every time the Court and its prospects were mentioned the Duchess d'Avila's face wore an even prouder expression than usual.

At such moments I saw clearly that even in the most devoted friendship, one can detect inequality of class. When, a few days later, we dined at the Duchess of Sidonia's, Duke Velasquez's equerry announced the visit of his master. The Duke was at that time in the bloom of youth. He had a handsome face and the French clothes he always wore, distinguished him among all men. Even his loquacity marked him as different from Spaniards who often do not speak at all and who, probably for this reason, seek escape in playing the guitar and smoking cigars. In contrast to them Velasquez moved easily from one subject to another and always found an opportunity to pay our ladies a compliment.

Toledo was undoubtedly cleverer, but cleverness is rarely visible, whereas loquacity is always at hand. We were not sorry to talk with Velasquez and he himself noticed that his listeners were not indifferent to him. Turning to the Duchess de Sidonia, he broke into hearty laughter and said:

"Well, I must admit, it would be wonderful!"

"What would be wonderful?" asked the Duchess.

"Yes, Señora," replied Velasquez, "you have beauty and youth; you will be, without doubt, the youngest and the most beautiful mother-in-law in the world."

The Duchess had not thought of that. She was twenty-eight years old.

"Believe me, Señora," added Velasquez, "I am telling you the plain truth. The King charged me, in the name of the young Marquis Medina, to ask for the hand of your daughter. It is his Majesty's urgent desire that the race of Sidonia should not die out. All the grandees share this anxiety with him. As for you, Señora, what could be more enchanting when you lead your daughter to the altar? The admiration of all would be divided between mother and daughter. If I were in your place, Señora, I would appear in a gown exactly like your daughter's—a white atlas gown embroidered in silver. I advise you to send to Paris for the material, I can recommend the most distinguished shops for it. I have already promised to furnish the little bridegroom with a white peruke after the French fashion. I will leave you now, ladies; Portocarrero intends to send me on numerous errands. I wish he would always charge me with equally pleasant ones."

As Velasquez spoke he looked at both ladies and gave each one to understand that she had made a greater impression on him than her neighbor; he bowed again several times, then made a pirouette and left the room. In France that was called in those days *"savoir-vivre."*

After Duke Velasquez had gone there was a long silence. The ladies were dreaming of silver embroidered gowns, but Toledo called attention to the present situation of the country.

"Can it be possible," he cried, "that the King cannot find any better men to use than the Duke d'Arcos and Velasquez—the most frivolous men in all Spain? If that is the way the French party handles affairs, we shall have to turn to Austria."

And in fact Toledo went immediately to Count Harrach, at that time Imperial Ambassador to Madrid. The ladies drove to the Prado and I followed them on horseback. Soon we met a marvelous carriage in which the ladies Uscariz and Busqueros were making a great show. The Duke d'Arcos rode beside them, with Busqueros assiduously following. Busqueros had just received the Calatrava Order that day and wore it on his breast—a sight that gave me quite a start. I myself had the Calatrava Order and thought I had received it for my services, above all for my deportment in commerce, that had brought me famous and powerful friends. When I now saw the same order on the breast of the man I most despised I was, I admit, completely at sea. I stood there on the same spot where I had encountered Señora Uscariz's carriage. After Busqueros had made the rounds of the Prado and saw me at the same place as before he approached me confidentially.

"You can be sure, my friend," he said, "that different roads lead to the same goal. Like you I am a knight of the Calatrava order."

I was highly indignant.

"So I see," I answered. "But knight or no knight, I warn you, Señor Busqueros, should I catch you spying in any house I frequent, I shall treat you as I would the lowest scoundrel."

Busqueros put on the sweetest expression he could manage. "Dear stepson," he replied, "I really should demand satisfaction from you, but I cannot be angry with you. I am, and shall always be, your friend. As proof I should like to discuss several very important matters that concern you and the Duchess d'Avila. If you are interested and would like to hear about it, give your horse to the groom and come with me to the nearest pastry shop."

Filled with curiosity and worried about the peace of the person nearest my heart, I let him persuade me. Busqueros ordered iced drinks and began to tell me a rambling, completely disconnected story. We were alone, but later several officers of the Walloon Guards came in, sat down at a table and ordered chocolate.

Busqueros leaned over to me and said half aloud: "Dear friend, you were rather angry because you thought I had sneaked into the Duchess d'Avila's house; however I heard a few words there that have been going round in my head." Here Busqueros began to laugh boisterously and looked over at the Walloon officers; then he went on: "Dear stepson, the Duchess said to you: 'There Beatrice's husband, here Leonore's widower.' "

As he said this Busqueros again laughed boisterously and at the same time looked over at the Walloon officers. This game he repeated several times. The officers rose, went into a corner and began to talk about us. Suddenly Busqueros jumped up and without a word, rushed out of the shop. The Walloon officers came up to my table and one of them turned to me with exquisite courtesy and said:

"My comrades and I would very much like to know what your companion found so amusing about us."

"Señor knight," I replied, "your question is fully justified. In fact my companion almost burst with laughter, but I cannot imagine the slightest reason for it. I can only assure you that the subject of our conversation had nothing to do with you, but that it concerned a family matter in which it would be impossible to find anything comical."

"Señor caballero," replied the Walloon officer, "I admit that your answer does not fully satisfy me although it unquestionably does me honor. I shall go and inform my comrades."

The officers apparently took counsel with each other and quarreled with the one who had spoken to me. In a little while the same officer came back to me and said:

"My comrades and I do not agree as to the conclusion we are to draw from your explanation. My comrades think we should let it go at that; unfortunately I am of a different opinion. I should really challenge Señor Busqueros, but the latter's reputation does not promise to bring me any fame in a duel. On the other hand, Señor caballero, you were with Don Busqueros and when the latter laughed you even looked over at us. I think therefore it would be correct for us, without giving this incident too much importance, to end our explanation with the sword that each of us wears at his side."

The captain's comrades tried again to convince him that there was no reason for him to fight with them or with me; but as they knew the man they had to deal with, they finally gave up trying to dissuade him and one of them offered to be my second.

We then went to the duelling ground. I gave the captain a light wound, but at the same moment received a thrust over the right breast which felt merely like the prick of a needle. But the next moment I suffered a deathly chill and fell to the ground, unconscious.

When the gypsy came to this part of his adventure, he was interrupted and had to leave us to attend to the affairs of the tribe.

The cabalist turned to me.

"If I am not mistaken," he said, "the officer Señor Avadoro wounded was your father?"

"You are by no means mistaken," I replied. "The record of duels my father kept refers to it and my father added that because he had feared the unnecessary quarrel with the officer who did not share his opinion, that very evening he fought with three of the others and wounded them."

"Captain," said Rebecca, "your father showed unusual prudence. Fear of an unnecessary quarrel compelled him to fight four duels in one day."

Rebecca's jest about my father greatly displeased me and I was about to answer her when, at that moment, the company separated and we did not meet again until the following morning.

The fifty-eighth day

That evening the gypsy went on with his story.

CONTINUATION OF THE STORY OF PANDESOWNA

When I recovered consciousness again I noticed that I was being bled on both arms. As though through a mist I saw Beatrice, the Duchess of Sidonia and Toledo; they all had tears in their eyes. Then I lost consciousness again. For six long weeks I lay unconscious in a condition like death. As they were afraid for my eyes, the shutters were constantly closed, and when the physicians were treating my wound they bandaged my eyes.

At last I was allowed to see and to speak. My doctor

brought me two letters: the first came from Toledo who informed me that he had gone to Vienna, on what mission I could not make out. The second letter was from the Duchess d'Avila, though not in her handwriting. She told me that the house in the rio de Retirada had been searched and there had even been attempts at spying in her own house. She had lost patience and had gone to her country seat or, as they say in Spain, to her estates. After I had read both letters, the physician ordered the shutters closed again and left me to my thoughts. This time I began to reflect seriously. So far life had seemed to be a path of roses, but now I was beginning to find the thorns.

At the end of fifteen days I was allowed to take a drive in the Prado. I wanted to get out of the carriage and walk around a little, but I did not have enough strength so I sat down on a bench. Soon the same Walloon officer who had served as my second approached me. He told me that during my entire illness my opponent had been in the greatest despair and that he now implored me to give him a chance to embrace me. I consented; my opponent fell at my feet, then pressed me to his heart and said:

"Señor Avadoro, give me an opportunity to fight a duel for you. That will be the finest day in my life."

Shortly afterwards I saw Busqueros who came up to me with his customary impertinence and said:

"My dear stepson, you received too sharp a lesson. To be sure I should have shared it with you, but I would not have brought it off so well."

"Dear stepfather," I replied, "I do not complain about the wound that brave officer gave me. I wear my sword in anticipation of an adventure like that. But as for the part you played in this incident, you should be given a sound hiding."

"Come, come, my stepson, that last remark is quite unnecessary," said Busqueros, "and under the present circumstances anything but courteous. Since we separated I've become an important person, a sort of assistant minister second class. I must tell you some of the details.

"When His Eminence Cardinal Portocarrero saw me several times in the company of the Duke d'Arcos, he smiled at me with particular favor. That encouraged me to pay him my respects. One day His Eminence came up to me and said in a low tone:

" 'I know, Señor Busqueros, that no one is so well informed about all that goes on in the city as you.'

"Whereupon I replied with astonishing presence of mind: 'Your Eminence, the Venetians, who are not considered the poorest managers of your country, count this knowledge as one of the indispensable requisites of any man who wishes to interest himself in diplomacy.'

" 'And they are right,' added the Cardinal whereupon he spoke to several other persons and then departed. A quarter of an hour later the Lord Chamberlain came up to me and said:

" 'Señor Busqueros, His Eminence charges me to invite you to dinner and it seems that he wishes to speak to you immediately afterwards. I warn you not to prolong this conversation for His Eminence is a heavy eater and cannot do without his sleep.'

"I thanked the Chamberlain for the friendly advice and remained with more than ten other guests to the midday meal. The Cardinal ate almost a whole pike. After dinner he sent for me to come to his study.

" 'Well, Señor Busqueros,' he said, 'have you heard anything interesting today?'

"The Cardinal's question greatly embarrassed me for actually I had not discovered anything interesting either that day or the day before. However, I thought for a while and then replied:

" 'Your Eminence, today I learned of the existence of a child of Austrian blood.'

"The Cardinal was greatly astonished.

" 'Yes indeed,' I added. 'Your Eminence will recall that the Duke d'Avila was wed in a secret marriage to the Infanta Beatrice. After his death there remained from this union a daughter named Leonore, who later married and had a child. Leonore died and was buried in the convent of the Carmelites. I have seen her gravestone, which however has vanished in the meantime without a trace.'

" 'That could greatly harm the Avilas and the Sorientes,' said the Cardinal.

"His Eminence would perhaps have said more had not the pike made him so sleepy; I therefore felt it proper to withdraw. This all happened three weeks ago. In fact, dear stepson, the gravestone has really disappeared from the place where I saw it. And yet I remember perfectly the inscription on it "Leonora Avadoro." I refrained from mentioning your name to His Eminence, not because I wanted to protect your secret, but to save this news for later."

The physician who accompanied me on my walk had moved off a few steps. Seeing me suddenly turn pale and on the point of fainting, he told Busqueros that his duty forced him to break off the conversation and take me home. Once back home, the doctor had cooling drinks prepared for me and closed the window shutters. Then I gave myself up to my thoughts; several of Busqueros's remarks had greatly depressed me.

So that's the way it is, I said to myself, and that is what happens to everyone who consorts with people of higher rank. The Duchess entered into a marriage with me which, in reality, is no marriage at all. Because of a pretended Leonore I am suspected by the government and in addition have to listen to the gossip of a man I despise. On the other hand, I cannot prove my innocence without exculpating the Duchess, and she is much too proud ever to admit her marriage with me.

Then I thought of the little three-year-old Manuela whom I had clasped in my arms in Soriente and whom I did not dare to call my daughter.

My darling child! I cried aloud. What sort of a future does fate have in store for you! The convent perhaps! But no, I am your father, but if your future depends upon it, I am ready to foreswear any claims. I shall be your protector even if I have to pay for it with my life.

The thought of my child had so moved me that I was bathed in tears and shortly afterwards in blood for my wound had broken open again. I called for the surgeon. They bandaged me again, whereupon I wrote to the Duchess and sent the letter by one of her servants she had left behind with me.

Two days later I went back to the Prado where I noticed great excitement on all sides. I was told that the King lay dying; from which I assumed that my affairs would be forgotten. The King died the next morning. I immediately sent a second message to the Duchess to tell her this news.

Two days later the King's will was opened and it was learned that Philip of Anjou had been called to the throne. The secret had been strictly kept up to this moment and when now the news was spread abroad, everyone was greatly surprised. I sent a third message to the Duchess. She answered all three letters and arranged a meeting in Soriente. As soon, therefore, as I had recovered some of my strength I hastened to Soriente; the Duchess arrived two days later.

"I was lucky enough to get away unnoticed," she said. "That scoundrel Busqueros was already on the right trail and would have been certain to discover our marriage. I would have died of grief. Of course, I feel that this is not right and I know that when I scorn marriage I am raising myself not only above my own sex but also above yours. An unholy pride has taken possession of my soul; but even were I to use all my strength to conquer it I can assure you it would be in vain."

"But what about your daughter?" I asked. "What is to become of her? And am I never to see her again?"

"You will see her," said the Duchess. "But do not think of her now. Believe me, I suffer more than you do under the need to conceal her from the world."

It was true the Duchess did suffer, but to my suffering she added humiliation. With me too, pride was bound up with my love for the Duchess. Now I was receiving the punishment I deserved.

The Austrian Party had chosen Soriente as the place for a general assembly. I saw the arrivals one after the other; Prince Oropesa, Prince Infantado, Count Melzar and many other distinguished persons, not to mention those who seemed to me suspect. Among the latter I discovered a certain Uzeda who called himself an astrologer and made a great effort to win my friendship.

Last of all came an Austrian named Berlepsch; he was the favorite of the widowed Queen and was to replace the ambassador after Count Harrach's departure. Several days were spent in conferences and at the last they opened a formal meeting around a great table covered with a green cloth.

The Duchess was permitted to join the conference, and I was convinced that pride or rather a longing to play a role in government affairs was uppermost in her mind.

Prince Oropesa turned to Berlepsch and said:

"My dear sir, you see gathered here together all the persons with whom the last Austrian ambassador conferred on Spanish affairs. We are neither French nor Austrian, we are Spaniards. If the French King accepts the late King's will, his grandson will undoubtedly be our king. To be sure we cannot foresee events that can happen only in the future, but I can guarantee that none of us will start a civil war." Berlepsch assured him that all Europe would rush to arms to prevent the Bourbons from taking over such widespread territory. Then he requested that the gentlemen of the Austrian Party should send their plenipotentiary to Vienna. Prince Oroposa looked at me and I thought he was about to propose me, but then he became thoughtful and said that the time to take such an important step had not yet come. Berlepsch declared he would leave a trusted representative in the land; moreover he could easily see that the gentlemen attending the meeting were merely waiting for a favorable moment to protest.

When the meeting was over I went into the garden to join the Duchess and told her that Prince Oropesa had looked at me when there was talk of sending an emissary to Austria.

"Don Juan," she said, "I must admit that we have talked about you for this post, that I myself proposed you. You seem to be inclined to reproach me for it. I am guilty, there is no question about that, but at least I want to explain my situation to you. I was not made for love, but your love succeeded in touching my heart. I wanted to know the raptures of love before relinquishing them forever. What do you say to that? You could not change my way of thinking. The right I have given you over my heart and my person, though to a limited extent, can no longer exist. I have erased the least trace of you from my life. I planned to spend several years in the great world and if possible to have a hand in influencing Spain's destiny. After that I intended to found an order of noble virgins with myself as the first Abbess.

"As for you, Don Juan, you should go to the Prior Toledo

who has left Vienna and is now in Malta. But, as the party which you are to represent, may make difficulties for you I shall buy up your entire fortune and carry it over on my estates in Portugal and in the kingdom of Algarve. This, Don Juan, is not the only change you will have to meet. There are in Spain regions, unknown to the government, where one can spend one's whole life undisturbed. I shall recommend you to someone who will show them to you. My words seem to astonish you, Don Juan. Before, I showed you more tenderness, but Busqueros's spying has frightened me and my decision is irrevocable."

After she had said this the Duchess left me to my thoughts which, as regards the aristocracy of this earth, were not very friendly.

"May they go to perdition!" I cried, "the half-gods of this world to whom the rest of us mortals mean nothing! I was merely a plaything for a woman who used me to find out whether her heart was made for love, who now sends me into exile and who, in addition, considers me more than lucky because I can sacrifice myself for her causes and her friends' causes. But nothing will come of it! Thanks to my unimportance I shall be able to live in peace and quiet in spite of them."

I had spoken these last words fairly loud and suddenly a voice answered me:

"No, Señor Avadoro, you cannot live in peace."

I turned around and saw the same astrologer, Uzeda, whom I mentioned before.

"Don Juan," he said to me, "I overheard part of your monologue and I can assure you that no one succeeds in finding peace in times of storm. You are under a powerful protection, you should not repudiate it. Go to Madrid, complete the sale the Duchess proposed and then come to my castle."

The longing to see my child dispelled my anger; moreover, it really was not proper for me to leave my protector. I went to Madrid and, declaring that I was going to America, I turned over my house and all my possessions to the Duchess's lawyer. Then I set out on my journey accompanied by the servant the Duchess had found for me. After losing our way a number of times we came to Uzeda's castle, in which you have been, and in which today his son, our honored cabalist here, lives. The astrologer received me at the gate, saying:

"Don Juan, here I am no longer Uzeda but Ben Mamun Ben Gerzon, by religion and descent a Jew."

After that he led me through his observatory, his laboratory and every corner of his mysterious dwelling.

"Kindly explain to me," I begged him, "how much reality there is behind your art. For I have been told you are not only an astrologer but even a sorcerer."

"Would you like to make a test?" asked Ben Mamun. "Look in this Venetian mirror. In the meantime I shall close the window shutters."

At first I could see nothing clearly, but after a while the surface of the mirror became bright and I saw the Duchess Beatrice with the child in her arms.

As the gypsy finished speaking and we were all waiting eagerly to know what came next, one of his men appeared to report on the day's work. The leader went off with him and we saw him no more that day.

The fifty-ninth day

All the next day we waited impatiently for the evening to come. The gypsy, finding us already assembled, was pleased by our interest and of his own accord began to tell us the rest of his story.

CONTINUATION OF THE STORY OF PANDESOWNA

I have told you how my glance was caught in the Venetian mirror in which I saw the Duchess with the child. After a while the vision vanished. Mamun opened the shutters.

"Most honorable sorcerer," I said to him. "You do not need the aid of evil spirits to bewitch my eyes. I know the Duchess. She has deceived me more than once and most surprisingly. In a word, seeing her picture in the mirror I have not the slightest doubt that she is here in the castle."

"You are not mistaken," replied Mamun, "and we shall immediately have breakfast with her."

He opened a secret door and I knelt at my wife's feet. Though at first she could not hide her emotion at seeing me, she quickly gained control of herself.

"Don Juan," she said, "as I told you that time in Soriente, I had to say what I did, for it was the truth and my decisions are irrevocable. But after you had left I blamed myself for my lack of tenderness. It is natural for my sex to abhor any heartless act. Following this instinct I decided to wait for you here to bid you a last farewell."

"Señora," I replied, "for me you are and will always be a dream that must replace reality. Forget Don Juan forever. I will agree to that, but do not forget that I leave the child with you."

"You will see her soon," said the Duchess, "and together we shall entrust her to the one who is to have charge of her upbringing."

It seemed to me then, as it still seems to me now, that the Duchess was right. Could I have lived with her then, I who was her husband and yet was not? Even if we had been able to avoid the shrewdness of the people around us, we would have been exposed to the glances of our servants and the secret could not have long been kept. There is no doubt that in this case the Duchess's entire life would have been changed. It seemed to me therefore that right was on her side. I bowed to her decision and soon I was to see my little Manuela, who was called Undine because she had been christened only with water and not anointed with oil.

We dined with our host.

"Señora," Mamun said to the Duchess, "I think Señor Avadoro should be told certain things it is important for him to know. If you agree, I shall so inform him." The Duchess consented and Mamun turned to me and spoke as follows:

"Noble Don Juan, you are standing here on ground whose deeper regions are hidden from the eyes and knowledge of most people, but whose mysteries every dweller of those regions guards zealously. Here, deep down in this chain of mountains lie spacious caves and underground passages. Moors, who have never left them since the days they were driven out of Spain, dwell in those underground regions. In the valley that spreads out before your eyes, you will meet gypsies, some of them Mohammedans, others Christians, and even some that have no belief at all. On the summit of this rock you see a belltower with a cross on its top. It belongs to the Dominican monastery. The holy Inquisition has reason to look aside at all that goes on here and the Dominicans are pledged not to see anything. The house you are in is occupied by Israelites. Every seven years Portuguese and Spanish Jews assemble here to celebrate the Sabbath year; the next one will be the four hundred and thirtieth since the jubilee celebrated by Jesus. I have already told you, Señor Avadoro, that among the gypsies down in the valley some are Mohammedans, some Christians, and some have no belief at all. These last are heathens, descended from the Carthaginians. Under the reign of King Philip II several hundreds of these families were banished. Some found shelter around a little lake formed by a volcanic eruption. There the Dominicans have a chapel. Now, Señor Avadoro, we have planned the following for little Undine who will never know the truth about her birth. The duenna, who is completely devoted to the Duchess, will be known as her mother; a beautiful house on the shores of the lake has been built for your daughter; the Dominicans from the monastery will teach her the fundamentals of religion. The rest we shall leave to Providence. No prying eyes can spy out the shores of Lake Lafrita."

While Mamun was speaking, the Duchess shed a few tears and I myself could not keep from weeping. The next morning we came to this very lake where we now are and brought little Undine here. The following day the Duchess had recovered her usual proud, haughty manner and I must confess that our parting was not very tender. I did not remain at the castle, but went aboard ship, landed in Sicily and persuaded the captain to take me to Malta.

I went to Prior Toledo's dwelling where my noble friend embraced me tenderly, led me to a separate room and closed the door. Half an hour later the Prior's house marshal served me a bountiful meal and towards evening Toledo entered, carrying a large bundle of letters, or, as statesmen call them, dispatches, under his arm. The next morning I was already on my way, bearing a communication to the Archduke Don Carlos.

I met His Royal Highness in Vienna. As soon as I had delivered the dispatches, I was taken to a special room. An hour later the Archduke himself appeared and took me to the Emperor.

"Your Imperial Apostolic Majesty," he said, "I have the honor to present the Marquis Castelli, a Sardinian nobleman, and at the same time to ask for a Chamberlain's key for him."

Emperor Leopold gave his underlip as pleasant an expression as possible and asked me in Italian when I had left Sardinia.

I was not accustomed to speaking with monarchs, and even less to lying, therefore instead of replying I made a deep bow.

"That is good," said the Emperor. "You shall be attached, my good sir, to my son's suite."

In this fashion I unexpectedly became a Marquis Castelli and a Sardinian nobleman.

The same day I suffered unusually severe headaches; the next morning fever set in and two days later small pox developed. I had caught it at an inn in Corinthia. My illness was severe and extremely dangerous, but I recovered and even benefitted by it, for the Marquis Castelli no longer bore any resemblance to Don Avadoro. I had already changed my name, now my appearance was changed. Less than ever could anyone have recognized in me the Elvira who was once to have been the Vicereine of Mexico. As soon as I was well, I was entrusted with the correspondence with Spain.

In the meantime Philip of Anjou ruled over Spain and India and even over the hearts of his subjects. However, I cannot understand what devil pursues us at such moments and interferes in our affairs. King Philip and his wife, the Queen, fell under the influence of the Princess Ursini.

Moreover, Cardinal D'Estrées, the French ambassador, was appointed Privy Councilor which infuriated the Spanish. In addition the French King, Louis XIV, who thought he could do anything he pleased, garrisoned French troops in Mantua, whereupon the hereditary prince, Don Carlos, felt that his hope of ascending the throne had improved. It was at the beginning of the year 1703 when one evening the Crown Prince sent for me. He walked toward me and embraced me tenderly. This reception, I knew, was a sign of something out of the ordinary.

"Castelli," said the Crown Prince, "have you had any news from Prior Toledo?"

I replied that so far I had heard nothing.

"He was a marvelous man," the Crown Prince added after a pause.

"What do you mean—was?" I cried.

"Yes," replied the Crown Prince, "he was. Prior Toledo died of typhus in Malta, but you will find in me a second Toledo. Mourn your friend but be loyal to me."

I wept bitter tears over the loss of my friend and realized that now I could never cease to be the Marquis Castelli. Involuntarily I had become the slave and tool of the Crown Prince.

During the next year we went to London and from there the Crown Prince left for Lisbon. I myself had departed earlier to join the troops of Lord Peterborough whom I had had the honor of meeting in Naples. I was at his side when he forced Barcelona to surrender and by a noble and at that time, much praised deed, showed his true character. During the capitulation several sections of the allied army had forced their way into the city and had begun to plunder it. Duke Popoli, at that time commander-in-chief representing King Philip, complained to Lord Peterborough,

"Let me enter the city for a few minutes with my Englishmen," said Lord Peterborough, "and I give you my word I will restore order."

He did what he said, then withdrew from the city and offered it an honorable capitulation.

Shortly after that the Archduke who had conquered almost all Spain came to Barcelona. I resumed my post in his retinue, still under the name of Marquis Castelli. One evening as I was walking around the main plaza in the Archduke's suite I saw a man who, by his peculiar gait now slower, now hurrying, reminded me of Don Busqueros. I gave orders to keep an eye on him and was informed that the man was wearing a false nose and called himself Dr. Robusti. I did not doubt for a moment that this was my old familiar scoundrel who had slipped into the city with intent to spy.

I told this to the Archduke who gave me carte blanche to do with him whatever I felt was right. First of all I gave orders to lock the wretched fellow in the guardhouse; then when it was time for the parade, I placed two rows of grenadiers from the guardhouse to the harbor, every man armed with a flexible birch rod. The men were separated from one another just far enough to be able to use their right hand freely. As Don Busqueros came out of the guardhouse, he realized that those preparations concerned him and that he was, so to speak, "king" of this ceremony. He therefore ran at top speed and in this way avoided half of the blows though at least nearly two hundred struck him. At the harbor he flung himself into a sloop that took him to the deck of a frigate where he was allowed to stay until his sore back was cured.

It was now time for the gypsy to attend to the affairs of the tribe. He therefore left us and saved the rest of his adventures for the next day.

The sixtieth day

In the evening the gypsy continued his story:

CONTINUATION OF THE STORY OF PANDESOWNA

For ten long years I remained at the side of the Archduke. The best years of my life passed sadly, though, in truth, for other Spaniards they were not much more enjoyable. Every day it seemed that the general unrest would come to an end and every day fresh disturbances broke out. Don Philip's followers were in despair over the King's dependence on the Princess Ursini and Don Carlos's party had no cause for rejoicing either. Both parties had made countless mistakes; the feeling of weariness and indignation was general.

The Duchess D'Avila who, for a long time, had been considered the soul of the Austrian Party, might probably have gone over to Don Philip's side had she not been frightened off by the Princess Ursini's indomitable arrogance. The latter was finally forced to leave the scene of her activities and return to Rome; soon however she was back and more triumphant than ever. The Duchess D'Avila then went to Algarve where she interested herself in establishing her convent. The Duchess of Sidonia lost her daughter and her son-in-law, one after the other. The Sidonia family died out completely, its estates went to the Medina-Coeli family, the Duchess herself moving to Andalusia.

In the year 1711 the Archduke followed his brother Joseph on the throne and became Emperor Charles VI. All Europe now looked with envious eyes at the new Emperor instead of at France. They did not want Spain under the same sceptre as Hungary. The Austrians departed from Barcelona leaving behind the Marquis Castelli, whom the inhabitants trusted completely. I spared no effort to make them see reason, but in vain. I can't imagine what madness possessed the Catalonians; they thought they could defy all Europe.

In the midst of these events I received a letter from the Duchess d'Avila. She signed it as Prioress of Val-Santa. The letter contained these few words:

> Go to Uzeda as soon as you can and try to see Undine. But do not fail to speak beforehand with the Prior of the Dominican Monastery . . .

Duke Popoli, King Philip's commander-in-chief, was besieging Barcelona. The first thing he did was to erect a fifty-foot gallows which was intended for the Marquis Castelli. I called a meeting of the leading citizens of Barcelona. "Gentlemen," I said to them, "I appreciate the honor you do me in placing your confidence in me, but I am not a soldier and therefore I am not the man to lead your army. Moreover, if you are forced to capitulate the first demand the enemy will make on you will be to surrender me and that could be very troublesome for you. It is therefore better for me to say farewell and leave you forever."

However, when people have started down the devious path of folly they like to take as many men as possible with them. They therefore refused to let me leave, but my plan had been prepared long in advance. A boat awaited me on the shore; I went aboard at midnight and the evening of the following day I landed in Floriana, a fishing village in Andalusia.

After I had richly rewarded the sailors, I made my way deep into the mountains. For a long time I could not find the way, but at last I came to Uzeda's castle where I found the owner himself who, in spite of his astrology, had great difficulty in remembering me.

"Noble Don Juan, or actually Señor Castelli, your daughter is well and extraordinarily beautiful. As for the rest, you will discuss that with the Dominican prior."

Two days later I saw a very tall monk coming towards me.

"Señor," he said to me, "the holy Inquisition of which I am a member, feels obliged to overlook many things that go on in these mountains. It does so in the hope of converting the wandering sheep of whom there are quite a number here. The example of these misguided wanderers has had a harmful influence on young Undine. She is, to be sure, a girl of strange ways of thinking. When we instructed her in the basic principles of our holy faith, she listened attentively and did not show that she doubted the truth of our words; but shortly thereafter she began to pray Mohammedan prayers and to take part in a heathen celebration. Go to Lake Lafrita, Señor, and try to fathom her heart to which you have a right."

I thanked the worthy Dominican and went to the shores of the lake on a peninsula, facing north. I saw a sailboat gliding swiftly over the water and admired its graceful lines. It was long and narrow, shaped like a skate and fitted with two masts whose counter-weight prevented it from canting. The sail was raised on a strong mast and beside it stood a young girl who seemed to hover the water without touching it. This unusual boat landed at the spot where I was standing. The young girl came ashore. Her shoulders and legs were bare, a green silk dress clung tightly to her body, her hair fell in luxuriant curls over her snow-white neck; she shook it now and then like a mane. This sight reminded me of the wild inhabitants of America.

Undine, Undine! So that is our daughter!

I went to her house. Undine's *dueña* had died several years before; the Duchess herself had come at that time and had put her daughter in the care of a Walloon family. Undine, however, refused to recognize any authority over herself. She was a silent girl who liked to climb trees and rocks, to swim in the sea. Nor was she lacking in talents; for example, she herself had built the graceful boat I have described. One single word only could compel her to obey—the name of her father. As a result if anyone wanted her to do anything, they mentioned his name. When I entered her house, the caretakers decided to send for her at once. She came in, trembling, and knelt down before me. I pressed her to my heart and showered caresses on her, but I did not succeed in getting a single word out of her.

After the noonday meal Undine went back to her boat again and I went with her. Seizing both oars she rowed out into the middle of the lake. When I tried to start a conversation she put down the oars and appeared to be listening to me attentively. We were near the east bank of the lake, very near the steep rocks that enclosed it.

"Dear Undine," I said, "have you followed the teachings of the convent fathers carefully? Undine, you are a sensible girl; you have a soul, and religion is meant to help you on your way through life."

As I was in full swing and about to give her my fatherly admonitions, she suddenly leaped into the water and disappeared before my eyes. Filled with anxiety, I returned as quickly as possible to the village and called for help. I was told there was nothing to worry about; in the rocks there were many caves or arches connected one with the other. Undine knew those passages; she appeared now here, now there, and often did not come back for hours. This time she did not stay away long, but I refrained from scolding her. As I have already said, Undine was not lacking in receptivity, but brought up in seclusion and thrown entirely on her own resources, she had not the slightest notion how to deal with other people.

A few days later a brother from the monastery came to me

on behalf of the Duchess, that is, from the Abbess Beatrice. He gave me a cowl similar to his and led me to the Abbess.

We walked along the seashore as far as the mouth of the Guadiana from where we came to Algarve and finally reached Val-Santa. The construction of the convent was almost finished. The Abbess received me in the parlor with that special dignity of hers; but after she had dismissed the witnesses, she could not restrain her emotion. Her proud dreams had faded; only nostalgic regret for the love she could not bring back remained. I wanted to talk to her about Undine, but sighing, the Abbess begged me to wait until our next meeting.

"We will talk about you," she said. "Your friends have not forgotten you. Your fortune has doubled in their hands; but now the question is in what name you can begin to enjoy it. It is impossible for you to continue to be known as the Marquis Castelli; the King will not forgive those who took part in the uprising in Catalonia."

We discussed this matter at great length without coming to any definite conclusion. A few days later Beatrice gave me a strictly confidential letter she had received from the Austrian ambassador. In flattering terms the letter invited me to come to Vienna. I admit few things in life have made me so happy. I had served the Emperor faithfully and his thanks seemed to me the sweetest reward.

Nevertheless, I was not deceived by the alluring hopes the letter held out; too well I knew the customs of the Court. I had been permitted to enjoy the favors of the Crown Prince as long as the latter fought in vain for the throne, but I could not expect to be tolerated by the side of the leading monarch in Christendom! Above all, I feared a certain Austrian gentleman who had always tried to do me harm—a certain Count Altheim who later became very important. Ignorant of this situation, I went to Vienna and embraced the knees of His Most Christian Majesty. The Emperor discussed with me the question of whether it would not be better for me to keep the name of Castelli instead of taking back my own and he offered me a high position in his kingdom. His kindness touched me, but some instinct warned me not to accept.

In those days a number of Spanish gentlemen had left their native land and settled in Austria, among them the Counts Lorios, Oias, Vasquez, Taruca and others. I knew them all well and they all advised me to follow their example. That was my intention also, but the enemy, I have already mentioned, was on the watch. He learned everything that had taken place in my audience with the Emperor and informed the Spanish ambassador. The latter thought he was performing a diplomatic duty in having me followed. In the course of an important conference, the Minister voiced his suspicion of me and made several remarks about my person and the role I had formerly played. And in so doing he attained his goal. I soon noticed that my situation had changed completely. My presence seemed to embarrass the courtiers. As I had already foreseen something of this sort before my arrival in Vienna, I was not so much alarmed. I asked for a farewell audience and was granted it. I then went to London and did not return to Spain for several years. When at last I visited Algarve, I found the Abbess pale and near exhaustion.

"Don Juan," she said, "you will certainly have noticed the changes time has worked on me. I feel that my end is approaching, the end of this life that has no more charm for me. Dear God! How many reproaches I deserved from you, Don Juan! Listen to me: my daughter died a heathen and my grand-daughter is a Mohammedan. The mere thought of it is killing me. Here, take this and read it." And she handed me Uzeda's letter which ran as follows:

Noble Lady Abbess! As I was searching for the Moors in their caves, I learned that a woman wished to speak to me. I went to her dwelling where she told me the following:

"Señor Astrologer, you who know everything, will you explain the adventure that has happened to my son? After wandering all day in the mountains among gullies and abysses, he discovered a charming spring. There a strange and beautiful girl came towards him. He fell madly in love with her although he thought she was a fairy. My son has gone off on a long journey and has begged me to clear up this mystery." The woman spoke the language of the Mauritanians and I discovered immediately that the fairy was our Undine, who had the habit of going down into one cave and coming up in another. To calm the Mauritanian woman I gave her several vague answers and went to the lake. Though I made every effort to find Undine, I did not succeed. You know, Señora, that she does not like to talk. But soon after that I no longer needed to ask for her figure betrayed her secret. I brought her to the castle where she gave birth to a daughter. But as she longed for the lake, she fled shortly afterwards from the castle, resumed her former untrammeled existence again and several days later became severely ill. I cannot recall that she had ever professed any religion. As for Undine's daughter, she inherited from the father the purest Moorish blood and must inevitably become Mohammedan—otherwise we would draw down upon us the vengeance of the underground dwellers.

"You can understand, Don Juan," the Duchess added and in her voice was a note of greatest despair, "how unhappy I am over this. My daughter died a pagan, my granddaughter must remain a Mohammedan! Dear God! How fearfully you have punished me!"

As the gypsy ended with these words, he noticed that it was very late and he went off to join his men. The rest of us went to our tents.

The sixty-first day

We realized that the gypsy's adventure was drawing to a close and therefore awaited the evening with all the greater impatience. We were tense with excitement when the chief began to relate the following:

CONCLUSION OF THE STORY OF PANDESOWNA

The highborn Abbess of Val-Santa would not have broken under the burden of cares if she had not prescribed strict penances for herself which her exhausted body could not withstand. I saw her slowly fading away and I did not have the courage to leave her. My monk's cowl allowed me to enter the convent at any time and one day the unhappy

Beatrice died in my arms. The Duke of Soriente, the Duchess's heir, was staying in Val-Santa at the time. He showed great frankness towards me.

"I know," he said to me, "your former relations with the Austrian Party to which I too belonged. If you ever need anything, come to me. I would consider it a favor. As you will understand I cannot enter into open relations with you without endangering us both."

The Duke of Soriente was right. The party had written me off. I had first been raised on high only to be allowed to drop to the depths. All that was left was a large fortune that could easily be made over to me as it was in the hands of the Brothers Moro. I wanted to go to Rome or to England, but when it came to making a definite decision, I could not do it. The mere thought of returning to the great world made me shudder. My dislike of social relations had become a mania with me.

Uzeda, who knew that I was hesitating, uncertain what to do, urged me to enter the service of the Sheik Gomelez.

"What sort of a service is that?" I asked. "Would that not be working against the peace of my native land?"

"Not in the slightest," he replies. "The Moors, who are hidden in these mountains, are preparing a revolution of Islam, based on politics and fanaticism. They control enormous sums which they use to further their cause. Several of the most famous Spanish families have, in their own interest, entered into relations with them. The Inquisition draws large amounts of money from them and permits things to go on in the depths of the earth that it would not tolerate on the surface. Do try, Don Juan, to learn to know the life we lead in our valleys."

Bored with the world, I decided to follow Uzeda's advice. The Moslems and the heathen gypsies accepted me as the man destined to be their leader and vowed stanch obedience to me. But it was the gypsy girls who influenced my final decision. I was particularly attracted by two of them; one was named Quitta, the other Zitta. Both were entrancing, and I did not know which one to choose.

They noticed my uncertainty and helped me out of the dilemma by saying that polygamy was permitted in their religion, and one did not need a religious ceremony to confirm the marriage bond. In deepest shame I must confess that I let myself be inveigled into this licentiousness. Unfortunately, there is only one way to adhere to the path of virtue—one must avoid all paths that are not brightly lighted. The moment a man conceals his name, his actions, his plans, he will soon have to conceal his whole life. I could be criticized for my marriage with the Duchess only because I was obliged to conceal it, and all the secrets in my life have been a noteworthy result of that first secret. But an innocent enchantment also held me in these valleys, namely the attraction of a pure life. The broad sky that spread over our heads, the coolness of the grottoes and the forests, the fragrant air, the crystal-clear waters, the flowers that sprang up under our feet—all nature, in short, with its allurement—soothed my soul, tortured by the tumult of the world.

When my two wives presented me with two daughters, I began to pay more attention to the voice of conscience. I had seen how grief had brought Beatrice to the grave. I decided that my daughters would be neither Mohammedans nor heathens; I would have to protect them—there could be no hesitation. I myself remained in the service of the Gomelez. I had been entrusted with very important matters and tremendous sums of money; I was rich in my own right; therefore, I asked nothing for myself and, with permission of my superiors, devoted myself as much as possible to charity. And many a time I was able to save men from great misfortune.

In general I led the same life in the depths of the earth as I had led on its surface. I became a diplomatic agent again; I went to Madrid several times and made many journeys to lands beyond the borders of Spain. This activity restored my lost efficiency and I clung more and more to life.

In the meantime, my daughters were growing up. On my last journey I took them to Madrid where two young noblemen won their hearts. The families of these young men maintain connections with our underground dwellers, and we did not fear that they would repeat what our daughters told them about our valleys. As soon as both girls are married, I shall retire to a monastery, there to await in peace the end of my life which, even though not wholly free of mistakes, could not be called criminal.

"You asked me to tell you my adventures. I hope you do not regret your curiosity."

"I would really like to know," said Rebecca, "what became of Busqueros."

"I can tell you that at once," replied the gypsy. "The flogging he received in Barcelona cured him forever of spying, but as he was flogged under the name of Robusti, he thought that would not injure the reputation of Busqueros. So he offered his services to Cardinal Alberoni and became a subordinate schemer in the Cardinal's ministry and at the same time the faithful image of his protector, who was a famous intriguer.

"Later on an adventurer named Ripperda ruled Spain. Under his rule Busqueros enjoyed a number of happy days; but time which limits even the most brilliant career robbed Busqueros of the ability to use his legs. A cripple, he had himself carried to the Plaza del Sol and there continued his activities, stopping passers-by and meddling in their affairs as far as possible. Recently I saw him in Madrid beside the most comical figure in the world, in whom I recognized the poet Agudez. Age had robbed the poet of the power to see, but he comforted himself with the thought that Homer had been blind. Busqueros told him the gossip of the city, Agudez put it into rhymes and sometimes the rhymes were even quite pleasant, though they were only a feeble copy of his former skill."

"Señor Avadoro," I asked, "what has become of Undine's daughter?"

"You will learn that later. For the present, kindly prepare to continue our journey."

We set off on our march and after a long journey came to a deep valley that looked as if it were cut out of the rocks that completely surrounded it. When the tents had been pitched, the gypsy chief came to me and said:

"Señor Alfonso, take your hat and sword and follow me."

We walked about a hundred steps and came to an opening in the rock through which I could glimpse a long, dark corridor.

"Señor Alfonso," said the chieftain, "we know your courage; we also know that you are not treading this path for the first time. Follow this corridor and then descend into the depths of the earth as you did before. Farewell, this is where we must part."

Remembering the first journey, I walked in darkness for several hours. At last I saw a small light and approached the grave where, this time too, the old dervish knelt in prayer. At the sound of my footsteps, the dervish turned.

"Greetings to you, young man!" he said. "I am genuinely pleased to see you again. You have kept your word and you have preserved silence regarding the part of our secret with which we entrusted you. Now we shall reveal the rest of it and not ask you to keep silent any longer. In the meantime, take a good rest and gather your strength."

I sat down on a stone and the dervish brought me a basket containing meat, bread and wine. After I had fortified myself, the dervish pushed against one of the walls in the vault, swung it aside and showed me a flight of stairs.

"Go down here," he said to me, "you will see what you have to do."

In the dark I counted about a thousand steps and then came to one that was lighted by a lamp. I discovered a stone bench on which, neatly arranged in a row, lay steel chisels and hammers. In front of the bench glistened a vein of gold the size of a man. The metal was dark yellow and seemed to be quite pure. I realized that I was expected to dig out as much gold as I could.

Grasping the chisel in my left hand and the hammer in my right, I set to work and, in a short time, I was quite an expert miner. But the chisel became dull and I had to change it frequently. After three hours I had dug out more gold than a man could carry.

Then I noticed that the cave was filling with water; I mounted the little flight of steps but the water rose higher and higher so that at last I had to abandon the cave altogether. I found the dervish in the vault; he blessed me and pointed to the spiral staircase that led upwards. I began to climb and after I had climbed about a thousand steps I found myself in a circular room, illumined by many lamps whose light was reflected in sheets of mica and opal glass that covered the walls.

At the end of the room stood a golden throne on which sat an ancient man, his head covered with a snow-white turban. I recognized the hermit from the valley. Beside him stood my two charming cousins, adorned with costly jewels, and, on either side of the throne, a number of dervishes in white robes.

"Young Nazarene," the Sheik said to me, "you recognize in me the hermit who welcomed you in the valley of the Guadalquiver, and you have guessed that I am the great Sheik of the Gomelez. You certainly have not forgotten your two wives. The prophet has blessed their pious caresses; both will soon become mothers and founders of the family to whom it will be granted to restore the Caliphate to the race of Ali. You have not disappointed our hopes; you returned to your camp and did not reveal—even by the slightest word—what took place in our underground kingdom. May Allah grant that the dew of happiness fall upon you!"

After this speech the old man stepped down from the throne and embraced me, and my cousins followed suit. The dervishes were dismissed, and we went into another room where an evening meal awaited us. There were no more formal addresses and no one tried to persuade me to accept the Mohammedan faith. Instead we spent the greater part of the night in joyous dalliance.

The sixty-second day

Early the next morning I was sent back to the mine where again I dug out the same amount of gold as the day before. In the evening I went to the Sheik where I found both of my wives. I begged him to satisfy my curiosity—there were so many things I wanted to know; in particular I was eager to hear his own story. The Sheik replied that the time had now come when they must reveal the whole secret to me and he began with the following words:

THE STORY OF THE GREAT SHEIK OF THE GOMELEZ

In me you see the fifty-second descendant of Massud Ben Taber, the first Sheik of the Gomelez, who built the Kasar which disappears on every last Friday in the month and does not appear again until the following Friday.

Your cousins have already told you a number of things; I shall round out their account by revealing all our secrets to you.

The Moors had been living in Spain several years when they decided to retire into the depths of the Alpujarra valleys, which were inhabited in those days by a people called Turdulans or Turdetans. The natives called themselves Tarsis and claimed to have formerly lived in the neighborhood of Cadiz. They had retained many expressions of their ancient language in which they could even write. This language, however, was considered in Spain to be *"descunoscidas"* (*desconocidas*-unknown). Under the rule of the Romans and later of the Visigoths, the Turdetan paid rich tribute and in return were allowed to have unlimited freedom and to retain their old faith. They worshipped God under the name of Jahh and offered sacrifices to him on a mountain, called Gomelez Jahh, which in their language means the Jahh mountain. The Arab conquerors hated the heathen, or those who were said to be heathen, even more than they hated their enemies, the Christians.

One day in the underground passages of the castle, Massud found a stone on which were carved ancient letters. He moved it and discovered a flight of stairs leading down into the interior of the mountain. Sending for a torch, he went down alone into the depths. He saw rooms, passageways, corridors, but fearing lest he lose his way, he turned back. The next day he examined the underground adobe again and in so doing discovered that the floor was covered with smooth, shiny little stones. Collecting a number of these stones, he took them back with him and discovered that they were pure gold. He then undertook a third excursion and, following the trail of gold dust, came upon the vein of gold on which you have been working. Startled by the sight of such a treasure, he hurried back as fast as he could and promptly took every imaginable precaution to keep his treasure hidden from the world. At the entrance to the underground cave he had a chapel built and announced that he would devote himself to prayer and meditation and to leading the life of a hermit. Meanwhile he continued to work steadily on the vein of gold and dug out great quantities of the costly ore. It was extremely slow work for not only did he not dare to take on any helpers, but he also had to supply in secret the steel tools needed for working in the mine.

Massud, who in those days had more gold at his feet than any man on earth, soon realized that wealth alone does not lead to power. He had expended incredible efforts on excavating the vein; now he did not know what to do with the gold or where to hide it.

Massud was a zealous disciple of the Prophet and a fanatical adherent of Ali. He believed the Prophet himself had led him to this gold and given it to him, that the Caliphate of his family, that is, the descendants of Ali, would be restored to power and the world converted to Islamism. This thought was uppermost in his mind. He gave himself up to it with all the greater passion as the reign of the Omayyad in Bagdad was now being contested and there was hope that the descendants of Ali might come to the throne. And in fact the Omayyad were conquered by the Abbasid, an event that did nothing to help the race of Ali; on the contrary one of the Omayyad even crossed over to Spain and became Caliph in Cordoba.

Massud saw himself more than ever surrounded by enemies and he was wise enough to keep well hidden. For the present he abandoned his plans, but altered them so that they could be carried out in the future. Choosing six chiefs from his tribe, he pledged them to secrecy under a sacred oath and as he told them about the vein of gold he said:

For ten years this treasure has been mine and I could not make any use of it. If I were younger, I would call together many warriors and rule by gold and by the sword. But I discovered my fortune too late. I am known as the follower of Ali; I would be murdered even before I could form a Party. I hope that some day our Prophet will restore the Caliphate to Ali's race and that then the whole world will profess his faith. The time has not yet come, but we must prepare for it. In Africa where I secretly support the followers of Ali, I have connections, but we must also make our race powerful in Spain. Above all we must keep our great wealth secret. It is not wise for all of us to bear the same name. You, therefore, my relative Zegry, will settle with your family in Granada. My family will remain in the mountains and keep the name Gomelez. Others will go to Africa and there marry daughters of the Fatimid. In particular, we must keep an eye on our young people, probe their ways of thinking and put them to various tests. Perhaps some day a youth will appear who is blest with unusual talents and great courage: he will undertake to drive the Abbasid from the throne, to destroy the Omayyad and to restore the Caliphate to the descendants of Ali. In my opinion the future conqueror should assume the title of Mahdi, which means the twelfth Imam, and the prediction of the Prophet, who has announced that some day the sun will rise in the West, will be realized.

This was Massud's plan. He wrote it all down in a book and from that day never undertook any project without asking the advice of the six chieftains. In the end he gave up his honorary title and entrusted one of the chieftains with the position of the great Sheik and with the Castle Kasar—Gomelez. Eight sheiks followed one after the other. The Zegry and the Gomelez acquired the most beautiful estates in Spain; some of the Sheiks went to Africa, where they held important posts and married into the most powerful families.

At the end of the second century of the hegira one of the Zegry dared to declare himself the Mahdi, that is, the rightful leader. He founded the capitol of Kairuan that lies a day's journey from Tunis, conquered all Africa and became the head of the Fatimid caliphs. The Sheik of Kasar-Gomelez sent him a vast amount of gold, but was obliged to do so in great secrecy for the Christians were beginning to be victorious, and there was danger that the Kasar might fall into their hands. Soon another anxiety tormented the Sheik. The cause for that was the rise of the Abencerrages, a member of our race, but hostile to us, whose way of thinking was diametrically opposed to ours. The Zegry and the Gomelez were savage, reserved and zealous defenders of the faith; the Abencerrages on the other hand were gentle in manner, courteous with women and friendly towards Christians. They penetrated our secrets to a certain extent and laid many traps for us. The descendants of the Mahdi conquered Egypt and were recognized in Syria as well as in Persia. The power of the Abbasid collapsed. Turkoman princes subdued Bagdad, but in spite of that, the faith of Ali spread very slowly and Sunnismus constantly kept the upper hand.

In Spain the Abencerrages were ruining the customs of the country. Women appeared in public unveiled, men sighed at their feet. The Sheiks of Kasar-Gomelez no longer left the castle and did not touch the gold. This condition lasted a long time till finally, to protect the faith and the kingdom, the Zegry and the Gomelez fell upon the Abencerrages in the lion's court of their palace—known as the Alhambra—and put them to death.

This unhappy event robbed Granada of its best defender and hastened the fall of the city. Following the example of the rest of the country, the inhabitants of the Alpujarra valleys surrendered to the conquerors. The Sheik of Kasar-Gomelez destroyed his castle and sought refuge in the bowels of the earth, in the same rooms where you saw the Brothers Zoro. Six families hid here with him, the rest sought shelter in the adjoining caves that open into other valleys.

Some of the Zegry and the Gomelez accepted the Christian faith or at least they announced that they had done so. To that branch belonged the Moro family who had formerly owned a bank in Granada and whose descendants later became Court bankers. They did not have to fear a lack of money, for the entire underground treasure was at their disposal. Relations with Africa, especially with the kingdom of Tunis, still continued. All went exceedingly well until the time of Charles, the Emperor and Spanish King. Thanks to Ottoman conquests in Europe, the faith of the Prophet, which no longer shone with the same effulgence as in the time of the Caliphs, began to spread.

At this period, the lack of unity that disturbs everything on earth had penetrated beneath the earth too, that is, into our caves, where lack of space and narrow quarters caused quarrels to flare up with great violence. Sefi and Billah fought each other for the title of Sheik, which was well worth such a battle, as it gave the winner the right to administer the inexhaustible gold mine. Convinced of his weakness, Sefi wanted to join the Christians: Billah plunged a dagger in his breast. After that, he considered the best way to insure the safety of the inhabitants of the Kasar. He had the mystery of the subterranean secret written down on parchment and then cut in six vertical strips so that it could be deciphered only when all the strips were put together. He entrusted one strip to each of the six tribal chieftains, forbidding them under pain of death to show them to anyone. The initiates wore the strips on their right shoulder. Billah retained the right of life or death over all underground inhabitants and those who dwelt in the neighborhood. The dagger he had plunged into Sefi's breast became the symbol of his reign and was handed down to his successors. After he had thus established a strict rule in his subterranean kingdom, Billah concentrated his tireless energy on the situation in Africa where the Gomelez had seized several thrones. They reigned in Tarudant and in Tlemcen; however, the Africans are frivolous people who follow the call of their passions—which is why the activity of the Gomelez did not have the expected results.

Around this time, the persecution of the Moors in Spain began. Billah cleverly took advantage of this situation. With incredible slyness he arranged a mutual protection system between his underground kingdom and certain highly placed dignitaries. The latter thought they were merely protecting a few Moorish families who wanted to live in peace, whereas in reality they were unconsciously serving the plans of the Sheik who, as a reward, opened his purse to them. I learned also from our annals that Billah reverted to the earlier plan of making the young men undergo tests to prove the soundness of their characters. Before Billah's time, these tests had fallen into disuse. Soon after that came the expulsion of the Moors. The current Sheik of the subterranean domain was named Kader. He was a clever man who left no means untried to strengthen the safety of the tribe. The Bankers Moro were blood relations and important men, who professed sympathy for the Moors; under this pretext they helped them in many ways, for which they were handsomely rewarded.

The Moors exiled to Africa brought with them a lust for revenge which constantly spurred them on. One might have thought that this part of the world would rise as one and tear all Spain asunder; but soon thereafter the African states declared themselves against the revolutionaries. In vain did blood flow freely in internecine wars, in vain did the Sheiks of the subterranean domain spend gold lavishly—the implacable Mulai Ismael took advantage of the Hundred Years' struggle and founded a kingdom that to this day still exists.

I now come to the time of my birth and from then on will tell you about myself.

As the Sheik was speaking, dinner was announced, and we spent the evening in the same way as the evening before.

The sixty-third day

Early the next morning I was again sent underground. I dug out as much gold as I could; however, by now I was accustomed to this work for I had already spent several days at it. In the evening, when I went to the Sheik, I found my cousins there. I urged him to tell me more of his adventures, which he did in these words:

CONTINUATION OF THE STORY OF THE SHEIK OF THE GOMELEZ

I have already told you the story of our subterranean kingdom; now I will tell you about my own adventures.

I was born in a little cave adjoining the one in which we are now sitting. The light came from the side—we could not see the sky; but every now and then we stepped outside for a breath of fresh air between the cracks in the rocks. There we could see a little piece of the sky and often the sun too. On the surface of the earth we had a small plot where we planted flowers. My father was one of the six tribal chieftains, and therefore he and his whole family lived underground whereas his relatives, who were Christians, inhabited the valleys. Many of them had settled in Albaicin, a suburb of Granada. You know there are no houses in Albaicin and the inhabitants live in rocky caves carved in the side of the mountain. Several of those strange dwellings were connected with certain caves in our subterranean kingdom. Those Moors who lived nearest us met every Friday at our place to pray; those who lived farther away came only to the important celebrations.

My mother spoke Spanish with me, my father Arabic, so that I knew both languages well, especially the latter. I had learned the Koran by heart and often became engrossed in its commentaries. From my earliest youth I was a zealous Mohammedan and loyally attached to the faith of Ali: a violent hatred of Christians had been instilled in me. All these feelings were, so to speak, born in me and developed in the dark of our caves.

When I reached my eighteenth year, I felt that the caves had oppressed me and my spirit for years. I longed for fresh air: this feeling affected my health, I became weak and was visibly wasting away. My mother was the first to discover my condition and she began to question me. I told her how I felt, describing my laboured breathing and the strange agitation in my heart, though I found the latter difficult to explain. I added that I absolutely had to breathe a different air, to see sky, woods, mountains, ocean, people, and that I would die if I were not allowed to have that. Tears streamed down my mother's face.

"Dear Massud," she said, "your illness is all too common among us. I have had it myself and at the time I was allowed to take several trips outside. I went to Granada and even beyond. But with you the situation is different. Important events lie before you; soon we shall throw you out into the world even much farther than I would like. But come to me tomorrow at dawn. I will see that you breathe fresh air."

The next morning I met my mother as arranged.

"Dear Massud," she said, "you are asking for a freer air than the air you breathe in our caves. Be patient. If you crawl for a short distance under these rocks you will come to a deep but narrow valley in which, however, the air is much fresher than it is with us. In many places you can even climb the rocks where you will see a measureless horizon spread out at your feet. The narrow passage over which you reach this place was at first only a fissure in the rock that led to other fissures. Therefore, take a piece of charcoal with you and when you come to a crossroads, mark the way you have come; only so will you keep from going astray. Take this bag of provisions with you; water you will find in plenty. I hope you will not meet anyone, but for safety's sake stick a 'jatagan' in your belt. Do not stay out too long, for I am running great risks to satisfy your wishes."

I thanked my good mother, began to crawl, and soon came to a narrow passageway cut out of the rocks but now overgrown with grass. There I caught sight of a beautiful little bay and, farther on, interesting ravines. For the greater part of the day I wandered about. The rush of a waterfall claimed my attention and I climbed down to the place where the brook ran into the bay. Overwhelmed with admiration, I stood there a long time; then hunger began to torture me. Taking my food out of the bag, I washed as the law of the Prophet decrees and ate my midday meal. When I had finished, I washed myself again, and thought about going back underground by the same route over which I had come. Then I heard an extraordinary rushing noise. Turning, I saw a young girl emerge from the waterfall. Her wet hair covered her almost entirely and beneath it she wore a tightly clinging green silk dress. The fairy stepped out of the water, hid behind a bush, and then came back wearing a dry dress and with her hair pinned up.

She climbed the rocks as though she wanted to enjoy the view, then she came back to the waterfall. Involuntarily, I moved in front of her to halt her. At first she was startled, but I fell on my knees and this humble attitude seemed to reassure her. Coming up to me, she grasped my chin in her hands, raised my head and kissed me on the forehead. Then, like a flash, she sprang into the water and disappeared. I was sure she was a fairy or, as we say in our Arabian tales, a *peri*. Nevertheless, I went to the bush behind which she had hidden and found a dress hanging over it to dry.

As it would have been useless to wait, I went back to our underground home again. I embraced my mother, but I did not tell her about my adventure, for I had read that fairies like to have their secrets kept. Seeing me so unusually animated, my mother rejoiced that the freedom she had granted me had had such a good effect.

The next morning I went back to the waterfall. As I had marked the spot with charcoal, I easily found it again. Once there I called with all my might for the fairy and asked her to forgive me for having dared to wash in her stream. Nevertheless, I washed in it this time too; then I spread out my provisions, of which I had instinctively brought enough for two. Even before I had begun to eat, I heard the water rushing in the source and the fairy, laughing merrily, stepped out of it and spattered me with water. Running over to the bush, she put on the dry dress and sat down beside me. She ate like an ordinary mortal, but she did not say a word. I assumed this to be the habit of fairies and did not object to it.

Don Juan Avadoro has told you his story so you will already have guessed that my fairy was his daughter, Undine, who went down under the rocky caverns and swam out of her lake into the bay.

Undine was innocent, but more than that, she knew neither guilt nor innocence. Her figure was so bewitching, her manner so simple and endearing that I, dreaming I had become the husband of a fairy, fell passionately in love with her. This went on for one whole month. One day the Sheik sent for me. I found the six tribal chieftains with him, my father among them.

"My son," he said to me, "you are to leave our caves and go to the happy lands where people profess the faith of the Prophet."

At those words, the blood in my veins froze. To part from the fairy was the same as death.

"Dear father," I cried, "grant that I may never leave this underground kingdom."

Scarcely had I spoken these words, than I saw all six daggers raised against me. My father seemed to be the first ready to stab me to the heart.

"I accept death," I said, "but permit me first to speak to my mother."

They granted me this grace: I threw myself in her arms and told her of my adventure with the fairy. My mother was greatly astonished.

"Dear Massud," she said, "I did not know there were fairies in the world. However, there are many things beyond my comprehension. Not far from here lives a wise Hebrew whom I shall ask about this. If she whom you love is a fairy, then she will find you wherever you are. But you know too that among us the slightest disobedience is punishable by death. The old men have great things in mind for you; submit at once and try to deserve their favor."

My mother's words made a deep impression on me. I also imagined that fairies were all-powerful and that mine would find me even at the end of the world. I went to my father and vowed blind obedience to all his commands.

The next day I set out on a journey, in the company of an inhabitant of Tunis named Sud-Ahmed. He took me first to the city where he was born, one of the loveliest cities in the world. From Tunis we went to Zaghouan, a little town famous for the making of red caps known as "fez"—I was told that there was a beautiful building not far from the town that consisted of a chapel and a pillared portico that extended in a half circle around a little lake. The water poured out of the chapel and filled the lake. In ancient days the water had been piped out of the lake to Carthage. It was also said that the chapel was dedicated to a divinity of water sources.

Fool that I was, I assumed that my fairy was that divinity. I went to the source and summoned her with all my might. The echo was the only answer. In Zaghouan I heard of a haunted castle whose ruins lay several miles deep in the desert. I went there and saw a round building that had been constructed in a handsome and most unusual style.

There was a man sitting amid the ruins, drawing. I asked him in Spanish whether it was true that spirits had built this palace. He smiled and replied that it was a theatre in which the ancient Romans had staged combats between wild animals and this place, now called El-Deschem, had formerly been the famous Zama. The traveler's explanations did not interest me; I would rather have met spirits who might have brought me news of my fairy.

From Zaghouan we journeyed to Kairuan, the former capital of Mahdi. It was a gigantic city with one hundred thousand turbulent inhabitants who were always on the point of revolting. We spent a whole year there. From Kairuan we went to Gadames, an independent little country that was part of the Blad el-Djerit, the land of the date-palms—that is what the region that lies between the Atlas mountains and the Sahara is called.

In this land date-palms flourish so abundantly that one tree can nourish a man who is a moderate eater—as are most of the people here—for a whole year. There is no lack of other food, like corn, called "durra," and long-legged rams without wool whose flesh has an excellent taste.

In Gadames we found a great many Moors who had been born in Spain. There were neither Zegry nor Gomelez among them, but many families connected with ours; it was a land of refugees. A year had not yet passed when I received a letter from my father that ended with these words:

> Your mother says to tell you that fairies were real women and even had children.

I understood that my fairy was a mortal like myself and this thought somewhat dampened my imagination.

As the Sheik finished speaking, one of the dervishes announced that dinner was served; whereupon we all repaired joyfully to the table.

The sixty-fourth day

I did not fail to go down to the mine the next morning and I spent the whole day busily exercising the trade of a miner. In the evening I went to the Sheik and urged him to continue his story.

CONTINUATION OF THE STORY OF THE SHEIK OF THE GOMELEZ

I told you I had received a letter from my father from which I deduced that my fairy was a real woman. At that time I was in Gadames. Sud-Ahmet accompanied me to Fezzan, a land greater than Gadames but not so wealthy and where the inhabitants are all black. From there we went to the oasis of Ammon where we were obliged to wait for news from Egypt. The servants we had sent out returned two weeks later with eight dromedaries. The gait of those animals was unbearable, but we were forced to endure it for eight hours at a stretch. When we halted to rest, every dromedary was given a little ball of rice, gum and coffee; we rested four hours and then went on our way again.

The third day we stopped in Bader bela-ma; that means at the "sea without water"; it is a wide, sandy valley covered with mussels; we saw no signs, either of animals or of plants. By evening we came to a lake where the water is rich in natron, a kind of salt. There we left our guides and dromedaries and I spent the night alone with Sud-Ahmet. At dawn eight strong men appeared, put us on stretchers and carried us across the lake. In places where the ford seemed quite narrow, they walked single file. Natron crackled under their feet which they had bound in leather to protect them. In this fashion we were carried more than two hours. The lake ran into a valley enclosed by two white granite rocks and ended beneath a huge arch carved out by nature but completed by the hands of men.

Here the guides made a fire and carried us about a hundred paces farther to a kind of pier where a boat awaited us. Our guides offered us a light repast; they themselves took hashish, partly drinking it, partly smoking it, a drug made of hemp-seeds. Thereupon they lighted a resinous torch, which illumined the region in a wide circle around us, and made it fast to the end of the boat. We got in, our guides transformed themselves into oarsmen and the rest of the day we were rowed across the underground water. Toward evening we came to a bay out of which ran several arms of the canal. Sud-Ahmet told me this was the beginning of the famous labyrinth of Osymandias known to antiquity. Today all that remains is the subterranean part of the building that is connected with the caves of Luxor, the subterranean kingdom of the Thebans.

Our men stopped the boat at the entrance to one of the inhabited caves; the helmsman went off to arrange for food for us after which we wrapped ourselves in our "shaiks" (cloaks) and fell asleep in the boat.

The next morning our rowers bent to their oars again.

Our boat glided among broad galleys covered with bright stones of unusual size; many stone slabs were written over and over with hieroglyphics. Finally we came to a harbor and went up to the garrison. The officer on duty led us to his commanding officer and the latter introduced us to the Sheik of the Druses.

The Sheik offered me his hand in a friendly fashion and said to me:

"Young man from Andalusia, our brothers from Kasar-Gomelez write me flattering reports of you. May the blessing of the Prophet rest upon you!"

The Sheik had apparently known Sud-Ahmet a long time. No sooner was dinner served when suddenly a number of curiously dressed men rushed in and began to talk to the Sheik in a language I did not understand. They spoke violently and pointed at me as if they were accusing me of some crime. I looked around for my travelling companion, but he had disappeared. The Sheik flew into a terrible rage; I was seized, chained hand and foot and thrown into prison.

This prison was one of the caves cut in the rocks from which several openings led into corridors that appeared to be connected one with the other. A lamp illumined the entrance to the caves. I saw a pair of dreadful eyes and then horrible yawning jaws with enormous teeth. A crocodile shoved his body halfway into my cave, with the obvious intent of devouring me. I was chained and could not move; so I said my prayer and waited for death.

However, the crocodile was on a chain too; the Sheik had merely been trying to test my courage. In those days the Druses formed a sect with numerous followers in the East. Their origin goes back to a fanatic named Darasi, who was actually a tool of Hakim bi-mir Allah, the third Caliph of the Fatimid in Egypt. This ruler, known for his godlessness, tried by every means to reinstate the old Isis belief, allowing himself to be worshipped as the incarnation of the divinity and indulging in the vile debauchery to which he also encouraged his followers. At that period the old mysteries had not been altogether discarded but were still celebrated in subterranean labyrinths. The Caliph had himself initiated; later his insane schemes collapsed; his followers were pursued and sought refuge in the labyrinth.

Today they profess the Mohammedan faith and practise it, but in the same way as Ali's sect which, even before that, the Fatimid had joined. They called themselves Druses to avoid the generally hated name of Hakimides. From the old mysteries, the Druses retained only the custom of the test of courage.

I was present at such a test and I have seen the Druses use physical means which would undoubtedly have given the most important European scholars food for thought; moreover, I believe that the Druses know special degrees of initiation that have nothing to do with Mohammedanism, but only with things that are completely unknown. At the time, however, I was much too young to investigate them. I spent a whole year in that subterranean labyrinth, but went frequently to Cairo where I stayed with people who were allied with us through secret treaties.

As a matter of fact we had traveled here and there to learn about the secret enemy, the Sunnite religion, which was at that time the predominant faith. We journeyed to Muscat where the Iman had declared himself firmly against the Mohammedans. That famous priest received us courteously, showed us the list of the Arab tribes loyal to him and declared he could easily drive the Sunnites out of Arabia. But his teachings were contrary to Ali's creed, therefore we had nothing to do with him.

From there we traveled by water to Bassora and reached the Safi kingdom by way of Shiraz. Here we found Ali's creed predominant everywhere, but the Persians had given themselves over to dissipation and domestic quarrels and paid little attention to the progress of Islam outside of their own country. We were advised to visit the Isid, who lived on the summit of Mt. Lebanon. The name, Isid, was given to various kinds of sectarians, the ones here being really known under the name Mutawalis. Leaving Bagdad we took the desert road and arrived at Tadmora, which you call Palmyra. From there we wrote to the Sheik of the Isid. He sent us horses, camels, and armed men to escort us.

We found the entire tribe assembled in the valley not far from Baalbek. A hundred thousand fanatics shouted curses against Omar and praises in honor of Ali. They arranged a memorial ceremony in honor of Hussein, Ali's son. The Isid stabbed themselves on their shoulders with knives, many in their frenzy cutting through their arteries and dying in a welter of blood.

We stayed with the Isid longer than I had expected, but at last word came from Spain. My parents were no longer alive and the new Sheik was prepared to adopt me.

After three years of travel I was glad to return to Spain. With the customary ceremonies the Sheik accepted me as his son and soon thereafter I was instructed in matters unknown even to the six tribal chieftains. They wanted me to become the Mahdi. First I had to be acknowledged by the Lebanese. The Egyptian Druses declared themselves for me. Kairuan also came over to my side; I was urged to choose that city as my residence and if all the wealth of the Kasar-Gomelez could have been transported there, I would soon have been the most powerful ruler on earth.

This was not such a bad plan, but first of all I was too young, and secondly, I had no idea what war was like. It was therefore decided that I should join the Ottoman army which was then fighting the Germans. As I was too gentle by temperament to take any pleasure in war, I would have been inclined to oppose this plan, but I had to obey. I was fitted out as became a warrior of importance, went to Istambul and joined the Vizier's suite. A German commander named Eugen inflicted a decisive defeat on us and forced us to retreat beyond the Tana, that is, the Danube. After that we tried to attack again and pushed forward to Transylvania. We were moving ahead along the Prut when the Hungarians fell upon us from behind, cut us off from our base and defeated us. I received two bullets in the breast and was left for dead on the battlefield. Tatar nomads picked me up, bandaged my wounds and gave me a little sourish mare's milk as my sole nourishment. That milk, I can truly say, saved my life. Nevertheless for a whole year I was so weak I could not mount a horse and when the tribe changed their camp, they laid me on a wagon beside some old women who took care of me.

My mind had become as weak as my body and I could not understand one word of Tatar. At the end of two years I met a Mullah who spoke Arabic fluently. I told him I was a

Moor from Andalusia and begged him to arrange for me to return to my home land. The Mullah interceded on my behalf with the Khan and the latter gave me the money for the journey.

At last I returned to our caves where they had already given me up for lost. My arrival occasioned general rejoicing; only the Sheik was not pleased when he saw me so weakened that my health was endangered. In this condition I was less suited than ever to be a Mahdi. However a messenger was sent to Kairuan to test the sentiments of the people, for they wanted to establish me there as soon as possible.

Six weeks later the messenger returned. Everyone gathered around him, everyone was greatly excited when, suddenly, in the midst of his report, he fell to the ground, unconscious. Help was summoned, he recovered consciousness and tried to speak but could not collect his thoughts. All we could understand was that the plague had broken out in Kairuan. The man was taken away, but it was too late; many hands had touched the traveler, his baggage had been moved and all the inhabitants of the caves came down with the terrible plague.

That was on a Saturday. The following Friday the Moors came from the valleys to pray and bring us food—they found only dead bodies, with me, the sole survivor, crawling around on the ground with a large abscess under my left breast.

As I was not afraid of any further contagion, I took over the burial of the dead. While undressing the sick tribal chieftains I found six pieces of parchment, put them together and discovered the secret of the inexhaustible gold mine. Before his death the Sheik had opened the water conduit. I let the water run off and gave myself up to the overwhelming sight of my riches, though I did not dare to touch them. Up to that point my life had been so stormy that I needed calm and rest: the honor of being the Mahdi did not allure me.

As I did not have the secret of our understanding with the Africans, the Mohammedans from the valleys did not come to the caves anymore but prayed by themselves, so that as a result I was quite alone in the subterranean kingdom. I put the mine under water again, took possession of the jewels I had found in the caves, washed them carefully in vinegar and, styling myself a Moorish jewel merchant from Tunis, I went to Madrid.

For the first time in my life I saw a Christian city. I was amazed at the freedom of the women and offended by the profligacy of the men. Filled with nostalgia I longed to retire to a quiet Mohammedan city, perhaps to Istambul to live there in luxury and forgetfulness and now and then to visit the caves to replenish my fortune.

Such were my plans. I thought no one knew about me—I was wrong. To make my appearance as a merchant more plausible, I made a point of appearing in public places and spreading out my jewels there. This attitude on my part gained me much respect and earned me large sums which were, for that matter, wholly unimportant to me. And yet wherever I went, whether to the Prado, the Buen-Retiro or to some public locale, I was followed by a man whose sharp, piercing eyes seemed to read my very soul.

That man's unflinching stare made me extremely restless.

The Sheik was silent, lost in thought as if he were reliving his experiences. Then dinner was announced and he postponed the sequel to his story until the following day.

The sixty-fifth day

Again I went to the mine, dug out a goodly supply of beautiful gold and was rewarded for my industry by having the Sheik continue his story that evening.

CONTINUATION OF THE STORY OF THE SHEIK OF THE GOMELEZ

I told you that wherever I went in Madrid, I was followed by the eyes of a stranger who, through his constant spying, caused me intolerable anxiety. At last one evening I made up my mind to speak to him.

"What do you want of me?" I asked. "Are you trying to devour me with your eyes? What have you to do with me?"

"Nothing," replied the stranger, "I merely intended to

murder you in case you should betray the secret of the Gomelez."

Those words made my situation clear to me. I realized that I must give up all thought of peace and I was filled with a profound apprehension, the inseparable companion of all treasure.

It was late. The stranger invited me to his house, ordered an evening meal served, then carefully locked the doors, knelt before me and said:

"Monarch of the caves, receive my homage! But if you fail to keep the secret I shall murder you as Billah murdered Sefi."

I bade my unusual vassal rose, take a seat and tell me who he was. The stranger obeyed and began with these words:

THE STORY OF THE UZEDA LINEAGE

Our family is one of the oldest in the world, but as we do not like to boast of our ancestry, we content ourselves with tracing our family from Abisua, the son of Pinchas, grandson of Eleazir and great-grandson of Aaron, the brother of Moses and a high-priest, in Israel. Abisua was the father of Bukki, the grandfather of Usi, the great-grandfather of Seradja and the great-great-grandfather of Merajoth, who was the father of Amaria, the grandfather of Ahimaaz, the great-grandfather of Asarja and the great-great-grandfather of Asarja the Second.

The latter was the high priest of the famous Solomon Temple and left memoirs which one of his descendants continued. Solomon, who had done so much to honor Adonais, defamed his altar by allowing his wives to worship false gods openly. Asarja wanted at first to punish this criminal impiety, but then he reflected and realized that elderly monarchs must have certain consideration for their young wives. He therefore overlooked those outrages he could not prevent and he died a high priest.

He was the father of Amarja the Second, the grandfather of Zadek, the great-grandfather of Ahitob, the great-great-grandfather of Sallum who was the father of Hilkia, the grandfather of Asarja the Third, the great-grandfather of Seraja and the great-great-grandfather of Jozadak who was carried off to a Babylonian prison.

Jozadak had a younger brother named Obadia from whom, in a narrower sense, we are descended. The latter was not yet fifteen years old when he was made a page in the king's retinue and his name was changed to Sabdek. There were other Hebrews there whose names had also been changed. Four of them refused to eat food prepared in the royal kitchens because of the impure meats that were cooked there. They therefore nourished themselves only on roots and water and were nevertheless just as fat as the others. Sabdek, on the other hand, ate all the food intended for all four men and grew thinner and thinner.

Nebuchadnazar was a great monarch, but he was altogether too arrogant. In Egypt he had seen gigantic statues almost sixty feet tall; he ordered a statue of himself made in the same height: it was gilded and he commanded everyone to fall on their knees before it. The young Hebrews who would not eat impure meat, refused likewise to make that obeisance. Paying no attention to their protests, Sadek bowed zealously and in his memoirs even commanded his descendants always to bow before kings, their statues, their favorites, their mistresses, even before their little dogs. Obaja, or Sabdek as he was called, was the father of Sealthiel who lived in the days of Xerxes whom the Jews called Ahasuerus. The Persian king had a brother Haman, who was a peculiarly proud and haughty man. Haman announced that whoever did not make obeisance before him would be hanged. Sealthiel was the first to fall on his knees before him, even touching the ground with his forehead; when Haman was hanged, Sealthiel was the first to pay the same homage to Mordecai.

Sealthiel was the father of Malachiel and the grandfather of Safad who at that time as Nehemia's governor lived in Jerusalem. Israelite women and young girls were not very attractive, the Moabites and Asdodites being preferred, Safad married two Asdodite women. Nehemia cursed him, beat him with his fists and, as that holy man himself tells in his story, tore a handful of hair out of his beard. Nevertheless in his memoirs Safad advised his descendants to pay no attention to the opinions of Jews if other women pleased them.

Safad was the father of Naasson, the grandfather of Elfad,

the great grandfather of Zorobit. Uzabit lived at the time when the Jews were beginning to rise against the Maccabees. As a natural-born enemy of war, he took with him what he could and sought refuge in Kassiat, a Spanish city in those days inhabited by Carthaginians.

Uzabit was the father of Jonathan, the grandfather of Kalamil; when Kalamil heard there was peace in his homeland, he went back to Jerusalem, but kept his house in Kassiat and also estates he had formerly obtained in the environs of the city. You remember that at the time of the Babylonian slavery our race was split into two branches. Joyadak, the head of the older line, was an honorable and pious Israelite and all his descendants followed his example. I do not understand why such a stubborn hatred arose between the present lines, that the elder line had to emigrate to Egypt and there devote themselves to the service of the God of Israel in the temple built by Onias. This line has died out or rather its last descendant is Ahasuerus who is known as the Wandering Jew.

Kalamil was the father of Elipha, the grandfather of Eljasib and the great-grandfather of Ephraim in whose day it pleased the Emperor Caligula to set up his statue in the temple of Jerusalem. The whole Sanhedrin assembled: Ephraim, who belonged to it, demanded that they should erect in the temple not only the statue of the Emperor, but also the statue of his horse which was already a consul; Jerusalem however rebelled against the pro-consul Petronius and the Emperor gave up his plan.

Ephraim was the father of Nebaroth in whose day Jerusalem rose against Vespasian. Nebaroth did not wait for events to develop but emigrated to Spain where, as I have already said, we had a handsome fortune. Nebaroth was the father of Jusub, the grandfather of Simron and the great-grandfather of Rephain, who was the father of Jeremiah. Jeremiah however became court astrologer for Gunderich, the King of the Vandals.

Jeremiah was the father of Ezben, the grandfather of Uzego and the great-great-grandfather of Jerimoth who was the father of Anathoth and the grandfather of Alemeth. In Alemeth's day, Jussuf ben Taher invaded Spain to conquer and convert the country. Alemeth appeared before the

Moorish commander-in-chief and asked permission to go over to the faith of the Prophet.

"You know well, by friend," the commander-in-chief said to him, "that all Jews will be turned into donkeys at the Last Judgment, the believers on the contrary will go to Paradise; if therefore you come over to our faith we would not have enough porters."

This was not a very courteous answer. But Alemeth comforted himself with the reception given him by Massud, the brother of Jusuf. Massud kept him with him and sent him on several missions to Africa and Egypt. Alemeth was the father of Sufi, the grandfather of Guni and the great-great-grandfather of Jessev, who was the father of Sallum, the first Sarraf, that is, the treasurer at the Court of the Mahdi.

Sallum settled in Kairouan and had two sons, Mahir and Mahab. The former stayed in Kairouan, but the latter came to Spain, entered the service of the Kasar-Gomelez and aided the connections of the Gomelez in Egypt and in Africa.

Mahab was the father of Jefelets, the grandfather of Malchiel, the great-grandfather of Behre and the great-great-grandfather of Dehod, the father of Sachame, the grandfather of Suoh, the great-grandfather of Achiog, the great-great-grandfather of Borog, who had one son Abdon.

When Abdon saw that the Moors were being driven out of Spain, he became a Christian two years before the conquest of Granada. King Ferdinand stood godfather to him. Nevertheless Abdon remained in the service of the Gomelez; in his old age he rejected the Nazarene Prophet and returned to the faith of his ancestors.

Abdon was the father of Mehrital and the grandfather of Azel; in Azel's time Billah murdered Sefi, the last lawgiver among the inhabitants of the caves.

One day the Sheik Billah sent for Azel and spoke as follows:

"You know that I murdered Sefi. The Prophet destined him to this death that the Caliphate may be restored to the tribe of Ali. I have therefore formed a society out of four tribes; from the Isid and the Lebanon, the Kabyle in Egypt and the tribe of Ben-Azaron in Africa. The heads of these three families have promised, in their names and in the names of their descendants, to send a brave, clever, even crafty man, experienced in the ways of the world, into our caves every three years. His duty would be to see that everything is in order there; in case the law were broken he would have the right to murder the Sheik, the six tribal chieftains, in a word, anyone who is proven guilty. As a reward for his services he would receive seventy thousand pieces of pure gold which, in your reckoning, is one hundred thousand sequins."

"Mighty Sheik," replied Azel, "you named only three families. Who will be the fourth?"

"Yours," said Billah, "for this you will be given thirty thousand pieces of gold; you must, however, pledge yourself to uphold the old alliances, to write letters and to take part in the management of the caves. If you fail in any of these tasks, one of the three families is duty bound to murder you."

Azel wanted time to think it over, but lust for gold won out and he took over these duties for himself and his descendants. Azel was the father of Gerson. Every three years the three chosen families received seventy thousand gold pieces. Gerson was Mamun, my father. Faithful to my grandfather's obligations I served the rulers of the caves and from the time of the plague, paid out of my own money the seventy thousand gold pieces that were owing to the Ben-Azars. Now I have come to do homage to you and to swear eternal fealty to you."

"Noble Mamun," I said, "have pity on me. I already have two bullets in my breast and I am not fit to be either Sheik or Mahdi."

"As for the Mahdi," replied Mamun, "you need not worry. No one thinks about that any more. However, you cannot refuse to accept the honors and duties of the Sheik if you, together with your daughter, do not wish to be murdered within three weeks by the Kabyls."

"My daughter?" I cried in astonishment.

"Yes," said Mamun, "the daughter you had from the fairy."

Dinner was announced and the Sheik interrupted his story.

The sixty-sixth day

I spent the day again in the gold mine, and, in the evening, in answer to my plea, the Sheik continued his story.

CONCLUSION OF THE STORY OF THE SHEIK OF THE GOMELEZ

As I had no choice, I therefore took up with Mamun the old activities of the Gomelez and entered into relations with Africa and several of the more important Spanish families; but the African Gomelez were in a bad way, their male children died or came into the world weak-minded. I myself had only two sons from my twelve wives. Both sons died.

Mamun persuaded me to choose from among all the Christian Gomelez who might be converted to the faith of the Prophet, inclusive of those who descended from the female line of our race.

In this way Velasquez had the right to initiation; I decided to make my daughter his wife, the same Rebecca you saw in the gypsy camp. She was brought up by Mamun who taught her various doctrines and cabalistic expressions.

After Mamun's death, his son succeeded him at Castle Uzeda; with him we have worked out all the details of your reception; we hoped you would be converted to the Mohammedan faith or would become a father, but at least on this last point our hopes have been realized. The children your cousins bear in their wombs will be hailed by all as descendants of the purest Gomelez lineage. You must come to Spain. Don Henri de Sa, Governor of Cadiz, is one of the initiated and he is the one who recommended Lopez and Meschito[1] to you. True, they deserted you at the spring of Alcornes but in spite of that you pressed on bravely as far as the Venta Quemada where you found your two cousins. You were given a sleeping potion and laid under the gallows of the Zoro brothers, beneath which you awoke the next morning. From there you made your way to my hermitage, where you met the terrible maniac Pacheca, who in reality is nothing but a Basque acrobat. The poor fellow lost an eye as the result of a dangerous leap and called on us for charity. I thought his sad story would make such a strong impression on you that you would break the oath of silence you gave your cousins. But you kept your word of honor loyally. The next morning we put you to a much more dreadful test; but even the false Inquisition that threatened you with the terrible rack was unable to shake your courage.

Because we wanted to know you better, we let you come to Uzeda's castle. Looking down from the height of the gardens, you thought you recognized your two cousins; and they were actually there. But when you entered the gypsy's tent, you saw only his two daughters, with whom—you can be sure of this—you had no relations. As we were obliged to keep you with us a fairly long time, we feared you would be bored, and we therefore arranged various distractions for you. Uzeda taught an old man, who was one of my subordi-

[1] Alfonso van Worden's two servants.

nates, the story of The Wandering Jew which he took from a family manuscript and which the old man recited to you. In this case, pleasure was combined with instruction.

Now you know the whole story of our subterranean life which probably will not last much longer. Soon you will hear that earthquakes have destroyed these mountains; for this purpose we have already collected enormous provisions of combustibles, and this flight shall be our last.

Go now, Alfonso, wherever the world calls you. We have arranged a bank draft for an unlimited sum, commensurate with the desires we think we have discerned in you. Remember that soon there will be no more subterranean kingdom, and try to make an independent life for yourself. The Brothers Moro will supply you with the means to do so. Once more, farewell; embrace your wives. The stairs with the thousand steps will lead you to the ruins of Kasar-Gomelez where you will find a guide to Madrid. Farewell!"

I sped swiftly up the spiral staircase and as soon as I glimpsed sunlight I also saw my two servants, Lopez and Meschite, who had deserted me at the spring at Los Alcorneques. Both men joyfully kissed my hands and led me to the old tower where an evening meal and a comfortable bed awaited me.

Wasting no time, we set out on our journey the next day. By evening we came to the Venta in Cardeñas where I found Velasquez. As usual he was absorbed in some task of computation that looked to me like squaring the circle. At first the famous mathematician did not recognize me. I had to remind him little by little of all the events that had occurred during his sojourn in the Alpujarras mountains. Then, at last, light dawned on him. He embraced me and expressed great joy at meeting me again but at the same time he informed me that he found the separation from Laura Uzeda, as he now called Rebecca, exceedingly painful.

Epilogue

On June 20, 1739, I arrived in Madrid. The following morning I received from the Brothers Moro a letter with a black seal that, to my mind, indicated bad news. And in fact I learned that my father had died as a result of a stroke, and that after my mother had leased our Werden estate she had entered a convent in Brussels where she would live in retirement on her income.

A day later Moro, in person, sought me out and advised me to keep the Gomelez secret inviolate.

"So far, Señor," he said, "you know only part of our secret, but soon you will learn all of it. At this moment all the initiated are busy investing your fortune in every country in the world; should any one of you suffer a loss, we would all come to your aid. Señor, you had an uncle in India; he died and has left you practically nothing. I, however, have spread the rumor that you received a large inheritance from him, so that no one will wonder about your sudden wealth. We must buy estates in Brabant, Spain and even in America; but let me attend to this. As for you, Señor, I know your courage and do not doubt that you will board the ship *St. Zacharias* that is carrying reinforcements and provisions to Cartagena which is being besieged by Admiral Vernon. The English ministry does not want war, but public opinion is forcing them to it. Nevertheless, peace is near and if you let this opportunity to see a war slip by, you will not find another one so easily."

The plan Moro laid before me had long since been worked out by my protectors. I boarded the ship with my company which belonged to a batallion chosen from various regiments. All went well on the voyage and we arrived in time to join the brave Esclave in a fortress. The English abandoned the siege and in March, 1740, I returned to Madrid.

One day as I was on duty at Court, I noticed among the Queen's ladies, a young woman whom I immediately recognized as Rebecca. I was told she was a princess from Tunis who had fled from her country to become a convert to our religion. The King stood godfather for her and conferred on her the title of Duchess d'Alpujarra, whereupon Duke Velasquez asked her to marry him. Rebecca noticed that we were talking about her and gave me a meaningful look, warning me not to betray her secret. Shortly thereafter, the Court moved to San Ildefonso but I remained with my company in billets in Toledo. I rented a house on a narrow street not far from the market-place. Opposite me lived two women, each of whom had a child and whose husbands—probably naval officers—were at sea. The two women lived in complete seclusion and apparently busied themselves solely with their children who were as beautiful as angels. All day long the mothers did nothing but rock their babies, bathe them, dress them and feed them. This touching picture of motherly devotion made such a deep impression on me that I could not tear myself away from the window. To be frank, curiosity was just as strong a motive, for I was eager to see my neighbor's faces, but they always kept them veiled. In this way two weeks passed. The room facing the street was given over to the children, and the women did not eat there; but one evening I saw the table being laid in that room and apparently preparations being made for a party.

At the head of the table stood a stately armchair that was decorated with a wreath of flowers and was obviously intended for the lord of this feast; on either side of the table high chairs were placed for the children. Then my two neighbors came to the window and invited me by signs to call on them. I hesitated for I did not know what to do in this situation, whereupon they raised their veils, and I recognized Emina and Zibeddé. I spent six months with them.

Meanwhile, Pragmatic Sanctions and quarrels ever the throne of Charles VI set off a war in Europe in which Spain was soon active. I then left my cousins to become the adjutant of the Infante Don Philip and remained at the side of this prince during the entire war. After peace was concluded, I was appointed a colonel.

While we were in Italy, the representative of the Moro Bank came to Parma to call in some securities and to set in order the money affairs of that principality. One night this man came to me and informed me secretly that I was being eagerly awaited at Uzeda's castle and I must immediately set out on my journey. He also mentioned one of the initiated whom I was to meet in Malaga.

I took leave of the Infante, boarded a ship in Liverne and, after a sail of ten days, arrived in Malaga. The man who had been apprised of my arrival was waiting for me at the pier. On the very same day we left Malaga and the next morning arrived at Uzeda's castle.

There I found a great company assembled; first of all, the Sheik, then his daughter Rebecca, Velasquez, the cabalist, the gypsy with his two daughters and sons-in-law, the three Zoro brothers, the fictitious maniac and finally various Mohammedans from the three families who knew the secret. The Sheik explained that, as we were now all together, we should immediately go down to the subterranean kingdom.

And actually at nightfall we all set out on the way and

arrived as dawn was breaking. We went down under the earth and spent a little time resting. Then the Sheik called us together and made the following speech which he repeated for the Mohammedans in Arabic:

"The gold mine which for thousands of years has constituted the fortune of our family was apparently inexhaustible. Convinced of this, our ancestors decided to use the gold taken from it, to help spread Islamism, in particular the religion of Ali. They were the keepers of a treasure whose protection cost them endless difficulties and efforts. I myself have suffered the most terrible trouble, and to rid myself finally of an anxiety that has daily become more unbearable, I decided to find out whether the mine really was inexhaustible. I tested the rocks in a number of places and found that everywhere the vein of gold was running out. Señor Moro undertook to calculate the remaining wealth and to ascertain what portion would fall to each one of us. The calculation showed that a million was due to each principal heir, and to each of the interested parties fifty thousand sequins. We took out all the gold and carried it to one of the caves far from here. First of all, I shall take you to the mine where you can see for yourselves that I am speaking the truth; after that, each man shall receive his share."

We descended the spiral staircase, came to the sepulchre and from there into the mine which we found to be completely empty. The Sheik kept urging us to make haste and return. No sooner were we all safely back on the mountain than we heard a tremendous detonation. The Sheik explained that explosives had blown up the subterranean kingdom we had just left. We thereupon proceeded to the cave where the rest of the gold had been stored. The Africans took their share. Moro took over mine and the shares of almost all of Europeans.

I returned to Madrid and presented myself to the King who received me with indescribable kindness. I purchased large tracts of land in Castile, was granted the title of Count Penna-Florida and was given my place among the leading Castilian *titelades.* In addition to all my wealth, my services to my country were also appreciated and at the age of thirty-six I was made a general.

In the year 1760 I was given command of a squadron with

orders to make peace with the Berber states. I sailed first to Tunis in the hope of finding the least difficulties there and that the example of this state would influence the others. Dropping anchor at the mooring below the city, I sent an officer into the city with word of my arrival. This was already known and the entire Goletta Bay was covered with gaily flagged boats that had come out to escort me and my suite to Tunis.

The next day I was presented to the Dei. He was a young man of twenty with a most attractive manner. I was received with full honors and invited to Castle Manuba for the evening. There I was shown into a remote arbor and the door closed behind me. A little private door opened, the Dei came in, knelt and kissed my hand.

Another little door creaked: three veiled women entered, threw back their veils—and I recognized Emina and Zibeddé. They led a young girl by the hand—my daughter. Emina was the mother of the young Dei. I cannot describe the strength of that fatherly love I felt in my heart. My joy was clouded only by the fact that my children were members of a faith that was my enemy. I said that this was very painful to me.

The Dei confessed that he was deeply committed to his religion, but that his sister, Fatima, who had been raised by a Spanish slave, was at heart a Christian. We decided that my daughter should move to Spain, that she should be christened there and become my heir. This all took place within the year. The King graciously consented to be Fatima's godfather and conferred on her the title of Princess of Oran. The next year she married the son of Velasquez and Rebecca, who was two years her junior.

I guaranteed her my entire fortune by proving that I had no near relatives on my father's side and that the young Moorish girl, who was related to me through the Gomelez, was my sole heir. Though I was still young and full of life, I was already thinking of a place where I could enjoy the sweetness of relaxation. The position of governor in Saragossa was open: I asked for it and was granted it.

After I had thanked his Majesty and taken leave of him, I called on the Brothers Moro to ask them to return the sealed roll of paper I had deposited with them twenty-five years before. It was a diary covering the first sixty-six days of my sojourn in Spain.

I wrote it by hand and laid it in an iron casket where, someday, my heirs will find it.

This book was designed by Wladislaw Finne. Composition, printing and binding were done by the H. Wolff Book Manufacturing Co., New York. The text was set in linotype Baskerville with display in Spartan Heavy.